Merry Christmas,
To Daddy from Patsy
1950

The Adventurer

ALSO BY MIKA WALTARI

THE EGYPTIAN

The Adventurer

BY MIKA WALTARI

TRANSLATED BY

NAOMI WALFORD

G. P. Putnam's Sons New York

Contents

BOOK I.

Michael Bast: Furfoot

I

I WAS born and bred in a distant region that cosmographers call Finlandia, a beautiful and far-flung country unknown to most educated people. In the south men fancy that such a northerly land must be bleak and unfit for human habitation, and that those who do live there are savages who clothe themselves in the skins of wild beasts and are the slaves of heathendom and superstition. No idea could be more absurd. Finland even boasts two large cities: the fortified town of Viborg in the east, and in the south Aboa, or Åbo, where I was born. As to heathendom and superstition, be it understood that for many centuries Finland belonged to the one true Church. In these evil days its people may indeed be accused of backsliding, since under the rod of the hard-hearted and rapacious King Gustaf the land has adopted the Lutheran doctrine and is already accounted a lamb strayed from the Christian fold. What wonder then if the people plunged again into savagery, ignorance, and sin? Although for this, I would blame a bad government rather than those governed. Finland is far from poor. The forests are full of game, and in every place along its mighty rivers salmon fishing is profitably pursued. The burghers of Åbo are active in overseas trade, and on the Bothnian coast the art of building ocean-going ships is well understood and practiced. Timber is plentiful; and besides the dried fish, the skins, and the cunningly fashioned wooden bowls that are shipped abroad from Åbo, there is also pig iron smelted from the ore of the inland lake region. The traffic in dried fish and salt herring in barrels is so rich a source of income that in the long run the country cannot afford to adopt a false doctrine that ignores fast days, for the proper observance of these as ordained by the Catholic Church is essential to the prosperity of many a devout citizen.

I have said this much of my native land to show that there is nothing of the heathen about me.

One night in late summer when I was six or seven years old, Otto Ruud, the Jutish Admiral, came rowing up the river past the sleeping guards in Åbo fortress, and at dawn launched his surprise attack upon the city. And since this hideous sack of Åbo took place in 1509, five years before the beatification of St. Hemming, I must first have seen the light of day in 1502 or 1503.

2

I remember waking between soft linen sheets. A fur rug was spread over me and a great dog was licking my face. When I pushed its nose away it was pleased, and taking my hand gently between its teeth, it would have played with me. Much later a thin, gray-clad woman approached the bed; she surveyed me with cold gray eyes and offered me broth. As I fancied that I had passed through death I was surprised to see that she had no wings, and asked shyly, "Am I in heaven?"

The woman felt my hands, my throat, and my forehead; and her hand was as hard as a board. She asked, "Does your head still hurt you?"

I touched my head and found that it was bandaged, and then I shook it in answer to her question, but in doing so felt a sharp pain at the base of my skull.

"What is your name?" asked the woman.

"Michael," I answered. This I well knew, as I had been named after the holy archangel.

"Whose child are you?"

I could not immediately answer this, but at last I said, "Michael the Tinsmith's son. Am I really in heaven?"

2

"Eat your broth," said she curtly. "I see. You're Michael's daughter Gertrude's boy. . . ."

She sat upon the edge of the bed and gently stroked the ache at the nape of my neck.

"I am Pirjo Matsdotter of the Karvajalka (Furfoot) family. You're in my house and I have nursed you for many days."

I remembered the Jutes then, and all that had happened; and her name so frightened me that I lost my appetite for the broth.

"Are you a witch?" I asked her. She started and made the sign of the cross.

"Is that what they say behind my back?" she demanded angrily, then checked herself and said, "I'm no witch, but a woman who cures sick people. Had not God and His saints bestowed on me the gift of healing, you and many others would have perished during these days of affliction."

I was ashamed of my ingratitude, yet I could not ask her pardon, for I knew that she was indeed the notorious witch of Åbo, of the Furfoot line.

"Where are the Jutes?" I wondered.

She told me that they had sailed some days ago, carrying with them priests, burgomasters, councilors, and the wealthiest citizens as prisoners. Åbo was reduced to poverty, for during recent summers the Jutes had bought the burghers' best ships, and now had even looted the Cathedral of its most precious treasures. For more than a week I had lain in Mistress Pirjo's cabin gravely injured and in a high fever.

"How did I come here?" I asked, staring at her; and as I stared I saw her head transformed into that of a benevolent horse. Yet I was not afraid, knowing that witches could change their shape. The dog padded up with wagging tail to lick my hands, and I saw her as Mistress Pirjo once more. I now had no doubt that she was a witch, yet somehow I trusted her with my whole heart.

"You have a horse's face," I said humbly.

At this she was offended, having all a woman's vanity although the best marriage years were far behind her. But she went on to tell me how she had bought immunity from the looters by tending a Jutish ship's captain who in his eagerness for plunder had been the first to leap from his vessel, and in so doing sprained his ankle. On the third day one of the Jutes had carried me to her cabin and paid her three silver groats to make me well again. No doubt he performed this act of mercy to expiate his sins, for the looting of the Cathedral had stung

3

the consciences of many. From her description I took him to be the same man who had slain my grandparents.

When Mistress Pirjo had related to me the manner of my arrival at her house she said, "I have washed the blood from your shirt and your breeches are hanging on the peg. You may dress yourself and go where you like, for I have kept my word and wrought a cure upon you worth more than three silver pieces."

There was nothing to be said to this, so I dressed and went out into the garden. Mistress Pirjo locked her door and set forth to visit those sick and wounded who had not been taken to the monastery or to the House of the Holy Ghost, and who preferred to die, if die they must, in their own homes. I sat down on the sunlit doorstep because my legs were still weak from my illness, and stared at the rich summer grass and at all the strange plants in the herb garden. The dog sat down beside me, and because I did not know where to go I laid my arm about its neck and wept bitter tears.

Here Mistress Pirjo found me when she returned at dusk, but she merely shot me a sideways glance of annoyance and went indoors. Presently she brought me a piece of bread, saying, "Your late mother's parents are already buried in a common grave with other poor people whom the Jutes murdered. The whole town's upside down and no one knows where to begin setting it to rights again; but jackdaws are screeching at the eaves of your house."

I did not understand what she meant, and she explained, "You no longer have a home, poor wretch. You can't inherit because your mother was unmarried. The monastery has taken house and land according to a verbal promise made by Michael Michaelsson and his wife for their souls' salvation."

I had nothing to say to this either, but a little later Mistress Pirjo came to me again and slipped three silver groats into my hand.

"Take your money," said she. "May it be accounted a merit to me at the Last Judgment that from compassion and without thought of gain I restored you to health, poor lad, though it might have been better if you'd died. Be off now, out of my way."

I thanked Mistress Pirjo for her kindness, patted the dog in farewell, and knotted the three silver coins into the tail of my shirt. Then I trudged homeward along the riverbank, noticing as I went that the doors of rich men's houses were smashed and that the glazed windows of the town hall had been stolen. No one had time to heed me, for the burghers' wives were busy sorting out the crazed cattle that had been

4

driven in from hiding places in the woods, while neighbors poked about the deserted houses and saved any gear that was still fit for use lest it be lost or fall into the hands of thieves.

I stepped into our cabin and found nothing there, neither spinning wheel nor water tub, neither cooking pot nor wooden spoon, nor the least rag to wrap about me. Nothing was left but pools of congealed blood, which the beaten earth floor could not absorb. I lay down upon the earth bench and wept myself into a deep sleep.

3

I was awakened early in the morning by the entry of a black-clad monk, but I was not afraid, for his face was round and friendly. He wished me God's peace and asked if the place was my home. I told him it was, and he said, "Be glad, for St. Olav's monastery has adopted the dwelling and so freed you from all the cares that worldly possessions bring with them. By the grace of God you have lived to see this joyful day—for you must know that I've been sent here to cleanse this hut from all the evil that haunts the scenes of sudden death."

From vessels he had brought he began to sprinkle salt and holy water over the floor and about the stove, in the hinges of the door and upon the shutter, crossing himself meanwhile and reeling off powerful Latin invocations. Then he sat down beside me on the bench where I had slept, brought out bread, cheese, and dried meat from his wallet, and bade me eat also, saying that a bite between meals was needful after such taxing work.

When we had eaten, I told him I would like to buy a Mass for the souls of Michael Michaelsson and his wife, to free them from the pains of purgatory; for I knew that those pains were worse than any on earth.

"Have you money?" asked the good monk. I unknotted the tail of my shirt and showed him my three silver coins. He smiled still more kindly, stroked my hair, and said, "Call me Father Peter, for Peter is my name, although I'm no rock. Have you no more money?"

I shook my head and he looked sad, for a Mass could not be had for so small a sum.

"But," said he, "if we could persuade for example St. Henry, who himself suffered a violent death at the hand of a murderer, to intercede for the souls of these good people, I don't doubt that the power of his holy intercession would be greater than that of the best Mass."

5

I asked him to teach me how to put my request before St. Henry, but he shook his head.

"Your modest little prayer would hardly weigh with him; indeed I fear that it would drown like a mouse in the torrent of prayers that in these days beat about his throne. If on the other hand a really strong man of prayer—one who has dedicated his whole life to poverty, chastity, and obedience—were to take the matter upon himself; if he were to pray at each canonical hour for a week, let us say, for your departed grandparents, St. Henry would certainly incline his ear to find out what was wanted."

"Where can I find so strong a man of prayer?" I asked.

"You see him before you," replied Father Peter with simple dignity, and so saying he took the silver from my hand and slipped it quickly into his purse. "I will begin the prayers today at sext and nones, and continue with them at vespers and compline. My constitution is not equal to vigils, for which reason our good Prior often excuses my attendance at the Night Office; but your beloved kinsfolk shall not suffer by this. I will increase the number of prayers proportionately at the other hours."

I did not understand all he said, but his tone was so persuasive that I knew I had put my case in the best hands, and I thanked him humbly. He propped the door to when we left, made many signs of the cross, and gave me his blessing. We then parted, and I returned to hang about Mistress Pirjo's cabin, not knowing where else to go.

I was afraid that Mistress Pirjo would be angry when she saw me, for I had already found her to be an austere woman. So I hid; but when it began to rain I crept into the byre. The walls were overgrown with moss, grass and flowers grew on the roof, and the only inhabitant was a pig. Surveying its fat shoulders, I became very envious of this beast, which had a roof over its head and no anxiety about food and drink. I fell asleep upon the straw and woke to find the pig beside me, and there we lay side by side to keep one another warm. Mistress Pirjo came in with pig swill in a tub, and was exceedingly indignant at finding me there.

"Didn't I tell you to be off?" she exclaimed. The pig gave me a friendly nudge with its snout and rose up to eat. The food consisted of pea pods, chopped turnips, milk, and oatmeal. I asked timidly if I might partake of the food if the pig would let me. I made this request not so much because I was hungry—I was all too sorrowful to feel hunger—but because the pig's supper seemed to me more savory than

6

anything I had eaten in my grandparents' house for a very long time.

"You ungrateful, impudent boy! Are you hinting that I should learn compassion from the pig, which warms you in its bosom and shares its swill with you? Have I not given you three silver pieces? For that sum even a grown man can find himself bed and board for a month or so. A burgher or a brother of some guild would house you for a year and bind you apprentice if you approached him civilly. Why don't you make use of your money?"

I told her I had already done so and had given them to Father Peter, that he might pray for my grandparents' souls and free them from the pains of purgatory. Mistress Pirjo sat upon the threshold of the sty, one hand holding the trough and the other supporting her long chin, and she stared at me for a long time.

At last she said, "Are you out of your mind?"

I said I hardly knew. No one had mentioned it to me before, but since the injury to my head life had seemed very strange and bewildering.

Mistress Pirjo nodded.

"I could take you to the House of the Holy Ghost. They might admit you with all the other disabled and blind people, and epileptics —for I've no doubt they'll think you queer in the head when they hear you talk. But if you can hold your tongue and look intelligent I might perhaps get a word with the brethren of Michael the Tinsmith's guild, and induce them to pay for your keep until you're old enough to earn your own living."

I begged her pardon for my unready speech; I had never talked much with anyone, for when Michael the Tinsmith spoke one must listen in silence, and when my grandmother spoke it was only of hell's torments and the terrors of purgatory, and of these things my knowledge was so small that I could not answer her.

"But," said I, "I know many words in German and Swedish and even Latin."

I was eager to show off to Mistress Pirjo, for no one else had ever spoken so kindly to me, and so I reeled off all the foreign and mysterious words that for some reason had stuck in my memory: words from church, from the merchants' houses, from guild meetings, and from the harbor, as for instance *salve, pater, benedictus, male spiritus, pax vobiscum, haltsmaul, arsch, donnerwetter, sangdieu,* and *heliga kristus*. When I halted breathless, Mistress Pirjo was holding her hands over her ears. Nevertheless I went on recklessly to tell her that I knew

7

many letters by sight and could write my name. When she would not believe this, I took a stick and wrote in the dirt as well as I could: MICHAEL. She could not read, but she asked who had taught me. No one, I said, but I was sure I could soon learn to read if someone would show me how.

The day had drawn to its close as we talked, and it was growing dark. She took me into the house, lit a candle, and began to press the wound in my head with her hard fingers. She told me that she had stitched up my torn scalp with needle and thread; but now the wound had festered, and she bathed it, spread mildew and cobwebs on it, and bound my head afresh. She gave me food and let me sleep in her bed.

Thus it was that I came to live with Mistress Pirjo and made myself useful to her, collecting the droppings of black cocks, hairs from horses' tails and from the necks of rams in the burghers' sheepfolds, and helping her to find places where healing herbs grew and to pick them at the new moon. But, most important of all, Father Peter at her request taught me to read and write, and instructed me in the art of solving many useful mathematical problems by means of a rosary.

4

My head injury seemed to have brought about a complete transformation of my life and character; nor did its influence lessen as the wound healed and hair hid the scar. I continued to be lively, inquisitive, and quick to learn, and forgot that I had ever been a whimpering brat afraid to open my mouth to a stranger. Mistress Pirjo neither struck nor frightened me, but treated me well and respected my talents. Learning, which for many is toil and weeping and gnashing of teeth, was for me a blithe game; and the more I learned, the greater became my thirst for knowledge. I cannot say whether at last I learned more from Father Peter's pious tales or from Mistress Pirjo's teaching when on clear winter nights she spoke of the stars, or on fragrant summer evenings led me by the hand through groves and along the banks of streams, and told me which herb was best for this or that disease. For Mistress Pirjo was known as a woman skilled in healing, and she lived in charity with the clergy and with the brothers of the monastery.

At first Father Peter took my instruction as a joke, but when he saw what great progress I had made in the course of a single winter—although it was only once or twice a week between the hours of prayer that he passed the time at Mistress Pirjo's cabin, and even then spent most of it in eating and drinking—he began to speak seriously with his hostess, telling her that I had better enter the monastery or the Cathedral School, so that as a pupil of Father Martin I might study grammar, rhetoric, and dialectic according to the rules of those arts.

"In the name of the Virgin and all the saints!" he exclaimed, wiping the grease from his lips with his black sleeve. "If I had a son like Michael—which the blessed saints forfend—I'd set him upon the school bench without delay in the certainty that in time he'd prove a credit to the Church. He might become a canon, or even a bishop, for already he knows his Pater Noster and Ave by heart, and has his Latin numbers pat up to twenty—and even I can't get much further."

He took a draught of wine and praised its refreshing and cordial effect.

But Mistress Pirjo said, "You forget, Father Peter, that Michael is alone in the world, and baseborn. The Church won't take whores' brats into her service; and what joy would he have of his learning if he could not be ordained?"

"In your place I should use the scholarly and seemly word 'bastard,'" observed Father Peter. "It's a word that hints at lofty origins, and those hearing it will at once try to recollect all the noble lords and legates who have visited Åbo of recent years. But if you tell Father Martin that the boy is a common come-by-chance, he will at once assume that Michael's father was a mere seaman, or a man-at-arms, or an ox-driver, and will laugh at your petition."

"But you wouldn't have me lie about his birth?"

"Now you're talking nonsense," was the scornful retort. "*Pro primo,* the boy's finely chiseled features, his silky hair, and his small hands and feet, to say nothing of his intelligence, talents, and good conduct, bear witness that he comes of eminent stock. *Pro secundo,* it's a question merely of a term which among high or low denotes the same thing: the fruit of a sinful act—*fructus inhonestus et turpis*—irrespective of the rank of those committing it."

I felt my hair, which was unusually stiff. My hands were not soft, nor even clean, and I rubbed my grimy leg with the other foot in some embarrassment.

"Believe me, noble and compassionate Mistress Pirjo," continued Father Peter, waving his tankard persuasively, "call upon Magister Martinus and speak to him. If you were to unfold a handsome piece

9

of cloth, large enough for a tunic, and set upon it a good fat ham, and jingle a few silver pieces modestly together, he would certainly listen to your request, however singular it might be. Then whisper mysteriously in his ear, 'The boy's a bastard!' His curiosity will at once be aroused. Show fear; say that you have sworn dreadful oaths never to breathe another word of the matter, and you'll find that Magister Martinus will show more regard for Michael than for any of his other pupils, since the ham and the pure silver will speak for him."

Father Peter's words gave Mistress Pirjo much to think of, and indeed they evoked a painful echo in my own mind. She sat and stared at me longer than usual that evening, propping her chin in her hard palm and murmuring to herself. I believe that Father Peter had convinced her that I was indeed a bastard.

5

I was the youngest in the Cathedral School, and so my life there was harder than it might have been. Beside me in the straw sat many youths whose beards were already growing and whose shameless behavior revealed more love for the vanities and abominations of the world than for Latin declensions. Magister Martinus and his assistants had no materials for instruction other than the birch suppled in brine, and at times I fancied that they were in error as to the part of the body most receptive to learning. Nevertheless, it does seem that those rules of grammar that have been imprinted upon the hinder parts remain most securely in the memory; and somehow the more we learned the more we came to love that murky school whose massive stone walls entombed our youth. We promised each other solemnly that we in our turn would not spare our successors; and when, in framing our own Latin phrases, we found the beaten-in grammatical rules hastening like obedient slaves to serve our thought, our hearts rejoiced indeed.

The most distinguished ecclesiastical gathering I witnessed during these years was the solemn enshrining of St. Hemming's bones. By then I had been four years at school and together with some ten other advanced pupils was preparing to study dialectic. Most of my comrades would have had handsome beards if scholars had been permitted to go unshaven.

It must be owned that I did not feel particularly solemn when we pried up the flagstones of the Cathedral floor with crowbars and began to dig out the holy bones, amid the hideous stench of corruption that filled the church despite the copious incense and the perfume of the sacred olibanum. I had recently distinguished myself by celebrating in verse Bishop Hemming's earthly sojourn, and his miracles, and was therefore accorded the honor of disinterring his bones. We found them in great numbers, and in washing and rubbing them clean of all impurities amid the chanting of the priests, we were filled with a marvelous strength and with a sense of consolation, as though we had drunk wine or had received the Holy Ghost. Our cheeks glowed, our eyes brightened, and suddenly we became aware of the fragrance of celestial balsam. This grew especially strong when we held his brown skull in our hands, in the jawbone of which a few broken teeth still remained. We handed up the bones one by one for Bishop Arvid and his fellow dignitaries to anoint with oil and lay in a new coffin, until at last the right reverend Bishop called out sharply that there were now bones enough. So it will perhaps not be accounted a sin that I scooped out another vertebra and a tooth and hid them in my pocket.

Before the ceremony of reinterment, we clerks had the troublesome task of catching live doves and chaffinches for the celebrations. Had we known of the matter the previous winter, we could have snared waxwings and bullfinches, which to my mind would have been a greater adornment to the feast. But in summer it was impossible to catch them.

The Cathedral was decked with garlands, wreaths, coats of arms, and pictures from the saint's life painted on canvas and illuminated from behind. There were thousands of wax candles and at least a hundred lamps, so that the interior was bathed in brilliance. The flagstones were raised once more and the sacred bones were swathed in costly stuffs and laid in a lofty gilt shrine. As the relics were borne in procession round the Cathedral among the kneeling congregation, we boys began to throw down tufts of burning tow containing gunpowder through a hole in the vaulted roof so that the people shrieked aloud in amazement and terror, believing it to be lightning. I have since wondered how it was we did not set fire to the whole building, for the loft was dusty and tinder-dry, and jackdaws were flapping and screeching about our heads unceasingly.

Next we released the doves and chaffinches one at a time to circle under the roof, and strewed flowers and Communion bread over the faithful to stimulate their liberality. Indeed the Cathedral gained from their offerings many times the cost of the festival, so one may say that St. Hemming paid his way generously. But the satisfaction was mutual, and Mistress Pirjo freely acknowledged that she had had her full money's worth of beauty and edification. An old man who had kissed the shrine threw away his crutches and began scampering about on sound limbs, and a dumb woman who for years had dwelt in the House of the Holy Ghost now received her speech again—albeit many accounted this a misfortune rather than a blessing, since she proved to be singularly foulmouthed.

This account is designed to show that my schooldays were by no means fraught with fear and oppression alone, but that they brought with them also some uplifting spiritual experiences.

6

Thanks to my tender age and to Mistress Pirjo's goodness, I did not have to spend my holidays like other clerks in wandering from parish to parish begging my bread and money for my schooling. Mistress Pirjo gave me food and clothes, firing, houseroom and light, and even bought me a book, so that I was the first of the dialectic students to possess one. With her permission I inscribed on the title page the name MICHAEL BAST: KARVAJALKA, and the date: A.Dni MDXV. Below this I added a powerful malediction in Latin on anyone who stole my book or sold it without leave. Mistress Pirjo had bought it cheaply, and the names on the cover and the tattered pages showed that it had passed through many hands. Yet for years it was my dearest treasure. Its title was *Ars Moriendi, etc.,* or in other words *The Art of Dying.* From this, everyone will know what book it was, for it is still read and surely ever will be, a precious guide to death and the life to come.

But why Mistress Pirjo so benevolently cared for me and incurred such expenses on my behalf I could not understand—or rather I never once troubled my head about the matter and accepted it as naturally as she did. It may be that because of her kinsfolk and her secret trade she was obliged to live too much apart from others, and in course of time had wearied of having only her dog and her pig for company.

On holidays she would often take me with her and teach me many useful things, and at other times I would read to her from my book and expound it to her. While declaring its arguments to be self-evident to any sensible person, yet, said she, it sounded very wise in Latin.

In the spring, when cattle were led out to pasture, and Father Peter had done what he could to ensure their thriving, all prudent people came to Mistress Pirjo, well knowing that unless she bore their live-stock benevolently in mind cows would go dry, calves be stillborn, lambs break their legs, and horses stray into the bogs. To this there were so many trustworthy witnesses that Mistress Pirjo collected a cattle fee from every well-to-do house.

Among her regular visitors I soon took special note of Master Laurentius, whom on cold winter evenings she would treat to mulled spiced wine. Sometimes he brought provisions with him in a stained leather pouch, but I was never able to see what else the pouch contained. He wore a splashed leather jacket and seemed always very melancholy. Mistress Pirjo addressed him by the title of "Master," but I gave no thought to what his craft might be until the first time I saw him practice it. He appeared at dusk and went after dark, and I never saw him in the town, although to judge by the cordial esteem in which Mistress Pirjo held him he was evidently one of Åbo's most consequential citizens.

Such was their friendship that I began to see Master Laurentius as a faithful admirer who had not lost hope despite Mistress Pirjo's oft-expressed resolve to remain single all her days; the surest sign of this seemed to me to be that she served him his wine in a silver cup. I had nothing against Master Laurentius, for he was always friendly, and I found him a serious, solid person who liked to talk of death and to listen to precepts from my book on how we should prepare ourselves to take leave of this world.

One spring day, when the birches were out and the fields were turning green, Magister Martinus gave us a holiday to attend the hanging of two pirates who had recently been captured, for he believed that we should derive edification and benefit from the spectacle. That same evening Master Laurentius came again, and Mistress Pirjo gave him wine in the silver goblet. I had greeted him after the execution, despite the astonished glances of my companions, and now on seeing me again he rubbed his hands in embarrassment and avoided my eye.

I told him shyly that I had never thought a man's life could leave his body so swiftly and easily; and taking my words as a compliment to his skill he said, "You're a sensible lad, Michael—not like so many others of your age who take to their heels when they see me, and hide, or throw stones. And their parents are as bad for that matter. In the tavern I must sit alone, and all the fun stops when I come in. The hangman's life is a lonely one, and his craft is most usually handed down from father to son, as in my own family. Tell me frankly, Michael: Aren't you afraid to touch me?"

He held out his hand, and I grasped it without fear. Maintaining the clasp for a while, he looked me in the eyes, sighed heavily, and said, "You're a good fellow, Michael, and if you'd not done so well at school I'd have bound you apprentice to my trade—for I have no son. The hangman's business is the most important in all the world. Before him princes and even kings must bow the knee. Without him the judge is powerless and his sentence void. So the pay is good, and even during times of peace the executioner can be sure of a living, since human nature is incorrigible and crime unceasing. In turbulent times many have grown rich. The art of politics above all has proved a boon to us."

He fell silent and gulped some wine as if ashamed of his talkativeness, but I urged him to tell me more, and having gained Mistress Pirjo's permission he went on.

"The chief quality required of a good hangman is the knack of winning the confidence of his clients, in which respect his work may stand comparison with that of the priest or the physician. You saw today how stoutly my two friends mounted the ladder of their own accord. It's a reflection on the executioner if his client has to be dragged by force, or if he howls and screams to the people for mercy and declares his innocence. The great art is to induce him to meet his death like a wise man, full of Christian humility and in the conviction that life is vanity, and a swift, painless death the best gift the world can offer him."

It was some time before I dared express the ugly thought that had flashed into my head when I saw the helpless feet of those criminals dance their last dance upon the gallows.

"Master Laurentius! In your experienced hands I saw a man die so painlessly that I began to wonder whether after all there *is* anything —beyond death?"

He crossed himself reverently and answered, "That is godless talk I don't wish to hear. Who am I, a poor man, to seek proof of what can't be proved?"

But he spoke hesitantly, and when I had once more pressed him for an answer, he said, "You've guessed rightly, Michael. As a servant of death I have often pondered on these things, and my thoughts have moved in such a direction that I no longer speak to my clients of bliss and eternal life; I leave all that to the priests. But when some poor soul in terror of damnation begs me to tell him what I know of death,

14

I bid him imagine that out of an icy winter's night he steps exhausted into a dark, warm cabin and lays himself down on a soft bed. There he may sleep soundly without fear of being roused by a knock on the door, and being dragged out again into the cold. This is what I say; if it's a great sin, may it be forgiven me for the sake of the comfort it has brought to many whose faith was weak."

Although I knew that Master Laurentius had fallen into error here and was talking heresy without knowing it, his fancy afforded me special consolation, for my mother was often in my mind and my heart ached for her sake. It soothed me to suppose that when she drowned herself she slipped away from the shame and humiliation of life into a sleep whence none could wake her.

7

Such reflections were a sign that I had already lost my childish innocence and that the devil had begun to lay snares for my destruction. The same can be said of my breaking voice, which lost me my place as chorister; and the changes now taking place in my body gave me great concern.

One Saturday evening after Mistress Pirjo had bathed me in the bathhouse, she examined me with care, and when we were back in the house she said gravely, "Michael, from now on it would be better if you washed your own hair and back. And it's no longer seemly for you to sleep in the same bed as myself as it might expose you to temptation. You must have a bed of your own and wear a man's clothes, since a man you will soon be."

Her words saddened me, but I knew she was right, and knew also why sometimes on spring nights she would lie and sigh so deeply. I had already begun to reflect upon the relationship between men and women, and in such matters had never been left in any uncertainty, for the other scholars were coarse fellows who did not mince words. But when they boasted of their exploits, I reddened in shame. I had lofty notions of love and felt not the smallest desire to seek it when I learned how low and bestial was its physical aspect.

Nevertheless my mind was troubled with manifold and restless thoughts. When the nights grew lighter, I could not sleep, but wandered about the outskirts of the town, breathing the scent of the bird cherries and listening to the hoot of the owl and the quack of ducks among the reeds. I longed for friendship, but among my schoolfellows

I had no friend to whom I could lay bare my thoughts. So Father Peter became my confidant, and confession meant a great deal to me, although he could not always answer my anxious questions.

Father Peter had no doubt many failings, which he bore with Christian humility, but he was for all that a wise man; for when he had had a long talk with Mistress Pirjo she called me to her and said, "You've often begged to be allowed to wander about the country like other boys during the holidays. In these godless times you would only incur spiritual and bodily harm by this; and yet it's time you began to contribute toward your keep. Therefore Father Peter and I have decided that during this long vacation you shall go to work with a German gunmaker who has lately come to this town. He is seeking a decent, steady assistant—one who can write—to help him in the powder mill and the saltpeter boilery."

When she had come so far she wept.

"It's not that I wish it—I would gladly bear you in my hand like a flower, still—but Father Peter says it's not good for you to live alone with an unmarried woman without the company and teaching of men. But you must keep away from the powder mill and take care of yourself; and you must come home every Saturday so that I can give you a store of food—indeed I would never let you learn so dangerous a trade if this master, whose heathen name ties my tongue in knots, hadn't promised good payment. And Father Peter says that a boy of your age shouldn't be coddled."

Master Schwarzschwanz had sailed that year from Germany as soon as the waters were open, and had taken service with the constable of the castle. He had signed a contract of many clauses concerning gun founding, improvement of the powder mill, and the installation of a saltpeter boilery. This was taken by many as an omen of troublous times to come.

Master Schwarzschwanz was a short, broad-shouldered man with a swarthy face and flashing black eyes. He bellowed his orders under the impression that this would help the powder boys to understand him. When he had assured himself that I knew his language and could write, he kicked out the tippling clerk whom he had employed hitherto for lack of a better, and opened his heart to me. He reviled the constable and also the burgomaster, and damned the whole oafish nation to the hottest region of hell for having got him there on false pretenses. He tore off his cap, dashed it to the ground, and stamped upon it to give emphasis to his words. I had never seen so terrible a man. I gazed at him goggle-eyed and tried to memorize the unfamiliar oaths and curses of which he, a great traveler, had an inexhaustible supply.

I feared he would prove a stern master, but finding me steady and trustworthy he grew milder in his behavior, and treated me kindly, never roaring at me even when I made mistakes. He saw that I did my best to please him and admitted that I was quickly learning the principles of his craft.

The old mill stood at some distance from the town on the riverbank, since water was necessary to moisten the powder, and also to quench fire in the event of an explosion. But Master Schwarzschwanz practiced the caution of experience, and ground the sulphur, saltpeter, and charcoal separately between wooden discs. We did not have the trouble of preparing our own charcoal, for we were able to trade with skilled charcoal burners whose product was so excellent that my master vowed he had never seen its equal, especially that of birch, which gave such strength to the gunpowder as to admit of smaller proportions of saltpeter and costly sulphur.

Master Schwarzschwanz was now trying to ascertain the proper proportions of these ingredients, and would not rely upon set tables when using birch coal. He had a yardstick furnished with a movable plummet under which he would fire powder compounds of equal weight, noting the height to which the plummet was thrown by the explosion. I recorded the different proportions and their results until he had determined which were most effective.

After some days of experiment there came a suitable wind that blew steadily from the west, and we mixed the required quantities of sulphur, saltpeter, and charcoal in a rotating drum. My master linked the drum to the mill and bade the mill boy see that it turned evenly. Making the sign of the cross with reverence, he said, "Let us go, Michael." As we strolled over the flowery meadows within sight of the mill, he told me that many experts had their favorite winds for the mixing of powder. Some claimed that the north wind gave it strength, others preferred the south, and there were some who held by the southeast.

"But that's all superstition; it may impress laymen, but never seasoned brothers in the craft. So long as the mill runs smooth and cool, with plenty of grease in the bearings and no risk of a spark, the wind can blow from what quarter it pleases."

When he saw by the angle of the sun that time enough had elapsed, he roared to the boy to lock the sails; they ceased turning and we stepped in to inspect the mixture. The master took a handful of it, smelled it, tasted it, and said he was content. With wooden shovels the boys spread the powder on smooth boards to be moistened, pressed, and sieved into grains. Schwarzschwanz used only water for the moistening, although he received several gallons of costly brandy from the castle for this purpose.

"Brandy's useful in damp weather, or in the winter, or when the powder is needed at once, for it evaporates more quickly than water," he told me. "But that's a trade secret. For every four bushels of gunpowder I claim half a gallon of brandy from the castle, and it's no business of the constable's—plague take him—how I use it."

While he was speaking, he pressed the powder into brittle cakes and showed the boys how to sieve them, so as to give the powder the necessary "corned" quality, since finer grains could be used only in small arms. Then he ordered it to be spread out to dry on planks, on a warm, sunny slope out of the wind; and finally it was poured into tubs whose heads were driven home by wooden mallets. The powder boys were forbidden to carry the smallest metal object about them, and were shod with slippers of soft leather or birch bark.

The gunpowder stood up to the usual tests, and the gray-haired gunners at the castle acknowledged that it was of exceptionally fine quality, dust free and evenly corned. Next followed practice shooting in the presence of the constable, and my good master showed that with three shots from a cannon royal he could hit a rowboat on the river. That is to say, he hit a land target at the equivalent distance, for cannon balls are costly and must be collected and brought back after firing. The only mishap during the exercises occurred when we used the bombard, for a stone ball as big as a barrel struck a rock and burst, although the ball was bound with iron.

"None but backward countries like this one use stone balls!" spat my master in contempt. "The only cannon ball worthy of the name is smooth and perfectly round; and this can only be achieved by casting, which makes for cheapness and accuracy of aim, since the balls are all of the same size and weight. But I'm unversed in the art, for it remains a foundry secret, and so we must continue to forge our missiles."

The constable, who usually listened willingly to what he had to say, now retorted indignantly, "Stone was good enough for our fathers and their fathers before them. This is a poor country, and it's plainly the Creator's intention to make up for the want of metal by stone and cheap labor."

When the constable had gone, Master Schwarzschwanz flung down his cap and stamped upon it, and swore till the old gunners' faces relaxed in melancholy smiles.

"God's blood!" he cried when he was calmer. "The constable's gone against our agreement, and wants me to make him iron guns. Neither he nor perhaps the whole country can afford the copper and tin necessary for gunmetal. But a nation that says it can't afford it, with its belfries full of bells and its burghers' cupboards packed with tankards, is doomed to go under."

When we returned to our lodging, he admitted gravely that he found himself in a dilemma. In his view, one bronze gun was worth ten of iron; even when cracked it was safe and fit for service, for bronze was tough and would not fly to pieces.

"Only fools or madmen can be hired to serve iron pieces," he said. "Experienced gunners won't do it. But we find ourselves now in a difficulty, for I've bound myself to supply the fortress with ordnance; and I'm not an ironfounder. I cast bronze only. And furthermore I will not be responsible for the injury and death of innocent gunners that must attend the use of iron pieces."

I reminded him that there were highly skilled smiths in Finland whom he could teach to forge the guns. He scratched his ear and observed that though he had seen it done he was hardly fit to impart the knowledge. His perplexity was great, but when he had drunk a tankard or two of ale he recovered his spirits and talked of hiring a smithy, and a master smith who could teach others as soon as he had become proficient in the new methods.

8

I have given a full account of these things because they led to another incident that was to have a great influence on my life. While Master Schwarzschwanz was laboring to install a forge, my holidays came to an end and I was obliged to trudge back to school. I had grown used to independence, and even the subtleties of dialectic now seemed musty. Magister Martinus considered me so advanced that he employed me as assistant teacher, and I had to ram the elements of Latin grammar into the skulls of newcomers. In just this way does a master craftsman delegate the rough work to his apprentices and apply no more than the final polish himself.

Magister Martinus now appeared only in the morning, at noon, and again in the evening, to thrash all his new pupils impartially from the eldest to the youngest. It fell to me to comfort them by telling them that I had been through the same ordeal; that the steam bath of learning scalded the skin indeed, but brought the reward of scholarship and good appointments; and that bear suet was the most soothing and efficacious ointment.

Magister Martinus thought it needless for me to study the breviary, since my birth disqualified me for ordination. So I became his unpaid assistant, which I bitterly resented as it meant that in any case I must exchange my gay breeches for the gray gown of a scholar. Forbidden fruits are ever sweetest, and I could not conceive of any greater happiness than that of being admitted to the Holy Order of priesthood in the fellowship of the Church.

Plunged in such reflections as these, I was walking along the street one day, oblivious of my surroundings, when I was startled by a terrible bellowing and shrill cries of distress. Stampeding citizens collided with me and knocked me flat. As I struggled to my feet again, I had hardly time to see a raging bull thundering down upon me before it had caught me on its horns and with a heave of its powerful neck had tossed me roof high. As I fell to earth again, I saw a strip of my gown hanging from one of the beast's horns. It had broken its tether and rubbed the bandage from its eyes, and now panted and snorted till the dust flew, pawing the ground and threatening to gore me where I lay. I believed my last hour had come and was so rigid with terror that I felt no pain, nor was I able to stammer the briefest prayer for my soul's sake. But at this instant a powerfully built peasant lad stepped up to the bull, gripped it coolly by the horns, and forced it over onto its back.

While the animal lay kicking and bellowing most frightfully, the boy turned his head to me and asked, "Are you hurt?"

Only then did I feel pain. My whole body began to tremble, and I mumbled prayers of thanksgiving for my preservation. Men rushed up, bound the bull's legs, and blindfolded it. The peasant who had been leading it to the butcher vowed repeatedly that it was the quietest, best-behaved bull imaginable and that I must have been teasing it. To my great joy the creature tossed its head so violently that it dislocated the man's shoulder, causing him to cut short his nonsense and to complain that Åbo town was possessed of the devil and that he ought never to have brought his virtuous bull to such a place.

I turned my eyes to my rescuer and surveyed him closely, for I had him to thank for my life. He was a head taller than I, and his gray eyes had a sleepy look in them. He had shoes and a knapsack of birch bark, and his ragged jacket showed him to be poor.

"You're strong to be able to throw a bull with your bare hands," I said. "I have you to thank for saving my life."

"That was nothing," he replied, and seemed embarrassed. I noticed that blood was running from my breast. There was a sharp pain in my ribs, and I was so giddy that I had to lean against the wall.

"Where are you going?" I asked him.

"I'm following my nose," he said, and seemed to find my question needless and indiscreet. Undeterred, I begged him to come with me to Mistress Pirjo's, for my knees were so weak that I could not have reached home alone.

A few moments before, when I had been lying on the ground staring into the snorting nostrils of the bull, I felt I would gladly give all I owned to the Church if I might be spared, but now I was thankful for the hard bump that had stunned me before I could make any rash promises. And as I tottered home leaning on the young peasant, followed by a flock of scared and pitying people, I thought of giving him my silver-mounted sheath knife and the money I had saved from my summer's wages. Yet by the time we arrived at Mistress Pirjo's cabin I was already cursing myself for unnecessary extravagance, and felt that three silver groats would be too much for a young man who could seldom, if ever, have held a minted coin in his hand.

Mistress Pirjo wept bitterly when she saw my pitiable plight and heard what had happened. She undressed me as if I had been a child again, and hastened to rub in salves. Careful examination showed her that two of my ribs were broken, and having bound my breast so tightly that I could scarcely breathe she tucked me up in her own bed. Meanwhile the peasant sat placidly on the threshold, munching a chunk of hard bread and some dried mutton he had taken from his knapsack. The children who had run after us gathered in a group to stare at him, picking their noses, and scratching their legs with the soles of their feet. At last Mistress Pirjo chased them away and asked the boy to come in.

"What's your name and your father's name? Where do you come

from? What's your trade? Where are you going? What brought you to Michael's rescue?" demanded Mistress Pirjo.

The youth, who seemed slow witted, scratched his ear.

"Eh?" he said. But presently his mind cleared, and he told us that his name was Andy Karlsson from Letala parish. He had come to town to learn the trade of a smith, since by a mishap he had broken the anvil of the blacksmith in his own district, and this man in his rage had chased him from the forge.

"How could you break an anvil?" I marveled. Andy's honest gray eyes were upon me as he replied.

"The smith put the sledge in my hand and told me to strike, and I struck. Then he said 'Strike harder,' and I struck harder. But he went on with his 'Harder, harder' and at last I took the biggest hammer and knocked the beak off the anvil."

Mistress Pirjo stared at him in amazement. She said, "This cabin of mine has settled at one corner so that the floor slopes. When I scrub it the water all runs down to that corner and rots the timbers. I've often thought it should be seen to. Could you lift the corner of the cabin for me so that I could push a stone or two under it?"

"Willingly," said Andy. They went out together and soon afterward there was a tremendous creaking, my bed rocked as if on stormy seas, and Mistress Pirjo cried out anxiously, "Don't knock the house down, you oaf! That'll do, that'll do!"

When they came in again, Andy was not even out of breath. Mistress Pirjo sat with her chin in her hand, looking at him. At length she asked, "Are you quite right in the head, you poor boy?"

After some reflection Andy looked at her and said humbly, "I may be a bit slow, but I never do wrong on purpose. Of course I never meant to wreck your cabin just now. I just can't control my strength. That's my whole trouble. That's what drove me from home, and from the smithy too."

I begged him to tell us of his home.

"I come from a poor place and a poor family. My father and mother had nothing—nothing but their children. One born every year and sometimes two at a time. We were eighteen mouths to feed, and I don't think mother was quite sure of all our names, for her memory began to fail as she lost her teeth. I was useful of course, because I could pull all the carts. But then when I put my back into it Dad had so much trouble mending them that he said a horse would be cheaper. You see, I wanted to eat as much as a horse when I was doing a horse's work,

22

but Dad didn't agree, because food's scarce in a poor house even though the bread's half bark."

He rubbed a tear from the corner of his eye and went on.

"I don't know why it is—why I've been blessed with more strength than there's room for in a little village. My father and mother are both puny, and when I played at tug of war with my brothers I could lift all ten of them from the ground if the pole held. But they say my granddad was a strong man who wasn't afraid to tackle a bear with his ax; one of them hugged him to death. My father thought I should do best as a soldier. But I don't fancy that at all, because I'm scared of brawling and hard words. Mother broke a loaf and gave me half when I left, and whispered to me to learn the blacksmith's trade. I'm trying to do as she said—but how shall I fare in this big city? Maybe I shan't even have enough to eat!"

He broke into hopeless weeping, grown man though he was, and faltered through his tears the story of how he left home.

"It was hard leaving those well-known places. I stood a long time at the gate looking back before I took heart enough to set out along the path. And then by ill luck I fell in with a bear. He reared up and challenged me. I was very frightened, but I remembered my grandfather and my homelessness, and felt that to die in the beast's hug would be the best thing I could do, for I was only a trouble—even to my own people. I meant to wrestle fairly with him, but he batted me in the face till I sat down with my head buzzing like a wasp's nest. He's left his marks on me. So then I lost my temper, though I'm a quiet chap by nature, and I got a grip of his paw and twisted it until he roared with pain and fled along the path. I followed, roaring louder than he did—being so angry—and he climbed a tree to get away from me. I shook the trunk till he fell down and there I bashed his head in with a rock. Then I went on to the village with the bearskin on my shoulders and began work at the forge. But the smith soon threw me out. And so here I am."

When he had finished his tale and wiped the tears from his face, Mistress Pirjo exclaimed, "You wouldn't fool us, would you, Andy Karlsson?"

He stared at her round eyed with astonishment and asked, "Why should I lie about a thing like that? Besides, he was a fine he-bear and I kept his tool—they say sorcerers pay good money for such things and use them for all sorts of black arts."

He drew forth the organ from his knapsack. I had never seen one

23

before and took a fancy to it, but Mistress Pirjo forestalled me and snatched it for herself, saying, "I'll pay you as much as anyone for this —whatever you ask—for it's excellent for love philtres, and one never knows when it may come in useful."

Andy said, "Take it as a gift, noble lady, and help me rather with advice; for if anyone needs it I do."

But Mistress Pirjo made warm protest.

"Virgin and saints forbid that I should take advantage of your simplicity. We're your debtors. St. Nicholas himself must have sent you to defend Michael in his hour of need, and he means to knit your lives together. You may sleep here tonight and I'll find you food and clothes while we consider how you and Michael may best serve one another."

"There's nothing to consider!" I exclaimed. "Master Schwarzschwanz has engaged a master smith who needs assistants; they needn't be fully trained, since the smith himself must first learn the art of forging guns under my master's direction."

Thenceforward Andy Karlsson's destiny was linked with mine.

9

This incident took place in 1517, which was, when I now think of it, the world's last happy year and my own happiest time, although the poisonous seeds that were to bring ruin on mankind were already germinating. I had the first hint of what was to follow from a conversation in Mistress Pirjo's house between Master Laurentius and Father Peter.

Father Peter said, "The Estates of Sweden have deposed our most reverend Archbishop Gustaf Trolle from his sacred office. Such a thing has never been known in this realm, and I dread to think what the Holy Father in Rome will say to it."

"That's not a matter we need trouble our heads about," said Master Laurentius, rubbing his hands in satisfaction. "The Kingdom will be placed under the interdict: no baptism, no sacraments, and no joining in matrimony, and the churches will be closed. This has happened for lesser offenses."

I joined in the talk here, and said, "Far be it from me to defend a godless act, but I've heard it said on good authority that His Grace the Archbishop is a confirmed supporter of the Union and thus an enemy to the country. We've made a lasting peace with the Czar and sealed it with a kiss upon the cross, so Denmark is now our only danger. And

24

we know that danger is at hand, for we're making gunpowder and forging cannon, as I myself can witness, having toiled from cockcrow till vespers all this summer to strengthen the country's defenses— though no one thanks me for it."

"Worldly honor and reward are but vanity," returned Father Peter piously. "On the Last Day we shall be weighed and judged according to our own merits. But the interdict! It would cause great hardship to the obedient servants of the Church by depriving them of their lawful dues, for services rendered to their flock. We may be greatly impoverished."

Master Laurentius rubbed his hands again even more complacently.

"Weeping and wailing are of no avail. When the storm gathers, the wise man makes up his mind quickly whether to be Jute or Swede, Unionist or anti-Unionist, for or against the Archbishop, and acts accordingly. This is called politics, and is the greatest of all arts, for sooner or later adherence to either party will lead to one and the same end. Let a man choose as he will, the moment must come that brings a sword in the belly, a club on the head, or a rope round the neck. The executioner alone is impartial, since both Jute and Swede have need of him. He's as necessary to ecclesiastical as to secular judges. *He* has no reason to complain of times when his services are most sought after."

Mistress Pirjo set aside the silver cup and wooden mug, saying, "Keep such pleasantries to yourself, Master Laurentius. Don't you see the boy's gone as white as a sheet, and even Andy's hair's on end, slow witted though he is? At least we're lucky to live in peace, far from the intrigues and squabbles of the nobles. We're content to appoint or depose kings and regents as Stockholm may direct. It's all the same to the people whether they pay tax to Jute or to Swede, so long as they're left in peace to earn their livings. We in this penniless country are fortunate; we can look on and bide our time until one of the parties wins and we see which side to take. I'm glad Michael has chosen the goose quill rather than the sword, for he that takes the sword shall perish by the sword, as the Scriptures say."

Master Laurentius maintained stubbornly that the world had altered, and that now a stroke of the quill could give the executioner more work than the rattle of swords and the roar of harquebuses; but I was too young to understand what he meant. Mistress Pirjo set the porridge bowl on the table and dropped a dab of butter in the middle of it. We crossed ourselves and dipped our spoons into the dish con-

25

tentedly. The world could not be so bad when poor folk had buttered porridge to eat.

But with the last vessels to make the harbor before the sea froze came strange news from Germany. There was talk of a great uproar among the monks on account of a certain Doctor Luther, who had nailed upon the door of a church in Wittenberg a list of ninety-five points, in which among other things he condemned the traffic in indulgences, thereby rendering suspect the Holy Father's temporal heritage as the one keeper of the Keys of Heaven. Yet these rumors appeared to me as no more than evidence that the Germans were a restless and discontented people, a fact I had already noted in Master Schwarzschwanz's company. I never dreamed that any man of sense could question the articles of faith revealed by Holy Church, which made life so simple and relieved mankind of much unnecessary thought.

BOOK 2.

Temptation

I

ONE mild day in the new year Magister Martinus sent his pupils home and asked me to go with him to his room. He sat down at his table, rubbed his narrow and ever bedewdropped nose with thumb and forefinger, and giving me a searching look he said solemnly, "In the Name of the Father, Son, and Holy Ghost. Michael, my son, what do you mean to be?"

His words struck at my heart. I fell on my knees before him, weeping, and said, "Father Martin, my dearest hope has been to devote myself to the service of Holy Church, and my soul is as bitter as wormwood because many who learned their first lessons with me are now tonsured priests. True, I'm younger than these comrades of mine, or so I believe, but I'm ready to toil night and day to increase my knowledge. Yet I'm told that my hopes and labors are in vain. I have already sought to enter the cloister, so that after a year's novitiate I might assume the black habit and serve the Church all my days, but Father Peter has counseled me against this. He says that I cannot expect any other position in the monastery than that of a lay brother—even were I to be received—since I have no worldly possessions to renounce."

"Michael," said Magister Martinus gravely, "who speaks with your tongue: the Lord God or the Devil?"

His question bewildered me. He let me reflect for a while and then continued.

"You're a talented boy, but your tendency to plunge into the profoundest matters and to put questions fit to puzzle the most scholarly has given me much concern. I fancy it is not Christian humility that works in you but most damnable pride when in disputation you seek to snare your preceptor in his own words, and put shame upon him, as happened latterly in the matter of Jonah and the whale."

"Father Martin, I am not as wicked as you suppose, and my heart is as soft as wax. Give me hope, and I will amend my ways; I will walk barefoot in the snow and fast for weeks on end to be worthy of your blessing."

He sighed heavily, but when he spoke again it was in a tone of anger.

"I've no doubt you would do anything to gratify your morbid ambition and outdo your fellows. Year after year I have awaited some sign from above that should show me your proper station in life, but none has come. Years pass, your origin sinks ever more deeply into obscurity, and soon there will be no one left who remembers your mother. Is it not best for you to accept your allotted path in life, and learn to fulfill with honor some worldly appointment?"

"Do you cast me out, Father?" I cried in a great fright, for the school was the one fixed point in my life, and for all my grumbling I dreaded leaving it.

"I do not cast you out, you stiff-necked wretch! On the contrary, I have felt an unreasonable fondness for you because your passion for books and your fiery enthusiasm remind me of my own youth. The path of learning is strewn with thorns. I had to sell my inheritance in order to study at Rostock University; yet for me no sacrifice was too great, such was my thirst for scholarship. So I understand you, Michael. But look at me now and see what came of it all: I'm just an ill-natured old man who will soon be blind from overstudying in my youth. In death my sole consolation will be the simple one that is offered to every soul, clerk and layman alike, that is to say, Extreme Unction and the forgiveness of sins. In this respect I'm no better than the meanest cowherd, for all my talents. For your own sake I tell you: You gain nothing by clinging so desperately to scholarship. You would be wiser to submit humbly to your destiny, to engage in some useful writer's work, and cease sighing for the moon."

"So be it," I answered bitterly, my eyes brimming with scalding tears.

28

"I will go and be a cowherd, since that is all the wisdom life has taught you, Father!"

He relented then. He patted my cheek with his veined, trembling hand and said, "A worldly appointment leaves you free to enjoy the pleasures of this life. You can wear a feather in your cap and run among the girls, and later settle down amid the perpetual joys of a good wife and obedient children."

I replied sulkily that neither marriage nor a pack of squalling brats in a poor writer's hovel held any charms for me.

"And besides," I added, "every priest—every bishop even—has a mistress and children and no one considers it a sin. They enjoy all the advantages of marriage and suffer none of its drawbacks. Only a secret marriage is the unforgivable transgression for those in orders. But these are not my reasons for aspiring to the priesthood. For a poor youth like me ordination is the only door to continued study and perhaps to some university appointment and the enjoyment of a benefice."

Hardly had I uttered these words than I blushed in confusion, for in inadvertently disclosing my most secret dreams I had given Magister Martinus valid grounds for accusing me of godless ambition.

But my teacher and guardian no longer rebuked me. He said sadly, "Do you not see, Michael, how wrong it is of you to regard the Church and Holy Order merely as the means to gratify your lust for scholarship? It's for the Church to choose her servants, and out of your own mouth you stand condemned as a petty fortune hunter and hypocrite. You would make the very monstrance your footstool if it could raise you an ell higher. In time you'll understand this, and be ashamed."

"Father Martin," I said, "I possess nothing in the world but my head and my hands—and Holy Church, which has been my one unfailing hope. Why should I be scorned when many who are stupider than I are thought worthy? Why am I rejected simply because I have neither possessions, nor family, nor any relatives who can buy me dispensation at the Papal Court for my mother's sin? Why?"

"Do you now cast doubts upon the Church's teaching?" he said sternly. "Who are you, little worm, to rise up and question her decisions? I warn you, Michael, you are not far from heresy!"

These terrible words frightened me, and I was humbled, although defiance yet glowed in my heart. Nevertheless in the end it appeared that Magister Martinus did not want to drive me from the school. He even promised payment if I would go on instructing the younger scholars in grammar, and this he secured by a generous recommendation of me to Lars Goldsmith, as a tutor for his two sons.

2

With the freeing of the waters in the spring came disturbing news. We learned then of King Christian II's intention to sail to Stockholm, reinstate the Archbishop, punish the swaggering Swedish lords, and set upon his own head the crown of the Kingdom of Svea, which was his lawful inheritance. Part of the Åbo garrison took ship for Stockholm to support Sten Sture, the Regent, and the castle was put in a state of defense. It was generally held, however, that Åbo's resistance would be useless if Stockholm fell, and would lead merely to turmoil and destruction. There was less talk now of the cruelty of the Jutes, and the people preferred to await the event in silence. But I longed for war, for it suited my mood. And what had I to lose?

At midsummer, on the Feast of St. John the Baptist, I went to church —which I had not done for a long time—to implore the Mother of God to help me live a better life. I had come as far as the town hall when I heard Andy calling to me pitifully from the vaults beneath it. He was clinging with both hands to the grating so that I could see his tousled hair and his broad face, which was so bruised and bloody that I hardly knew him.

"Jesus, Mary!" I cried in horror. "What have you been doing?"

"That's what I should like to know," he lamented. "I seem to have been mad drunk. Who'd have thought brandy could do this to a quiet chap like me? I'm black and blue all over. But I can't have been the only one—there must have been others fighting too, for a man could never do himself so much damage, though he should roll head-over-heels downhill over rocks."

"I'll run to church and pray that you mayn't fetch up at the whipping post, or be fed to the crows for manslaughter," I suggested, to comfort him.

But Andy answered wrathfully, "What's done is done, and whining won't help it. Be a Christian, Michael—get me some water and a bite to eat. My stomach's like an empty oven, and I've more regard for that than for my skin."

The city watchmen were not to be seen, and I brought him water in a bucket. But he could not get at it through the grating, and so fierce

30

was his thirst that he put forth his strength and wrenched the bars apart so as to ease the vessel in between them.

I was alarmed to see the mortar cracking, and said, "You mustn't damage civic property, Andy, or they'll give you an even harder punishment. But if you want to escape, now's your time; you might be able to wriggle through the hole you've made."

"I'm not going to escape," retorted Andy loftily. "I mean to bear these insults and this well-deserved punishment with Christian humility, and win back my self-respect before God and men."

I had a few coins in my purse, having intended to light a candle to St. John the Baptist, a virtuous man who chose to be beheaded rather than succumb to the lecherous Herodias. I ran to the Three Crowns and bought an earthenware bowl full of turnips and herring, and an armful of bread. But I could not linger with Andy, for the burghers were beginning to pass by on their way to High Mass.

"Keep your heart up," I told him. "I'll try to sneak back this evening with more food."

"Keep my heart up! Easy, isn't it, with frogs hopping all over me and rats gnawing my nose every time I try to get some sleep! Still, maybe after a bellyful the world will look a little brighter."

I left him then and hurried to the Cathedral; but Satan sets his snares more cunningly than we suppose. When I came from Mass, full of contrition, I was detained in the porch by a youngish man whose cheeks were speckled black, as if at some time he had been peppered with gunpowder. As he girded on his sword, he addressed me in German, saying that he had heard a good report of me. He was a stranger in the city and with his sister was staying at the inn that stood next door to the Three Crowns tavern. He told me that he was in need of the help of some clever youth, and asked me to call upon him that evening. I should not regret it, he said. His manner was suspiciously oily, yet he had a winning smile. He was dressed in tight-fitting hose and a velvet doublet with silver buttons, and it seemed to me that I should lose nothing by doing as he asked.

When Mistress Pirjo heard of Andy's pitiable plight, she prepared a bag of food for him, and as evening drew on I carried it to the town hall. There in the courtyard I met the jailer, a one-legged man-at-arms who had taught me to handle a sword.

"You can go in," he said in a friendly tone. "You're not the first visitor."

I stepped down into the cellar, which was now lit by a cheerful

31

tallow candle. There sat the hostess of the Three Crowns with Andy's head in her lap, stroking his cheeks and speaking tenderly.

"Michael," said she gravely when I appeared, "a better, nobler boy than your friend Andy it would be hard to find. When I'd come home to bed last night, after the midsummer bonfire, I was roused at dawn by a hideous din. A score of drunken apprentices had smashed down the door and broken into the house. They threw my poor husband into an empty kneading trough and piled stones on the lid, and then forced me to serve them with beer and brandy and food. This good lad happened to come in, and when he saw my distress he set about the fellows singlehanded with his bare fists, like St. Samson at the walls of Jericho; and he threw them out, though they fell upon him with cudgels and stakes and logs, and he could hardly stand on his feet, tired as he was from the midsummer night's doings. When at last the watchmen turned up, they rebuked me very insolently for serving customers at unlawful hours, and this young man misunderstood their intentions and threw them out, too, to protect the peace of my house. Then he fell asleep on the floor, worn out, but the watch came back and kicked him and beat him and hustled him off to prison, since they could find no one else to arrest. They shall get their bellyful for this rascally business, so help me God! And so says my poor old man, whom I forgot to let out until this morning."

She stroked Andy's cheek and said, "You're in good hands, my friend, for as sure as I hold a tavern license and pay tax, I'll get you out of this. So drink up that beer—it's my best—and restore your strength."

Seeing that Andy lacked for nothing and was being well cared for, and that my presence was superfluous, I went to drink a quart of ale at the Three Crowns, where the landlord bore out every word of his wife's account.

The strong ale braced me and gave me courage to enter the inn and inquire for the stranger who lived there with his sister. He appeared to enjoy a reputation for wealth and liberality, for I was shown to his room without delay. On entering, I was at once aware of the pleasant smell of sealing wax; a taper was burning on the table where the stranger sat writing. His writing materials were of fine quality, and were such as could be carried in a copper case at his belt. He recognized me, rose from the table with a friendly greeting, and took my hand. This was flattering, for he had the easy, distinguished air of a true

32

gentleman to whom fine lodgings, wine every day, splendid clothes, and good service were matters of course.

He told me that his name was Didrik Slaghammer and that he was the son of a Cologne merchant who had been knighted by the Emperor. Ever since his youth he had traveled in foreign lands, and had been trading lately in Danzig and Lübeck. Tales of the holy places of Finland, which were famed all round the Baltic, had lured him to Åbo; for although in his young days he had led a wild life, he had grown steadier since his thirtieth year, and now took pleasure in praiseworthy acts such as pilgrimages to holy places, when these were not too inaccessible. He gave me to understand that he needed me as interpreter-guide on these pilgrimages.

Greatly delighted, I told him of St. Henry's Road, of the sun of Nådendal, of the Holy Cross in Anianpelto, of Reso church, which the giants built, and of many other holy places. His thoughts wandered as I spoke. He stifled a yawn, which bared his feline, predatory teeth, and began to fidget with a dagger that lay on the lid of his traveling chest.

"People have tried to scare me with tales of this savage country, and of its wild beasts and robbers," he remarked, "and so I've brought with me a pair of these newfangled horse pistols, which have helped me out of many tight places."

He showed me two short-barreled weapons in a double holster that could be slung over the horse's back, so that the heavy leaden butts rested within convenient reach. Yet his interest in such matters seemed hardly consonant with his professed piety.

Suddenly he asked me whether I had heard that King Christian was arming against Sweden, and what the Finns in general thought of it. I replied that such rumors had greatly damaged trade. Åbo merchants dared not send their ships into the open sea for fear of Danish men-of-war. The vessels had to set their course to Lübeck through dangerous coastal waters where contrary winds often sent them aground, leaving them a prey to pirates from Ösel and the Esthonian coast. And although these Åbo traders sought the protection of Lübeck convoys, the citizens of Lübeck were disinclined to afford them this protection now that the Åbo city council no longer reserved half their seats for German members, as in former years, but kept all civic appointments for men of their own nation. I boasted also of the powder mill and the guns that were being cast, and said that the Jutes would have a warm reception if ever they ventured within range of Åbo fortress.

Herr Didrik toyed absently with his gun, pulling the trigger and

33

sending bright sparks from the flint. He said with a smile that war held no terrors for him, but he had his sister to think of, and therefore it would be reassuring to learn how many pieces of ordnance there were at the castle and of what caliber, how large the garrison was, how it was paid, who was in command, and where the troops came from. It might also be well to know the names of the most eminent citizens and how far they were to be trusted in matters of state.

He seemed a nervous fellow; indeed this was already evident from the fact that he kept weapons handy at a peaceful inn. So to reassure him I told him what I knew of the garrison, at the same time reminding him that I was a clerk and no soldier, and advising him to consult my good friend and former master the gunfounder. Indeed I would have fetched him on the instant, but the friendly stranger restrained my eagerness, being unwilling to disturb so respected a craftsman on St. John's Day—a craftsman moreover who had met with base ingratitude and was therefore easily angered. For he had heard this of Master Schwarzschwanz and was already aware that I had been his secretary; therefore he would be content with what I could tell him, especially as he found me so intelligent. How many bombards were there at the castle, he wondered; how many cannon royal, culverins, falcons, falconets, swivel guns, and harquebuses? I tried to recall what I knew, and he made swift notes of the figures, but in front of these he scrawled only mysterious characters. This seemed to me no fit occupation for a merchant or a devout pilgrim. My speech began to falter, and I gave him reserved answers when he went on to question me about the soldiers' equipment and the sailings from Åbo. His curiosity seemed boundless.

All at once he noticed my misgivings, swept his papers together, and locked them up in his traveling chest, saying with a laugh, "I see you're startled at my excessive curiosity, Michael. But I was born with an insatiable thirst for knowledge of all kinds, and I'm in the habit of collecting useful information wherever I go. One never knows when it may be needed. But I have pestered you enough. Let us eat, drink, and be merry. You shall be my guest this evening."

He led me into an adjoining room where stood a table laden with delicacies and lit with the soft splendor of wax tapers. Yet it was not the table I gazed at. The loveliest and most expensively dressed woman I had ever seen was coming toward me. Her petticoats made a swishing sound as she advanced; she held her head proudly, and Herr Didrik bowed courteously to kiss her hand.

34

"Agnes, my dear sister," said he. "Allow me to present to you Michael the scholar, an able youth who besides his priestly learning is also proficient in the art of making gunpowder, and was at one time secretary to a gunfounder. He has had the great goodness to promise to help us in perfecting our knowledge both for worldly profit and for our souls' sake."

At this the lady gave me a warm smile and held out her hand. I had never before kissed a woman's hand, and shyness forbade me to raise my eyes to her beautiful and aristocratic face. Clumsily I bowed and let my lips touch her fingers; they were warm and white and smelled of fine ointments.

She said with a laugh as merry as her brother's, "Let us not be stiff with one another. We're all young, and I'm weary of sitting shut up in my room away from cheerful company. And sir, I am no wolf to devour you! You may safely raise your handsome face and look me in the eyes."

I was thrown into even deeper confusion when she addressed me as "sir" as if I had been a gentleman born, and spoke flatteringly of my appearance. But I looked up at her mischievous brown eyes, and she gave me such a wanton smile that the blood rose to my cheeks. In my simplicity I did not then know that her lips were painted, that her eyebrows were plucked, and her cheeks dusted with white powder. She seemed to me in the soft, clear light of the wax candles the most wonderful, the most beautiful woman I had ever seen.

We sat down at the table to oxtongue and roast goose spiced with saffron and pepper, and we drank sweet Spanish wine from the finest goblets the inn could furnish. I had not the remotest idea of how much such a meal might cost, but all my misgivings vanished and I ate as neatly as I could, cutting the meat with a knife into small pieces that could be picked up in the fingers, instead of gripping the bone with both hands in the vulgar manner and gnawing at it with a greasy mouth. The fiery wine went quickly to my head; I forgot all my wretchedness and felt as if I were in heaven surrounded by kindly angels. And while we ate, the one-eyed flute player from the Three Crowns played sweet airs in the adjoining room until Herr Didrik sent him ale and dismissed him, no doubt because he could not endure such miserable music. Instead, he proposed that we should sing, and we rendered a few godly student songs concerning the evanescence of earthly joys.

The lady soon found the room somewhat warm, and dropping her gauzy scarf she revealed her shoulders. Her bodice of green velvet was embroidered with pearls, gold thread, and red hearts which somehow led one's eyes to her breasts. Never had I seen a gown cut so low, and the beholder could be in no uncertainty as to the lady's figure whenever she made a rash movement, although now and then she would pull up the front of her dress.

Herr Didrik followed the direction of my gaze and said smiling, "My sister Agnes was named after the saint, and when we sit in good company I could wish she might be favored with a miracle similar to hers. My sister is a faithful follower of court fashions; but don't let it disturb you, Michael. In these joyous times no woman is required to hide her fairest charms. Indeed the most discreet lady is encouraged to reveal whatever may be worth revealing."

My face felt rather hot, and I asked what miracle had happened to St. Agnes. In Finland her cult had been overshadowed by that of St. Henry, and to me she was unknown. Herr Didrik explained that a Roman judge had sent her naked to a brothel because being a Christian she had refused the hand of his son. But the Almighty in His grace had caused the holy Agnes's hair to grow so long as to form a concealing cloak in which she was able to wrap herself and so protect her chastity from shameless eyes and hands.

"As you see, my sister has dyed her hair red in the Venetian manner," he went on. "It would be splendid to see her enveloped in so fiery a mantle. But I am perplexed by a problem which only a learned clerk could solve. If such a miracle were to be repeated—which I fancy is unlikely, since my sister is not notably shy—would her hair be red throughout its length, or would the part nearest the head retain its natural color, so that the dark cloak would have only a wide red border?"

I admitted that the point was too knotty for me with my poor learning to pronounce upon, although a more perfect scholar might win a doctor's degree by a disputation on this theme at any learned university. I ventured to affirm, however, that the world would be deprived of much delight if Madam Agnes were to be honored with such a miracle.

She smiled in acknowledgment of my compliment, and Herr Didrik said, "At princely courts even ladies of high rank have grown envious of the courtesans and now permit themselves to be portrayed stark naked by famous painters to show that they have no blemish to be ashamed of. And what could be more delightful than life at the medicinal springs, where men and women may in all decency spend days together in warm baths wearing no more than a loincloth—and even play backgammon and enjoy meals together at floating tables?"

I remarked that men and women in Finland were in the habit of taking steam baths together, but that this was among the common people and for cleanliness only, not for pleasure. Herr Didrik was curious, and asked me if I often took such baths with young girls, which I firmly denied. He saw that I was embarrassed, and, exchanging a glance with his sister, began to talk of other things.

The table had by now been cleared. He fingered his drinking cup and asked, "Michael, what do you think of the action of the Estates in deposing and imprisoning the Archbishop of Sweden?"

I was taken aback by this abrupt question, but replied cautiously, "Who am I to pronounce upon such high matters? The Archbishop is suspected of intrigues against the State, and the most reverend bishops were parties to his dismissal. Shall I be wiser than they?"

Herr Didrik retorted hotly, "Is young Sten Sture the State, then, in your opinion? Isn't it rather the arrogance of his whole family that has taught them to regard the Kingdom as their property, despite the Union of Kalmar by which King Christian of Denmark is the only lawful ruler?"

I remarked that the Jutes had brought nothing but bloodshed and disaster to the Kingdom of Sweden and that there could be no enemies more cruel and more faithless. To scare an Åbo child into good behavior it was enough to say "The Jute'll get you!"

This surprised Herr Didrik, and he answered angrily, "I thought you were a sensible boy, Michael, but I see you're content to repeat what others have said, without attempting to think for yourself."

He began to explain what a resolute, able, and merciful monarch King Christian was. He told me that there was nothing His Majesty hated more than oppression by the nobles and that he always took the people's part against them. His intention was to crush Lübeck's mastery of the Baltic and make Copenhagen a mighty center of commerce; vessels from here should sail the seas unhindered, to the profit of his subjects, and it would not be long before his Kingdom was powerful and wealthy.

"It's only a question of time," Herr Didrik persisted, "before the haughty Swedish lords will be forced to give way. War is at our gates, and any day now King Christian may set sail with his navy against Sweden. A wise man reads the omens and by his present behavior

37

insures his future place in the King's favor. He is the mightiest ruler in the North, and I believe he will go down in history as King Christian the Great."

His words made a deep impression on me, for I had never heard anyone speak out so confidently about King Christian before. The lady Agnes also gave me many examples of the King's kindness to the poor, and told me that he listened more readily to advice from an old Dutch peasant woman than to that of the nobles about his court. Yet I ventured to tell them of my personal experience of Jutish cruelty, of which the scar on my head was to that day a reminder; and I added that a merciless Jute had murdered my grandparents.

Herr Didrik could turn this upside down, too, and said, "Who has driven the Danes to harry the Finnish coasts? Who but the stubborn Swedes, by rebelling against their lawful King? And rebellion has been passed down from generation to generation, to the great prejudice of the common people, who follow their lords blindfold."

Lifting his cup he said challengingly, "We will fence no longer, Michael! I know more about you than you think, and my heart aches at the contemptuous treatment you have received. Tell me, has any Swedish or Finnish noble ever shown you favor, or helped you with his patronage? The Church has cast you out and refused you ordination—and what can one expect of prelates who snatch the miter from the head of their own Archbishop to curry favor with their godless masters? Good King Christian will foster scholarship and afford the same opportunities to all men of talent, regardless of status or birth. He is a faithful son of the Church. The greater his power, the greater will be his influence at the Papal Court, so that even a poor man may attain to priestly eminence at a word from him. For I fear that before long there will be many empty choir stalls in Finland, to be filled by men who are devoted to the King and to Holy Church."

His words were so alarming that I glanced behind me to assure myself that no one was listening.

"Sir! Madam!" said I in a voice that trembled. "Would you lure me into treason? I'm neither soldier nor conspirator; I'm a peaceable scholar, and know as much of politics as a pig knows of pewter."

But Herr Didrik rose, lifted his cup, and said in persuasive tones, "Far be it from me to think of any such thing! But is it treason to prepare the way for the rightful King into his own country? Can it be called conspiracy to defend the Church against blasphemers and mockers who, through their selfish ambition, have forgotten what is due to their sacred office and are unworthy to be servants of the Church? No, Michael. All I hope is that like an honest and right-thinking man you will drink a toast to King Christian and his aims, and to your own advantage now and in the future."

I could do no less than obey, and emptied my cup. The heady wine flowed like fire in my veins, and Madam Agnes laughing with excitement wound her arms about my neck and kissed me on both cheeks.

Herr Didrik said gravely, "Let me dissemble no longer. As a man of honor I am not ashamed to own that I am heart and soul for King Christian, and have come to this country to further his interests. Such is the trust I place in you; and between ourselves I can tell you that there are more in Åbo than you imagine who are secretly King Christian's men. But if you should be tempted by some rich reward to betray my confidence, let me remind you that you have already imparted many military secrets, and I can easily prove that you have drunk the King's health with me."

"I'll not betray you," I said sulkily. "But now you must let me go, for it's already late. I've drunk too much wine and have a great deal to think about."

They did nothing to detain me, once we had arranged our next meeting; but it was hard for me to leave their company—to go from the clear light of the wax tapers and the worldly wealth there displayed. I felt as if tough threads bound me to them, not knowing that these were Satan's meshes. I believed in my hosts and in their honor.

I need not speak at length of how by stratagems and promises Herr Didrik and especially his sister made of me a faithful and obedient ally. For several months I served him as his secretary and made myself useful to him in his dangerous intrigues. But let it be said in my defense that I thought less about my own prospects, which Herr Didrik painted for me in such glowing colors, than I did about peace and the general good, for which I was persuaded I was working. My conscience was soothed also by the knowledge that Herr Didrik had soon become very much at home in Åbo, and had won the goodwill of even the wealthiest burghers. He was invited to weddings and funerals and was also the guest of the Three Kings' Fraternity, the highest honor that could be shown to anyone in the city. So, since my employer had already learned what he wanted to know from other sources, I could not see that I was doing any harm.

He gave liberal alms to St. Olav's Monastery and St. Örjan's Hospital, and all marveled at his affability. He was not too proud to converse with men-at-arms, seamen, and apprentices; nor was it long before he was openly praising King Christian and his many noble qualities.

If any became offended by this, he would look them frankly in the eyes and say, "I respect every man's views, and I hold that each has a right to think for himself. But I claim the same right—with the more justice in that I'm a foreigner. Standing as I do outside your national disputes, I'm able to take a wider view than those who are concerned in them."

All had to admit that he spoke wisely and well, as befitted such a knightly gentleman; though the less enlightened added that he did not know the Jutes, who were treacherous and false.

I derived great pleasure from our journeys, since in order to conceal his purpose Herr Didrik visited every shrine in the neighborhood of the city. Once we rode to Nådendal, where Madam Agnes wished to buy lace that was made at the convent there and was said to rival that of Flanders.

I need not say how blinded and enchanted I was by her graciousness and beauty; but I was conscious of my humble position, and too young and inexperienced even to imagine that I could aspire so high.

On our return from Nådendal, I was about to take leave of her at the door of the inn when she looked deep into my eyes, sighed heavily, and said, "I'm weary of this tedious city and the oafs who live in it. Come in with me, Michael, and drink a cup of wine. My brother leaves me alone all day, and I'm at a loss how to pass the time."

She led me to her room, which was so full of perfumes that we seemed to pass from the many nauseous odors of the inn into a rose garden.

When we had sipped our wine, Madam Agnes broke out passionately, "I wish to God the business might be settled one way or the other. This eternal waiting oppresses me. My wandering, restless life has got into my blood so that I can never bear to remain long in one place. I know I can be of no use in this country; my skill is needless, since even experienced men run their heads into my brother's snares of their own accord. But now I know that the King's fleet lies off Stockholm, and any day now we may have news of the battle. That will be the signal for action here, too, unless the King is able to avoid bloodshed by means of negotiation."

"Madam," I said, "what is to be my share of all this? Each morning I wake with a deadly ache in my breast, not knowing whether I'm

40

doing right or wrong. I can't endure much longer the searching, suspicious looks I encounter everywhere and that hurt me as if they were open accusations. If blood flows in my home town, every drop of it will burn my conscience, and I shall never know another moment's peace."

She laughed a clear laugh, stroked my neck, and said, "You have a weak, slender throat, as befits a clerk; it would be easily severed! But remember, Michael, omelettes cannot be made without breaking eggs. Statecraft may be likened to omelette making, and if anything at all is to be achieved the eggs must be well beaten."

"That is irresponsible, sinful talk," I answered. "A human being is not an egg to be broken."

"No?" She spoke softly and took my hand in hers. "You Finns are indeed a slow and unenterprising race, and I wonder whether anything could blow you to a flame. You too, Michael; you out-Joseph Joseph! I can only suppose that I've grown old and ugly in this accursed town, for anyone else alone with me and with wine before him would have found other things to talk of than omelettes. Don't you understand that I'm exceedingly bored, Michael?"

I could not believe my ears, and asked, "Can you mean, madam, that I should abuse your confidence and deceive your brother, who has entrusted me with your honor—that I should sin against you, and lead you into temptation that might be too strong for both of us?"

She broke into such a ringing laugh that I too was compelled to smile despite my uneasiness. Ruffling my hair with both hands she said, "You're a youth of splendid virtue, Michael; an almost incredible phenomenon in this evil world. Perhaps I wear a Venetian belt to protect my chastity. Haven't you the smallest desire to find out?"

Trembling all over, I fell on my knees before her.

"Madam, you are more beautiful and desirable than any woman I have met, and your many good qualities have won my heart. Therefore I beseech you to send me away at once, and lead me not into temptation—for I can never be worthy of you, or offer you the position to which your birth, breeding, and beauty entitle you."

She laughed even more merrily, and said, "A little play between good friends is an innocent amusement and binds one to nothing. Believe me, the art of love is a precious one, requiring perception and much practice, like all other useful and valuable accomplishments. It is the eighth of the liberal arts, and you shall be my pupil, Michael."

She spoke so persuasively and with such candor that I fancy a wiser

41

man than I would have succumbed; and she seemed unusually proficient in the subject. As instructress, she was easily understood, and had complete mastery of her materials. Her own body was the copybook, and she did not hesitate to grasp the pen herself if I seemed perplexed. But we had not progressed further than the elements before a sudden peal rang out from the church bells and a noise of tumult reached us from the harbor.

Madam Agnes released her hold at once, pushed me away, and began calmly rearranging her dress, while I stood trembling and discomfited in the middle of the floor.

"Something has happened," she said in a cold, controlled tone. And at that moment came a hammering at the door. As she did not immediately draw the bolt, Herr Didrik began to batter on the panels with his sword hilt, amid a torrent of oaths.

"God's blood!" he cried when he had been admitted and had seen us. "Look at you both! Shameless woman, you should be dragged by the hair to the pillory. But never mind that now. We must think and act quickly. A fast-sailing sloop has arrived with news of King Christian's defeat at Brannkyrka, wherever that may be. His troops are deserting in flocks to the Swedes and he's trying to re-embark as many as he can. It's hard to say how much of this is exaggerated, but they're singing the Te Deum in the Cathedral, and in the market place the mob is turning ugly. They threw dung at me when I tried to force my way through them to the inn. All our work has been wasted, and there's nothing to be heard now but singing, and howls of 'Victory!' and 'Long live Sten Sture' and 'Death to the Jutes!'"

"Herr Didrik," said I, "what has happened has happened, and no doubt it is God's will. But both in the city and the castle there are many who have drunk King Christian's health at your expense. Let us muster them and make a bold assault in our good and rightful cause!"

He growled, "God has nothing to do with it. It's the number of troops, their arms, and the skill of their leaders that determine a battle. If we're to come off with life and honor, there's nothing for it but flight. My sister and I are not in mortal danger, being foreigners—but with you it is different."

He sat down and emptied his sister's wine cup, then sucking the boss of his sword hilt he looked at me reflectively.

"With you it is different," he repeated. "You know the names of all who have drunk the King's health. The good name and fame of too many men lie in your hands for me to spare your life, Michael."

42

"But Herr Didrik!" I exclaimed in bitter indignation. "Do you think I would betray these secrets to save my life? If so you're entirely mistaken, and do me grave injustice."

"A man is no more than a man," he answered. "No one in the world is to be trusted except oneself—and oneself only in moderation. My dear sister," he continued, turning to Madam Agnes, who was already stowing away her possessions in her traveling chest. "Be good enough to step into the next room, or at least avert your eyes. I am obliged to kill this young man for our safety's sake."

She seemed startled, but came up to me, patted both my cheeks, and kissed me on the forehead. Two bright tears glistened in her eyes.

"It grieves me that we must part so, Michael," she said, "but you must see the wisdom of what my brother says."

I was so bewildered at this sudden development that even now I could not believe that they were in earnest.

"Sir!" I stammered. "Do you really mean to murder me in cold blood? If you have no fear of the Last Judgment and the fires of Hell, at least consider the temporal and ecclesiastical courts, both of which will condemn you."

He pondered a little, but his fair sister made haste to put in her word.

"It would be easy for me to put my dress into disorder again, and even tear it, for this is a gown I am now quite tired of. Everyone heard you thundering on the door and swearing, and will at once assume that you slew the young man in defense of your sister's honor when in a drunken fit he sought to outrage her."

Such hideous treachery was incredible to me. I could only whisper "Jesus, Mary!" and stare at them as though I were seeing them for the first time. Herr Didrik's powder-speckled face now appeared to me profligate and malignant, and his sister Agnes was neither so young nor so seductive as I had fancied while still under Satan's spell. Her hair was dyed, and her face was smeared with eye-black and the red paint from her lips. Men and the world of men appeared to me starkly for the first time, and in that hour I aged by many years. But if they thought to pay me in false coin, I could at least give them counterfeit change for it, now that the scales had fallen from my eyes.

I therefore poured the last drops of wine into my cup with hands that shook, and said boldly, "Sir and Madam! You will permit me to drink a last toast to all the wrong, malice, and treachery in which you have so well tutored me. To prove to you that I have been an apt pupil, I will acknowledge that I have not believed in you without some reservations. Nor do I hold any very high opinion of Madam Agnes's virginity and honor. It is only my warm regard for her that prevents my calling her a common whore."

Madam Agnes turned pale, and her brown eyes began to flash.

"Do not hesitate, Didrik my dearest!" she cried. "Silence that shameless mouth, for I have never been afraid of the sight of blood, and now it would double my love for you."

But Herr Didrik was studying me, and feeling the edge of his blade absently with his finger.

"Let the boy speak," said he, "for I've seldom heard so much sense from him, and young though he is he is rising in my estimation. Go on, Michael. You must have something up your sleeve or you would never dare to speak so boldly."

"Sir, since I am forced to it, I'll be frank with you. For my own peace of mind and because I suspected your motives, I entrusted to the keeping of good Father Peter of St. Olav's a written statement in which I have recorded in detail all your actions and have given a list of those who drank King Christian's health. The seal of the confessional forbids Father Peter to open the letter, but if any evil should befall me he is empowered to let the Bishop read what I have written. I did this merely to save my skin should our plans fail, but I see now that the paper may be more urgently needed than I thought."

"Is this true?" he demanded. But looking him fearlessly in the eye, I held my peace. He judged my nature by his own, and so was ready to believe this of me. With a sigh he thrust his sword back into the scabbard and smiled sourly.

"I hope you'll forget my little joke and forgive me for putting your loyalty to so exacting a test. I see now why you were so diligent in taking notes—and even if you're lying I can't afford to take the risk of its being true."

But Madam Agnes broke into bitter weeping, and said, "He has betrayed us, the graceless boy! And just now he all but seduced me. I couldn't have believed such wickedness of you, Michael. I fancied you were a good, ingenuous youth, and I should have been glad to lead your pure young heart into the gardens of Paradise. All too late I see that we've been cherishing a serpent in our bosom."

Herr Didrik snorted, "Cover your breasts and hold your tongue, you drab! We owe Michael many thanks, and the least we can do for him is to get him safely aboard ship and out of the country, until the dawn of the new day when he can return home in honor and triumph.

44

Let us remain friends and confederates, Michael, for this you will find most profitable in the end. Be content now with a few gold pieces, since my funds are running low, and I'll see you safely to the continent, where you may bide your time at some university. I promise to do all I can to persuade King Christian to endow you with a purse for your studies, since you can be of great service to him on your country's behalf."

This was more than I expected; I had hoped merely to save my skin. Glancing at his sword, which appeared to me to sit loosely in its scabbard, I said, "Most excellent sir, my gratitude to you will be undying if you will indeed help me to fulfill my dearest wishes. Let us as you say forget this trifling, and shake the dust of the city from our feet while there is yet time."

He answered, "There's a vessel from Lübeck lying in the harbor, in which I have already taken a passage for myself and my sister and which is to sail tomorrow if the weather is favorable. What more natural than that my faithful secretary should accompany us? Come down to the harbor at dawn and we shall meet on board, God willing."

So pious was his tone as he said this that I became suspicious and said quickly, "Of your great kindness, sir, you mentioned gold. Allow me to suggest that you hand it to me at once, for I should find myself in a tight corner were you to meet with some hindrance and fail to appear."

But I did the man an injustice, for when once he had made a decision, he adhered to it. Indeed it was as much to his advantage as mine to bring me aboard in a good humor. Without protest he gave me five papal ducats, three Rhenish gulden, and a number of silver coins as well, so that in a moment I was richer than I had ever been in my life.

In great spirits I left the inn by the back door and succeeded in reaching Mistress Pirjo's cabin without any hostile encounter. I explained to my foster mother that because of the pressure of his affairs Herr Didrik was obliged to leave Åbo at once, but that he had offered to take me abroad with him so that I could enter some university. I did not yet know whether I should set my course for Rostock, Prague, or even Paris. This, I assured her, was the greatest good fortune, and I begged her to make haste and equip me for the journey. She made no attempt to oppose my plans and indeed seemed somewhat relieved, which surprised me, as I had not supposed her to be aware of my master's intrigues.

To avoid the crowds whom victory had driven wild, I borrowed a boat and rowed down the river to the monastery; for above all I desired to see Father Peter and confess myself to him. I had no wish to leave my homeland with so black a conscience.

The office of nones was already over and Father Peter came to meet me at the monastery door. He had girded himself to take part in the rejoicings, but when he heard of my solemn errand he led me up the hillside and heard my confession.

He made the sign of the cross many times as I spoke, and at last he said, "I thought Herr Didrik was a good fellow, but it seems he's a blackguard. Nevertheless, thanks to a protecting Providence, all has turned out for the best, and your hopes seem likely to be fulfilled. The way that lies before you is certainly rough, and strewn with more thorns than you can conceive of. Many have gone abroad in search of knowledge, never to return. But you have acted very foolishly. You must understand that it is wrong and offensive to God to seek to bring about changes so long as everything is running smoothly. We know nothing of these new ideas, and they're just as likely to lead to evil as to good. However, I cannot see that you have offended against the Church; and it's therefore in my power to give you absolution—though for your soul's sake I charge you to pray at every holy place you come to on your way."

I was filled with wholehearted contrition, and kissed the greasy hem of his habit. Then I remembered that in my haste I had forgotten to mention the lesson that Madam Agnes had given me. This seemed to me the blackest sin of all, and I described as well as I could what had happened.

Father Peter put many questions, so as to shed the clearest light on the matter. Then he sighed deeply and said, "You've been the victim of seduction, Michael, and it was hardly to be expected that one so young and inexperienced as yourself could resist so great a temptation. Even I, perhaps, could scarcely—but now to talk of practical things. I urge you to go at once to Magister Martinus and ask him for a letter of recommendation and a scholastic report. Then after vespers I will come at once to Mistress Pirjo's, that we may watch and pray together before you take the step that will decide the whole course of your life."

His advice and consolation cleansed my soul, although I was nervous of presenting myself to Magister Martinus. But he also received me smilingly, his pale cheeks now rosy with wine. He was astonished and gladdened by my news, which he considered important enough to be communicated to the Bishop. Indeed he dared not set his name to any letter of recommendation without the Bishop's permission. And, as Magister Martinus was on his way to him now, to attend a banquet in celebration of Sten Sture's victory, he bade me go with him and present my petition.

We strolled side by side past the Cathedral and St. Örjan's Hospital, where the two lepers of the town begged alms of us. One had no nose, and the face of the other was covered with silvery hair. I grew melancholy at the thought that I should never see their well-known features again.

The most savory odors floated out to us from the Bishop's house. I halted on the threshold, cap in hand, while Magister Martinus went in on my behalf. He returned shortly to bring me before the austere prelate. Bishop Arvid Kurk was also in a gay mood, and at once began to recall how as a student he had wandered singing along the roads of Europe, although he had had an influential family and a benefice to back him. His one concern appeared to be the wise choice of a university. Father Martin began to speak of Rostock, which lay nearest, and from which I could most easily return if my difficulties proved too great.

But the Bishop bade him be silent, and spoke thus, "So evil are the times that I cannot recommend any of the German universities, where the false doctrines from Wittenberg are now rife. In such places the young man might come to spiritual harm. No, Michael, if you have the means you should try to reach the University of Paris—my university, where I and many others who by God's grace have held the See of Åbo acquired our learning."

The stern Bishop would no doubt have lost himself in reminiscence had not Magister Martinus been bold enough to interrupt him and beg permission to write a letter of recommendation for me at once, fearing lest his fingers should be incapable of holding a pen after the banquet. The Bishop without more ado determined on Paris University, and in his own name dictated the letter in which he submitted my case to its learned professors.

"Michael," he said, "when you have found a good tutor and have been accepted as his pupil, you will enjoy the rights and privileges of the University. But remember, many have trodden that perilous path never to return. And many have returned broken in soul and body, after having devoted themselves more to the seven deadly sins than to the seven liberal arts. But, if you do your best and in due course take

47

your baccalaureate, I will seriously consider what I can do for you. Let the first examination be the touchstone to prove that you are of true temper."

I was tormented by the thought of what the good Bishop and my tutor Martin would say when they came to hear of my activities in the Jutish cause, for I had no doubt that such news would not be long in reaching their ears. Moved to tears after my terrible suspense, I made humble and heartfelt thanks; and good Master Martin also wept.

Bishop Arvid, himself not unmoved, said, "Make use of my name, poor boy, if you find your way beset with difficulties or if sickness saps your strength, for I can say without boasting that I was the most eminent of the Finnish students at the University of Paris, and I don't doubt that mention of my name will always be worth a meal or a cup of wine to you, at the St. John's Head or the Master's Gown, although nearly twenty years have passed since those days. But to show my favor in more tangible fashion, let me make a small addition to your funds."

So saying, he dug into the well-stuffed purse at his belt and gave me three Lübeck gulden, of which one was underweight. Magister Martinus also was moved to give me three silver pieces. And thus it was that I, whose rightful place was the jail or the whipping post, met with nothing but goodwill. Bitter remorse burned away the last remnant of my arrogance, and I was filled with good resolutions.

In Mistress Pirjo's cabin a solemn silence reigned, and the table was spread with enough delicacies to regale the town. She had filled a big sack with provisions of every kind, and in a battered chest, which Master Laurentius had brought me as a present, she packed my clothes and many changes of linen, and laid on top of all my tattered book, *Ars Moriendi*. Master Laurentius himself sat in a corner with his elbows on his knees. I thanked him for his present, though inwardly I shuddered at the thought of the materials he had carried in that chest from parish to parish. Andy sat in another corner with his chin in his palm. I thought he was sulking because of my journey, but later it appeared that he had other preoccupations.

After vespers Father Peter came. He had borrowed the Prior's seal, and in the name of the monastery had written a recommendation for me to all communities of Black Friars, so that from them I might receive supper and a night's lodging as I traveled the long road to Paris.

"I've set my own name to the letter," he remarked, "so it is not a forgery, and I fancy no one will remember who happens to be Prior of such a remote little community. It should save you much expense, and you may present it at any religious house, no matter what the Order, for the Lord takes no account of whether His lambs be black or gray or brown, and you yourself are a layman."

There is little more to relate of this sorrowful evening. We wept, and Mistress Pirjo stroked my hair. She had packed a box of medicines in my chest, a handsome box painted red and green containing her best nostrums for fever, ague, coughs, and fluxes. Bear's grease and hare's grease were not forgotten, and costly theriac was there also.

Of a little horn filled with strong-smelling fluid she whispered, "I don't know whether I'm doing right or wrong in this, but men are men, and I've filled the horn with the most powerful love potion I know. A few drops of it in wine or mead will melt the most virtuous woman."

After much advice and admonition she gave me five big silver pieces, charging me to change them to gold at one of the more respectable merchants' houses in Lübeck, and to beware of accepting clipped coin, for which money changers were notorious.

I am not ashamed to say that I felt as limp as a rag because of the kindness that I, all undeserving, had received from everyone. At the hour of the Night Office we were still awake and praying, though lauds found Father Peter and Master Laurentius slumbering on Mistress Pirjo's bed, and Andy had disappeared.

When the first wan light of the autumnal dawn glimmered through the green glass windows, we were already afoot. Father Peter and Master Laurentius staggered to the shore, bearing my chest between them. Mistress Pirjo carried my pack, and I took the haversack of food. The east was reddening when with many blessings they helped me into the ship's boat. From aboard the vessel itself I could still see them waving. I saw the mighty tower of the Cathedral above the low houses, the blue-green fields of cabbage and the long rows of hop poles on the slopes of the hill. The great ship glided down the river; and, when we had passed beneath the somber walls of the castle, I prayed and bade farewell to my former life as I set my face toward an unknown destiny.

BOOK 3.

The Learned University

I

MY COMPANIONS had their cabin on one of the decks in the high-built stern of the vessel, but I had to shift for myself. Herr Didrik advised me to make friends with the purser, and this bull-necked Lübecker let me move into a little pantry off the galley. Thus I was saved from having to sleep with the sailors in the forecastle—if indeed there had been room for me among them. But it was all the same to me where I lay; for when we had come out into the archipelago and were rocking on smooth green rollers, the fresh sea wind blew away all my heaviness, and I felt my heart swell with joy and courage.

Great was the shock, however, to behold my friend Andy Karlsson creeping from one of the numberless corners of the ship, scratching at his matted hair and looking dazedly about him.

"Jesus, Mary!" I cried. "What are you doing here? Did you creep on board to sleep it off? Quickly, jump over the side and swim ashore while we're still among the islands."

But he said, "I came aboard lawfully to work my passage as boat-swain's mate. I thanked my master for teaching me what little he knew of his honorable craft and gave him my word to requite him for his trouble. I've also committed my fellow 'prentices to God's protection—which they sorely need—and have forbidden them to slander me in my absence. I ought perhaps to have stood them a farewell drink, but it was late, and Mistress Pirjo's ale had gone to my head. It's time I went out into the world to perfect myself in the most important of crafts. So I'm coming with you, away from my native land, and without undue regret, for that land ever gave me more hunger than bread, and more harsh words than warm corners by the fireside."

"Andy, you fool! Go back at once. You may yet be pardoned if you beg humbly enough."

But Andy answered stubbornly, "I don't want a bullet in my chest. My affairs took an unlucky turn, and the landlord of the Three Crowns has been blinded by the devil. He's out for my blood. He keeps a loaded gun and a smoldering match behind the bar in readiness for me."

"But why?" I demanded in amazement. "I thought you were their best friend! The mistress of the house stroked your cheek whenever she saw you and gave you the customers' leavings."

Andy surveyed me seriously with his honest gray eyes and answered, "Michael, if life is dear to you, never let a woman stroke your cheek, for no good can come of it. In all innocence I became the friend of the hostess of the Three Crowns—or rather she sought my friendship from the time I saved her from the robbers. And I saw no evil in it until like St. Potiphar's wife she told me to come to bed with her when her husband was looking the other way."

"Andy!" I said. "Adultery is a black sin! I could never have believed such wickedness of you."

But in injured tones he replied, "How was I to know? I'm an obedient fellow and do as I'm told. Unluckily the landlord surprised me when I was doing his wife's bidding, and there was nothing for it but to put him into the same kneading trough from which I once rescued him. And he flew into such a mad passion, although he's a weedy little man, that I had to set a cask of salt meat on the lid. At this he was still more enraged and as soon as he got out he borrowed a gun from the council, 'To prevent strangers from ploughing and sowing his field,' as he put it, and I had to make myself scarce. His wife with tears in her eyes gave me a well-stuffed haversack, so I shan't starve while we're at sea. And on land a strong man can always earn his living."

I reproached him no further, for what was done could not be undone, and our wisest course was to look to the future. I could only marvel at the way in which our lives were bound together. On the same day, and perhaps at the same hour, Andy had been as near death as I when at the point of Herr Didrick's sword. It seemed indeed our Creator's purpose that we should travel together. We sealed the agreement with a clasp of our hands, but neither of us could foresee how inseparably and for how long this pact would bind us.

2

I will say no more of the voyage than that during the next three weeks we encountered two storms—which the seamen called slight squalls—and that, although we sighted other ships we fell in with no pirates, who were said to swarm between Gotland and Ösel. In due course, therefore, we berthed safe and sound in Lübeck.

Herr Didrik, amiably disposed once more, would have persuaded me to continue with him to Copenhagen, and he held out fair promises of honor and wealth and the favor of King Christian. But I had had my warning, and the precarious life of an adventurer held no charms for me now that the gates of learning were opening before my mind's eye. I thanked him, therefore, and bade him farewell, and he promised to remember me in more auspicious times. Being anxious about my baggage, I persuaded a party of merchants to let me join them, and in return for liberal payment they loaded my chest and bag of provisions onto their wagons. It was a day or so before I realized that they would willingly have carried my belongings for nothing, since they were conveying valuable merchandise and wanted as many men as possible to travel with them, for safety. It was by then too late to retrieve my blunder.

Soon Hamburg also was left behind, and we went forward among yellow fields and over many rivers. Every day the landscape smiled more warmly in the autumn sunshine, and I never ceased to wonder at the fertility of the soil and at the wealth and number of the German cities. We could hardly go a day's journey without encountering a gibbet on its hillock, warning us that we were approaching a populous place where laws were held in reverence.

In the good city of Cologne on the mighty Rhine we remained some days because of bad weather. I blessed the delay, which permitted me to tend my feet and to secure a hundred days' absolution by prayer in the Cathedral. Andy and I had already seen an abundance of cities and churches, but the sight of this magnificent temple struck us both dumb. We felt like worms when we raised our eyes to the cloud-wreathed spires in the giddy heights above us. It seemed to me that the whole town of Åbo could have been contained under its roof. I could not wonder that the sick, the blind, and the maimed had been healed after praying here, for I have seldom if ever felt nearer the majesty of God than in this mighty Cathedral. It was hard to realize that it had been built by human hands.

In Cologne I entrusted my traveling chest to a merchant bound for Paris by a longer route than ours, while with God's help Andy and I continued our journey alone, for autumn was by now far advanced. We reached Burgundy and France and began to have difficulties with the language, but in every town and village I met with God-fearing priests and monks who gladly directed us, since I spoke Latin. Necessity proved a good teacher; I have an ear for languages and soon found that French was Latin's daughter, although her disguise was at first somewhat bewildering. We walked through bright beech woods, and on fine days the sun shone through a haze that cast a dreamlike veil over the landscape. On All Souls' Day we stood upon the hill of Montmartre and looked down over the towers and roofs of Paris, which lay locked in the green arms of the Seine. Falling upon our knees, we thanked God for bringing us safely to the end of our long, long journey. We hastened on winged feet down the slope, and I knew how Moses felt when from the mountaintop he gazed at the Promised Land.

But we had given thanks too soon, and our fate came still nearer to being that of Moses, who never entered Canaan, for a flock of beggars and thieves rushed out from their hiding place among some chestnut trees at a bend in the road and fell upon us with cudgels, stones, and knives. I have no doubt they would have slain us in cold blood, stripped us, and hidden our naked corpses among the bushes where none would have made inquiry, had not Andy's strength been so gigantic that with a few blows of his staff he beat them off. They took to their heels shrieking and howling, convinced that they had attacked the Evil One himself. But I lay bleeding in the road without the power to rise, having been struck on the head by a stone. Thus for the second time Andy saved my life.

So stunned was I that I felt no particular pain and seemed to hear nothing but the chiming of bells and the singing of angels. This is the strongest proof of how near I came to the gates of Paradise. Supported by Andy, I staggered on, and for part of the way he carried me in his sturdy arms.

At the gate of the city we were halted by the guard, who did not want to admit us because I was injured and my head bloody. To their thick wits I seemed a ruffian. I told my story many times and sought in vain to move their compassion, and no doubt they would have locked us up had not an old, barefoot monk come to our aid. When he had seen my papers, he told the men that he would answer for my good faith and reputation. With the greatest kindness he led us over the island to the other side of the river, where the University quarter lay, and showed us a modest inn on the bank where we might spend the night.

The slatternly landlady seemed accustomed to the sight of broken heads. She fetched warm water and rags without waiting to be asked, and at my desire scraped cobwebs and mildew from odd corners to apply to the wound. After drinking a cup of wine, I felt better and my giddiness passed, though the angels' song lingered in my ears for many days afterward.

I had much help from that good woman, who had fed and sheltered many students and knew how I should set about joining the University. First I must choose a tutor, so that in due course I might qualify, by disputation in his school, for the first degree of scholarship. University privileges could be enjoyed only if one were sponsored by a tutor. My nation was the Almain or Germanic, to which belonged all who were born beyond the borders of France. I had therefore to choose an English or German tutor if I could not find a Swede or a Dane. Such men, having attained the Master's degree, must according to the statute give two years' free tuition in the faculty of arts while pursuing their own studies in one or other of the three higher faculties. But the landlady had never heard of such outlandish heathens as Swedes or Danes.

"The farther students are from their homes, the more they drink and the worse they behave," she observed somberly. "If you've really come as far as you say, I'm not at all surprised that you had a broken head before you arrived. A poor mortal must bear with the trials God sends—and the students, He knows, are not the least of them! These faraway, fair-haired fellows are frigid without and hot within, like all dwellers in cold countries, and therefore they need to take more liquid on board than the dark-skinned ones. So much natural philosophy even a simple creature may learn in the Latin Quarter."

"Good mother," said I, hurt, "I have come to this queen of universities with worthy ambitions only, and for the sake of scholarship.

54

Hereafter let my drink be water and my food moldy bread until I have attained the threshold of high scholarship. For to be frank, I am poor, though courteous and well disposed, whatever you may think."

At this the landlady sighed deeply and lost all interest in me. She did indeed give us food and a bundle of straw to lie on, but apart from that we might have been a couple of rats about the place.

On the following morning I would have hastened out to find a tutor, since the vacation was long since over and term begun, but Andy restrained me, saying, "Brother Michael, the good God never created hurry, only time—that is, if I've well understood what the Black Friars preached. It would not be suitable for you to appear before your learned professor with a black eye and a bandaged head, and might well give him a false notion of your character."

I had provided myself with a handful of Paris deniers from a money changer on the bridge, and soon found that life in this restless city was very dear in comparison with conditions in my poor birthplace. If I continued to live at the inn, one denier a day would not suffice for even a miserable meal and a heap of straw among the other guests in the sleeping room. I tried to find a Swedish or Danish college, but no one knew of such an institution. Only a venerable gray-bearded beggar seemed to have heard that there had been a Swedish college a hundred years or so before. Danish students had not been seen for the last twenty years, and the beggar said that Danes were forbidden to study beyond their own borders since the founding of Copenhagen University. This really respectable and wise old man was the only one to give me sensible advice during these first days. He spoke faultless Latin and told me he had plied his trade by the Cathedral bridge for more than fifty years.

A drunken student condescended to speak to me when notwithstanding my straitened means I offered him wine, but all he would do was to teach me a French poem with witty rhymes enumerating a great many of the street names of Paris. My knowledge of the French language was still so limited that I did not fully grasp the content of the poem, though I learned it by heart to please him. It cost me one evening and two and a half deniers, and it was not until long afterward that I discovered to my indignation that this poem, which comprised forty-eight verses, mentioned only such streets as contained houses of ill fame.

But these first outgoings of mine were the sort of school fee that every newly arrived young student must pay. A few days' assiduous trudging gave me a rough notion of the Latin Quarter and the University buildings, and of the many churches and monasteries. There were something like six thousand students, twice the population of Åbo. Between them, the different nations and sundry pious foundations possessed at least thirty colleges, but only a fraction of the students could be accommodated in these, and it was vain to seek admission to any of them since term had begun on St. Denis's Eve and it was now nearly Christmas.

When my elation at having arrived was somewhat abated, I began to feel seriously uneasy at being still only on the bottom rung of the ladder. Luckily my head healed within a few days so that I could remove the bandages and spruce up my appearance. My traveling chest arrived with the good merchant from Cologne; and, having arrayed myself in my best clothes, I boldly sought an interview with the bursar of the Almain nation, to obtain his advice about my studies. This youthful scholar began by rebuking me severely because I had wasted half a term, but, having read the letter of recommendation from Bishop Arvid, he acknowledged that my journey had been long and arduous. The letter and my neat appearance must have led him to suppose me wealthy, for he at once asked whether I intended to pay my tutor. All instruction was free in principle, he told me. But it was clear that the unpaid masters in the faculty of arts would devote more attention to pupils who could make them presents. He was a Hollander by birth and could at once lay his hand on a Dutch tutor for me, a certain Magister Pieter Monk, who at present had only a few pupils and under whose guidance therefore I should be able to make exceptionally rapid progress in preparing for the examination. He gave me Magister Monk's address in the Rue de la Harpe, and his blessing.

It was fortunate that I had been given clear instructions, for hardly had I left him when two men wearing the biretta of the Master's degree, and attended by a crowd of students, bore down upon me in the anteroom and began loudly extolling the merits of themselves and their tutors. When I told them that I was on my way to Magister Monk, they warned me against him with one accord, attributing to him the most dreadful qualities, such as drunkenness, gluttony, and even heresy, so that I began to feel quite nervous about meeting him. Nevertheless, I placed more reliance on the bursar's word than on that of these touts.

The Rue de la Harpe lay near the river and the inn at which I was still staying. I hastened to my lodging and changed into my plain

56

traveling clothes, retaining only my good boots, for I did not want to give the master an exaggerated idea of my means. The learned man lived in the house of a signet-engraver; it was narrow and several stories high. The engraver directed me to the topmost flight of the dark stairs, and at last, in a cold, squalid room I found the scholar writing at a rickety table. He was young, pale, and half starved, and for warmth rather than dignity he wore his biretta and his entire wardrobe. He gave me a searching look with his tired eyes. Frankly and respectfully I told him my errand, stressed my thirst for knowledge and my small means, and promised to serve him in obedience and steadfastness if he would take me as his pupil.

"In these stern times, Michael," he replied, "the Queen of Sciences has become a malignant stepmother who often gives her children stones for bread. I'm only twenty-five but I have chewed stones till my teeth ache. To be frank with you, I received my *licentia docendi* only last year. 'Yesterday bachelor, today master, tomorrow doctor' runs the proverb. But those days are as long as years and filled with ceaseless anxieties, struggles, and spiritual wrestling. In the winter one freezes, and in the summer one breathes the foul stench of the streets. Bad food and rotten eggs are the heritage of learning, and the only reward of the diligent is hollow teeth and a stomach disordered for life. Yet I see from the look in your eye that you're filled with the desire for scholarship, and will not shrink from toil, or sleepless nights and troubled days. So that is all the warning I'll give you. I will do my best to further your studies according to your means."

He then interrogated me closely for an hour, at the end of which I felt as if he had turned me inside out like a glove and knew more of my acquirements than I did myself.

But shaking his head he told me, "Michael, my son, you're quick to learn and you're well grounded in Aristotelian logic. But your vocabulary is out of date and your knowledge better fitted to a churchman than to a scholar. It's plain you have never had access to modern books and commentaries. But if you attend my morning lectures regularly and listen each week to disputation, we may perhaps come far enough this year for you to determine the theses and defend them in disputation with my other pupils. I don't doubt that after a year's hard study you may venture to come up before the appointed examiners to take your baccalaureate. So much I promise, though my own progress depends on yours, since a master is judged by his pupils."

He bade me come after Mass next day to the church of St. Julien le

Pauvre, and added hesitantly, "Michael, it is usual for a pupil to give his master a present proportionate to his means. I have no wish to rob you, but the truth is I cannot have any supper today until the printer has paid me for these proofs which I'm correcting; and your coming interrupted the work."

He showed me the manuscript, and the sheets still damp from the press. It was a pamphlet by a Hungarian scholar, a gruesome picture of the peril that had threatened all Christendom since the previous year, when the cruel and bloodthirsty Sultan Selim of Turkey conquered Egypt and seized control of the trade routes to India. Selim had brought the whole Orient under his sway and could now gather his forces for the overthrow of Christendom. In some embarrassment Magister Monk began to tell me of the contents, to give me time to consider, and to estimate what I could afford.

I was fighting a severe battle with myself and could give little heed to his words, but at last I handed him one of my few gold coins, a Rhenish gulden of full weight.

"Magister Pieter, my good tutor," I said frankly, "take it while money yet remains to me, for this is certainly the best and wisest thing I can do with it. God willing, it will bring me in good interest. In return, I beg that you who have yourself suffered want will advise me how I may eat and lodge most cheaply—and will perhaps lend me one or other of your books from time to time. For my hunger for books is keener than my bodily hunger and I swear to guard them as the apple of my eye."

Magister Monk turned very red and made many refusals before at last he took my coin. I was growing ever more convinced that among all the scholarly crows who preyed upon new students I had found a good and honest tutor. He promised that I should borrow his books whenever I wished, and even read them in his room if I could find no other quiet place. It appeared that many of his pupils lived in the same house, since the seal-engraver let his rooms to students. The Magister was glad to have them gathered together in this way, for unlike the older masters he had no regular lecture room.

"In youth a man is content with little and is prepared to deny himself," he said, "but there's a limit to such austerity that cannot be exceeded without detriment to health. Many a scholar must pay for the want and hardship of his youth with lifelong suffering and an early death. Winter lies before us, Michael, and therefore you must always have at least a bowl of hot soup every day. I'll find out whether three

58

or four of my pupils would be willing to let you share a room with them, to bring down the rent and increase the warmth—for in winter it's best to sleep many in a room. You must also take care of your health, and if the worst comes to the worst and your money goes sooner than you expect, we shall find some way of helping you, since from now on I hold myself responsible for your welfare."

3

Thus began what was one of the more happy times of my life, for I was still young and my heart unstained, and I had had a severe and wholesome warning against worldly temptation. The boundless realms of knowledge opened out before me, and as a free student I could enter doors that few might even peer through. I was intoxicated with the feeling that the mind of man knew no obstacles, and that no power was greater than that of knowledge. I had companions who were as young, poor, and enraptured as myself. In the evenings we talked together, we enlarged our minds, sharpened our reasoning, and felt how we were growing in spirit beyond the narrow confines of our distant homes and entering the great brotherhood of a common speech and a common, international culture.

It may be that I suffered cold and hunger that winter, but I remember nothing of it. I remember only the enchantment of learning. It may be that I chewed barren stones amongst the true knowledge, but I had the strong teeth of youth and did not know the meaning of doubt.

We looked like a flock of needy sparrows when we assembled shivering in the dawn before our church, with at most a mouthful of wine and a piece of bread in our stomachs, to await our master and go forth with him in search of an empty room. The older and more celebrated tutors in the faculty of arts had an audience of hundreds, but we were never more than twenty. Yet the profit we derived was the greater, for our dear Dutch Magister became our friend.

We had come from many countries in a torn and turbulent Europe; like sparks we had been blown together from near and far to the greatest school of all ages. Noble Theology, the Queen of Sciences, reigned here—the finely polished product of centuries of evolution. No problem, human or divine, lay outside its scope, and within the framework of the Church's approval it could furnish exhaustive answers, based on precedent and tradition, to every intelligent question. But only a finished master who was already perfect in secular philosophy was considered ripe for the study of divinity, and we had five or six years before us. I never came so far, as I shall tell, yet I realized that never before had human thought created—and perhaps never again would create—an intellectual structure so complex and superb as the theology of my time, which reached its peak just before the great dissolution.

Youth is greedy and swallows indiscriminately all knowledge that is set before it, and I availed myself to a dangerous extent of Magister Monk's permission to read his books. He lent me two works by his compatriot Erasmus Roterdamus, that I might have some stimulating reading outside my proper studies. One book was called *Moriae Encomium,* or the Praise of Folly, and the other *Colloquies,* or Conversations; the second one had the appearance of a harmless Latin reader. The two works were written in a consummate Latin style, and I devoured them in a few evenings. My head threatened to burst with the riot of thought they evoked, and I sat up far into the night beside my rape-oil lamp.

I had never read more perplexing books. The biting irony of the writer's exposition worked in my mind like poison and awakened misgivings in my heart. For in praising folly the learned humanist turned everything upside down and demonstrated convincingly that man's wisdom and knowledge were no more than specters of the brain— and cold, terrifying specters at that. Folly alone, in suitable measure, gave substance and savor to the deeds and strivings of men. He alleged that only a fool could be happy in all he desired and did, and adduced evidence of this with startling penetration. He taught me to discern in my own surroundings and in the most solemn circumstances the grimaces of Mistress Folly. But the *Colloquies,* which had only recently come from the press, were even worse. In his fictitious conversations he did not hesitate to question even the efficacy of the Sacraments for those who did not themselves change and reform their lives. He went so far as to affirm that a few lines of pagan Cicero were more nourishing and reviving to the soul than all the doctrines of the schoolmen. For, said he, clear thinking is capable of clear expression.

When I had read these books I felt wiser than ever before, for they evoked thoughts in me that I had not dared think for myself. My spirit was filled with glowing admiration and disturbing doubts. I paid him homage as a great teacher and a fisher of souls, yet I could not be easy until Magister Monk had assured me that Erasmus was a priest and an obedient son of the Church, and that the Holy Father himself had read his books with pleasure.

Every Sunday after Mass we gathered about our good master and together ate the most palatable meal of the week at a little tavern on our own street. Often we conversed on worldly topics also, until late in the evening. The memory of a day in early spring when the sun's rays had begun to shed a little warmth on us remains with me yet. I see before me the thin, rapt face of my teacher, under his black biretta. I see the stubborn face of a Basque boy, I see the pale, effete young English nobleman who paid most and was the favorite pupil, and I see the freckled son of a Dutch weaver.

The Englishman had ordered wine for us all, and raising his cup, our master said, "May the soul of the late Emperor rest in peace! I give you a toast now to the happiness and prosperity of the young King Charles: May he who already wears the crowns of Spain and Burgundy add to them the Imperial crown and become the mightiest Christian ruler of all time; one who shall avert the Turkish peril and root out heresy!" The Englishman said, "Courtesy requires that I join you in the toast. But my own King Henry VIII is competing for the Imperial crown, and our respect for the good city of Paris and for the King of France bids us remember that he too has the same ambition."

The sulky young Basque said, "I owe little gratitude to King Charles, since the Holy Inquisition has made life in my country intolerable for a free scholar who desires to study Jewish and Arabian medicine. But this must be my farewell toast, for my money's gone and I'm thinking of returning to Spain and taking service as an army surgeon beyond the ocean. I've heard that a man by the name of Cortez is looking for bold fellows who will help him to a conquest in the New World. He promises each soldier as much gold as he can carry."

The Dutch burgher's son said, "No one has yet won riches in the New World, and even Columbus returned from there a poor man, and in chains. But I wish you well on your journey, since you have more faith in old wives' tales than in sensible advice."

The Englishman said, "Shall we drink this toast or shall we not? I am paying for the wine, and needless talk dries the throat."

We drank the toast together, and expressed the pious hope that the chosen Emperor would prove a blessing to Christendom; but we named no names. This did not please a vagrant scholar seated nearby who had been secretly listening to us, as with inky fingers he scrawled a poem.

This man, who had the look of a tippler, stepped up to our table and said, "Have I heard aright? Are strangers, who by sheer goodwill are permitted to enjoy the privileges of this city and its University, so lost to decency that they hesitate to raise their cups to noble King Francis in his hopes of the Imperial crown? He is the one most worthy of it. And he has a right to greater veneration from people who take the fullest advantage of the privileges which he is graciously pleased to accord them—although to judge by your talk their talents are not worth a turnip."

Magister Monk, deeply insulted, made answer, "I'm a man of peace and consider it beneath my dignity as scholar and priest to correct a tramp who seems to have drowned in his cups what little wit he ever had. But if any of you, my dear pupils, feel the wish to give him a dressing down—with all restraint and courtesy—I will not hinder you, but will afford you the protection of my authority."

We looked dubiously at one another, and the Englishman said gravely, "The fault is mine, since I so indiscreetly urged the toast. I don't doubt that between us we could throw the shameless fellow out and chastise him well for his insolence. But the question has many implications and is political in its nature, for this sly ink-dabbler affects to defend the honor of his King, whereby he can land us in a very painful predicament. We are naturally bound to show suitable deference to a ruler whose goodwill and protection we enjoy. Therefore the simplest solution seems to me to be a fresh toast. I raise my cup to the noble and chivalrous King Francis: His happiness and prosperity! We'll ask this gentleman to join us in this toast, provided he will first beg our pardon for the insult, in fitting terms."

Hardly had he finished speaking than the stranger's grotesque, drink-sodden face was wreathed in smiles. He raised his inky hands in deprecation and said, "Respected Magister! Learned scholars! I see that I've made a grievous error and I deeply repent the words which in my hasty choler I let fall. I was moved only by regard for my King and not by any wish to pick a quarrel."

Without so much as a by-your-leave he sat himself down at our table, though we eyed him with distaste because of his evil smell. He felt the necessity of overcoming our repugnance and began boasting of his many journeys in foreign lands, and of the distinguished patrons whom he had lost through persistent ill luck, so that he had never found peace but was a perpetually rolling stone.

"But," said he, "my misfortunes vex me less than before, since disaster is now to overwhelm the world. If you care to know it, we have at most five years of life left to us. On this point I'm fully informed, having lately returned from the great city of Strasburg."

He broke off, peered with amazement into his empty cup, and began to move his mouth as if his tongue had suddenly stuck to his palate. But he had aroused our curiosity, and at a sign from Magister Monk the Englishman readily filled the stranger's cup.

He then continued, "I won't vex your ears with the tale of my misfortunes. No one can avoid the fate which the stars have marked out for him, and for many years now, in hours of wretchedness, I have regarded the gallows as my only earthly bride, which one day will receive my poor body with open arms. But that you may place reliance on what I shall now tell you, you must know that my name is Julien d'Avril. I was born in April and my life has been as uncertain and capricious as that month. While in Strasburg, I happened to read a printed prophecy based upon a conjunction of planets to occur in February 1524. According to this prophecy the world is threatened by a second deluge. I pursued the matter further and found that many learned men—among whom I need only mention the court astrologer at Vienna and a stargazer in Heidelberg whose heathen name escapes me, as also Thriremus himself in his writings—had alluded to this planetary conjunction and suggested an interpretation. In a word, I am satisfied that all the planets will then meet in the Sign of the Fish, and am at present engaged in preparing for publication my own views on the event."

Magister Monk nodded, saying, "I've heard of this remarkable conjunction, and without doubt it portends upheavals, but I cannot agree that these will take the form of a deluge, since that would conflict with the Bible's unequivocal promise, of which the rainbow is our constant reminder."

Julien d'Avril assented, and went on, "There are those who maintain that they can best interpret the meeting of these planets by means of images; these say that the state of the world will resemble that of seething waters. They believe that emperors and princes will fall, that the meanest in every land will rise up against the mightiest and empty the fishpools of monasteries and of the nobles. But we can find a simpler explanation if we rightly read the signs, and it amazes me that no one has hit upon it."

Uninvited, he stretched out his hand to the pitcher of wine, refilled his cup, and resumed, "The terrible and most inhuman Grand Turk

Selim has waged war in Syria, Persia, and Egypt, and has united the Orient beneath his standard. His highest ambition is to fulfill the commandment of his prophet Mohammed and crush the Christian peoples, whom the Turks call Unbelievers, although they themselves follow a false prophet. The Venetians are never weary of demonstrating how boundless is the cruelty and bloodlust of the Turks, but these qualities are the result mainly of their prophet's ban on the use of wine. The bloodthirsty people of Islam must content themselves with water; therefore to me at least it is evident that their ruling sign must be that of the Fish."

"This is indeed *sat sapienti,*" put in Magister Monk eagerly. He had become acquainted with these matters through the Hungarian pamphlet.

"Ay, is it not?" agreed Julien d'Avril, elated with wine and his own wisdom. "In February 1524 the planets will bestow their united powers upon the Fish, which means that the world will come under the sway of the Turks. It is a hideous thought, yet we cannot doubt what is plainly written in the stars, and it will be wise for us to take proper measure. I, for example, mean to exhort the winegrowers of France to store up and conceal as many casks as may be, that Christians need not perish of thirst during the first years of Turkish rule. The Turks might even be won over to a moderate use of wine, whereby their power would be lessened."

The Englishman snatched the wine jar from the stranger's hand and tipped the last few drops into his own cup.

His face quivered as he said, "Britain is an island and need fear nothing that occurs under the Sign of the Fish. Gentlemen, you may be sure that England will resist every assault upon her coasts, though the Emperor and all Europe should fall."

Julien d'Avril returned politely, "God forbid that I should give the smallest offense to our good host, who regales us with this refreshing wine. I freely acknowledge that the Turks would most likely go astray in the fog if ever they sought to take your capital city by storm."

The wine of our liberal English brother had gone to my head also, and it seemed to me that the pursuit of knowledge, or any other human activity, was indeed vain if the world were destined for some great cataclysm.

The Basque youth said, "Sir, I'm grateful for your prophecies, for they do but strengthen me in my resolve to return home as quickly as possible and take service in the New World. I have the feeling that here in the Old we're tossing in a moldy, worm-eaten ark which at any moment may go to the bottom. What can I hope for in a world where princes lack honor and women virtue, and where Holy Church has decayed into idolatry and stoops to jugglers' tricks?"

Magister Monk laid his hand upon the boy's mouth, bidding him be silent and threatening him with his displeasure. When he had quieted the boy he looked gravely into the eyes of each one of us, and said, "Every true Christian may mourn in his heart the present debased state of Holy Church, but it is not for us to make bad worse by open censure. We must humbly trust that the purification that is due will come from above when the time is ripe. Let each one of us do penance and seek amendment in his own heart, for of that we all have need. It is through our own individual lives and actions that we must find peace for our souls, and joy everlasting."

"Amen. So be it," responded Julien d'Avril reverently. "Yet I would suggest that a long pilgrimage is often of benefit when our evil deeds weigh too heavily upon us or when we suffer oppression by our neighbors. I've often been compelled to avail myself of this well-tried expedient, and I make you a present of the suggestion."

It was in this way that I made the acquaintance of Julien d'Avril. It was a mixed blessing, but I learned much from his endless tales.

I saw spring come to Paris, when the flowery candles of the chestnuts gleamed white along the banks of the green Seine. But more wonderful to me than spring was the University and its learning, and my only care was the threat of destitution. The school year closed at the end of June, on the feast of the martyrdom of SS. Peter and Paul. Good Magister Monk returned to his home in Holland and my companions were scattered to the winds. But the road to Åbo was too long and arduous for me to think of taking; moreover, I had a wholesome dread of being arrested and tried as an adherent of King Christian and the Union.

My limp purse was emptied of its last coin that summer. I had not seen much of Andy, for he was working at a bell and cannon foundry on a lower reach of the river. He had visited me now and then on feast days, but I was so deeply engrossed in my studies that I had no time to do more than assure myself that he had enough to eat.

But there came a Sunday morning when I remained stretched upon my straw mattress, too weak to rise and hear Mass. The carrion stench that summer brought with it drifted in through the window and I would not have given much for my life just then. For many days I

65

had existed only on bread and water, and in order to buy that I had had to sell my best doublet, being more willing to part with it than with my books.

Andy stepped into my room, sniffed the air, and said in his blunt manner, "What's the matter—did you drink too much last night? Or why are you lying there with a green face in all this stench? Look at me, the honest craftsman, fresh as a daisy and up at cockcrow to come and see you! That's what you gain by avoiding strong drink and swapping even thin table wine for more bread."

"Brother Andy," I began, and burst into tears. "You've come in time to hear my last requests. This isn't drink but hunger and too much study, and I see that I must die among strangers in a strange city for my sins. Give me Christian burial, and God and His saints will reward you."

Andy looked anxious. He felt my neck and wrists with his steady hand.

"You're like a plucked bird," he said. "I wonder your ribs haven't worn holes in your skin. But are we among heathen? Is there no Christian in all this fine city who will take pity on you and give you a meal?"

"To what end?" I asked miserably. "On the strength of Father Peter's letter I've had so many meals with the Black Friars that I daren't show myself there again, and the landlord of the Angel's Head has fed me so long on credit that I can't go there either. I'm still too well dressed to beg in the streets—and why prolong my wrechedness? I mean to lie here and meekly await my end."

Andy said, "It seems to me foolish to throw your ax in the lake while it's still sharp. But you're wiser than I am, Michael. Otherwise I would gladly have invited you to a modest meal at the Angel's Head —for this I fancy my purse is still equal to."

I rose quickly and dressed myself.

"Brother Andy," I said, "why should I refuse you? Am I not your only friend in this strange city, and one who speaks your language? Let us therefore hasten to the Angel's Head, for I stand in great need of a generous bowl of soup."

The tavern keeper greeted me cordially despite my debt to him, perhaps because he feared that by a cold reception he might lose his money altogether. And there we met Julien d'Avril, who frequented the place whenever he had not been taken into custody by the watch for shameless behavior and brawling in the streets.

66

Greeting Andy politely, he said to me, "Your comrade looks a stout, good-natured fellow, and no doubt he'll stand me a stoup of wine when he hears that I'm a learned man and an astronomer, and have published a printed book. Explain to him that I'm far from particular, and will be content with the lees that our host draws from the bottoms of the casks and sells for a farthing."

The tavern keeper brought us each a bowl of good strong broth and a chunk of bread, and, since it was Sunday, Andy ordered wine.

So feeble was I that even the broth went to my head, and I said to Julien d'Avril, "Learned brother, advise me what I'm to do, for want knocks at my door and only my natural diffidence has prevented me from revealing my destitution."

Julien d'Avril answered in great indignation, "Witless ass, why didn't you tell me this before? We could have gone to Frankfurt together and done our little bit in the Imperial Election. My experience and your guileless face would have worked wonders. But Charles V is now Emperor without our help. If we're to put our two clever heads together, Michael, you must realize at once that people of our order can't grow rich by following the narrow, thorny path of virtue. You must choose a broader road if you're to earn enough during the summer to support you next winter in this miserly city."

Andy also said he had observed that no one made money by honest work, although it could teach one many useful lessons.

Julien went on, "Were it just a matter of keeping you alive, I don't doubt I could persuade some honorable citizen to give you your meals in exchange for your teaching his children to read; but such an expedient would be of no lasting benefit. You have of course the Bishop's tooth, which is an effective remedy for toothache, as I've found, and many other heathen medicines from your native land; but were you to turn quacksalver you would soon fall foul of the Faculty of Medicine, who are jealous of their privileges. Then again, your powerful companion could force locks and your slim body could creep through the narrowest windows if I were to point out to you the houses where silver spoons are to be found; but I fear your piety would forbid your laying hands on your neighbor's goods. However, in the course of this summer I've been hatching certain laudable projects which you might help me to carry out. I'm beginning to be too well known in this town, and it would be healthier for me to change my place of residence. The grape harvest is approaching and I've been seized with a yearning to behold the smiling vineyards of France. Moreover,

67

both peasants and winegrowers are wont to be in a good humor at this season, and the company of your stout friend would be a protection against violence."

I asked him what these laudable projects might be, and he replied, "When I'd written my book and noted how reverently simple people read and believed the printed word, even I began to dread the Turkish peril that I had described in it. I've therefore resolved to journey to the East and devote my life to the conversion of Islam. I mean to accustom the Turks to the use of wine, thereby mellowing their savage nature before the fatal hour is upon us. But in order to achieve this pious end, I must have the support of all good Christians."

To this I said, "Learned brother, such lies wouldn't impose on the stupidest peasant, far less induce him to open his purse."

But Julien shook his head.

"You're young, Michael. You've no idea how readily people will believe the biggest lies. It's the very insolence of the lies that deceives them."

The further he unfolded these schemes of his, the further he confused my judgment. The slow-witted Andy he tickled with tales of the autumn slaughtering, and the plenty then prevailing in the country districts. And—how he contrived it I cannot guess—the very next day he showed me a document hung with many ecclesiastical seals, whereby all true Christians were exhorted to help him and support his devout and praiseworthy mission, which was to be of the greatest service to all Christendom. He arrayed himself in a pilgrim's habit and girded his waist with a cord, and from the printer he bought—on credit—a crateful of copies of his own book. It was to be my task to sell them. Andy he arrayed in a strange costume which he declared to be that of a Turkish warrior.

When we had come two days' journey from Paris, Julien d'Avril took his stand before a poor-looking village church and began to summon the people with a loud voice. The simple-hearted priest came and blessed our zeal, and bought a copy of the prophecy; and the innkeeper bought another for his guests to read aloud. Julien addressed the people and presented Andy as a Turkish Janizary whom he had converted to Christianity, and having bidden Andy say a few words in his mother tongue, he declared that this was Turkish. Next Andy performed some feats of strength that caused the onlookers to cross themselves in awe, while Julien demanded loudly what they thought they could do against a swarm of such creatures when they overran Europe

68

like locusts. If each and every one contributed his mite toward the good cause, this terrible danger would be averted.

But the inhabitants of the place were poor and could not part with much, although they were liberal in the matter of food and drink. In the evening the priest took us to the castle and presented us to the seigneur and his ladies, and there we earned a gold piece. The seigneur told us that he had been in Venice and had seen Turks at an inn there. He assured us that they had been dressed like Andy and that their speech was similar to his, which greatly astonished Julien.

I do not willingly recall our journey, which lasted two months and took us to the south of France and back again. The exercise, fresh air, and good food improved my health, but I suffered continual dread of detection. Julien d'Avril, on the other hand, grew ever more impudent with his continued success, until at last he himself began to believe in the projected journey to the East—so strongly that he shed bitter tears as he described in a heart-rending manner the sufferings he might expect at the hands of the Turks.

In the larger towns he would hasten to wait upon the highest dignitaries of the Church, and he gave a bag of earth to an old bishop with the assurance that he had brought it himself from the Holy Land. If no money was forthcoming, he contented himself with other offerings; we ended by possessing two horses, which carried a great variety of food and clothing. His own steed was a donkey, for as he drank himself insensible every evening he was unable to walk next day. Yet he never stayed more than a day in any one place and made us promise to lash him to the saddle every morning if he should prove incapable of remaining there by himself.

St. Denis's Day approached and we set our faces toward Paris. During the last days of our journey, we begged no more, to my relief, and made great haste, for Julien d'Avril told us he had had a bad dream, which he took to be an omen. When we had come to within a day's journey of Paris, we sheltered for the night like other law-abiding travelers, at an inn. For once, Julien abandoned his practice of drinking himself into a stupor.

He seemed grave and preoccupied, and said, "Brother Michael and my good son Andrew, tomorrow we must share out our gains and part from each other; but I would like to thank you now for your friendship and faithful care during this journey of ours. Let us now go to rest with blithe hearts and restore our bodies from the exertions of the day, for tomorrow we shall behold the familiar towers of Notre Dame."

Both Andy and I slept heavily and well, for we had led our pack-horses a full day's march. When we woke, Julien d'Avril had disappeared, having fully discharged our joint reckoning. The innkeeper handed us a letter that read as follows:

"Michael my dear son,

The bitter pangs of conscience that have beset me this night compel me to continue my journey without delay, and I have not the heart to wake you and your comrade, who are sleeping the deep sleep of youth under the saints' protection. I am leaving one of the horses, as it is awkward to lead two when riding a donkey. I hope you will bear me no grudge for taking the money, and that you will find consolation in the thought that thanks to me you have learned a lesson beyond price, which is that money is easily won upon the broad road, and as easily lost. Should my printer pester you for payment for the books, console him by telling him that I mean to return as soon as possible to discharge my debt; if he believes this, so much the better for you. You will ever be remembered in my prayers; that you may ever continue in the same innocence of mind is the hope of

Julien d'Avril."

Cut to the heart, I read the letter aloud to Andy. When we had reflected upon its contents, we sat staring at one another.

At last Andy said, "The drunken swine has cheated us! Were we not to share the money?"

"So it was agreed," said I. "But we were collecting for his journey and we can only hope that he will indeed set forth to convert the Turks. But I confess I have from time to time withheld a little silver for myself, and have suffered needless qualms of conscience on that score."

Andy said, "It was no doubt my patron saint St. Andrew who led me to slip my hand into Julien's purse when I put him to bed at night, for he was often so drunk that he didn't know how much he had collected."

On counting our savings, we found that together we possessed ten gold pieces and a pile of silver. We succeeded in selling the horse for a good price, and the provisions fed me for a month. The gold and silver we divided fairly, and when my money was spent I borrowed weekly from Andy's share.

By leading a frugal and industrious life, I won the wholehearted approval of Magister Monk, and after Christmas he allowed me to appear before the six elected examiners. I answered all four questions correctly and to their satisfaction and received a diploma to which was appended the faculty's seal, testifying that I had now attained the degree of baccalaureate.

The first obstacle on the road to higher learning was now behind me, but this meant little, as my name was not yet entered in the books of the University. A further four or five years' study was required before I myself should be fit to teach, to receive the *licentia docendi* and obtain the degree of *magister artium*. Only then could I begin studying in one of the three higher faculties. And if I desired to qualify as Doctor of Divinity, I must allow at least fifteen years. But I gave no thought to this, being filled only with a boundless joy at this first success, and I felt well repaid for all my labors and pangs of conscience.

A few days later I was cruelly bereft of my hopes by a letter from Father Peter, written the previous autumn. It was to the effect that in these troubled times I would be wise to keep away from Finland, and that good Bishop Arvid was greatly incensed against me. King Christian was preparing a new campaign. He was levying troops to attack Sweden, and all suspected Unionists in Åbo were being persecuted.

I had based all my hopes on the possibility of returning after my examination, of falling humbly upon my knees before the Bishop, and begging forgiveness for the youthful follies into which I had been lured by Herr Didrik. These hopes were now vain, my money was at an end, and I could only exist from week to week by borrowing from Andy. I also owed the Almain nation six deniers and was in danger of losing my privileges as a student.

Nor in my despair could I even kneel before the altar of the Blessed Virgin in Notre Dame Cathedral to purify my spirit; for when the Prior handed me Father Peter's letter he glared at me suspiciously and asked, "Michael de Finlandia, are you not a Swedish subject?"

I assented respectfully, but added, "I might as well be a sparrow in the snow for all the help I get from that country, and I haven't one influential patron. My only friend is the good Father Peter who writes to me."

The Prior said, "Though you have neither joy nor succor from your country, you may at least share its trials. I've been told that the stiff-necked Swedes have been placed under the interdict and the Holy Father has authorized the good King of Denmark to put the ban into effect. It's my duty to tell you that being a Swedish subject you are included in this ban. You may enter no church; you may not receive the Blessed Sacrament. Your very presence is desecration to the building and would entail reconsecration at great cost. Yet I am certain you could purchase dispensation, and I advise you to do this as quickly as may be, for it is a terrible thing for a Christian to be denied the Sacraments."

"Jesus, Mary!" I cried in horror and bewilderment. "I have no money! Indeed I'm so destitute that I would have ventured to beg yet another bowl of soup from you, for I've eaten nothing today."

He was saddened on my account, and having reflected for a long time he said, "Michael de Finlandia, I know nothing against you, or nothing more than against other students, although I hear you're studying Greek, which smacks unpleasantly of heresy. I don't want to be hard on you, but you must leave here quickly and not come back, lest you desecrate the monastery. As I see it, your only course is to pray humbly for good King Christian's victory over the enemies of the Church—that is, if God hears the prayers of those lying under the interdict."

4

It was the end of winter, and the unrelenting cold and lurking hunger increased my wretchedness and desperation. But since the previous winter I had altered, and no longer felt inclined to submit so meekly to my destiny. There were times when I missed Julien d'Avril, despite his double dealing, for the humor of that gay gallows-bird had often blown through my mind like a fresh breeze when self-pity loomed too large. Rebellious thoughts and wild doubts began to sprout in my heart, like rank weeds that soon stifle all wholesome plants, and they could not have found better soil than hunger, cold, and loneliness. I grew negligent of my studies, and too often sought relief in drinking with blithe companions. Hitherto I had been content with the intoxication of learning, but now my eyes were sharp to see both the prodigal brilliance and the black wretchedness of the city. The path of knowledge was long, and its obstacles were insurmountable for a poor man, whose only reward was tears and a back bent before its time. The rich, on the other hand, could readily purchase a bishopric and its benefices, and the

Pope could appoint his fifteen-year-old favorite son to the office of cardinal.

When spring came with its thaw, and the roads were slushy, hunger and the effects of a drinking bout drove me to seek help from Andy in the middle of the week. His master had taken him back into his service after the previous summer's escapade because Andy was a skillful craftsman and also because he had bribed his companions to stand by him and plead in his defense. I trudged the whole way to Saint Cloud and was invited to dinner at the master's house. While the others took a nap after the meal, Andy walked with me on my homeward way until, without noticing it, we had reached Paris. Andy resolved then not to return to his place of work. The sun shone brightly after a cloudy morning, the fields were turning green, and the black lime trees had begun to veil themselves in a pale mist. The ice had not yet broken up along our distant Baltic shores, but we were both tormented by cruel homesickness.

It was almost dark when we reached the city, and in the street we came upon a carriage that had lost a wheel. A coachman with a stupid face was vainly trying to coax the wheel back into place, and beside the coach stood a veiled woman, beautifully dressed and with furs over her shoulders, who seemed greatly agitated.

She addressed us, saying, "For the love of God, good friends, help me by finding a chair for me to continue my journey."

I told her it would be quicker to walk than to try to find a chair after dark, but she explained that the man had to stay with the horse, that she had no other companion, and that it was not safe for a gentlewoman to walk the streets of Paris alone by night—or by day either, for that matter.

In this I was bound to agree, and I said, "I am a poor bachelor of arts and my brother is a brassfounder, but if you will entrust yourself to us, we will escort you safely home. And if you fear to soil your shoes and gown, we can carry you over the worst of the mud."

She hesitated and examined us searchingly through her veil, but the need for haste overcame her misgivings and she replied, "My husband must be very uneasy about me, for I ought to have been home by vespers from the visit I've been paying to my old, sick nurse."

The servant gave us a torch and we set out, I carrying the torch and Andy the woman until we came to drier and better-lighted streets. We had to go as far as the monastery of St. Bernard before, with a sigh of

73

relief, the woman halted before a solidly built stone house, and struck the ironbound door with the knocker.

Wiping the sweat from his forehead, Andy turned to me. "Thank God we've arrived! Satan has tormented me the whole way with temptations, and only by repeating many Aves could I resist them."

"Is she then so fair?" I asked, although I had already noted the woman's youth and beauty.

"What if she is?" retorted Andy. "No; as I carried her I heard the clinking and jingling of much jewelry, and I believe she has upon her a hundred ducats' worth of gold and precious stones. I can't think why a fine lady should wear velvet and jewels in order to visit an old nurse. But to each land its customs, and far be it from me to judge. At any rate, Satan cruelly tempted me and showed me how in an instant we could have put out the torch, plucked off her jewels, and thrown her into the river. The thing could have been done in a twinkling, and you and I left with enough to keep us respectably for years."

I began to look at the gentlewoman with new eyes, but just then the door was opened with the clanging of many bolts, and she, after the manner of her kind, began rebuking the porter for his delay.

Then she invited us to enter, saying, "My husband will certainly wish to thank you for your ready assistance."

But her husband, who was a short, irascible old man with a matted beard and swollen red eyelids, showed no particular gratitude.

He shook his staff at his wife and barked, "Where have you been? Why do you bring thieves and miscreants to my house? Look at your dress! Truly God has punished me in my old age in giving me such a cross as you to bear."

"Noble sir," said Andy, "such a cross is light and agreeable to bear. Many have worse ones than yours, such as poverty, hunger, and thirst, by which my brother and I are tormented; for we've gone far out of our way to bring your fair lady safely home. Nevertheless, if you wish it, we'll gladly relieve you of this cross and carry it back to the place where we found it."

The malignant old man thumped his staff on the floor and shot dubious glances from his weeping wife to us and back again. Finally he dug into his purse and offered Andy and me a denier for our trouble, but at this his wife wept even more bitterly and demanded whether her honor were worth no more to him than that. The matter ended by his inviting us, despite his indignation, to share their supper, which had already been waiting some time. During this meal the lady de-

74

scribed her adventure in great detail and spoke much of the sick nurse, taking us to witness that the matter was as she said. Soon she was smiling and laughing, which made her lovely in my eyes, and I was soon much taken with her. Her husband also was mollified; he smiled toothlessly in his beard and called us decent fellows. After supper he gave us sweet liqueurs such as monks make, and asked us questions about ourselves.

He was especially delighted with Andy's physical strength, and said, "In these godless days honesty and virtue among the young are hard to find. I need a strong, trustworthy fellow to guard my house and accompany me on long journeys, for thieves and ruffians lurk about my dwelling and threaten my possessions at every inn."

Andy replied modestly that the Master of the King's Ordnance had offered him three gold ducats monthly if he would enter His Majesty's service. The old man crossed himself in horror and pointed out that Andy must allow for good board and lodging, clothes, security, and peace of mind among beneficent relics; for our host, Hieronymus Arce, was a dealer in such things.

"The blessed saints must have led us to the succor of your gracious lady," said Andy. "My comrade Michael and I are linked together, and if he also may enjoy your good food and have new clothes like me, I will gladly guard your house, at any rate for the time being. Although how long we shall stay here I can't say, for I have my trade to learn."

He said that jokingly, but to my astonishment Master Hieronymus eagerly assented and sealed the bargain with a handshake.

His wife, the beautiful Madam Genevieve, added her word.

"If this young student is to take his meals in our house, I hope he will often entertain me and pass the time by reading aloud edifying legends of the saints. And I would gladly learn to read myself, if he considers my poor woman's intellect capable of it."

Thus Andy became porter in Master Arce's house and wore a handsome blue doublet with silver buttons. Thanks to him, I ate every day with the other servants, and Madam Genevieve often called me to the inner rooms to read aloud to her from one or other of the many French books in the old man's possession. Master Hieronymus padded about the house in felt slippers and was careful to see that the door of his wife's room was always open when I was with her. Now and again he peered through the crack, but soon grew easier when he found that I was up to no mischief.

He carried on a copious correspondence with other countries. As a

75

reward for writing his letters for him, he once took me down to his strong room in the cellar. As soon as the many-locked, ironbound door was opened, I smelled the incense and was dazzled by the great quantity of treasures he had amassed. The most precious of these was a fragment of the True Cross. In a golden casket with a glass lid were a few grains of yellowish dust—the remains of two drops of the Blessed Virgin's milk.

He showed me also a very notable object, part of a plank from the boat in which the apostles were sitting when they saw Our Lord walking upon the water. Master Hieronymus was just then negotiating the sale of this relic to a rich shipowner, who was anxious to discover how efficacious it might be in protecting vessels from tempests. There was also in that chamber a yard of the rope with which Judas hanged himself, and two fine cocks' feathers from the cock that crowed for St. Peter.

I had my private reasons for helping Master Hieronymus and for lingering in his house, for from the moment I first set eyes on Madam Genevieve I had come under her spell, and to sit beside her was to be on fire. Her dark glance, her languorous mouth, and her softly rounded shoulders had bewitched me, and I could think of nothing else. She made me read to her all sorts of frivolous tales which were anything but edifying, and as I read she would often heave deep sighs, resting her chin on her hand and gazing before her.

Our acquaintance had lasted about a week when she took advantage of her husband's absence and said, "Michael, my friend, can I rely upon you?"

I assured her that she could do so fully and confidently, for I respected and admired her with all my heart, and thought of her as I would think of the Blessed Genevieve herself.

At this she sighed and said, "You may think otherwise when I've revealed my mind to you. But is it not unjust that a young and beautiful woman like myself should be bound in marriage to an ugly, bad-tempered old man like Master Hieronymus?"

I replied that I had wondered at it myself, and supposed that her parents or kinsmen had forced her into this unnatural union.

But at this she was offended, and retorted in some indignation, "No one has forced me. I myself did all I could to lure him into marriage, since he's immeasurably wealthy and liberal enough to give me many valuable jewels and beautiful clothes. But I'd been led to believe that sickly old men of his age never last more than three years when a young and warm-blooded woman does her best to please them and fulfill all their desires. I can assure you I've done what I can, but to my dismay he has grown all the younger and livelier for it, and is now in better health than when I married him, although I've kept him awake many nights. I can only suppose that he has some secret relic that gives him this strength. And now his mere touch is hateful to me. But that's of little importance. What is worse is that some months ago I met with a misfortune that I didn't foresee when I married, and that torments me both day and night. It is as though countless ants were ceaselessly crawling over my body."

"Dear God, madam!" I cried in the most heartfelt concern. "I've heard that the French pox—or as the French people prefer to call it, the Spanish pox—often begins with such symptoms as these."

She told me sharply to hold my tongue and not talk nonsense.

"I'm in love, Michael," she said, looking deep into my eyes. "I've become the slave of a passion for a noble knight in the King's suite. I should never have met him if he had not borrowed money from my husband—for his money affairs are in hopeless disorder, as are those of most gallant knights. I was not coming from my sick nurse when you and I met in the street. At great risk to my honor I had been visiting my beloved."

My heart ached and my eyes filled with tears as I pictured Madam Genevieve in the knight's embrace, although I could not feel the slightest jealousy of Master Hieronymus.

I rebuked her, saying, "Madam, do you not see what a terrible sin this is? By deceiving your good husband you hurl your soul to perdition!"

She was the best judge of that, she replied, and her salvation was a matter between herself and her confessor.

"This has nothing to do with my soul's welfare. You can have no notion of what a lover he is. He has carried me to the seventh heaven in his arms, and my whole body turns to wax at the mere sight of him. But alas, he has no love for me. . . ."

Here she broke out into weeping, laid her head on my knees, and sobbed, wetting my stocking with her tears.

"How is it possible for him not to love you?" said I, moved to the bottom of my heart. "Who can help loving you who has once seen you?"

"He seduced me only to get money. He thought I should be able to persuade my husband to lend him more. And once I succeeded—but

77

only once. So he despises me and withholds his favor. Last time we met he never once took me in his arms, but abused me with harsh words and said he never wished to see me again. I don't blame him, for it's clear that a noble knight such as he must need a great deal of money. But it would be easier to squeeze gold from granite than from my husband, when adequate pledges are lacking. My husband won't accept his word—although my lover has pledged his honor as a gentleman in security for the loan—and says he wouldn't advance a denier on such a poor guarantee."

"But what can I do?" I asked in wonder.

Madam Genevieve gripped my arm and pleaded, "I want you to write him a letter in my name and deliver it to him. You must say that by many falsehoods I've been able to wring fifty gold ducats out of my husband, and that I humbly pray to meet my noble lover once more and give the money into his own hand, although I blush for so small a sum. If he will but propose time and place, I will speed to him, though it were through hell-fire."

Her distress melted me. I knew how she felt, for I too was in love.

"Madam," said I, trembling in every limb, "what reward will you give me if I compel him to love you?"

She laughed.

"You speak of impossibilities, Michael, but if you could indeed do this I would name you in my prayers every morning and night of my life, and would deny you nothing that is in my power to give."

"Madam, this is witchcraft, and it may be that I shall deliver myself into the hand of the Evil One by helping you, but I have a love philtre that my foster mother tells me is irresistible. Trick him into drinking it when next you see him!"

She went pale, and her eyes darkened and sparkled. Then she wound her arms about my neck and kissed me on the mouth.

"Michael, if this is true, you may ask anything of me and I will not deny you."

I kissed her face and her bare arms, trembling as I did so, and said, "I'm ashamed to tell you my desire. But from the first moment I saw you I've not had an easy day, and at night I dream of your eyes, which are like dark violets. I long for you with all my heart, although this is a great sin—perhaps even a greater sin than to kindle love by witchcraft."

She withdrew from my arms in dismay, and rebuked me.

"Michael, I've been greatly mistaken in you, and I cannot understand how you dare address such words to an honorable woman. Your behavior compels me to believe that you've conceived a sinful desire toward me, which is a thing I should never have suspected."

I saw how deeply she despised me, but her resistance only inflamed me further and made her more desirable in my eyes. She was indeed beautiful as she eyed me with the flush of anger in her cheeks, her crossed hands laid protectively upon her shoulders.

"Madam Genevieve," said I respectfully, "remember that it may be in my power to bewitch the noble heart of your lover so that he can no longer live without you, and will fulfill your dearest wishes. Remember that your well will not dry up merely because you allow a thirsty wretch to drink from it—and no one need know."

The temptation was great. She began to wring her hands in distress, and to seek with tender words to dissuade me. She caressed my cheeks and gazed into my eyes, but I never for an instant forgot that I was imperiling my soul's salvation by helping her with black arts, and therefore I insisted on my reward, which as I saw it would cost her little trouble.

"I will give you the elixir of love," said I. "Neither of us can tell how it will work, but my good foster mother has never lied to me, so I have every reason to trust her in this matter also. If it should prove successful, your happiness will be so great that you won't grudge me a fraction of it. When you meet your lover, ask him for something to drink. Then, having secretly poured a few drops of the elixir into the cup, ask him to share your wine with you."

She snapped at me to hold my tongue, since she knew quite well what to do. This gladdened me, for it showed me that she was becoming reconciled to our bargain. I wrote the necessary letter and set forth with it myself, having received careful directions as to where he lived and how to address him.

The lover stood in his garden, training a young hawk whose eyelids were sewn together. The bird sat helpless on the falconer's glove and dared not raise its wings in flight. I admit that I was much astonished at the sight of this noble gentleman, for he was slenderly built and of shorter stature than myself, and his legs in their red silk breeches were thin and bandy. His haughty features were disfigured by black birthmarks, and on his chin grew a sparse beard.

When he had read the letter, he dismissed his servant. Shooting me a malignant glance, he demanded, "Do you know what is in this letter?"

I told him that I did, since I had written it.

He reddened with fury, flung glove and falcon from him, and exclaimed, "Fifty ducats! A drop of spittle on a red-hot stove! Your mistress must be out of her wits to bother me with such trifles. Tell her to send me some money at once, and then betake herself to the nethermost pit, for I never want to see her again. Her mere presence would revolt me because of the way she has disappointed me, when I had such faith in her."

I replied that his words were too harsh and merciless for the ears of a woman, and hinted that he would lose nothing by devoting a few minutes of his time to receiving the fifty ducats from the lady's own hand, since she had something of importance to say to him.

When he perceived that he could come by the money in no other way, he uttered the most fearful oaths, blaspheming against the Trinity and even calling in question the virginity of Mary. At last he flung the letter in my face, bade me greet my mistress—whom he named whore and Jezebel—and tell her that she might bring the money on the following afternoon.

"But she need expect no kindness for fifty ducats," said he. "If it were five hundred, now, or a thousand—try at any rate to persuade her to find me a hundred."

He felt in the purse at his belt for something to reward me with, but finding the purse empty he merely assured me of his favor and let me go. For safety's sake, I picked up the letter from the ground, lest it fall into the wrong hands, and traveled the long road back to the city and the relic merchant's house. Madam Genevieve embraced me and kissed me on both cheeks when she heard of my success, and I could only marvel at the ways of women and their strange caprices.

That evening Master Hieronymus returned from one of his journeys with an armed escort. He was in an unusually sunny humor. He gave me a gold piece, and for his wife he had a bag of ducats with which he bade her buy some trinket or other from the goldsmith on the Pont Neuf. For Master Hieronymus had just succeeded in collecting a debt of nine thousand ducats from a client who had unexpectedly inherited from a distant kinsman in Normandy. The debtor in his joy at this unexpected windfall had at once discharged his obligations. Master Hieronymus, equally elated, abandoned his usual prudence. There was something sickening in the sight of him that evening, as he sat weighing and stacking the gold coins, and paring tiny strips from their edges.

On the following day he made no objection to his wife's request to visit her old nurse; on the contrary, he urged her to stay the night and not expose herself to the dangers of the road after dark.

Madam Genevieve washed her body many times, rubbed in fragrant salves, arrayed herself in her best gown, and put on her finest jewels.

I marveled that these preparations aroused no misgivings in the breast of Master Hieronymus, but he only admired his wife's appearance and said, "She is still young and seldom has an opportunity to wear her best clothes, since I'm not fond of company and there are few people with whom I would care to spend an evening. At my age a man has wearied of society, and all members of it seem alike to him. It is but natural that my wife should wish to show herself out of doors now and then, and I have no fear as long as your brawny brother Andy is with her to protect her from footpads."

5

All that afternoon I wrote letters at my master's dictation. He was anxious to invest his newly acquired money in some valuable relic, and he was also involved in negotiations with the Duke of Saxony, another enthusiastic collector of sacred objects. So I was kept very busy.

Andy came home while I was eating my supper in the kitchen, and remarked, "Nursing must be a paying trade in this country. I almost wish I'd been born a woman. Think what an incomparable nurse I should have made! Our mistress's nurse lives in a house with a wall round it, and so fine is she that I never even caught a glimpse of her, but only of her servants. They all wore bright-colored clothes with holes slashed in them, and they tripped about her door like so many cockerels. My mistress gave me a gold piece not to tell anyone this, and to say something quite different if I were questioned. But I don't count you, and the thing seemed so strange that I had to tell you of it."

The next day Andy went off to fetch Madam Genevieve. She was very pale when she returned and seemed utterly exhausted. Her eyes had a vague, distracted look, and there were dark rings around them. She seemed to be walking in her sleep; she would say not a word to anyone, but went straight to her room, threw herself on the bed, and slept like a log.

Our master was most uneasy, fearing that she had fallen sick, but Andy reassured him.

"I fancy my lady is simply in need of sleep. She's accustomed to a good bed and an easy life. She told me just now that she hadn't slept a wink and that she's been bitten all over by some vermin or other."

This was true, for when Master Hieronymus let us step into the bedroom and survey his sleeping wife, we saw that her neck and shoulders were indeed covered with red blotches. But she slept quietly and soundly, with a pillow pressed hard to her bosom.

Master Hieronymus screened her tenderly from our curious gaze, saying, "May this be a lesson to her not to sleep at her nurse's another time."

The whole of the next day I waited impatiently for an opportunity to speak to her, but she avoided me and I was not able to see her alone until Master Hieronymus had gone to benediction.

"I beseech you, madam, in the name of all the saints, tell me what happened to you! I've been sick with anxiety and I lay awake all night, fearing that I'd caused you some harm."

She responded willingly, and said, "My noble lover received me in his room and did not at first invite me to sit down. But when I gave him one hundred and fifty ducats he was mollified and bade his servant bring the cup of wine I asked for. As good luck would have it, his dogs began fighting in the garden, and when he went out to thrash them I was able to mix the potion with the wine as you showed me. At my request he drank from the cup, albeit unwillingly, and hardly had he swallowed the last few drops than he began to feel tired and sleepy. He began to yawn; he opened the shutter to let in a little fresh air and said that his body was burning.

"I tried to pass the time until the drug worked by telling him that my husband had come home with nine thousand ducats, but hardly were the words out of my mouth than he seized me in a passionate embrace, saying that his body was being consumed with such terrible fires that he must strip and plunge into the well to cool himself. My own condition was no better, though womanly modesty forbids me to enlarge on that. But I assure you he plunged into the well so many times that I lost count and swooned, and he never left me in peace all night. I fancy no woman ever had a more fiery lover. When I took my leave he assured me yet again of his passion and forced me to say that I loved him—but I must reflect upon all this, and my head aches, and I'm tired. You must leave me in peace, Michael."

I ventured to remind her of her debt to me, and she said, "Yes, yes, you shall have your reward, Michael; but you might have chosen a more appropriate time to claim it. I ache all over and cannot think of a man's touch without repugnance. Spare me now, and you shall be rewarded both for your trouble and your self-restraint."

With this she thrust me away with both hands and forced me to resignation.

Next day Master Hieronymus took me with him on a journey to Chartres, which had long been planned. He had meant to take his wife that she might pray before the miracle-working image of the Virgin, since they were childless, but she was still weary and begged her husband to spare her the fatigues of travel.

So completely can worldly desires blind a man that I remember no more of the wonderful Cathedral of Chartres than that its great towers differ entirely from one another, presenting a remarkable and awesome sight. Smoke from countless candles had turned the wonder-working Madonna as black as a Moor, but I could not pray before it with due fervor. My thoughts were ever upon the beauty of Madam Genevieve, for whom my desire was but intensified by absence. On the evening of the third day we returned to Paris, hungry and thirsty after a speedy ride. Andy was waiting for us in front of the house with an air of dejection.

He came up to us and said, "Master Hieronymus, my good master, a great misfortune has befallen our house, and I must be a bad servant indeed not to have guarded your property better. Madam Genevieve's costliest velvet gown has disappeared during your absence."

The relic merchant perceived from Andy's expression that something even worse had happened, and made to enter the house. But Andy held him back and said, "That is not all. Madam Genevieve has vanished with the gown."

In this considerate manner did Andy break the news to his master. Then he told him that the lady had taken with her all her clothes and jewels, and the table silver as well.

"With my own hands I carried out the coffer of gold from the cellar to the coach that came for her," he went on placidly. "So heavy was it that two ordinary men could scarcely have moved it; but my good mistress relied upon my strength and I wished to serve her to the best of my ability, as you ordered me to do."

Master Hieronymus was stricken dumb with dismay and could utter not one word.

Andy added, "The cellar door was fast, for you had forgotten to give my lady the keys, but I borrowed a sledge hammer and after great

83

effort was able to smash lock and hinges. You bade me always obey my lady as I obey you."

Only now did I grasp the full extent of the misfortune. My eyes filled with tears and I cried out, "Dear Master Hieronymus, your false and faithless wife has deceived us and betrayed our trust. May the good God hurl a thunderbolt from heaven to crush her treacherous head, and may her wanton body be torn asunder by curs!"

Master Hieronymus wept bitter tears also, but he said, "Not so, not so. God's just punishment is upon me for my blindness."

He tore his beard, flung his cap to the ground, seized his staff, and belabored Andy, who meekly submitted to the well-earned chastisement.

But when the dealer was weary he dropped the rod from his hand and said in the deepest dejection, "Blows and tears are of little avail, and the blame is not yours, since you're but a simple youth, and it was I in my folly who ordered you to obey my wife."

He walked unsteadily into the house; it gave me pain to see his bowed back. But I was sorrier for myself, for Madam Genevieve had broken her promise and I knew that I should never see her again.

Therefore I emptied the vials of my wrath over Andy, who answered calmly, "Madam Genevieve is a beautiful and capricious woman, and it's hard for a common servant to gainsay her. This you should know better than I, for it was her reference to you that overcame my misgivings. She told me that you supported her in the plan from the great love you bore her. She said she had you to thank for her happiness and that she was ready to pay you what she owed whenever you liked to claim it. But as I still hesitated, she gave me a little on account—and I must say she's a liberal woman who pays her debts with interest."

"Andy!" I cried, unwilling to believe my ears. "Were you so presumptuous as to lift your eyes to Madam Genevieve and lust after her in your heart?"

"Such a thing would never have entered my head," returned Andy seriously, "but when I saw what a good beginning you'd made I thought it only right to exact at least a part of your dues, that the whole might not be wasted."

The thought of Andy in her arms filled me with such blind rage that I began to drub him with both fists and to revile him with every injurious term I could think of. He let me exhaust my fury and then coaxed from me the secret of Mistress Pirjo's love potion.

When I had told him all, he regarded me with his gentle eyes and said, "Why didn't you give her the drug secretly, if your heart was really so bound to her? You might have won her and the nine thousand gold pieces into the bargain.".

The scales fell from my eyes and I could not understand how I had been so simple. But I would not admit this to Andy, and answered, "I withstood the temptation for the sake of my immortal soul. If I'd used witchcraft to win her, I should have been entangled in the snares of the devil."

"The grapes are sour," said Andy. "For my part I'd like to see many such snares in my path, although I admit it can be difficult to free oneself from them once one is well and truly entangled."

Neither of us dared to visit Master Hieronymus. We left him alone with his grief, for we had heard him weeping, sighing, and praying in his room.

Two days later he summoned us and said, "I trust you to keep silence about all that has happened. I'm an old man and my great mistake was to hope for love and companionship from too young a woman. Let me try to forget what has passed. You'll understand that I never want to see either of you again, since the mere sight of you must remind me constantly of my wife. Don't think that I'm sending you away in anger, or that I bear you any grudge. On the contrary, I pardon with all my heart any injury you may have done me, and I'm giving each of you five gold pieces to purchase your silence."

His red-rimmed eyes were bright with tears as he spoke, and when he'd counted out the money into our hands he smoothed his beard with trembling hands and dismissed us. He was wiser and nobler in his sorrow than he had been in the days of his false happiness, and I slunk from his house like a cur, deeply conscious of my guilt. Yet I found comfort in the thought that some such misfortune must have befallen him sooner or later without my help, and that grief was physic for his soul, since it brought him humility and wisdom.

We walked silently along the green banks of the river, and halting at the bridge we gazed at the shining white façade of Notre Dame.

Presently Andy said, "Brother Michael, take this money. It burns my palm strangely and I fancy it would prove no blessing to me."

I was amazed at his words, but hastened to take the money before he could change his mind. I thanked him warmly and promised him a good meal at the Angel's Head, where we would take counsel together on what was to be done next.

But there was no need to debate upon our future; fate had intervened. As we turned into the Rue de la Harpe we saw Herr Didrik coming toward us, stumbling over the heaps of garbage. He was handsomely dressed in the Danish colors, girded with a sword, and wearing a plumed hat.

He greeted me as if we had parted only that morning, and said, "What foul hole do you live in, and what becomes of you during the daytime? I've been up twice to find you. Tell me quickly where we can get a quart of wine, for I've something to tell you."

"Herr Didrik!" I exclaimed, making the sign of the cross. "Has the devil sent you here?"

"The devil or the King of Denmark—no matter which," said he. "I had your address from the Almain nation. Wind and weather drove me to Rouen with a shipload of Frenchmen rotten with wounds and chilblains. I'm to levy fresh men in their place, for the King has a battalion of Frenchmen in his pay. And you—you must make haste if you would claim your due and profit by the good times, for the haughty Sten Sture has fallen, and it's only a matter of time before the noble King has the whole of Sweden in his power."

I was so enraptured by his news that I took him to the Angel's Head and stood him and Andy a feast. I perceived of course that he would never have troubled to seek me out unless he had felt that there was something in it for himself. But our interests were common, and the more he told me the firmer grew my conviction that the hour of good fortune had struck for me at last, and that I should receive my reward for the work I had done on King Christian's behalf, if I could only get there by the time the booty was being shared out.

"Enemy resistance is melting with the snow," he said. "Fortresses capitulate without firing a shot. The Pope supports the King, who has the Emperor for brother-in-law and who has been financed by Fugger in exchange for the Swedish copper mines. Thus he has been able to hire mercenaries from Scotland who are so wild that they began to fight among themselves while they were yet in Copenhagen. One of them was mortally stabbed and tried to escape by crawling under the King's horse. This I saw with my own eyes. When I left Sweden there was already talk of a truce. So you would be wise to throw your books into the corner and sail at once with me to Copenhagen, and thence to Sweden."

In early May we reached Copenhagen after a stormy voyage, and there we learned that only a few days earlier King Christian had sailed

86

to conduct the siege of Stockholm and meet the Estates, whom he had summoned to attend him at the beginning of June. Having revictualed and taken more cargo aboard, we continued our voyage up the Swedish coast.

Throughout the whole journey, except on the days when I was seasick, Herr Didrik sang the King's praises and prophesied a golden future. If ever I had had doubts about the Union, they were now dispelled by the latest news of victory. And when in the middle of May we anchored off Stockholm I was firmly conv'nced that the age of northern greatness had dawned. Even old Doctor Hemming Gadh— agitator and bitterest foe of Denmark—had read the signs and had gone over to the King. He was now doing his best to win the realm for His Majesty without needless bloodshed.

The young green of the silver birches met my eyes, and for the first time I saw the spires of Stockholm rise above the waters. We sailed northward with the spring, and spring was in my heart as I surveyed the forest of masts of the King's fleet and the countless white tents in the camp of the besiegers. But I must write a new book to tell of King Christian and the siege of Stockholm.

BOOK 4.

Harvesttime

I

SEEN from a distance, a military camp in spring sunshine may have charms for the young beholder, but to live its daily life is to discover that there is no more pernicious nest of squalor, debauchery, excess, and indiscipline. The acrid smell of excrement, the clash of arms, loud oaths, brawling, and the yells of drunken soldiers assail the senses from several hundred yards away, and here they were carried as far as the sea. I am sure that the King's forces did themselves more harm during the three months' siege than was ever inflicted upon them by the defenders.

Herr Didrik was convinced that the city would capitulate as soon as the Estates had obeyed the King's summons. This was also the opinion of the mercenaries, who regarded the campaign as over. They had no desire to engage in any serious hostilities, and often contented themselves with firing no more than a shot or two in the course of a day, just to remind the besieged that a state of war existed. I was entirely dependent on Herr Didrik, and hung about him until he grew irritated at "the gadfly," as he called me. He achieved nothing, as the King was too deeply engaged with weightier matters to see him. I got in everyone's way and ran short of money, since I had to pay for my rations and for my sleeping place in the straw at the high camp rate laid down in the articles of war. Somehow I had to eke out my living until I was needed.

Andy, being a trained craftsman, lacked for nothing; he had immediately taken service under a German master gunner. I thought seriously of following his example, but when I accompanied him one day to the gun emplacements, a ball hummed past me and struck the ground nearby so that earth was spattered into my face. It crushed the stout timber screen in front of the gun, and if the port had not been closed while the boys were loading, my life might have been forfeit. This was a wholesome lesson; I was not born to be a soldier and realized I had better earn my living in some other way. I left Andy to his bombardment and returned hastily to the southern end of the camp, where I lodged with a Danish sutler.

On the way I met a German mercenary who, with an expression of utter bewilderment on his face, was staggering along with a hewn-off ear in one hand while with the other he strove to stem the flow of blood from the place where the ear had been. So drunk was he that he could scarcely walk upright, and half his tunic was sticky with congealed blood.

Seeing my gown, he took me for a surgeon, and hiccuped, "In the name of all the saints, noble Doctor, sew on my ear again, or I shall be mocked and spat upon when I get back to my village."

I helped him to a barn that served as a hospital, while he still steadfastly clutched the ear for fear of losing it.

A man of about thirty-five was sitting on the threshold, scratching cabalistic figures with his sword point on a piece of board. He swore at our coming and glared at us with strangely bright, penetrating eyes. He was a short but sinewy fellow with heavy pouches under his eyes, and young though he was he was already beginning to go bald, which showed him to be a man of learning.

"High-born, learned, and noble Doctor," said the German, humbly holding out the ear in his grubby fist, "may it please you to sew my ear on again and heal me, for I've been visited by a misfortune which only your devilish arts can cure."

"Perfect knowledge is of God, imperfect knowledge of the devil," returned the physician. "You drunken swine, you! Throw the ear in the bucket with the amputated limbs. I can bind up your wound, but that is all."

The German broke out into pitiful lamentations, but the doctor snatched the ear and tossed it into the bucket. Then, bidding me hold

89

the fellow's head, he washed the wound, dressed it with some ointment, and deftly bandaged it with clean linen rags. He then claimed his fee from the soldier and told him to come back in a few days for a fresh dressing. His speech and demeanor were marked by such unusual and masterful decision that I could not bring myself to leave him, but stood staring at his bright, sharp eyes as if bewitched.

"What troubles you?" he asked.

"Learned master," said I, "I'm a poor student awaiting commands from the King—and while I wait, I want. Master, take me as your pupil and teach me your art, for since my childhood I've been familiar with herbs and I think I may be of service to you."

He laughed scornfully.

"What can such a young cockerel do for me? Don't you know who I am? I am the great Doctor Theophrastus Bombastus Paracelsus von Hohenheim. I have studied at the universities of Italy and France, but they could teach me nothing. I have traveled in Spain, Granada, Lisbon, England, Holland, and many other countries. My learning is of nature, my book is nature's great book, and my light nature's light—and so men fear me, and call be black magician, devil, and sorcerer."

I feared and venerated him for these powerful words. He was imbued with a steady, burning faith in himself that swept me along like a withered leaf in a gale.

He fell into silent reflection, and then said, "On second thought, I do need an assistant, one who can speak the language of this country and help me to converse with barber-surgeons, wise women, gypsies, and executioners; for good knowledge may be found in murky corners. Every land has its own diseases, which must be studied, and its own remedies for those diseases."

Bidding me step into the barn, he opened his medicine chest and showed me many herbs, some of which I knew. Then he examined me as to their properties, comparing my replies with his notes.

Thus I became for a short time the pupil of Doctor Paracelsus, and learned to know his ways, which I found not altogether irreproachable. He sought the company of the vulgar and was often so drunk that he tumbled fully dressed upon his bed. He could as easily have frequented the learned and even the nobly born, since his reputation as a physician was daily rising, yet he preferred low company. He owned no man his master; he himself, like God, was master and healer of mankind.

He was an exhausting teacher, for in moods of restlessness he would rise in the middle of the night to gather herbs, when planetary aspects were favorable, or would converse with specters at the grave's edge. As summer wore on he marveled at the light nights when the stems of silver birches gleamed in the dusk and birds sang throughout the twenty-four hours. He feared neither the worms nor the stench of the burial pit, but stood there during the darkest hours invoking the spirits of the dead until cold shivers ran down my back.

He would instruct me in this matter, saying, "Man has an earthly body and an astral body which are dissolved simultaneously; but while the physical body turns to dust, the astral one is drawn back to the stars. For this reason a man with keen eyes can see these astral forms floating above the graves at every stage of dissolution, and he can do it most easily at the burial places of those who have fallen in battle or have met with some other sudden death. Daylight dims them, but at night they appear. These light northern nights are well suited to their observation."

I believed what he said, for when I had gazed long enough into the dimness above the burial pit I could distinguish floating human forms in the mist that rose from the graves. But what use he made of this I could not understand, and I resented the loss of my night's sleep.

2

During this time the Estates of the Swedish Realm assembled and ratified the peace treaty. By this they acknowledged King Christian as Sweden's ruler, and profited by his promise of pardon to all those who submitted. So far, all might have been well, but their number was not complete, no representatives from Finland having presented themselves, despite the royal summons. The palace and city of Stockholm maintained their resistance. Sten Sture's widow, Lady Christina, would have nothing to do with the Estates, far less would she bow to their decision. The city was well stocked with food and arms, and the mercenaries had not the smallest wish to storm its walls, which spat fire whenever they approached too closely.

These mercenaries were glad to idle about the camp this warm summer weather, and to be paid for doing it. But every day that passed cost the King untold sums, and His Majesty was soon compelled to return to Denmark for fresh supplies, and for loans to pay the army. Doctor Paracelsus was preparing to visit the Swedish mines, where he desired to study the diseases peculiar to those who worked in them, and no doubt I would have accompanied him had not Herr Didrik fetched me to meet Doctor Hemming Gadh.

Herr Didrik said with an oath, "It's scandalous that the obstinacy of one woman should delay this fortunate issue! The lords and burghers of Stockholm are childish to dance to the Lady Christina's pipe instead of listening to the notes of the King's horn. All might have been over by now."

I answered, "The King has promised to pardon all who submit, and it frightens me to hear the Danish captains complain that there are still not enough rich widows for them to woo, and that the Swedish peasant must learn to plough his field with one hand and one foot. Surely this is no more than a harsh jest? For His Majesty has already distributed salt and has promised to compensate all those who have suffered loss."

Herr Didrik said, "The Union has been in existence for a hundred years. During all that time there has been nothing but insurrection and bloodshed, simply because the greedy Swedish nobles will not resign themselves to accepting the King as their ruler, but take every opportunity of breaking faith with him. The war has cost so much already that Denmark is impoverished. We Danes who have sacrificed life and blood and possessions for the King have a right to full indemnity, and we must be assured that when the war is over Sweden will not once more secede from the Union. We shall stand no nonsense once peace is declared and all cities and castles are in the King's hand. But you must not say this to Doctor Hemming, who is an old man and weak in the head."

My heart grew heavier at his words. As he said, Doctor Hemming was an old man with a palsied head. He had put off the spurs and the plumed hat he had worn in the days of his strength, and had arrayed himself in the priestly cassock.

He spoke to me kindly, and said, "Herr Didrik has told me of you and says you are a man of peace who suffered harsh treatment in your own country for defending the cause of the Union. We must now forget the past and think only of our nation's good. All my life I fought against the Union, until at last my eyes were opened, and now I see that it is useless to kick against the pricks. King Christian has an invincible army and I am persuaded of his good faith and worthy aims."

"Yes, indeed," I answered. "Herr Didrik has made all these things clear to me. But in what way can I be of service?"

"I have written a long letter to Bishop Arvid, urging him to submit while there is yet time. You shall carry my message. As you were born in Åbo, you must speak to the city council and the people in general, and tell them that resistance is vain and harmful."

"Venerable Father," I said hastily, "my tongue is slow and I'm too young and quite unfitted for so important a mission. Moreover, the good Bishop Arvid has promised me a collar of tarred hemp if ever I return to Åbo."

"Modesty is the adornment of youth," he answered, "but he who would win anything must not be too modest. Herr Didrik's account of you fully satisfies me, and the message I shall give you will serve as a safe-conduct. If you fulfill this mission in a satisfactory manner, I can promise you the King's favor, and I intend also to speak a word for you to the papal legate, that you may obtain dispensation for your illegitimate birth. A stroke of his quill, his signet in the wax, and you are free to be ordained. I fancy Bishop Arvid will reward you with a good living in Finland."

"Father Hemming, I shall be ever grateful to you if you in your goodness think me worthy of this, and will say a word to the legate for me. But I cannot understand what such a matter can have to do with my journey to Åbo, for there I shall be spat upon as a blackguard and traitor, and shall not be able to look my childhood friends in the face."

Doctor Hemming started violently, his face reddened, and the fiery temper of his younger days blazed forth.

"Have I not proved by my actions and by the shedding of my own blood that I am the best of patriots? If my gray hairs can bear the accusations of the foolish, these are surely not too burdensome for your young shoulders. Will you do this thing, or must I believe that you're but a halfhearted supporter of our cause? If this is so, then neither Holy Church nor the King has any use for you. There is no room for the lukewarm in war or politics; in these a man stakes all he has."

His words gave me courage, and indeed they were the wisest he had yet spoken. I took his letter, therefore, and a few gold pieces that he gave me for my journey.

And this journey was far less dangerous than I had expected, for I was put ashore near Nådendal, where at an agreed rendezvous I was provided with a horse to carry me to Åbo. At each stopping place the people listened eagerly to King Christian's promises, and said that a meager peace was better than the fattest war. No one wanted war but the aristocrats, who were afraid of losing their estates and privileges.

I was not admitted through the gates of Åbo, and the guards bade me ride on to Kustö, where Bishop Arvid was superintending the defenses. Without delay I continued my journey and arrived in the evening of the same day. Work on the fortifications had not ceased, although darkness had fallen, and men were building and sawing and hammering by the light of torches and flares. Bishop Arvid, who had exchanged his gown for a shining breastplate, was passing to and fro among the smiths and carpenters and urging on the work. I greeted him respectfully and told him without preamble that I had come from Stockholm with a letter from Doctor Hemming. He took the paper, but at the same time raised his torch and gazed into my face.

He recognized me at once and shouted to the provost marshal, "Seize this man and string him up as a warning to all traitors, for it is Michael Whoreson, Michael Perjurer, from Åbo town!"

I thought my last hour had come, and falling on my knees before him I pleaded, "Father Arvid, deign to read good Doctor Hemming's letter, for it is my safe-conduct and I am his emissary. King Christian will sternly avenge my hanging. But if you treat me well I can do you and the whole country a good service."

Bishop Arvid was adamant. Sword and horse were taken from me and I was lowered into the fortress dungeon at the end of a rope, there to languish amid rotten straw, rats, toads, and every sort of filth. Here I had leisure to reflect upon King Christian's power and Doctor Hemming's wisdom. By dawn I would not have given a farthing for either of them. But a little later the trap door was opened, and the guards threw down the rope's end and drew me up for an interview with Bishop Arvid. I was so soaked and filthy from my sojourn below that the good Bishop gave one sniff and ordered me to be taken and given a bath at once, and directed that other clothes be lent me while my own were being cleaned. My spirits rose in the steam bath, and when I had had a bowl of soup and a wooden stoup of strong ale I felt bold again, and reflected that I had nothing to lose and everything to gain.

I stepped once more into the Bishop's presence, keeping a firm grip on my borrowed breeches, which were much too wide, and rebuked him boldly for his shameless treatment of the King's envoy, of which I threatened to inform His Majesty. The good Bishop was not angered by my plain speaking.

He was sitting with Doctor Hemming's letter before him. The letter was as crumpled as a rag and he smoothed it out again, read it afresh, and said, "Michael, my son, my heart is heavy and ill at ease. Of your charity forgive the rough treatment which my hasty temper meted out to you, and let us take it that you have atoned thereby for your support of the King. When a man like Doctor Hemming turns jackal to him, a weak, inconstant youth like you may be forgiven for doing the same. Tell me all you know of the King's military and naval strength, of the situation in Sweden and of the defense of Stockholm."

I gave him what information I could, as Doctor Hemming had instructed me to do, while the Bishop strode to and fro sighing.

He said at last, "I must believe you. Doctor Hemming tells me the same and he wouldn't lie to an old friend. But how can he trust the Danes? We know only too well how they eat their words and break their oaths, and how they offend against the laws and customs of Sweden whenever they seize power. I see that I'm fighting in a lost cause, but I have ever been the Lady Christina's ally and I cannot yield as long as she stands fast. In return for my loyalty she must obtain a free pardon from the King for me and certain other gentlemen in Finland.

"You shall return at once to Stockholm and, with Doctor Hemming's permission, convey a letter from me to the Lady Christina. Speak on my behalf to Doctor Hemming and through him to the good King Christian. Describe the military preparations you have seen here and assure them that I mean to sell my life as dearly as possible if the King refuses me the pardon."

Bishop Arvid then gave a me a safe-conduct and at my own request sent me to Åbo. There I was to wait until he had drafted his written answer, for he desired first to consult other leaders. My horse was restored to me, and when I complained of my meager funds he gave me a new suit of clothes to replace those that had shrunk in washing, and two Lübeck gulden. I then set off to Åbo attended by men-at-arms, like a fine gentleman, and I was flattered when people halted in the street to stare.

But when the mighty tower of the Cathedral rose before me and I saw the jackdaws flapping about it with hoarse cries as of souls in torment, I was filled with a wholesome humility. I dismounted, handed my reins to a horseman, and stepped into the Cathedral to pray. For Bishop Arvid, defying the papal interdict, kept his church open and celebrated Masses there as if nothing had happened.

When I stepped out again into the fresh air, I saw suddenly how little and poor the town of my childhood was compared with the great cities of the world. I did not want to swagger through it; it was perhaps to suffer bitter affliction because of many men's blind, foolish loyalty to a lost cause. While my attendants took my horse to the Bishop's stable, I went on foot to Mistress Pirjo's little cabin. How low it was, how crooked the turf-covered roof, how moss-grown the old pear tree! Burning tears blinded me as I stumbled over the threshold and hit my forehead against the blackened lintel. Mistress Pirjo was busied over something in the living room. She was bent and gray. Her chin seemed yet longer and bonier than before as she bent her piercing eyes upon me.

"My dear foster mother and benefactress, Mistress Pirjo," I said unsteadily. "It is I, Michael, who have come home."

"Wipe your feet, blow your nose, and sit down. Have you eaten, or shall I cut up a little pork sausage or make some porridge? You're very thin, but you seem well and your head's unbroken, so I suppose I mustn't scold you too severely."

She came up to me to touch my cheeks and shoulders, and her hand was as hard as a board. Suddenly she burst out weeping, and her words poured forth through her tears.

"Our good Bishop has sworn to hang you—and our beloved Sten Sture died of his wounds last winter on the ice off Stockholm—and salt is dearer than it has been for thirty years—poor Lady Christina a widow so young—such dreadful, dreadful times I have never seen—they say it's the end of the world and another deluge—I can hide you in the cellar and fatten you up like a pig in the sty, and no one will find you and stretch your poor thin neck."

"Mistress Pirjo," I returned with injured pride, "I am no pig but a *baccalaureus artium* from the learned University of Paris, and I enjoy the favor of His Majesty and Doctor Hemming. Moreover I have come straight from the good Bishop, who gave me this new doublet and two gold pieces, so you need shed no tears on my account."

"What did you say you were?" she asked.

"A *baccalaureus artium*."

"You may be a bucket of swill for all I care, but you're as thin as a rail and you start at every sound. You'd better eat and sleep until I've had time to make you some lace-trimmed shirts befitting your rank."

But having come safely home I could not rest until I had completed the work that Doctor Hemming had given me to do. First I wanted to meet Father Peter, who could give me the fullest information about

96

conditions in the city, without which I should run the risk of a good thrashing through talking to the wrong people, despite the Bishop's safe-conduct. I sent word to St. Olav's Monastery and Father Peter came scuttling, clutching the skirts of his habit, with his hairy legs flying like drumsticks. He arrived sweating, breathless, and very thirsty, but Mistress Pirjo had no ale in the house. We left her to prepare dinner and hastened off to the Three Crowns. The hostess was fatter and more melancholy than before, for her dear husband had tripped on the steep cellar stair and had broken his neck. She wept to see me, patted my cheek, and brought her best Lübeck ale. As I was telling Father Peter how the siege of Stockholm was progressing, a crowd of people gathered about us to listen and sigh and exclaim. I had not to concern myself with payment, for they urged me to moisten my throat at their expense and tell them more. It was not long before the clerk to the council arrived. Addressing me with respect he told me that the burgomaster would be glad to see me.

I remained some days in Åbo, awaiting the Bishop's letter. Copious drinking and rich food quickened my blood and I was flattered by the people who, despite some murmuring, showed great respect, listened carefully to what I said, and strove to turn their old thoughts into new channels. They had heard so many harangues on Jutish cruelty and treachery that hatred had entered their blood. So they were greatly confused when required to think only well of the Jutes. In their bewilderment, they confined themselves to hoping for the best from King Christian; the glory of this figure brightened the darker side of the Jutes and drew the veil of oblivion over the lootings and burnings of the army. What else could be expected from godless mercenaries? Many toasts were drunk at that time in Åbo to peace and to King Christian, and my head was never free of wine fumes—a circumstance that did my health no good.

3

By the end of July I was again in the King's camp. I delivered Bishop Arvid's letter to Doctor Hemming, who personally conveyed it to the Lady Christina without requiring a safe-conduct or a hostage as surety for his life. So far had negotiations for surrender proceeded. There is no doubt that the letter from the Bishop and the other Finnish leaders had its effect. A few days later a document was signed and sealed, guaranteeing a full pardon to the Lady Christina and to

97

all those bishops and nobles who had allied themselves with her, for their resistance and former offenses.

Church bells pealed, citizens in holiday dress thronged the streets of Stockholm when the King rode into his city, and it was a joy to witness the innocent happiness that flowed to meet him. At the gates he received the keys, presented to him on a velvet cushion by members of the council. The prettiest maidens of Stockholm in gay dresses strewed flowers in his path amid pipings and fanfares. Yet during all this rejoicing I had the uneasy feeling of having been fooled, for Doctor Hemming did not consider me worthy to join his party, and the meanest mercenary was lord and conqueror compared with me, who was compelled to look on from the thick of the mob.

But I was in demand again a few days later when the King dispatched warships to Finland to take possession of the castles there, and appointed Doctor Hemming to conduct the negotiations. When they sent for me I realized that I was necessary to them, and I demanded reward and acknowledgment for my services to the King. Doctor Hemming begged my pardon, saying that he was a troubled, absent-minded old man who had had no thoughts save for his country's good. He had forgotten to speak of me to the legate, but would do so at the earliest opportunity; and he led me to meet a haughty Junker in charge of the embarkation of horses. This officer and gentleman, who was standing hands on hips snorting through his snub nose, was a German named Thomas Wolf, who was to be Constable of Åbo Castle. On Doctor Hemming's recommendation he engaged me as his secretary because of my knowledge of the language. I was thus assured of food, clothes, and three silver groats a month. During the voyage I came to know Junker Thomas and found him to be an uneducated man who could barely write his own name. But he was no doubt an efficient commander, for on the least provocation he would ejaculate the most horrible and unchristian oaths.

So we set our course for Åbo. Beacons signaled our approach from island to island with columns of black smoke, and when the vessel cast anchor in the river the salutes began thundering from the fortress. Bishop Arvid received his written pardon, the city council was given similar assurances, and the castle was handed over to Junker Thomas with military honors, to the sound of fife and drum. Junker Thomas garrisoned the stronghold with his own men and made a careful check of the stores. He then asked me where he might lay his hand on a good hangman, and I warmly recommended Master Laurentius, who was summoned and tested by being given two men-at-arms to hang—fellows who had brawled in the Three Crowns, had offered violence to respectable citizens, and had raped a girl. This execution gave the greatest satisfaction to the townspeople, who commended Junker Thomas's severity and justice.

Doctor Hemming mourned at having to expose his old bones to the hardships of travel, now that the chill of autumn was nipping the fields, but it could not be avoided, for the governors of the various castles showed no inclination to come and meet him and negotiate the terms of peace, as he had hoped they would. He was compelled to ride with an escort of cavalry to Tavastehus, and thence to Viborg to win over Tönne Eriksson. I went with him as far as Tavastehus, where he met Åke Jöransson and spent many days in dispelling the doubts of this sulky lord. Doctor Hemming sent me back from here to Åbo with a message for Junker Thomas, saying that so far the negotiations had prospered. From Tönne Eriksson at Viborg came word that he would hand over his castle as soon as he received the King's pardon from Doctor Hemming's hand. Junker Thomas sent me back to Stockholm with this good news. His Majesty was to be ceremonially crowned there, and hailed as Sweden's anointed King, and I was aflame with eagerness to be present at the festival. But none of the Finnish lords accepted the invitation to attend, and even Bishop Arvid sickened and took to his bed at this most inopportune time, to Junker Thomas's great indignation.

I arrived in Stockholm on All Saints' Day, and saw the Estates greet their King with pomp and state on Brunkeberg Hill, which was bright with banners. They had renounced their immemorial right to elect their ruler, and had proclaimed their country to be the domain of King Christian and his heirs in perpetuity. It was indeed an event worthy of the most solemn ceremonial. Having learned wisdom through experience, I had availed myself of the credit that my Åbo appointment brought me, and provided myself with fine clothes. I had a bunch of feathers in my hat, a sword at my side, lace cuffs, and red shoes with silver buckles.

Since every man of rank must have at least one servant in attendance, I had sought out Andy and arrayed him also in suitable clothes, and was therefore received everywhere in a manner befitting my position as secretary to the Constable of Åbo, and his representative at the coronation. The next day, when His Majesty was solemnly anointed and crowned at the church of St. Nicholas in Stockholm,

99

I elbowed myself forward among my equals and was able to witness the ceremony, which the reinstated Archbishop Trolle performed as perfectly as if he had never done anything but anoint kings with holy oil and invest them with the insignia of power.

In the course of the lengthy ritual, I had time to look my fill at King Christian, and perceived that I served a noble master. He had a long face, level, black eyebrows, and his glance, shaded by weary lids, was at once brilliant and melancholy. As he sat enthroned for his anointing, I observed the strength of his body, naked to the waist, the swelling muscles of the forearms, and the growth of dark hair upon his breast. Then, the crown of Sweden having been set upon his head, he was pleased to confer knighthood upon a great number of Danish and German nobles. The Swedish lords looked on resentfully, outraged that the King had not regarded any of them as worthy to bear the regalia to church, far less to be admitted to the order of chivalry. Finally the envoy of the Emperor hung the Order of the Golden Fleece about His Majesty's neck.

Thus I witnessed a great historical event—the birth of a United North beneath the scepter of one King.

On the fourth day I lay in my lodging, bathing my head with wet cloths. Every hoof beat on the paving stones, as the coronation guests rode home, echoed painfully in my head. I lay in torment, unable to eat or do more than suck at a salt herring and gulp water from a jar to allay my abominable thirst. Andy walked into my room, his doublet torn. Holding his head in his hands he swore by all the saints never to taste strong drink again.

"Still, I'd rather be in my shoes than in their lordships'," he went on. "There are strange rumors abroad. It seems the King is holding a reception for the Lady Christina and many eminent gentlemen—a rather queer reception, for there are armed guards at the doors, and the Archbishop himself is said to be preaching amendment to those who have injured him."

I replied that all those old offenses were forgiven and forgotten, and I bade Andy be quiet and let me sleep. But that evening it appeared that he had spoken the truth. The Lady Christina, with a great assembly of distinguished churchmen and nobles, was placed under house arrest at the palace. In the Lady Christina's house a wall had been torn down and a document had been found in which the privy council and the spokesmen of the Estates jointly condemned the Archbishop, decreed the forfeiture of his appointment, and promised to stand together in defying the papal interdict that was to be expected as a penalty for this deed. The Lady Christina, basing her defense upon the document, declared that no one person could be held responsible for the Archbishop's dismissal, for which the whole nation and not her late husband alone must bear the blame. But I failed to see how anyone could be charged with acts which His Majesty had promised to forgive and forget. The following morning the matter was made clear to me by Herr Didrik, who called upon me before cockcrow.

"Dress at once, Michael!" he said hurriedly. "The King has been reluctantly compelled to set up an Ecclesiastical Court of Inquiry into alleged heresy, and this Court requires a clerk. Their Lordships find it difficult to come by a man of sufficient education who has not pressing business elsewhere. But you are learned, proficient in Latin, unexceptionable in character, impartial, and a Finn. Catch Fortune on the wing and hasten to the palace!"

He dragged me out of bed while I was yet drunk with sleep, and before I grasped what it was all about he was presenting me to cross-eyed old Master Slagheck at the palace, who instructed me in my duties. And so I found myself most unexpectedly in the distinguished company of the Lords Spiritual, there being present three bishops, eight canons, and Dominican Prior, and the Archbishop himself, all sorrowfully herded together behind closed doors. His Grace inquired as to my spiritual qualifications and was astounded to learn that I was not in priestly orders. Indeed he considered that this state of affairs should be instantly rectified, and with a hasty laying on of hands ordained me there and then. I knew not whether I stood on my head or my heels, and could not believe that as the result of so simple an act, bread and wine would henceforth be transmuted into the body and blood of Christ when I pronounced the words of consecration. But when I ventured to hint as much to the Archbishop, who was arrayed in full pontificals, he retorted sharply that he knew more of the matter than I. I felt it prudent to hold my tongue.

The meeting seemed distasteful to the prelates, who would have preferred to sleep off the effects of the recent festivities undisturbed. Most of them still found it difficult to collect their thoughts and debate so solemn a matter. The Archbishop took the lead at once, unfolding the bill of indictment that he had drawn up the previous day against the Swedish nobles, and also the secret act whose hiding place the Lady Christina had with feminine thoughtlessness revealed in order to defend the honor of Sten Sture, her late husband. This document, observed the Archbishop in tones of grief, aggravated still further the disgrace and degradation of which he had been the victim, since it disclosed the fact that surprisingly many gentlemen of high position, including the Burgomaster and Council of Stockholm, were implicated in this hideous and heretical conspiracy against Holy Church. It was no longer merely a matter of making good the injuries to the Archbishop. When King Christian took the oath he swore to defend the rights of the Church, and it was therefore his duty to discover to what extent the corruption of heresy had spread in his domains. This tribunal had been set up to investigate the matter and record their findings.

The first point His Grace put forward for discussion was whether any of the signatories could be held innocent of the charge, and with one voice the assembly declared that Bishop Hans Brask of Linköping should be at once acquitted of any complicity, since he had signed under duress.

General debate followed on the wording of the report, but on the findings themselves there were no divided opinions. The conspirators, by setting themselves in opposition to the Church and the Pope's authority, had fallen into heresy.

Bishop Jens, a good, singlehearted man, made this clear, and added, "Our task is a grievous one. Let us however comfort ourselves by recollecting that we are not passing sentence, and therefore we need feel no responsibility for the measures which the King may feel called upon to take. Heresy must be dealt with sternly, indeed; but the great number of the accused, their high positions, and His Majesty's sworn oath to overlook former offenses, are sufficient guarantee of his clemency."

The good Archbishop answered sharply, "It is not for us to speak of punishment. We must confine ourselves to fulfilling the task which has been laid upon us. The clemency you speak of is irrelevant here, since the King has no power to forgive offenses against the Church. We have already wasted much time in unnecessary talk. Let us now dictate our report and sign it, and leave His Majesty to decide what steps should be taken. We are not his counselors."

So at last the findings were committed to paper, and I engrossed them in as fair a hand as I was master of. The signatories were accused individually by name and the Court found that all except Bishop Hans Brask were notorious heretics. The Court therefore handed them over to the secular arm. I own that these terrible words froze the very blood in my veins, for canonical tradition gave both inquiry and decision a formidable scope, and I seemed already to smell the smoke of the burning.

The members of the Court signed their statement in glum silence, headed by the Archbishop. I lit the tapers on the table for the dignitaries to melt wax and affix their seals. Then His Grace smilingly urged the assembly to enjoy the repast which they had so well earned. He even deigned to pat me on the shoulder and invite me to join them, as I must be very hungry after my exacting and important task. His affability encouraged me to inquire once more whether I was indeed an ordained priest, and he replied that I could now assume the tonsure with an easy mind and claim my warrant from the Cathedral chapter. When I ventured to mention that I had not attained the canonical age, and had not even been born in wedlock, he smiled sourly and said that such points were of small significance beside the great service I had rendered to Holy Church that day.

Cold and hungry, we sat down to a long table in a comfortable dining room warmed by a bright, crackling fire. We were offered hot soup, blood sausage, and every kind of delicacy left over from the three days' feasting. Yet despite the strong ale, conversation languished, and we ate in gloomy and oppressive silence. Outside, a few snowflakes were falling from the gray November sky, and although my dearest hopes had suddenly found fulfillment I was very far from happy. All had come about so suddenly that I still hardly realized the import of what I had done, and I fancy that the bishops too—until the warmth and the ale thawed their intellects—had not fully perceived the far-reaching consequences of their act. For according to the ancient ecclesiastical law, death is the only penalty for incorrigible heresy, and it would be exceedingly difficult for the King, with the best will in the world and notwithstanding all his promises, to circumvent this law.

During the meal the notes of distant horns reached our ears, but we paid no attention to them. We arose at last. Bishop Jens had just said a short grace in thanksgiving for the good things we had enjoyed when an agitated servant rushed into the room crying that Bishops Matthias and Vincentius were being led out from the palace to execution in the Great Square.

We were transfixed, but the Archbishop reassured us, saying, "The fellow's raving."

Good Bishop Jens added, "God forbid we should believe His Majesty capable of raising a finger against such men as those." And when he was a little recovered from his dismay, he went on, laughing, "We know that no one in Sweden has done so much for the King since the capitulation as Bishop Matthias of Strängnäs. His Majesty could hardly have succeeded without his help."

But the Lords Spiritual had grown exceedingly uneasy; they walked to and fro and tried to peer out through the windows. Good Bishop Jens bade me see what was happening, and I slipped out and hurried down to the courtyard, where a mob of German mercenaries bawled at me to go in again. The King had just issued a proclamation that everyone in the palace and in the city should keep withindoors. But at that moment a door opened and Bishops Matthias and Vincentius stepped into the courtyard, between guards. Both men were wan from anguish and lack of sleep, but when the provost marshal stepped forward to escort them, Vincentius attempted to smile, and asked him playfully what was he to do?

The soldier greeted him with a deep bow and said respectfully, "Nothing good, my Lord! I beg your Lordship's pardon, but the order has gone forth that your Lordship's head is forfeit."

I do not think they believed him, but took his words for a grim jest, as I did, who knew the strange humor of the Germans. However that may be, the bishops were led away from the palace and the soldiers hustled me indoors again. I returned to the dining room and related what I had heard and seen, adding that it was certainly some rough pleasantry or other. Yet many of the prelates turned pale. Bishop Jens pressed his hand to his breast and complained of breathlessness, while one or two others became the victims of a sudden internal disorder. These the Dominican Prior, who knew his way about the palace, directed to a privy. After their return, when all were again assembled in the room, one of Bishop Matthias's servants ran in weeping bitterly, with a torn jacket, and blood streaming from his nose, to tell us that a scaffold had been erected in the Great Square, and around it a number of gibbets. The two bishops, he said, were at that instant kneeling at the block, and many other prisoners were on their way thither.

At this, many of the gentlemen cried out in horror and buried their faces in their hands.

But Bishop Jens said, "Let us hasten to the King and plead with him not to incur the guilt of such an atrocity!"

All but the Archbishop sped from the room, and I followed them, dumb with horror. But Master Slagheck advanced to meet us with arms outstretched and forbade us with many German oaths to disturb

His Majesty, who was already distracted with grief at the measures that the Ecclesiastical Court had forced him to take.

There was nothing for the prelates to do but to return to the dining room, where they prayed aloud to God for mercy. They dared not look one another in the face, and I was in no better case; I was icy cold and burning hot by turns, and I saw now why it had been so hard to find a clerk to copy out the findings of the Court. Yet I could not believe the worst, and fancied that the King wished to frighten the nobles—that he would behead some and let the others go. I wanted to see for myself, and to this end sought out Master Slagheck. He slapped me hard on the shoulder and with a ringing laugh bade me be of good cheer; miscreants alone were to receive a well-deserved punishment. At my desire he ordered a halberdier to attend me so that I might proceed safely and unmolested to the Great Square, and there see the sentence carried out.

Scared out of my wits, I trudged at the heels of the foot soldier through deserted alleys to the Square, where a great crowd of the common people stood aghast. Round about the scaffold, behind a forest of lances, stood the nobles of Sweden. The numbers of the condemned were constantly increasing, for many who had already left the city returned, only to be dragged from the saddle at the gates and taken to the Square. Many citizens were there also who had been seized at their honest occupations, one at his pickling tub, another at his scales. Many still had their leather aprons on and their shirtsleeves rolled up. On the balcony of the town hall stood some of His Majesty's councilors, who called out to the people now and then that they need not be alarmed at the punishment to be visited upon criminals, conspirators, and heretics. But many citizens among the accused shouted in reply that this was treachery and a lie.

"Good and honorable men of Sweden!" they cried. "Take well to heart the wrongs and injustices done to us, for the same fate awaits all those who put their faith in the words of despots, and who allow themselves to be shamefully betrayed. Strike down this tyrant! We shall pray in heaven that you may be given strength, and from the gutters of Stockholm our blood will cry out for vengeance!"

The provost marshal grew impatient at the continued uproar and ordered the drummers to drown it, thus depriving the prisoners of their right to speak to the people from the scaffold. They were denied even the Blessed Sacrament, and were left to pray alone and commend their own souls to the mercy of the Almighty. They did not look like heretics, for many of them knelt devoutly as they prayed; the strong comforted the weak, and the old people steeled the hearts of the young. But through the roar of voices and drums sounded the thud from the block, and the platform grew slippery from the blood that poured down in streams to the Square. Casks were filled with the heads of the victims, and the bodies were piled in heaps on each side of the platform. But commoners whose rank did not entitle them to beheading were strung up on the encircling gibbets.

In trying to keep count of the number of those who perished, I found to my amazement that the headsman was slaying many more than those whom the Ecclesiastical Court had named. Steam from the warm blood hung heavily in the cold November air, and soon the confusion grew so great that many who had come to the place by chance were dispatched without inquiry, whether in error or by design. This ghastly orgy so paralyzed the people that no one attempted resistance. The victims allowed themselves to be led up the steps of the scaffold like lambs to the slaughter; and I fancy that everyone present in the Great Square felt as guilty as they, for the condemned men had done no worse than the others. Men dragged forth from the crowd to the scaffold showed no surprise; they merely hastened to grope in their purses for money to offer the headsman, that he might do the business swiftly and with dexterity.

I too became so bewitched and stricken by the bloodshed that I could not so much as mumble my name when two of the provost marshal's men, in looking about them, caught sight of me and demanded, "Who's this stripling with inky fingers and the face of a scholar? He must be of the Swedish party. He has lace at his cuffs, so his proper place is behind the lances."

They pushed through the close ranks of the mercenaries to seize me, and I should certainly have been herded among the condemned for hanging or beheading had not Doctor Paracelsus stood nearby. Observing my desperate plight, he hurried forward and smote the men across the fingers with the flat of his sword. He defended me and told them my name, and an angel from heaven could hardly have been more welcome, for the Germans feared him as a notorious sorcerer and at once let me alone. The man-at-arms who had attended me from the palace had long since left my side, to crawl about among the other godless mercenaries and steal purses, rings, and buckles from the blood-soaked and headless dead. I leaned on my rescuer's arm and spewed up all the good food I had eaten; but I had no regrets, as it would have

106

poisoned me if it had remained in my stomach. I have recounted all this at length merely to convey the chaos and confusion that prevailed, and in no way to boast of my marvelous rescue.

It was by this time growing dark, and with the increasing chill of evening the reek about the headsman's block grew denser. Snowflakes brushed my cheeks. I was shocked to see that the balcony of the town hall and the doors of many houses were still decorated with juniper in honor of the coronation. As surely as King Christian had provided three days of lavish entertainment for his guests, he now offered them a draught that would free them from the resulting headaches, and indeed from all other earthly suffering.

Having somewhat recovered, I would have left the place, but Master Paracelsus held me fast, saying he wished to speak to the executioner when the bloody feast was over.

"I am no prophet," said he, "only a physician; but just as these eyes of mine, sharpened by nature's light, could discern the infinite wealth of ore hidden in the bowels of the earth—for I've been among the miners, studying their diseases—so I can see that King Christian, with every blow of the executioner's sword, is smashing his own brilliant crown into fragments. I noted on my journeys that there are men hiding in the woods—men who put no faith in the King's promise of pardon—and if there should be among them one fit to lead, they will choose him for their king. He need fear no rivals; King Christian in his folly has cleared them all from his path."

I replied that no other monarch could be thought of now that King Christian was crowned and anointed and the Estates had with oath and seal declared Sweden to be his and his heirs' domain forever.

And I added, "The people may pull wry faces, but they have cooked their own stew and must swallow it."

Master Paracelsus surveyed me through the deepening twilight with the terrible eyes of the seer, and observed, "I should like to know just what manner of stew it is that you have been busied with, Michael Furfoot! Remember, he who gives the devil a finger loses his whole body."

His remark silenced me, and I made the sign of the cross several times. But now at last the drums were stilled, the crowds began to disperse, and the executioner sank down upon the steps of the scaffold, panting with his exertions. He was drenched in blood from head to foot, and had to draw off his boots and empty them. Even the mercenaries withdrew from him in repugnance.

But Doctor Paracelsus led me up to him and said, "Sell me your glaive, Master Jörgen, that I may have a precious memento of Sweden. I promise to honor it as it deserves, for in all Christendom there is certainly no sword so impregnated with power as yours now is."

Master Jörgen contemplated his weapon, which was a two-handed broadsword with a cross hilt topped by a big round boss.

"To be frank with you," he said, "I'm a Godfearing man, and now when I come to think about it I fear my own sword because I feel it to be full of all the spirits and forces it has released this day. It is blunted too, and I think if I held it to the grindstone it would bite off my fingers. Take it, Master Paracelsus, and wear it in memory of me. I want no money, only another similar sword, ready-whetted. But that we can talk of later. My clothes have begun to freeze upon me and will be my death if I don't run to the baths and put on some dry things."

It was in this manner that Doctor Paracelsus acquired the executioner's sword which was steeped in such virtue and which he wore to his life's end. He cared not that men mocked him for its great length, which caused him to trip over it constantly, for he claimed that the blade held magic. Many have puzzled over the secret of this weapon, and therefore I have told how he came by it.

But I fell sick, and when at last I reached my bed I vomited continually and shook in violent ague. Few eyes were closed that night in the good city of Stockholm. From every house came the sound of sobbing. Mercenaries broke into the houses of the deceased, forced the women to surrender their keys, and then rifled chests and coffers, so that widows and the fatherless were made destitute. But I do not think this was done by order of the King, as was affirmed by many who were inclined by now to blame him for everything.

Throughout the following day the headless corpses lay in the Great Square, to the great horror of the people; but the King ordered wood to be dragged to the southern outskirts and there stacked into a pyre. On Saturday the dead were loaded onto carts and taken thither to be burned. The body of Sten Sture was exhumed also, to be consumed with those of the other heretics. The King's purpose was to show that the punishment was that laid down by the Church for heresy, and by no means a private act of vengeance. His henchmen did their best to spread this idea among the people at large, and it was not long before many burghers began to remark among themselves that indeed they had nothing to thank those haughty nobles for, who had done nothing but oppress them and encroach upon their rights. Great consolation lay also in the thought of the many civic posts that had fallen vacant in that fair city.

4

I too began to take heart again, but the notion of paying my respects to the Cathedral chapter was repugnant to me. I never wanted to see them again. Yet I dared not of myself assume the dress of a priest, or the tonsure. On Sunday evening, however, I was sent for and taken to a room in the palace where Master Slagheck was in the act of trying on Bishop Vincentius' miter. He had secured the good Bishop's apparel for himself, to save the expense of new vestments.

At my entry Master Slagheck interrupted his impious occupation, put the miter aside, and said, "Well, Michael! Are you a true King's man or a lazy good-for-nothing? Give me an answer, that I may know how to treat you?"

I replied that having chosen to ride upon the King's sleigh I must cling to it now, however giddy the pace.

This greatly pleased him, and he said, "His Majesty desires to meet you and to entrust to you an important task. You need not regret the course you have chosen, but may feel assured of the King's favor so long as you carry out your duty faithfully and well."

He led the way up a stair in the thickness of the wall and into a secret room, where the King himself was sitting with knitted brows, apparently suffering cruelly from the aftereffects of the feasting.

His Majesty addressed me thus, "You're a Finn, are you not? You were clerk to the Ecclesiastical Court that put me to the painful necessity of executing the heads of Sweden's noblest families. Few kings have been forced to so cruel a decision. Yet I believe that all right-thinking men have understood my difficulty and will give me their support."

I answered that I for one fully understood, and offered him the service of a faithful subject.

But I added, "Since by favor of the Archbishop I am now an ordained priest, I am bound as an obedient son of the Church to point out that Bishops Matthias and Vincentius were holy men whom even the Ecclesiastical Court held guiltless. It was therefore a great sin and an outrage against Holy Church to execute them and burn their bodies, without so much as allowing them to receive the Sacrament or to defend themselves at a trial."

The King shot a hostile glance at me with his great eyes, and exclaimed, "I require no answers to questions I have not put, and you'll be wise to remember that. These gentlemen whom you call holy were members of a gunpowder plot against my life; and this you may tell all in Finland who ask you. Yet tell it with due precaution as a secret, since such a threat to my life might arouse uneasiness among loyal citizens."

I was much shocked by this news, and realized that the two bishops had indeed deserved their fate if they had so far forgotten what was due to their sacred calling. Of this I had no evidence but His Majesty's word and the grimaces of Master Slagheck; but I could not bring myself to believe that the King would have met my eye so coolly with a deliberate lie upon his lips.

Observing my expression closely, he said, "A King's crown is no easy burden, and is weighted down by many cares. To God—and to God only—I must render an account of all I do. As clerk to the Court you will know that Electus Hemming Gadh set his name and seal to that heretical paper. This has deeply shocked me. I desired to think well of him because of his burning zeal on my behalf, but he is evidently an archheretic. I have reason to believe that his zeal was but the outcome of a heretical love of intrigue, and to forestall him I am compelled to endow him with a heavenly benefice before the news of the regrettable events here in Stockholm can reach his ears. Take this sealed warrant to Finland, seek out the man immediately, and have him beheaded without delay. My authority entitles you to every assistance in your lawful duty, and Master Slagheck will hand you ten silver marks for your expenses."

"Your Majesty cannot be in earnest!" I cried aghast. "Doctor Gadh is a servant of the Church and a warm friend to the Union. Your Majesty would never have won the Finnish castles had it not been for his persuasive tongue and the confidence which he enjoys. Such excellent services can never merit so hideous a reward."

The King returned impatiently, "As a servant of the Church it is your duty to root out heresy wherever you find it. And you need not remind me of his services. God knows they are too considerable for me to allow him with his widespread influence to retain his life after all that has passed. In the same swift and easy manner whereby he persuaded the Finnish lords to surrender he could raise them against me.

With a heavy heart I must do my duty and condemn him to death, my only comfort being that Doctor Gadh is an old man who has had more than his share of worldly joys."

Further objections might have imperiled my own neck, and to no purpose, since the King could easily have found another to run his dismal errand. Therefore I accepted the sealed death warrant and the King's authority to demand and receive assistance when required, and having been permitted to kiss His Majesty's hand I was given leave to go. Master Slagheck accompanied me to the treasurer and saw that I was provided with ten marks in pure silver—a fine fat purse, more than I had ever had in my hands before, which served to solace my oppressed and conscience-stricken spirit.

When I emerged into the fresh air, I felt as if I had left a dungeon or a tomb behind me, and I passed my hand uneasily over my neck, which was very fragile and slender. On returning to my lodging, I hastened to pack my baggage, and Andy, who was to accompany me, did the same. I then went to make my farewells to Doctor Paracelsus, who was shortly to visit Poland, and then Andy and I boarded a ship for Åbo.

We had a terrible passage, through the worst weather I have ever known, and it was fully a week before we stepped ashore at Åbo, more dead than alive. The news of "Stockholm's Blood Bath" had arrived before us in the form of rumors, and had run through the land like wildfire, despite Junker Thomas's efforts to dismiss the story as lies and slander.

Because of this I continued on my journey without delay, although I was still almost too ill to ride, leaving Andy in Åbo. Attended by two men-at-arms lent me by Junker Thomas, I arrived two days later at Raseborg, where Doctor Hemming was staying for the time with Nils Eskilsson Banér, the Constable of the castle.

My heart sank like a lump of lead at the sight of the black, surf-ringed walls of the castle, and I felt wretched indeed. The drawbridge was not lowered, despite my shouts, and the gate remained closed until the Constable himself appeared on the wall to see who had come. He called a greeting and explained that the vile rumors from Stockholm rendered it necessary to keep the gates locked against possible disturbances. He then ordered the porter to admit me instantly.

The drawbridge came down with a squeal, and the great gate rumbled on its hinges. As I passed in under the echoing archway, I said an Ave and a Pater and a Credo to keep up my spirits. As soon as I had reached the inner bailey, I ordered the men to close the gate at once, and called the captain of the German mercenaries, to whom I showed the King's seal and authority, bidding him render me all necessary assistance in obeying the royal commands. He nodded and at once ordered his drummers to sound the alarm. At this, Constable Nils came rushing bareheaded into the courtyard, demanding in the devil's name what the matter was, and whether he was no longer master here. But he quieted down at the sight of the King's seal and warrant, which he stood and fingered for a while with a look of indecision. At length he led the way indoors, although I was no longer a very welcome guest.

A huge fire was blazing in the great hall, where Doctor Hemming was. He hobbled toward me, his old head trembling, and when he saw who had come he stretched out his hands in blessing, which caused Constable Nils to soften toward me. I had hardly time to taste the ale they brought me before both men began bombarding me with questions: What had happened in Stockholm? Was it true that such or such a one had been treacherously slain? How much of all these hideous rumors were they to believe?

I pondered for a while, uncertain how to act, and then seeing no help for it, I rose and said, "All this is true, and more, but we have no time to discuss it now. Dear Doctor Hemming, it will be best for you to turn your thoughts from worldly concerns, and commend your soul to God. His Majesty King Christian has promised you a fair benefice—but in heaven. This very night you shall enter into the glories of Paradise. I have been given the task of helping you on your way, though I do it with a heavy heart. You have ever been kind to me, and treated me better than many a father treats his own son."

Although I had spoken as gently and courteously as I could, his reverence Electus Hemming was greatly agitated, and exclaimed, "This is outrageous, impossible! I refuse to believe in such black treachery, for I bear His Majesty's letter of safe-conduct and I refer you to that."

I handed him the warrant and His Majesty's written command, requested the Constable to read them also, and said, "The matter stands as I have said. Doctor Hemming's execution must take place immediately, and to this end the Constable is bound to assist me. Nevertheless I will gladly permit Doctor Hemming to receive the Sacrament before the painful event, which grieves all of us who are his friends. He shall also be given honorable burial, since I have no explicit orders to burn his body. I beseech both of you to act promptly, so as not to render my bitter duty yet more difficult."

The Constable retorted with an oath that he would rather dangle from the gallows himself than obey so shameful a command. He drew his sword and might well have run me through had not Doctor Hemming held him, and I was much shocked at his foolish and unruly behavior. He began bawling for his servants, bidding them arm and hold the castle; but none obeyed him, for good Captain Gissel of the mercenaries had already sent his men to their posts. His five harquebusiers were stationed in the bailey and upon the stairs, with their weapons in the rests and their matches smoldering, ready to shoot anyone who attempted resistance. When Captain Gissel heard the Constable's yells of rage, he entered the hall to bid him surrender his sword and obey His Majesty's commands. But even now Nils Eskilsson did not understand, and vowed that rather than obey so faithless a ruler he would rouse all true men in rebellion and sell his skin as dearly as might be.

And he added, "It is a pleasure to think of the price which that bloody tyrant will have to pay for his treachery!"

The good captain was obliged to summon two men-at-arms to corner him, and only then did he unbuckle his belt and let his sword fall to the floor.

At this Doctor Hemming turned pale, and in a quiet voice said to him, "It's useless to struggle when one is up to the chin in a bog. You should have listened to my advice, dismissed your garrison, and taken the castle into your own hands, to wait for the rumors to be confirmed or denied. We could then have determined our own future. But now we're bound hand and foot and driven like cattle. Be wise; submit, and beg these good men to pardon your rash words and forget what you said. As for me, my hoary head feels already the chill of death about it."

Turning to me and Captain Gissel, he went on respectfully, "Take my old head if you will; it is weary of the evil and the faithlessness that flourish in the world today. But spare this man, for he is yet young and of noble birth, and it would be wrong to harm him because he spoke a few thoughtless words."

The Captain bade Nils go to his room and kept him there under guard. A Dominican friar from the monastery at Viborg happened to be staying at the castle, and he at once heard Doctor Hemming's confession, absolved him, and administered the Sacrament. There was no headsman at Viborg, but a German mercenary volunteered to perform the execution for the customary fee of three silver groats. A sturdy birch log was rolled to the top of a rise near the castle, and a crowd gathered about it—house servants, maids, and people from the neighboring market. Many wept sorely, for the good Doctor had won the respect of everyone, and his reputation throughout the land stood high.

He came, alone and unsupported, to the block, and when he had emptied the executioner's cup he spoke to the throng.

"Do not weep for me, good people! I am to receive no more than the punishment I deserve for trusting to a king's fair promises rather than to my own heart and to my experience of the oaths of princes. I have nothing to say in my defense save that I believed I brought peace rather than a sword, and friendly alliance instead of ceaseless bloodshed. But events have proved otherwise and there can be no reconciliation with an enemy who consistently goes back upon his word. Weep rather for our poor country, for as long as this man sits upon the throne no man's neck will be safe, be he high or low, rich or poor; as a token of which you shall see my white head roll in the mire, although I am a man of God and under the wing of Holy Church."

Pausing for breath, he drew himself to his full height, and I saw in him the leader he had been in the days of his strength.

He lifted his face to the bleak December sky, and thundered in a terrible voice, "Hear me, God in Thy Heaven! May my blood cry out from the earth before Thy radiant throne! For here where I have set my feet I curse King Christian, that man of blood, for all the evil he has done. I curse him with all the spiritual power with which Thy Holy Church on earth has endowed me; and before Thy countenance, almighty God, I say: May he suffer now in this life the punishment for his iniquity! May he forfeit his lands and the crown which he has dishonored! May he perish a poor man, in misery, persecuted of all and denied by Thee! May all this befall him, according to his deserts. Hear my cry, most holy God!"

Such was the dignity and power of this anathema that even the mercenaries crossed themselves, and all the people raised their eyes, expecting the heavens to open. I too gazed upward for some omen, but saw only the gray winter sky. When Doctor Hemming had ended, he handed his purse to the headsman and humbly knelt in the mire, tucking the skirts of his gown beneath his knees. Then he laid his head upon the block and closed his eyes. The German raised his sword in both hands and swept off the head so neatly that it rolled upon the ground. Head and body were then shrouded and carried to the chapel, where the good Dominican said the Mass for the Dead.

Captain Gissel now regarded himself as Constable of the castle and begged me to say a word for him to Junker Thomas, that the appointment might be confirmed. We partook together of a lavish and well-deserved meal, and talked feelingly of Doctor Hemming and his good qualities, regretting that so good and so learned a man should come to so sad an end. But the thundering of the ex-Constable on his door disturbed us, and when we had emptied a jar of his best wine, Captain Gissel spoke sadly.

"What shall we do with this maniac? If we let him go, we shall bring a hornet's nest about our ears, and Junker Thomas will be displeased. If we keep him under arrest, he will be a constant danger, since I have no more than a score of greedy mercenaries under my command, who would be easily bribed. What are we to do with him?"

"Indeed I cannot say," I replied frankly. "And I've no wish to meddle with the functions of your office, although I admit that my coming has placed you in a difficult position."

He sighed.

"Learned sir, you have the King's authority. I must render you all necessary assistance. Yet the scope of your delegated powers is not clearly defined, since evidently much must be left to your own discretion. I'm bound to obey you in everything and if, for example, you were to order me to shorten Master Nils by a head I should have no choice but to do as you say. The matter would be attended to without delay and, I will admit, to my own great satisfaction, as it would be an excellent solution to this awkward problem."

"Honored sir!" I exclaimed, deeply shocked. "God forbid that I should issue so wicked an order. I have no power to do so."

"Yet you have heard the worthy gentleman swear to slit your belly when next he sees you, because, says he, you're a traitor and the Tyrant's jackal. He brought misfortune upon himself through not listening to Doctor Hemming's advice. Don't do the same by turning a deaf ear to me, so long as you have the King's authority to act. Should any questions be asked later, I'll undertake to stand by you and say that we took this step after mature consideration and solely in His Majesty's interests, since this one neck will save us the necessity of severing many hundreds."

I had to admit that he spoke like a sensible man, yet it was horrible to bear responsibility for a deed which the King alone had the right to sanction. I will give no further account of this somber conversation, which ended with Captain Gissel's ordering out the drummers, although the hour was late, and sending men to the prisoner's room to put Master Nils in irons. This was achieved only after a violent struggle. A couple of torches were lit in the courtyard, and the same German soldier did his work so neatly that the victim had scarcely time to grasp what was to happen. I regret to say that Master Nils died with his sins unrepented and his heart hardened, and to the last he volleyed imprecations against me and Captain Gissel and the King.

I was now so weary from my journey and the wine I had drunk that I retired to the room prepared for me and slept like a log until late next morning.

Stiff though I still was from my ride, I prepared at once to return to Åbo, having no wish to tarry longer in that grim fortress. I rode at walking pace over the half-frozen mire of the roads, but at length the sun came out and my heart was lightened with every step away from those brooding ramparts. At the halting places I had opportunity to talk with many honest farmers, who all cried out on Junker Thomas for his extortion when victualing the army. And while they seemed not unduly concerned at the beheading of the Swedish nobles, they sighed deeply over their cattle and corn, and muttered, "It looks ugly —very ugly!"

When I arrived in Åbo I found it as deserted and drear as Stockholm had been when I left it. People with red-rimmed eyes slunk along close to the walls and started at the least noise. I was not tempted to linger here and ask for news, and so I rode straight to the fortress. Junker Thomas received me cordially, and on hearing all that had passed he praised my calmness and presence of mind, and said many kind things of Captain Gissel.

"I too have striven to give a wide interpretation to the King's commands and avoid niggling measures," he said. "Harmful weeds must be uprooted before they grow too rank and smother more wholesome growth. I think I can say that the whole of this region is now quiet and won't cause the King or his faithful servants any trouble."

He blew through his tufted nostrils and stood rigid as a rock, while at his dictation I wrote a report to His Majesty of the great services that Junker Thomas had rendered him.

But having finished, I said to him respectfully, "The good Archbishop Gustaf has laid his hands on me and ordained me, and it's no

116

longer fitting that I should serve as a common secretary. I trust that Bishop Arvid will confer a suitable benefice upon me, so that I may continue my studies according to God's will."

Junker Thomas laughed loudly.

"You may return home if you like, and be my eyes and ears in the town; but cattle must go where there's grazing, and you'll soon find where your advantage lies."

I set off therefore to speak with the Bishop, but on the way my heart failed me and I stepped into the Three Crowns for a stoup of ale. When I entered the cozy barroom, conversation died away. One customer after another laid his coin on the table, rose, and went out, so that in a few moments the place was empty, to the great indignation of the hostess.

She greeted me and said, "I don't know what's the matter with people today. Some are angry because Junker Thomas has erected gibbets in the market place. It's never been done before; folk never minded walking to Gallows Hill to watch the hangings. But I'm as happy as a lark because your friend Andy has come back, and now lodges with me. Perhaps he'll be master gunner at the castle and a fine gentleman, for he has learned much on his travels abroad. But it might be better for you to come in the back way, Michael, and sit in the kitchen with Andy so as not to frighten away my customers. People have turned very queer these last few days."

The thoughtless words offended me, but nothing better could be expected of a foolish tavern woman, so I replied serenely that I would drink my ale at the inn rather than compromise my position in low resorts.

So to the inn I went, but the innkeeper seemed not at all glad to see me. He began at once to deplore the bad times and meager takings. The serving boy gave me stale beer and contrived to spill half of it into my lap, so that I had the greatest trouble in cleaning myself up to be fit to call upon the Bishop.

The innkeeper wiped my knees with his apron, saying, "Learned sir, don't be offended at an old man's words. But many have threatened to thrash you and throw you into the river, and I should be glad if you wouldn't visit me too often, as it may give rise to disturbance. No one would say a word if I were to serve Junker Thomas, because he's a foreigner and has sold himself hair and hide to the King. But you, Michael, were born in our good city; you grew up among us and have a Finnish name, though God knows where your father came from. And so some people can't make out why it is you fawn on the King and run his errands so officiously, to the great prejudice of your countrymen."

For a time I was at a loss for an answer. Not until I was on the stairs did I think of what I should have said, and I mumbled a few murderous words as I left his house behind me. Glowing with resentment, I passed the church and St. Örjan's Hospital, and wielded the knocker at the Bishop's gate so vigorously that the courtyard within resounded. The servant who hurried to open to me was white in the face, and Bishop Arvid received me at once. His hands were shaking when I stepped into his study.

"Who do you think you are?" he exclaimed. "Why this violence? We live in evil times and not even a bishop's life is safe."

"Gracious sir," I answered, "every man of honor, every supporter of the Union, enjoys full security beneath the protection of our good King, and only those who have something to conceal see ghosts in broad daylight."

"You're right," said the Bishop hastily, "and of course I have nothing to hide. Be seated, Michael, my dear son, and tell me how I may best serve you."

He asked me to tell him all I knew, and was deeply shocked to learn of Doctor Hemming's sad fate at Raseborg.

"God be praised that I was in no way connected with him," he said. "Doctor Hemming left me in anger. It is not for me to comment upon His Majesty's actions, but in this case he acted rightly, for Doctor Hemming was a rogue who trimmed his sail to every wind, and I can only thank my Maker for keeping me out of the net of his intrigues."

I further told how His Grace the Archbishop, with three bishops and eight canons in attendance, had ordained me priest, but emphasized that my mind would be easier if this ordination might be confirmed with the customary ceremony by the good Bishop Arvid himself, in Åbo Cathedral. It was also my hope, relying as I did on his favor and goodwill, that he would secure me a modest benefice that would enable me to continue my studies at the University of Paris, since I felt no great desire to remain in my own country.

But at this the Bishop became embarrassed and said, "This is a complex theological question which I must deliberate upon and discuss with my good canons."

I demanded in some indignation whether he considered himself wiser than the Archbishop, to which he replied, "Show me His Grace's written statement, or at least one from the Chapter, and the thing is done. At present I have only your word, and persuaded though I may be of your honesty, nevertheless your unsupported evidence is inadequate in resolving a knotty theological point that would puzzle even the learned doctors of the University."

I persisted with some heat and even threatened him with the Archbishop's displeasure, but he remained adamant. He assured me of his willingness to help me, however, if I would first obtain the necessary written authority from Uppsala. I saw no alternative but to write humbly to Bishop Slagheck and beg him to use his influence on my behalf.

The letter was dispatched before Christmas, but immediately afterward the sea froze and I had plenty of time to ponder my affairs while awaiting the reply. I was unwilling to return to the fortress and the service of Junker Thomas, having conceived a repugnance for his company, and was therefore obliged to settle in my former and only home at Mistress Pirjo's. She took care of me and protected me, for she knew the purity of my motives; nor did Father Peter cast me off in my wretchedness, but visited me often and consoled me with instructive legends about the transience of earthly happiness. Sometimes Master Laurentius, true to his old custom, would visit the cabin to drink mulled wine from the worn silver cup, and to talk of immortality and of specters. But these two good men were my only companions, for all other of my former acquaintance shunned my company and found every pretext for passing quickly on when we met by chance in the street and they were compelled by mere courtesy to greet me.

5

What wonder then that during that long winter I was plunged in the deepest melancholy! I lost my desire for company and was better pleased to be alone. No doubt if I had been brazen and importunate I could have persuaded the council to give me some appointment, but I had no desire to profit by scurvy blackmail, being still deeply hurt by people's attitude toward me and their inability to appreciate my good intentions. I told myself that in the evil days to come they might appeal to me and beg my help and favor, and the thought consoled me. But I found yet greater solace in books, for the good Bishop allowed me access to his library, to preserve my good humor at little cost. In order to prepare myself for the sacred calling which I kept constantly before my eyes, I read with fitting humility the works of the Fathers of the Church, including the *Summa* of St. Thomas Aquinas, which has given wiser men than I some hard nuts to crack.

Days began to lengthen out and the snowdrifts melted, but with the spring came disturbing news that the ski-runners and seal-fishers of the Bothnian Gulf brought with them from the Swedish coast. It was said that a fiery youngster named Gustaf Eriksson, whose noble father had been beheaded as a heretic in Stockholm with others of his peers, had raised the standard of rebellion in Dalarna and had gathered about him a great following of peasants who refused to surrender their arms to the King's constables and were resentful of the heavy taxes. These peasants had already taken the lives of a number of His Majesty's officers and innocent taxgatherers, and no Dane could travel without an armed escort between one Swedish stronghold and another.

In southern Finland also, in the region of Wanda and Raseborg, where snow still lay, swift ski-runners began to harry the taxation officials, and would attack heavily armed horsemen with arrows, well knowing that His Majesty's cavalry could never follow them into the recesses of the woods. The skiers robbed wagonloads of collected tax money, and once they locked a judge and all his attendants into the courthouse, barred the doors and shutters, and burned him and all his folk alive. No one knew whence these swift runners came or whither they went. If anyone guessed, he dared not hint it, for fear of having his throat slit or his cabin set afire some dark night. The result was that all peaceful, law-abiding citizens lived in an agony of dread, and were as frightened of the swift ski-runners of the woods as of Junker Thomas's horsemen, each of whom had a lissom rope slung at his saddlebow.

The skiers ventured as far as Åbo. One morning a notice was found nailed to the Cathedral door, to the effect that Danish tyranny and oppression would soon be at an end and that he who helped the Danes by word or deed did so at the peril of his neck. The Cathedral clergy seemed afraid to tear down this seditious paper, and not only left it where it was until the hour of High Mass, but even read it aloud to those who were illiterate, for a great number of the curious had gathered at the Cathedral doors to stare at the notice. Not until dinnertime did Junker Thomas come to hear of it, and he sent horsemen galloping through the city to tear down the despicable sheet. Nevertheless a few graceless apprentices ran away from their masters and disappeared, and the sons of some of the burghers followed their example, despite the tears and warnings of their parents. Everyone that spring bore some hidden fear in his heart, and to look into men's eyes was to find embers glowing beneath dead ashes. I could not but believe that sorrow and devastation must follow.

I had to wait until summer for Bishop Slagheck's letter. He had written it in great haste and regretted that he could not further my case, for Archbishop Gustaf was a madman whom no one of sense could deal with; it was not to be wondered at that the Swedish lords had removed him from his sacred office. The Archbishop had now allied himself with Bishop Jens against Master Slagheck and paid not the slightest heed to his warnings or advice, in his own ever burning desire to remain cock of the walk in Sweden.

But a rival cock had begun to crow; the young upstart Gustaf had so corrupted the people that Master Slagheck was compelled to exchange his crosier for a sword and to march against him at the head of an army. This campaign had ended in defeat not for the said Gustaf but for Master Slagheck himself, who had but narrowly escaped the spears and arrows of the peasants. It was unnecessary to speak of this in Finland, and Master Slagheck mentioned it only to make it clear to me that he had had other matters to think of than my cassock. Furthermore, if I could not look after myself, I had only my stupidity to blame, and he was not minded to drag me into high positions if I lacked the wit to get there by myself.

"But," he ended, "unless you are more foolish than I think, you must already have skimmed the cream from the bowl I set before you last winter and must now be a man of means. I will therefore content myself with sending you my blessing and wishing success to you in all your undertakings."

As I read these lines the scales fell from my eyes, and I felt as great an emptiness within me as when Julien d'Avril had shaken the dust from his feet and departed to convert the Turks, leaving me with his farewell letter at the little inn outside Paris. Nor could I understand what Master Slagheck meant by "cream." I would gladly have forced him to lap all the cream I had been given that winter in Åbo, where I had met with nothing but mockery and ill will both from laymen and clergy.

6

I was plunged in these dismal reflections that evening when Andy came in. He took off his cap without a word of greeting, sat down

121

in a corner with his chin in his hands, and heaved a deep sigh. I sighed as deeply again to show him that I had troubles of my own. But when we had sat sighing together for some time I became irritated and asked him why he had come to plague me thus.

"Don't be harsh, Michael," he answered. "There's a noose about my neck and I'm at my wits' end what to do. You're cleverer than me and a scholar, and you must help me out. All this winter I've been well cared for by the widow at the Three Crowns, as you know, and so far there's been nothing to complain of. But now my back's to the wall; she wants me to marry her!"

I heard him with amazement, but wished him luck most heartily.

"Andy, you're Fortune's favorite! The Three Crowns is the best tavern in Åbo, and the widow counts her gold with a shovel. What's more, she's experienced in her trade, and a chatty, agreeable woman."

But Andy said, "Ah, if it were only a question of victuals I wouldn't complain. But marriage—that's something I've always fought shy of. I'm young still, and she's twice my age. I feel as if she were driving me to the altar at the pistol's point. . . . And spring has made me restless. I can't hang about here any longer, although every morning and evening, and especially at mealtimes, I try to tell myself that it's a fine thing to be among old friends who speak a Christian language."

His gloomy words gave me something to think about, and after deep reflection I said to him, "It's plain that the stars have bound our lives together, Andy, for if you've suffered anxiety and affliction, I too have the sensation of one sitting on an anthill without his breeches. I've begun to feel grave doubts of King Christian's motives; and in any event he pays very poor wages. And so I too would be ripe for discharge and departure were it not arduous to travel as a poor man. And I can't think how to fill my purse."

Andy gave me a searching look and said, "A strange customer came to the Three Crowns last night, and when he heard that I was a trained gunner he began to tempt me with some very agreeable employment. It seems he's one of Grabbacka Nils's boys, and the work he has for me is in the privateering line, where a clever man is soon a rich one."

"Andy, Andy!" I warned him. "You talk of ungodly things—and you were never born to be a sailor. Junker Thomas has sworn to hang Nils from the yardarm of his ship the Finnish Prince. Moreover, Grabbacka Nils is a bloodthirsty man who has burned houses full of people and has even robbed churches."

"But," returned Andy wistfully, "he wants only young and unmar-

122

ried men in his service, and that's in his favor. The fellow at the Three Crowns can't say enough of his cunning. Nils declares that he robs the Danes in the name of God and of his country and of all good people. And he answers Junker Thomas's threats by saying that as sure as there's still justice and the fear of God in the world, Junker Thomas shall swing before he does. There are clerks and the sons of burghers among his men, and like other officers of high rank he needs a ship's chaplain who can write Latin and administer the Sacrament to his German and Danish prisoners before they're hanged, which shows him to be a man of piety and no heathen."

"Far be it from me to think of such a thing!" I cried. "I should not suit him, for to enter his service is to become chaplain to the devil himself. In any case, he would hang me without delay, for he was one of Nils Eskilsson's drinking companions at Raseborg, and has sworn to avenge his death."

Andy arose and assured himself that no one was listening behind the door. Then with a steady look at me he said gravely, "You need never set eyes on him, for Grabbacka Nils has a use for unseen men who can give him information. He wants to know which vessels are sailing from Åbo, the nature of their cargo and armament, particulars of the taxgatherers' journeys—when they leave the city and when they return—and many other facts that may be useful to a man of his occupation. My companion showed me a deep crack in the Cathedral wall opposite St. Örjan's Hospital. If some bold man were now and then to slip a letter into this crack, the same man might in that same place find his reward. But being an ignorant fellow myself, I mean to take to the woods and gather pine cones, to escape the bonds of matrimony."

"May God and the saints protect you, Andy! You're tempting me to hideous treachery. I can feel the noose about my throat at the very thought."

"It would be safest for you to go back to the castle and re-enter the service of Junker Thomas, if you won't take to the woods with me, or else you may find a knife in your ribs one of these fine days. Grabbacka Nils seems outraged at his friend's death. But even at the castle you would certainly have business at the Cathedral and the Bishop's house, and on your way you could examine the crack in the wall. Have no fear; those I take orders from shall never know who is the author of the letters."

He paid no heed to my warnings but slipped out of the town that night, to the great grief of the widow at the Three Crowns. But he had spoken the truth, for the very next evening I was set upon as I came from vespers, and so I felt it best to return to Junker Thomas and tell him I was no longer safe in Åbo. He received me kindly, having already wearied of his new secretary Måns, a simple Swedish clerk who never attempted to conceal his hostility to the Danes. But in me Junker Thomas had confidence, and he told me all his plans.

Time dragged at the castle, and I had no pleasure in the company either of Måns the clerk or in that of the chaplain, who preferred to swill beer and play dice with the mercenaries rather than converse on matters spiritual.

To while away the time I made a detailed list of all vessels sailing from Åbo, indicating their cargoes and how many guns they mounted, the names of their captains and the size of their complement. And I also reported upon the reinforcements that Junker Thomas meant to send to Raseborg, now threatened by pirates. In going to borrow the *Summa* of St. Thomas Aquinas from the Bishop's library, I slipped the paper into the crack opposite the blank wall of the Hospital. Whether or not it was my doing, many transports carrying provisions to Stockholm were attacked and sunk off the Åland Islands. The Swedish provinces could no longer victual the capital city, and therefore Junker Thomas had with great difficulty scraped together these necessities of life from the already plundered parishes around Åbo.

Later, on my way to the Bishop's house to return the commentaries, I paused to relieve myself against the church wall, and at the same time I put my hand into the crack. At the bottom of the hole lay a soft, heavy bag, which I joyfully hid in my pouch. Having hastened to Mistress Pirjo's cabin, I counted the money in it and found pieces of silver both large and small, coins from Stockholm and from Åbo, some Lübeck gulden, and a smooth ducat. I felt a wealthy man once more; this money would suffice for a journey of many months. For safety, I buried it beneath a flat stone by the pear tree.

My mood had changed, as when the sun breaks through and blue sky appears after long and heavy rain. I told myself that life was a gamble that in the long run could be won only by the lighthearted use of loaded dice, and by taking care not to get caught. King Christian and Master Slagheck had thought me simple in my trustfulness and had landed me in a situation of sorrow and vexation. I owed them nothing, and Junker Thomas still less, for he was a cruel man. Hitherto I had been as a lamb among wolves, and by their false promises they

124

had fleeced me. Now, beneath the shorn wool, I too would grow the hide of a wolf.

I visited the town often during the summer, and found no difficulty in slipping my hand into the crack from time to time. Strange birds began to take wing from Åbo to all the hiding places in the archipelago and elsewhere, returning in due course to lay gold and silver eggs in the wall.

Meanwhile ships from Stockholm brought grave news. It was said that young Gustaf's peasant rabble were drawing near to that city and surrounding it; while from the King's castles and fortified towns poured fugitives—gentle and simple, bond and free—to take service under Gustaf's banner. The Swedes had chosen him for their Regent, and with money from Lübeck he hired German mercenaries to form a sturdy backbone to his army. Junker Thomas could only marvel that the pirates off the Finnish coasts had grown so daring, and were so well posted as to his plans. Danish vessels now had to sail to Stockholm in convoy, which occasioned many delays.

It had been my intention to shake the dust of the city from my feet that autumn, and travel abroad, leaving the fighting men to settle the quarrel among themselves as best they might. I was a scholar and my sole weapon the goose quill. Yet I postponed my journey to Paris, for the rumor spread that the King of France was arming against the Emperor, and I was unwilling to jump from the frying pan into the fire. So in November, when Gustaf's forces landed and joined those of Nils Grabbacka, I was still in Åbo fortress.

BOOK 5.

Barbara

I

THE siege of Åbo is not worth recounting, for it brought honor to neither side. The besiegers had no artillery and spent most of their time lounging in the cabins swilling beer, while the unwilling inmates of the castle dozed in the armory, and drank and squabbled among themselves. They were exacting guests who evinced the greatest reluctance to take part in any sortie and were in the habit of wheeling and galloping off, with panting foot soldiers clinging to the tails of their chargers, at the first shot fired from the timber breastworks of the besiegers.

Good Bishop Arvid showed himself at last in his true colors and lent the assailants his own men-at-arms and culverins, as well as horses and ammunition and food, for Gustaf's followers were poor men. They were glad to idle in the warm cabins and stain their doublets with what little food Junker Thomas had allowed the townsmen to keep. When Gustaf's men first marched into Åbo, the citizens welcomed them with tears of joy, rang the church bells, and sang psalms of praise to God. But Christmas had hardly come before they began to sigh and to wonder whether it were not better to feed Junker Thomas's few wolves than the countless, rapacious rats of Master Gustaf.

It was not difficult to keep ourselves informed as to the strength, equipment, and morale of the attacking forces, since the only object of our sorties was to take some poor wretch prisoner. Junker Thomas welcomed all captives with equal satisfaction, and when he had squeezed and battered and roasted as much out of them as he could, he strung them all up on the ramparts, irrespective of rank and condition.

There was little Christmas cheer in the fortress, and Junker Thomas saw about him nothing but glum faces and averted eyes. Nevertheless he was an outstanding leader, if a trifle rough and ready in his methods. Before the coast became icebound, he sent away his warships and other vessels to join those of Admiral Severin Norby, of the King's Navy, that they might not fall into enemy hands. He undertook to hold the fortress until the spring, and as early as January he received as reward for his efforts the assurance of speedy help. His Majesty, greatly angered by the rebellion, charged him to hang any Swedes or Finns who might be in the castle, saying that he had issued the same command to every officer in the Swedish realm.

Junker Thomas was well pleased by this letter and blessed King Christian, saying that he was weary of looking at sour faces and that his only concern was lest there should be too few gallows. He could scarcely wait until the following day when the carpenters had finished erecting them, and then he hanged all Swedes and Finns as the King had commanded. Among them were two little boys of noble birth whom his men tore from their mother's skirts. Even Måns the clerk found a noose about his neck; Junker Thomas feared betrayal by him, although Måns was far too stupid to be a traitor. I was sorry for him, but suffered yet more upon my own account, being convinced that I must meet the same fate. I was a Finn by birth like the others, and when I saw them all dangling side by side on the ramparts my anguish was such that I went up to Junker Thomas and asked him outright when my turn was coming.

He was taken aback at my question, but after some reflection he crossed himself devoutly and said, "Perish the ungodly thought! I cannot hang one whom the Archbishop himself has ordained. I am a believer and hold the Sacraments in honor."

2

It was a mild winter, and spring came early. The sea cast off its icy shackles and it was not long before the carefree besiegers were aroused

127

by a terrifying sight. Norby, that merry admiral, was sailing with a following wind into the mouth of the river. All was confusion in the city. Gustaf's men fled in such haste that I found a soup plate half empty on the table in the Bishop's house. Indeed I found little else, for Nils Arvidsson, who had stored his powder in a stone building on the northern bank, blew the place up before he ran, starting a fire that destroyed a great part of the town. Stone buildings, such as the Cathedral, the monastery, the Bishop's house, and the hospital, escaped, but even there the leaded panes of the windows flew to pieces at the shock of the explosion. The good Bishop and the burghers had contrived to move their possessions long before this time, and the fire preyed chiefly upon empty houses. But both Admiral Norby and Junker Thomas were incensed over the fire, and thought little of Nils Arvidsson's generalship.

I was one of the first to hurry into the town while the fire was yet raging, and I sped to Mistress Pirjo's cabin in case she should need protection against looters. The cabin was still standing, though the windows were smashed and the door was torn down. When I entered, I saw that all usable furniture had been removed and the rest broken. Andy was lying on a heap of straw. He looked pale and wretched, and was too weak to raise his head. Beside him on the floor sat the hostess from the Three Crowns with her skirts spread around her, running at the eyes and nose like a gutter pipe.

"God bless you for coming, Michael!" said she. "My tavern's in flames, but I was just able to drag your brother here—for I guessed you'd come, and you're his only hope."

I heard the soldiers clattering and banging in the street, and on the spur of the moment could think of no other expedient than to spatter Andy's face with ink from my pencase.

When immediately afterward the men stormed in, I halted them, saying, "Here lies a man in the last stages of smallpox; and there's nothing left worth taking, as you can see."

They backed hastily out with many signs of the cross, for Andy with his black spots and terrified grimaces was indeed a fearful object.

When they had gone I turned to him.

"What has happened to you? Where is dear Mistress Pirjo? And why have you stayed behind to be hanged, you fool? Your friends could have helped you, or at least you could have found sanctuary at the altar."

Andy said sadly, "I've no friends in this vile world but you, Michael,

128

and this good widow who sticks to me like a burr. I fell out with my comrades and it's they who have dealt thus with me."

"And a quarrelsome fellow you must be if you can't even live at peace with your brothers-in-arms. No doubt you were drunk. Drinking will be the death of you—if by some miracle you escape the gallows."

Weak though he was, Andy retorted indignantly, "Would that I had been drunk, so that I might have fought better, for when I'm sober I'm as weak as a lamb. They half killed me when I tried to save your good foster mother. She's dead."

The hostess of the Three Crowns wiped her nose and confirmed this news. Seeing me so shocked that I could not utter a word, she went on eagerly to tell me that some days ago the burghers had taken it into their heads to accuse Mistress Pirjo of witchcraft. With the help of the maddened soldiers, they threw her off the bridge into the river, but thanks to her voluminous petticoats she floated neatly to the bank again like a true witch. So they stoned her to death and thrust her body into an old cask, that she might float downstream and out to sea as far as possible from the good town of Åbo, over which no doubt she had long brought malediction.

"They reviled her for bringing into the world such devil's spawn as you, Michael, and for harboring you in her house," she continued smugly. "They took revenge on her, having failed to catch you. But when Andy heard what had happened, he rushed at her assailants like a mad bull. He smashed the skull of one and drowned another, and he injured a great many more before the mob could overpower him. They would certainly have chopped off his head if I hadn't come and bought them off with beer and silver."

But Andy said, "Don't take this too much to heart, Michael. Mistress Pirjo begged you not to bewail her fate, for you were not to blame for it. She said she had always loved you as her own son. And she seemed not sorry to die. She was hard and stern to her last breath, and cried out that those who stoned her would soon be roasting in hell. The Bishop was standing on the bridge and looking on without raising a finger to help her, and to him she shrieked that he should not live to see blossom on the bird-cherries."

This hideous tale so appalled me that my knees gave beneath me and I sank to the floor. I could only rock my head from side to side, filled with hatred for Åbo town and all who lived therein. Surely they had brought disaster upon their own heads by stoning a defense-less old woman who had done them so little harm! My only consolation was that Mistress Pirjo had been strong in her wrath, for her death had been followed only a few days later by the gunpowder explosion and the fire that had ravaged half the city. Nor did I believe that Bishop Arvid could escape her curse, although he had fled.

But now there was no time to lose, for the wind was veering. When I looked out at the door I saw pillars of smoke and eddies of sparks, and a streetful of rats fleeing from the burning houses.

Almighty God was on Andy's side, for a badly burned Danish soldier came howling out of the smoke. Tearing the hot helmet from his head, he flung it from him. He had gone astray among the hovels while seeking plunder and it was an easy matter to knock him on the head with a stake. I took both helmet and breastplate and put them on Andy; then I tied the Dane's sash and sword about his waist. With great difficulty the widow and I contrived to support him as far as the riverbank, where we laid him in a boat. Then I rowed him across to the monastery, where Father Peter hid him in the cellar among the casks and carcasses. Father Peter and I fell upon each other's necks, weeping and bewailing Mistress Pirjo's fate, and he reviled the cruel prelate who had stood by while the mob stoned her. He told me that the Bishop had a vessel waiting in Raumo harbor, laden with his valuables, and that he meant to make for Sweden and put himself under Gustaf's protection.

At this news, being willing to avail myself of every advantage that offered, I sped back to the town and requested an interview with Admiral Norby. This jovial man was seated on a tombstone near the door of the Cathedral, from which his men were attempting to lure the fugitives. When I told him what I knew of the Bishop's movements he was delighted, declaring that he would not fail to make things hot for the worthy man. But as it turned out later, so powerful was Mistress Pirjo's curse that a fearful tempest arose and sank the Bishop's vessel with all on board.

Mistress Pirjo's death had plunged me into the deepest sorrow, but my desire to save Andy kept me from the apathy of despair.

Admiral Norby was most gracious, and at his dictation I wrote a letter to the Lady Christina, now held prisoner in Denmark with other distinguished ladies. The Admiral confided that he had been charmed by the proud, beautiful widow, who was of the noblest blood in Sweden, and that he desired to do what he could to help vanquish her grief and turn her thoughts again to the pleasures of this world.

My letter pleased him, and when he had taken it from my hand

130

he surveyed me kindly, and asked, "Why so hangdog, young man? Come to sea and be cured of your woes!"

His solicitude touched me deeply, and I answered weeping, "All this winter I've smelled nothing but the carrion on the gallows, and the screeching of crows has been my only music. My dear foster mother was stoned to death as a witch, and now my only desire is to make a pilgrimage to the Holy Land to beg forgiveness for my sins, and then to become a monk or a hermit."

"Every man to his taste," said the Admiral. But he went on to observe that I was young and bore little resemblance to a saint. He also spoke with sympathy of Mistress Pirjo when I had told him her story.

Seeing him favorably disposed toward me, I said humbly, "I have a foster brother, a useful, honest young fellow, albeit stupid. He was in the service of Nils Arvidsson as gunner, but was hurt in defending my foster mother. Take him into your service, sir, and save his life, for when you sail from Åbo, Junker Thomas is sure to hang him, and he has no refuge, since his own comrades have turned against him."

The Admiral reflected for a little, and answered, "I could find use for such a fellow. The sly Lübeckers are preparing for battle. Some of their warships have already sailed, but my spies there are either incompetent or drunk, or else they've been hanged, for I get no information from them. If you would care to help me, I'll hire both you and your foster brother, since he understands something of artillery —for I fancy you know less of men-of-war and guns than a pig knows of pewter."

"How can I get to Lübeck?" I asked. "And when I've done my work there, may I then take up my pilgrim's staff and set forth to the Holy Land?"

He laughed.

"You're a man after my own heart, Michael, for you know how to make up your mind. I assure you that as far as I'm concerned you'll be as free as a bird though I should have had no other news from you than that the sow has farrowed and has a litter of eighteen, by which I shall know that the Lübeck fleet, numbering eighteen sail, has put to sea. Without useful information such as this, I might as well sit with my head in a sack."

He told me to search among the harbor taverns in Lübeck for a man with a harelip and only three fingers on his right hand. With him I could safely entrust details of the pig market. If he had already been hanged, then I was to bribe some fisherman to sail to Visby, in

Gothland, and sell the pigs there. The fishermen and other poor folk in and around Lübeck were hostile to the arrogant city council, and I should find no difficulty in securing a willing messenger.

Thus it was that Admiral Norby took us both aboard his flagship when he put to sea again with the purpose of destroying the Lübeck fleet wherever he might encounter it. But before we sailed, I went to the place where Mistress Pirjo's cabin had stood, and there from under the charred pear tree I dug up my money. Then I went down into the cellar to bring out a quantity of her medicines, so as to be able to appear in Lübeck as a physician. It seemed wiser to enter that city openly, and, as it were, with flying colors and a band, than to slink about in it like a foreigner under suspicion.

3

I took leave of Junker Thomas without regret. After a few days' cruise in Lübeck waters, our jovial Admiral sent us ashore before seeking his base in Gothland, where he was to await news of enemy movements. I set forth at once in the direction of Lübeck, followed by Andy, who carried my baggage on his back. We mingled unchallenged with other wayfarers, and at the gates of the city I had only to state that I was Doctor Illustrissimus Michael Pelzfuss to be at once admitted; pure silver answered all further questions. The noble Admiral had provided me with German coins and Florentine gold ducats so that I might not betray myself with coins minted in Åbo or Sweden.

I took up residence at a good inn, as befitted one of my condition, and at once hired a drummer to make known to the public that I had opened a practice and would cure every sort of disorder, even those that baffled the physicians of the city. I was besieged by a horde of incurables and their relatives, while at the same time the doctors stormed into the city council with tales of an outlandish quack who was encroaching upon their privileges. Before I had had time to examine any of my patients I was haled before the judges to answer for my unlawful behavior, and was required to produce my diploma, to pay the fine, and to present a petition in form if I wished to practice as a doctor in Lübeck. As I had hoped, it occurred to no one that I might have another and more dangerous object.

In all confidence, therefore, I entered the High Court. Among the fur-trimmed velvet gowns of the assembled physicians I made great play with my studies at the University, and mentioned among other things that I had worked under the far-famed Doctor Theophrastus Bombastus Paracelsus. With one voice the physicians affirmed that I was too young to have completed my medical studies, and challenged me to a disputation on one or other of the subtler points.

But I appealed to the Council, saying, "The science of the physician is based not on Latin but on his power to heal. I challenge the physicians to meet me in this field. Let me treat a patient whom they have been unable to cure, and we shall soon see which of us possesses the greater ability."

At this the councilors began to draw in their horns, for they could not suppose that anyone would speak so boldly unless he was sure of his case; they looked at me with a certain respect.

But the doctors were greatly incensed and said, "Are the gentlemen of the council so indifferent to the lives and health of the good people of Lübeck that they would let this quacksalver attend them? Such a man may succeed now and again, by the use of devilish arts, in alleviating the suffering of an incurable case; but that is pure trickery, and we suspect this man of being a spagyrist, heretic, and necromancer."

After a noisy dispute I was forbidden to practice as a physician in Lübeck and was ordered to pay the costs of the trial. But I was not fined, for the innkeeper was able to testify that I had not had time to treat anyone. Thus the physicians won their case and I won a fair reputation.

One of the councilors sought medical advice from me immediately after the trial; for, as he said, neither law nor custom could prevent my treating people as long as I took no fee, nor was it illegal for sick people to give me presents if they so chose. In the course of our conversation, during which we discussed the war and the villainous Danish pirates who infested those coasts, he mentioned that Lübeck had sold ten fully armed warships to Gustaf Eriksson and held as a pledge from him a number of Swedish castles.

I returned to the inn, and while the waiting patients were yet protesting at my inability to treat them because of the jealousy of my colleagues, my attention was diverted from them by the arrival of a richly dressed lady. Her hair was dyed in the Venetian manner and her brown eyes widened in astonishment when they encountered mine. I seemed to feel the noose about my neck, but she feigned not to know me and passed straight through into her room. I asked the innkeeper who she might be, and he told me that she was a wealthy Swedish widow of noble blood who was staying in Lübeck until peace enabled

133

her to return to Sweden and regain possession of the estates which the ruthless King Christian had stolen from her, after the death of her husband in battle against the Jutes.

This story reassured me, for it seemed to indicate that Madam Agnes also was playing a double game. I was just debating with myself whether to visit her, speak to her frankly, and ensure her silence, when Andy returned, reeling drunk, from the harbor. I had sent him there to search the taverns for a harelipped man with three fingers, and now he was all for going back there at once if I would give him some more money. I had my work cut out to quiet him, but at last he suddenly rolled over onto the floor and lay there, dead to the world. This made me so furious that I kicked him as he slept, in which praiseworthy occupation I was surprised by Madam Agnes, who slipped into the room, wound her arms about my neck, and said that she had always missed me.

"Is it really you, Michael?" she cried. "How glad this has made me! Yet I grieve to see that your brow is furrowed and that you're no longer the downy fledgling of our first meeting. But Michael, my dearest, you must not seem to know me here in this wicked city, for it would harm me. No one here knows that Herr Didrik is my brother, and I'm leading a virtuous life in the hope of finding some good man to marry."

"I share your grief, Madam Agnes," I replied. "I've been told that you're a rich and well-born widow burning with revenge against wicked King Christian. Therefore you keep yourself informed of military operations in Lübeck, and all your admirers are eminent naval officers."

She blushed becomingly and answered, "Have you had the impudence to spy upon me? And you—what are you about? You'll end on the gallows if anyone discovers that in your youth you served the Danish cause."

"I'm no longer young," I told her, "but a venerable physician, and no one knows that I'm a Finn. My name is Michael Pelzfuss. You and I are in the same boat, fair Madam Agnes, and I've no desire to know you if you won't acknowledge me. But if I'm to dangle on the gallows, then by all that's holy you shall dangle beside me."

She pressed her hand to my mouth and shivered as she murmured, "Don't speak of such dreadful things! Put your arms about me—be tender to me, for I'm a lonely woman in great fear of the dangers to which my malicious brother has exposed me. Have you any money?"

134

I told her I had enough to support me modestly for some time, at which she rejoiced and said, "Give me ten gold pieces and I'll betray you to no one. As a pledge, you may ask of me what you will, even the sacrifice of my virtue and good name, if you can bring yourself to make so ruthless a demand."

But I refused very warmly, telling her that her pledges were valueless to me.

"Truth to tell," I went on, "I was about to call upon you and for the sake of old times beg the loan of a few gold pieces myself. I mean to journey to the Holy Land to obtain forgiveness for my sins, and by helping me you would he performing an act pleasing to God."

With a toss of her head she retorted, "That fellow of yours lying there was bellowing like a bull and I heard him mention a harelipped, three-fingered man whom you're seeking in the harbor. Will you give me a gold piece if I tell you where he is?"

"May God forgive us our sins!" I broke out in amazement. "It appears that you and I are serving the same master, dear Madam Agnes. You shall have the coin if you'll fetch the fellow here. Every rapscallion in Lübeck knows things undreamed of by the Danish Admiral."

The fair Agnes demanded first to see the gold piece, and having closed her shapely hand upon it she said innocently, "I can't fetch him here; you must seek him yourself. You'll find him at the gate of the arsenal, hanging in four pieces on the wall."

I was bound to believe her, and I was enraged at the loss of a whole ducat, as well as the loss of the silver that Andy had drunk. Having no choice but to trust her, I asked how well she was doing in the pig trade, since the mother sow had farrowed long ago. She replied that the trade had gone to pieces since the young had run from the sty, and that the Admiral had tarried too long in Finland to catch them in his sack. Lübeck's governors had ears in every tavern, and when they armed for war the first thing they did was to imprison or execute everyone who had shown an exaggerated interest in their warships.

"I feel as if I'd thrust my head between the jaws of a bear," she lamented. "It has never been possible to send one useful report to Visby, and here I sit with all my information, like a miser crouching over the gold he will never spend. In any event, I fancy that King Christian has lost the game. Lübeck has mustered in strength against him, and his fond uncle the Duke of Holstein thinks of joining his enemies. Even the Pope is angered because Christian has summoned heretical preachers to Copenhagen. It would be as well to seek other

135

hunting grounds. The Emperor and the French King are at war and need servants; and Henry VIII of England has declared war on France, for which the Pope has conferred upon him the title of Defender of the Faith."

She told me so much that was new and astonishing about European affairs that I felt I had lived too long in a dark hole. Having ordered wine and food to be brought to my room, I spent an agreeable evening in Madam Agnes's company, while Andy snored upon the floor. She told me that Selim the Turk had captured Belgrade and was threatening Hungary, making skillful use of the dissensions within Christendom itself, which were now more serious than ever before. By means of intrigue, the Emperor had succeeded in elevating his stern Dutch tutor to the chair of St. Peter, and this new Pope had taken the name of Adrian VI. Madam Agnes further related many frivolous anecdotes about the French court and the mistresses of Francis I. She was all shrewdness and malice, yet from time to time she would heave a languorous sigh and let her brown eyes dwell upon me.

At last she said, "You're young, Michael, younger than I, and I feel like an old woman beside you, although I'm not yet twenty-five—or at least not thirty. You're more of a man than I remember you. I find your self-mastery and your dark eyes quite disturbing." She surveyed me curiously. "What are you thinking about?"

I answered, "I was wondering how we might slip out while there's yet time, and I'm vexed to think of all the informers that perhaps lie as idle as we in this good city now that Admiral Severin, for all his subtlety, has fooled himself."

"Sufficient unto the day. . . ! And this day is now evening. The snores of your servant offend me, so let us continue our talk in my own room."

Andy's powerful snores disturbed me also, and I followed her. Memories of my youth rose up with poignancy at the scent of her ointments and perfumes, and although I had resolved never to approach a woman again, I betrayed the resolution more rapidly than one may repeat an Ave. All that can be said in my defense is that she was singularly amenable and taught me to understand much that had bewildered me about women's often quaint desires.

However, despite her pleading I did not remain with her to sleep, knowing how little she was to be trusted. I gathered up my clothes, my belt, and my purse, and returned to my room, locking the door carefully behind me. Andy lay snoring as vigorously as ever, but I,

136

weary though I was, could get no sleep. I lay wakeful and tense upon my bed.

The glow of the wine slowly faded. Through the open shutter came the smell of wet grass from the herb garden of the inn, and the gray light of dawn crept into the room. I seemed to be standing with one foot on the threshold of death, looking back upon wasted days. All those plans for the worldly advancement and honor that I was to attain by serving Admiral Severin were seen to be but vain and beguiling fancies. If my thoughts turned to political intrigue, I saw nothing but the gray sky, the gray snowflakes, and the steam rising from the warm blood in Stockholm market place. If I thought of my own country, I saw flocks of glossy black crows, and Mother Pirjo shielding her head against the whistling stones. For me there could be no return, and the thought filled me with a boundless sorrow. I felt no bitterness or hatred, but only the conviction that man is man's worst enemy.

Then I thought of Holy Church, and in the chill light of my own emptiness I saw that I had aspired to priesthood solely from morbid, selfish ambition. I had never regarded that sacred calling in a way befitting a would-be servant of the poor. To me it had meant seven, ten, or perhaps fifteen silver marks yearly, which would enable me to live and study as best suited me, to acquire higher degrees, and so preferment. Moreover, I had no joy of my learning, since I accepted meekly all that was taught me, and never dared to ask a question out of my own head for fear of falling foul of the Church—the fate of everyone at that time who overstepped the canonical bounds set to human knowledge.

In the gray light of morning, after a night of tenseness and consuming sorrow, the sudden wearying of my body brought with it a strange, painful ecstasy. The surrounding walls fell away, and all at once I knew that God and Satan dwelled in my own heart, and that in this heart slumbered infinite powers for good and evil. But beyond the confines of my heart there was neither God nor Satan; only a mad, meaningless world whose inhabitants wrestled with one another in a hideous combat that was born of desire and the fear of death. God and Satan were hidden within us and had no power beyond our innermost core, where they revealed themselves. All else was custom, convention, an edifice that man had raised up in lust and fear. The Son of God was made man, and if He had atoned with His blood for the world's sins, what right had the Church to barter His flesh and blood for gold? For wherever two or three were gathered together to seek

God in their own hearts, they could break the bread and bless the wine which in their hands became the body and blood of Christ as surely as in the hands of a consecrated priest.

Thus I became suddenly aware of all the heretical ideas that for so long had lain secretly maturing within me. Yet despite my ecstasy I was appalled, for the ideas were too strong a meat for my old self that had been wont to drift with every wind.

Yet in the morning when I awoke it was as if I had had no more than an evil dream, and the sight of Andy groaning on the floor with his head in his hands plunged me again into everyday concerns.

It was useless to chide him for his stupidity, and I went to the harbor myself in search of some way of getting word to the Admiral. But my journey was in vain. I saw only sweaty fellows in felt slippers carrying powder kegs into the ships; and on the heaps of garbage in the gutters lay numbers of soldiers who had been thrown out of the taverns.

We remained in Lübeck for more than a fortnight, and I amassed much information that would have been of service to the Admiral if it could have been conveyed to him. Every morning the fishing boats headed out to sea with their nets, but guard vessels followed them and would not allow any to sail out of sight. I myself lay under no suspicion, for I gave out that I was awaiting a safe passage to Danzig; and I ate and drank and showed myself often in company with Madam Agnes—who was now pressing to accompany me when I resumed my journey, at any rate as far as Venice—so that the innkeeper fancied I had begun to pay serious court to the fair and wealthy widow.

One day Andy came back from the harbor and said, "There's a wall-eyed fellow who's been sitting for four days down by the gate of the arsenal. He's trying to sell his pigs to the ships, but asks such a high price that no one will buy them, although he weeps and wails and prays all who pass to buy in God's name, or his stern mistress will thrash him to a rag."

It seemed to me that the walleye, like the harelip, might well be one of Admiral Severin's whims, for even a stranger could not fail to note it.

So I went straight to the harbor, approached the filthy, evil-smelling pig dealer, and said to him, "Are you out of your mind, fellow? This is the fourth day you have sat here trying to sell pigs at an outrageous price. Don't you know that the council has forbidden such dealing? The halberdiers will soon be here to flog you and confiscate your pigs

138

without giving you a farthing for them. Sell the pigs to me at once, and you'll have a good customer."

The walleyed man sighed and wept, saying, "The council has fixed only the price of carcasses or salt fish. For livestock a man may take what he will, and my mistress demands a high price for these beasts, for they're of good stock and they fatten well. In Stockholm they'd fetch their weight in gold; I hear they're eating rats and cats there already."

"Let my servant have an eye to your pigs for a moment," said I, "and come with me into the church, where we can discuss the matter quietly."

He did as I bade him, and when we had knelt to pray he murmured, "The noble gentleman whom I shall not name told me to look out for a man who, despite his youth, looks as if he had sold his butter and lost the money. Without doubt you are the man and you must tell me at once what you know, for I sail tonight. I'm to give you a gold piece for every pig you know of, or run a knife into your belly, as I see fit."

I told him all I had discovered, and begged him earnestly to take with him a certain well-informed and noble lady, for I did not see how else I was to be rid of Madam Agnes. As we talked, the bells rang out and jubilant people began streaming into the church to give praise to God.

I asked them what had happened, and they said, "There has been a great naval battle off Stockholm, and the proud Lübeck forces in Master Gustaf's service have annihilated a powerful Danish squadron that was approaching from Finland to liberate Stockholm. Not one vessel escaped, and Gustaf has hung the admiral, a certain Junker Thomas, who deserved no better fate."

The walleyed man sighed heavily and said, "Now I have more than enough to report, and the Admiral will surely hang me for my bad news. But it's high time for me to go, and I'll have no petticoats on board, for they bring misfortune at sea, and the voyage will be arduous and full of danger."

I begged and pleaded, and finally I said he might keep all the gold intended for me if only he would take Madam Agnes with him.

At this he changed his mind and exclaimed piously, "If she is disguised as a nun, I can smuggle her out of the city without arousing suspicion; and such a dress might trick the spirits of the storm into allowing us a fortunate voyage. Let her make ready. I will wait for her outside the Church of Our Lady after evensong."

But Madam Agnes was far from pleased to learn of the voyage she was to make. She wept and wrung her hands, cried out upon my faithlessness, and said she had been relying on my promise to take her to Venice.

"Dear Madam Agnes," I answered, "you have quite misunderstood me. I promised only to rescue you from your awkward predicament and help you reap your well-earned reward from the Admiral. Besides, he's a handsome fellow whom no woman can resist. Just now he's collecting at Visby all the plunder from the vessels he's captured, and there I fancy you will have few competitors."

After some further argument, she sighed and said, "It seems then that I must renounce the journey to Venice because of your cold, hard heart, Michael. No doubt this fate stands written in the stars, although I could not have believed that I should ever be forced to wear a nun's habit."

I wished her good fortune upon the journey, and she embraced me, seeking at the same time to cut with a small knife the straps holding my purse to my belt. But I held the purse firmly with my free hand as I kissed her, and her eyes filled with tears of unfeigned disappointment. She expressed the hope that on my way to the Holy Land I might fall into the hands of Turks, and so we parted.

When she had gone, I said to Andy, "We have fulfilled our task like men of honor and are now free to come and go as we choose. Let us travel southward to foreign countries beneath other stars. Let us leave our woeful memories behind us and sail from Venice to the Holy Land, to obtain forgiveness for our sins."

Andy asked if it was far to the Holy Land, and did not think his sins were yet so very great. Nevertheless he wished to put as much land and sea as possible between himself and the widow of the Three Crowns. I shed my fine clothes and with them my former life, and exchanged them for the gray mantle of a pilgrim, girding my waist with a coarse rope. I sold all superfluous baggage and retained only my medicine chest, which Andy assured me he could carry all the way to the Holy Land. When we had passed out through the city gates I cut myself a staff of ash. The masts, gray walls, and slender spires of Lübeck vanished behind us as we turned our faces south. The standing corn was ripening to harvest and we had fair weather throughout our journey. Summer and birdsong followed us and autumn was left behind in the darkening north.

Vagabonds along the highway, seeing me in the habit of a pilgrim and believing me poor, did not molest us, and Andy's broad shoulders and sturdy stick evoked in them a wholesome respect. Thus we wandered for sixty days, neither hurrying nor idling. At last, above green vineyards, we saw the Alps rising like shimmering blue clouds into the sky.

At this sight Andy looked grave; his eyes widened, and he said, "That's what I call a good stout fence! Can we climb it without splitting our breeches?"

True enough, I split mine before we even reached the foot of those ranges.

4

We spent that night in a walled town. In the taproom of the inn sat an irascible man whose cloak bore the cross of the Knights of St. John of Jerusalem. Seeing my pilgrim's garment, he demanded whither I was bound, and when I told him he declared positively that my enterprise was vain.

"Don't you know, friend," said he, "that the Turks have laid siege to the fortress of Rhodes? If this bastion of Christendom should fall, the galleys of our Order can no longer protect the pilgrim vessels. They will be captured and the pilgrims flung into cruel slavery. Therefore in these days no ship dare put out from Venice to the Holy Land, which we've now lost for the last time, since the devout men who serve the churches and monasteries of the Holy Sepulcher depend on pilgrims' offerings to pay the crushing tax the Sultan demands: eighty thousand ducats a year.

"But does Christendom break out in lamentation at the peril now threatening Rhodes, or take up the Cross, or at least pay for equipping a fleet in defense of the island? By no means! The Holy Roman Emperor and France's Most Christian Majesty are at each other's throats and care not a rap for the Pope's prayers and cries for help. Yet if Rhodes falls, Christendom falls, and Christians must endure stern punishment for their heresy and ever increasing godlessness. I know what I'm talking of, for I hold the post of revenue officer in the Order. Only with the greatest difficulty can I collect the indispensable annual rent from our estates.

141

"Venice too has betrayed the Christian cause by making peace with the Sultan. The Venetians demand usurers' prices for a passage to the Holy Land and the money finds its way into the Sultan's purse. You'd be well advised to renounce your purpose and offer your money as a contribution, against my seal and quittance, toward the relief of Rhodes."

I replied cautiously that I was a poor man who could barely afford a bundle of straw to sleep on and a bite of black bread; nevertheless if he would tell me more of Rhodes I would give him a silver piece in aid of the good cause. He then told me that the Turkish fleet lay off Rhodes—three hundred vessels in all—and that the Turks had heavy siege cannon with them. The Sultan himself had arrived at Rhodes by the land route at the head of an army of a hundred thousand men.

The stocky Hospitaler emptied his cup, crashed the flagon on the table with a swirl of his grimy cloak, and roared, "Here all is drinking, gambling, and fornication, without thought for the morrow! But if you had ears to hear you would catch the thunder of cannon from Rhodes across land and sea, and the yells of the infidels as they storm the walls and call upon their false prophet for help! This is the punishment for the sins of Christendom and for the false Lutheran doctrines preached in every village by renegade monks and married priests— though Luther himself has hastened to hide from the interdict. Or perhaps the devil has already taken him to himself."

The innkeeper wiped the table with his apron and brought fresh drink for the Knight, who went on more quietly, "The recruiting drums rumble on all sides to gather in more mercenaries for the Emperor's army, but name the Order of St. John and all ears are stopped. But the day will come when the Turks will unstop those ears, and slice them off—ay, and noses too! When they will flay men alive, impale children on spears, sell wives as slaves, and geld the husbands! Then it will be too late to mourn and bewail past foolishness, for they've abandoned the Order to its unequal battle—the battle for Christendom and the freedom of the Mediterranean."

When we had gone to rest, Andy asked if I were quite sure that we had not jumped into the wrong barrel, for he began to feel some misgivings about the journey. Venice itself was undeniably a sinful, viceridden city, but we were bound yet further: to the Holy Land whose customs differed greatly from ours, and where the manner of preparing food would certainly be entirely strange and possibly a threat to our health. He proposed that we should instead equip ourselves as mercenaries and take service under the Emperor's standard, since according to the recruiting officers the Emperor had already captured Milan and now aimed at subduing all France. In this way we might win renown: I might receive an earldom and he become master gunner to His Imperial Majesty.

I asked if he had not had his fill of wars and bloodshed, and told him that it was better to contemplate the wounds of Christ and his own immortal soul than to dream of plunder. Yet if he desired to take up the Cross and go to war against the Turks in Rhodes, it was a praiseworthy resolve and one which, if fulfilled, would lead him straight to Paradise. Moreover, it seemed to offer the only means of attaining the Holy Land.

Further argument proved needless, however, for it appeared that I had made too much play with my purse at that inn. Next day at dawn, as we were continuing our journey toward the "stout fence," misfortune overtook us. Andy, complaining of an internal disorder, retired into a hazel thicket to relieve himself. As I stood waiting for him in the road, two horsemen came up at a gallop from the direction of the town. One struck me on the head, and the other, the revenue officer from Rhodes, dealt me another blow on the back of my neck and threw me across his saddle. Or so I believe, for I knew nothing more until I came to my senses at midday in a wooded hollow deep in the forest. There was a severe wound in my head and I was miserably cold, for the man had stripped me naked and the leafy boughs that they had cast over me yielded no warmth. I had lost not only my purse but also certain gold coins that I had painstakingly stitched into my clothes for fear of robbers.

I awoke to the sound of a bird singing. It was uttering plain words in my native tongue, saying, "No good, no good, home again, home again!" So I fancied myself a little boy once more, waking from sleep while guarding Mistress Pirjo's pigs outside Åbo. Then, feeling the icy chill and the pain from my wound, I pushed away the branches and tried to sit up.

At that instant I heard a sweet voice saying, "God be praised that you're alive, fair youth! I have stayed by you, praying and praying that you might be restored to life, although I believed you dead. But spare my modesty and do not move the branches; I have already gazed too long upon you."

I had no notion of where I was or how I came into the wood, and

143

for the moment I had forgotten my identity and my quest. Having just heard the bird speak to me, I supposed that this gentle voice came from the ancient oak at my head and that I understood the language of birds as well as if I had swallowed the tongue of a white crow. But when, despite my giddiness and violent pains I succeeded in turning my head, I beheld a woman kneeling on the ground beside me, her red-striped skirts becomingly spread about her. She seemed quite young, and was gazing at me with a look of devotion in her yellow-green cat's eyes.

Conscious of my nakedness, I hurriedly replaced the foliage and asked, "Where am I and what has happened? Who are you? What are you doing in the wood and what's your name?"

She answered, "I am Barbara Büchsenmeister, born of honest parents in the good city of Memmingen, where my father's a gunsmith. I've come here to visit my dear uncle. We're not far from the town, and I'm in the forest gathering wormwood. Who are you? Are you a man, or a pagan wood sprite who has taken human shape to seduce me?"

Stretching forth her hand, she touched my shoulder to assure herself that I was indeed flesh and blood; her touch was not unpleasing.

"I am a man," said I, "and my name is Michael Pelzfuss—or so I believe, though just now I remember but little. I've been beaten and robbed and cast out into the forest as naked as when I was born— and indeed as poor, and as much in need of compassion."

The woman clasped her hands, praising and thanking God, and said, "The Almighty Father has then heard my prayer, and my dream has come true. I've long been tormented with restlessness, and for this reason I came hither to visit my uncle in the hope of finding a husband in this city, since in my own town where all know me I could find none. Yet here also I have failed, having left the best marriage years behind me. Lately I had a dream in which I was bidden to go into the wood to find a husband, and I've wandered here every day, talking to charcoal burners and woodsmen. And so I found you. The Creator has without doubt destined you for my husband, since He has left you here naked and destitute, sick and helpless, so that you cannot run from me as others do. And I have already taken a liking to you and have thought of my marriage portion, although womanly modesty has forbidden me to survey you too closely."

"Barbara Büchsenmeister," said I, "without doubt it was God and His saints who brought you to me, that I might not perish of cold or be torn to pieces by wolves. This I do not deny. Nevertheless you

144

should not busy yourself with fruitless schemes, for I'm a cleric on pilgrimage and can entertain no thoughts of marriage. As soon as I have regained my strength I shall once more take the road."

She seized my hand and pressed it ardently against her breast, saying, "Your memory deceives you, Michael Pelzfuss, and you're still dizzy from the blow. You have neither tonsure nor any look of a clerk, though certainly those hands of yours have never done heavy work. Besides, there are now priests and monks preaching the new doctrine who marry without hindrance. I will gladly embrace these teachings if necessary, and no doubt we shall meet with some wandering friar who would be willing to make us man and wife as soon as I have healed you and found you clothes."

I turned sick and giddy and I trembled from head to foot at the thought of my lost money and the journey that was now beyond my power to make. I raved and vomited and cried for Andy, and it was not until three days later, after many hideous dreams and visions of demons who held me in their claws, that I came to my senses once more, this time in a great four-poster bed. I was staring into Barbara's yellow-green eyes and she was holding my hands. I was so weak that I could hardly move my fingers, but the pain had left me and I felt cool and refreshed after the burning fever.

When Barbara saw that I was awake, she bent over me, kissed my lips shyly, and said, "My dear betrothed, you're well again and your head is clear. For three days and nights I've fought for your life, and have hardly closed my eyes. I have had to hold you down in bed by force, and the barber has bled you, so you're as wan as a specter. But the illness has passed. Now I shall feed and clothe you. If you will, you may speak with your companion who fears for your reason. Tell him he's free to go where he pleases, since we're betrothed, you and I. I will take care of you until we're made one at the altar of my church at home."

She called Andy, who entered, gnawing a crust and looking at me inquisitively.

"That's a queer head you have," he remarked. "It withstands the most horrible blows. I could have sworn you were going to die. But you're alive and have even found time to catch a sweetheart, and there's nothing left for me but to wish you happiness and prosperity. You're perhaps wiser to do this than to journey to the Holy Land and slavery among the infidels. Yet at the same time I cannot for my life imagine what you see in Mistress Barbara, or how you came to fall so suddenly a victim to her."

"Talk leads nowhere, Andy, and it's useless to cry over spilt milk. How much money have you left?"

Plunging his hand into his purse, he counted the coins therein and said happily, "Not quite one gulden. This is what comes of carrying all the money yourself! I only wish I'd drunk it, as you suspected I should, for you lost it before a cat could sneeze. I fancied God had swept you to heaven by the hair when I came back onto the road and found you gone. I heard horses, and ran after them till I was out of breath, but in the end I went back to the city full of sorrow, meaning to tell the priest of this miracle. But at the city gate I saw you in your sweetheart's arms on a hay wagon. So I followed you to this worthy house, whose only drawbacks are poor fare and strict rule."

"Brother Andy," I answered, "it's no doubt the Creator's intention that I should remain under the protection of this virtuous maiden. Without money I cannot continue my pilgrimage and I'm so weak that I can barely lift a finger. Should she require some return from me for house room and food and medical attendance and bloodletting, I have no choice but to marry her. I owe her my life. It's the simplest solution to all my troubles, for at this moment I crave only repose. Therefore you too must go out and find yourself a good wife, make a home for yourself, and ply your honorable trade."

Andy raised his hands defensively and said, "Your reason is still a little confused, I see. To lure your brother into the pit into which you have fallen is unworthy. Have no concern for me; I too have a sweetheart, and must now bid you farewell to follow her."

Only after close questioning did I discover that Andy, having wearied of Mistress Barbara's lean fare, had strayed to an alehouse where he had accepted three gulden from the recruiting sergeant. He had drunk this and his own money, and the sergeant had told such dazzling tales of Italy and of the Dukedom of Milan that he longed to see these wonders for himself.

"Forgive me," he said, "if I prefer to lie by my cannon than beside a shrewish woman."

Thus it was that Andy followed the Emperor's colors to the wars in Italy and France while I remained in Mistress Barbara's care. She nursed me tenderly and would not let me out of her sight for an instant. As soon as I was able to walk, she seated me on her traveling chest in an ox-wagon and took me to her parents' home in the good city of Memmingen. Barbara was the fifth and youngest of the gun-smith's children, and his only daughter. Her three elder brothers were artillerymen in the Emperor's service, and the fourth, a sullen fellow, was apprenticed to his father and in due course would succeed him as master.

I was still in a daze and remembered little of my past life, which only gradually emerged from oblivion. Barbara was gentle but firm; she managed everything for me, so that I need feel no anxiety for my livelihood. Two months elapsed in this way, and the leaves in the garden were turning red.

One day Barbara approached me shyly and hesitantly, and fixing me with her green eyes she said, "You're well and strong again now, Michael, and you must tell me what you mean to do. As a stranger you cannot well go on living in my parents' house and eating their bread. You're free to leave us if you wish, and I claim no return. But I am lonely and forsaken. Why should you not stay and receive by betrothal gifts, so that on All Saints' Day we may be married?"

She handed me a shirt she had beautifully embroidered, and about my neck she placed a copper chain from which hung the picture of a saint. Her hands lingered on my shoulders and her face was near to mine. She grew warm. She flushed so that her features softened. Her freckles disappeared and I saw only her green, compelling eyes, which drew all my strength from me and made her seem desirable.

Without really knowing how I felt, I put my arms about her, pressed her to me, kissed her lips, and said, "I'm in your power, Barbara, and have no choice. I long to share the bridal bed with you if you will bind your destiny with mine and not repent it—for there may well be a curse upon me, bringing misfortune to those I love."

She kissed me passionately many times, and said, "I rejoice with my whole heart that you have chosen me for your wife, and I promise to be a good and faithful one to you. You must settle my marriage portion with my father at once, and I will speak for you, since you're shy and unready with your words."

Thus it was that I received her betrothal gifts. And I had no regrets, although often before All Hallows came I would look at her from the side and note all too plainly that she was no longer young. But then she had only to bend her yellow-green cat's eyes upon me to be trans-figured. She was comely then, with softened features from which the freckles seemed to vanish; her teeth lost their stain and I would stare into those eyes as one bewitched.

One day when the preparations for our wedding were in full swing at the gunsmith's house, Barbara, impatient for the first time, slipped a silver coin into my hand and bade me go and drink ale at the Wild Boar's Tusk, instead of getting under the women's feet. Glad enough to obey, I set out for the tavern, which lay next to the town hall and was cool in summer and warm in winter, as a good tavern should be.

I had lived so long apart from others that I was disconcerted when the murmur of voices died away and all eyes were turned upon me. But I was wearing the seemly suit of clothes that Barbara had had made for me, so I sat down at the end of the table and ordered the landlord to serve me a tankard of his best ale. He hesitated, and loitered to wipe the table with his apron before drawing ale from the cask. Then he dumped the tankard down so hard that the froth splashed over onto my knees. The young men at the same table began whispering among themselves, and one of them spat venomously on the floor when he met my eye. But I paid no heed to him, since from his dress he seemed to be but a common apprentice.

I took more careful note of another lad seated in the middle of the group with an open book before him. He had a pencase of copper at his belt and the sleeves of his coat were puffed and slashed in the new fashion. His face was open and resolute, and his large, brilliant eyes were set wide under black brows, giving him a look of intellectual power. I drank my ale while he, having urged his comrades to be silent, continued reading aloud from his book—an occupation that my entry had interrupted. I listened attentively; the theme was familiar but some moments passed before I realized that he was reading the Gospel in German. It came as such a shock that I started and involuntarily made the sign of the cross.

The man who was reading took offense, and breaking off again he scowled at me and said, "If you're a stranger to the town of Memmingen and afraid of listening to the holy word of God, there's nothing to prevent you finishing your ale and running off to inform against me. And so that you may know who it is you're telling tales of, let me mention that my name is Sebastian Lotzer and that my father is a furrier. I work as his 'prentice when I am not declaring God's holy word to honest men in a language they can understand."

His companions began nudging one another and saying, "Let's throw out this monkish hanger-on, and break his bones! He's the whey-faced fellow betrothed to Barbara Büchsenmeister, and who knows from under which devil's tail he came!"

The uproar dismayed and offended me, and I withdrew to the door, brawls being beneath my dignity.

Yet I spoke in my own defense, saying, "My name is Michael Pelzfuss and I'm a *baccalaureus artium* from the noble University of Paris. You have no cause to hate me. But I'm newly recovered from a long illness, and it seemed to me just now that I heard you, Sebastian Lotzer, reading God's holy word from a book printed in German, although you wear a layman's dress and say you're a furrier by trade. Therefore I can only suppose that the devil is putting my faith to the test and has confused my hearing and bewitched my eyes."

Sebastian Lotzer smiled at me and said, "Your illness must have been prolonged indeed if you've not yet read the signs of the times. Sit down with us and listen to my reading, for my comrades and I have clubbed together to buy this sacred book, which cost as much as a good horse, that we may found our hopes of the Redemption on the words of the Holy Bible only, and through it alone assess the facts and events about us. This book is the New Testament, which Doctor Luther has translated into German, and is no invention of the devil. Indeed, Satan sought to oppose him with horn and hoof—to disturb him and hinder him in his work of translation, so that he was compelled to hurl his inkhorn at the snout of the Evil One. But now, despite the plots of devils and priests, the book is printed. Every honest man henceforth may read and expound the text, and I've found not one line or one word in the whole volume that forbids a layman to do so."

But Sebastian Lotzer's companions warned him, and said, "He shall not sit with us, for he's a white-faced man, and he's to marry carroty Barbara. But if he must join our evangelical fellowship, let him at least stand ale all round."

It was in this manner that I made the acquaintance of Sebastian Lotzer and heard him expound the Bible in a fashion altogether different from orthodox interpretation. He and his friends were not primarily concerned to find salvation by means of the Bible, but rather to discover whether it contained any justification for the paying of tithes, whether man was bound to adore the saints, to believe in purgatory and intercession, and whether monks and nuns had the right to compete with the poor weavers' guilds without paying taxes and other contributions to the civic revenues. Sebastian Lotzer declared

149

boldly that no one need believe or pay anything not explicitly enjoined by the words of the Bible. He declared also that nothing was said of monasteries in Holy Scripture. The cloister was the invention of the devil, intended to vex and oppress honest artisans and the poor. Weavers could no longer support themselves and their families, since they had to compete with the great monastic weaving shops, which were exempted from all tax.

Sebastian Lotzer added, "The justice of God is greater than the justice of the Church or of the Emperor, for the Church is a human institution and the Emperor is elected by the people. Therefore I shall strive day and night to understand God's justice, so that in due time I may testify of it to others through the clear words of the Bible, which every man may grasp. Surely it was never God's intention that monks should wallow and grow fat in their cloisters while peasants and townsmen toil and drudge for a bare crust. No, we must put an end to all this, for the blood of Christ has redeemed all poor sinners, and all are equal in the sight of God. God acknowledges neither bishops nor priests, neither monks nor nobles, and before Him all enjoy equal rights. The people must learn to read the signs of our times, for the patience of the poor is not endless."

The landlord of the Wild Boar's Tusk had listened reverently, but now, growing uneasy, he took away our empty mugs, wiped the table, and said, "I can serve no more on credit, Sebastian—and if your father heard you he'd thrash you till you couldn't stand. Take your reading elsewhere, for the good burghers will soon be meeting here for their choral practice—and that means time for 'prentices to get out, whether the Bible says so or not."

Sebastian Lotzer wrapped the precious volume in a piece of cloth and thrust it under his arm. We left the tavern together, and he said to me, "Let's be friends, Michael Pelzfuss, for I lack anyone of my own standing to discuss with me all the burning ideas that throng my head. And I should like to converse with you in Latin. I've studied the language by myself, and though I speak it but stumblingly I read a great deal of the Bible in it, before this incomparable book had come from the press."

He took me without hesitation to his father's house and into a room where the tall master furrier stood cutting up valuable skins with sure, swift strokes, to make borders for the mantles of eminent patrons. Father and son were alike in appearance, and their large, bright eyes were set equally far apart.

"I've found a friend," said Sebastian, and presented me to his father. "He's a stranger in this town, but a scholarly boy with polished manners. I beg your favor to him, father—and don't be displeased if today I talk to him instead of helping you with the cutting."

Master Lotzer gave me a lingering, appraising glance.

"Welcome to my house, Michael Pelzfuss," said he. "Bring no misfortune upon my son. He's young and impetuous and you must steady him. I know he was never born to be a furrier, for the goose quill runs more nimbly in his hand than the knife. I hoped he might follow the law, and I obtained a post for him as writer in the court of justice here, but he lost it through arrogance and a tendency to answer back. I'm a liberal-minded man and would have everyone think for himself —but my young son does not yet understand the difference between thinking and thinking aloud."

Sebastian hugged his father and gave a radiant smile. His proud head and noble bearing showed me that neither his father nor anyone else could be truly angry with Sebastian, but must ever be ready to forgive him his impulsive speech. He led me to his own room, where there were many books, a stove of gray-blue tiles, and a bed coverlet of gleaming furs. I realized that he was the cherished son of a well-to-do man and had never been forced to endure cold or want. For this reason it was easy for him to play with ideas which might deprive another of shelter and food, and lead perhaps to the stake. He talked with great enthusiasm and gave me little chance to put in a word.

But when at last he was silent, I said, "Sebastian, you know that on Saturday I'm to marry the gunsmith's daughter Barbara, and being a stranger here I have no friend to attend me to the altar. If as you say you desire my friendship, be my groomsman and afterward my guest at the house so that I need not feel ashamed before all the people."

His face darkened; he bit his lip and averted his eyes. After a little while he said, "Michael, do you know what you're doing? Do you know anything of red-haired Barbara and her family? She has a bad name—bad enough to set a gulf between her parents and all other citizens. She was once compelled to take the Oath of Purgation before the Spiritual Court. Believe me, she has an ill repute in this town and no one can believe that she caught such a man as yourself by natural means. I tell you this as a warning, that you may fully understand what you're about."

His words explained much that I had noted but to which in my illness I had given little thought. Yet I was vexed by the warning, having already resigned myself to the belief that Providence had destined me for her husband. So I related as much as I thought fit of our first meeting in the wood, and then asked Sebastian to give some grounds for the evil he believed of her.

"Ever since she was a child she's been different from other people," he said hesitantly, "and no one can account for the mysterious power she has over her parents."

I fingered the copper chain Barbara had given me, and retorted, "You too are different, Sebastian. You too have a remarkable power over your father. He never chides you, although he must have sound enough reasons for doing so."

Sebastian laughed in spite of himself, but went on, "You do not— or will not—understand. There was a boy once whom Barbara bewitched. All other children avoided her, striking her and pulling her hair when she tried to play with them. This boy was struck by lightning. Her mere glance can dry up a young mother's breasts. And once when Barbara was angered with the spice-dealer's wife she stretched out her hand and three black spots appeared on the woman's arm. So no one dares look her in the eyes, and those eyes have certainly cast a spell over you, Michael. For the best marriage years are behind her, and she's ugly and red haired and has worm-eaten teeth."

"This may all be true, Sebastian," I answered, "yet perhaps ordinary love is nothing but blindness and witchcraft, for a mother will love her ugliest child and think it comely. Every word you utter stings my heart, for in my eyes Barbara is not ugly. To me her complexion is warm and white and I love her green eyes. And it's not that I covet her father's money; I mean to support her as befits a husband as soon as I can find work suited to my talents. If you would be my friend you must atone for your wounding speech. Lash *me* with your tongue for a white-faced man and a stranger, but not Barbara, who is to be my wife."

Great rapture possessed me as I spoke these words to Sebastian. Not until he spoke evil of my betrothed did I perceive how dearly I loved her. I longed for her and desired to live my life with her, strange though this seemed even to myself. And Sebastian could not withstand me; the warmth of his heart overcame his good sense, and embracing me he promised to attend me to the altar in his best clothes, and afterward to come to the feast as my guest. He even lent me his velvet cloak with the collar of silver fox to wear over my shoulders in the bridal procession, since the weather had turned cold, and an icy wind blew from the Alps.

I will say nothing of my wedding but that I was blinded and happy and took no heed of evil omens, although people looked sourly at our procession as it passed and called out none of the customary blessings. Barbara's dowry sufficed to furnish me with all necessary clothes and linen and household goods, and there were also fifty Rhenish gulden which the old gunsmith carefully counted into a leather purse. I would have embraced him as my father, but he pushed me churlishly away, and no more than a week or so had passed before I understood that both he and his son earnestly wished us to leave their house.

I sought some fitting appointment for myself, but I belonged to none of the city guilds and was a stranger in the place. I was made bitter by many abrupt and humiliating rebuffs, which made me feel like some guttersnipe whom honest folk expelled from their society. Sebastian was my only friend, but he visited me merely to discuss points relating to his overruling passion, the justice of God. And since I felt more interest in theological than in juridical matters, we often talked at cross-purposes when interpreting the clear words of the Bible. His companions, the ignorant weavers' apprentices, avoided me and envied me his friendship; they continued to call me the white-faced man although I had regained my strength and healthy complexion.

My pride suffered from these things, and unknown to Sebastian I called on his father the furrier, begging to be accepted as his apprentice. But having handed me the knife and a moleskin and watched me do my best with them, he snatched the knife back, saying I was not born to be a furrier. Instead, he recommended me to an apothecary, but this man was a miserly, ignorant fellow who mixed his drugs in the strictest secrecy. I am persuaded that he fobbed off his customers with worthless remedies and therefore desired no assistant. Nor could I set up as a physician, being too young and lacking the University diploma, though doubtless I should have harmed the patients no more than the accredited doctors so long as I followed the simple principles of Doctor Paracelsus.

These were troubled times. The Empire waged incessant war against powerful and wealthy France. From the Swiss Confederation and from the north came the quarrelsome voices of heretics who demanded the purification of the Church. The little town of Memmingen was swamped and battered by these raging seas. Almost every day some monk who had deserted his monastery, or some wandering shoemaker's apprentice, would stand in the market place and preach against the sacred customs of the Church, and the monastic system. Then he would beg alms in order to continue his arduous journey to other cities. God's thunderbolts did not strike down these agitators, and neither ecclesiastical nor secular courts dared interfere with them for fear of uproar.

The seditious harangues of these itinerant preachers spread a spiritual plague over the whole Empire, just as true plague is bred in dry dust and transmitted through the breath so that no one is safe from its attack. The people listened laughingly or with indifference, or with gaping mouths, to these ragamuffins. Yet the words infected and corroded their minds, as is the way of heresy, and knowledge of the Bible increased among the lower orders in an alarming manner. Each man according to his means and opportunity had begun to eat of the forbidden fruit, and it was not long before everyone believed that by appeal to the Scriptures he could justify his evil desires.

Sebastian had introduced me to the elderly Rector of the city, who was from St. Gall in the Swiss Confederation. He was unfortunately a touchy, uncouth individual and plainly infected with heretical ideas, although he never ventured to give them expression in plain terms. Yet he was the more eager to win young men to his side by inviting them to discussion and ale drinking at his house. And there he gave weight to his arguments by thumping his fist on Erasmus's Latin translation of the Bible. For, while he did not acknowledge Luther, he had found a yet more virulently heretical preceptor in his own country, in the town of Zürich.

Sebastian and the Rector went to Zürich at the New Year and would have taken me with them, but I had not the means to make the journey. I stayed where I was and passed the time in feeding a little green bird in a wicker cage and staring out of the window over the neighboring roofs.

At last I could no longer master my despair. Laying my head in my wife's lap, I mourned most bitterly and said, "Forsaken, worthless wretch that I am! No one will speak to me and I can't even support my own wife. You made a bad bargain when you married me, Barbara. It would be better if I vanished from the world as I came into it."

Stroking my hair with her narrow hand, she said, "Don't distress yourself, Michael. I have a plan. The tax-assessor to the City Council is a drunkard. His hands are shaky, and before long he'll meet with some accident. Then I fancy you'll be able to purchase his appointment.

In the meantime win his friendship and relieve him at his task without payment; in this way the councilors will become accustomed to the sight of you and cease to shun you."

As she stroked my hair I was filled with a sweet if illusory sense of security, and did not take particular note of her words. However, I sought the company of the assessor and obtained it very simply by offering him ale at the Wild Boar's Tusk. Thereafter he often took me with him to his office or to council meetings, and allowed me to help him in the drafting of protocols, that he might return the sooner to the alehouse. I learned to handle the seals and was initiated into the most usual disputes relating to false weights and measures among the merchants, or to the control of prices to prevent undue competition. I never reflected how monotonous and tedious such occupation was, but dreamed of the joys of a peaceful life and of an unexacting task —of growing old with honor beside my good wife, with books and the company of friends as temporal delights. In the hope of these things I did my utmost to win the favor of the councilors, bowing deeply when I met them, appearing always neatly dressed, and engrossing documents in my fairest hand. Nor was I dismayed at the shabby, slovenly, ale-sodden appearance of my employer, or see in him the image of my own future in civic employment. I envied him his position and in my heart wished him ill.

Sebastian and the Rector returned from Zürich, drunk with zeal and triumph, and were besieged by the evangelical mob who desired both news of their sojourn, and instruction. The Rector of Zürich, Ulrich Zwingli, had so successfully defended sixty-seven theses on Christian freedom from the oppression of the Church that no one had been able to offer serious refutation.

"Is it possible," I exclaimed, "that God has given this agitator more of His grace than He bestowed upon the great Fathers of the Church, and upon all the blessed saints who for His sake endured torture and martyrdom? I cannot believe it, for Zwingli is the slave of his flesh, having abandoned celibacy and married. In other respects also he displays no marked sanctity."

Sebastian said, "You should have seen him, and looked into his eyes! Then you would have known that the Holy Ghost speaks through his mouth. And he's not content with what he has already accomplished. He has told his closest supporters that he will never be satisfied until saints' images in all the churches have been destroyed as idols, and until monastic houses have been converted into schools and workshops. Luther is a lukewarm appeaser compared to Zwingli; for Luther permits all that the Bible does not explicitly forbid, while Zwingli intends to allow nothing that the Bible does not explicitly enjoin."

"That I can well believe," said I, "for when once we slip our cable and abandon the saving anchor of the Church we have no reason to retain any other useless ballast. Let us jettison the Holy Sacraments at once, and let Satan blow with all his might into our sails."

I said this in mockery, but Sebastian regarded me with eyes in which fanaticism burned. He replied, "You speak more truly than you know. A storm is gathering whose roar may even now be heard! It will blow away all old and outworn things, that God's Kingdom may be founded upon earth."

Rector Christopher said, "The Pope himself has sought to tempt and bribe Zwingli by promising reform within the Church, but it is vain to cleanse a ruinous house. It must be torn down. Zwingli takes St. John's Revelation to witness that the Pope-governed Church is Antichrist, and unequivocal omens foretell its imminent fall; for when Pope Adrian was celebrating Mass at Christmas, in plague-ridden Rome, a great stone from one of the pillars loosened and fell upon the altar before him. This is a sign that every true Christian understands, although the Pope seeks to explain it away by saying that the fall of this stone signifies the capture of Rhodes, since it was on Christmas Day that the infidels penetrated the city to murder, plunder, and burn, although Rhodes had already surrendered."

At this I rose and said, "I believe indeed that Antichrist has appeared on earth, and that Satan has distorted men's vision, when the Holy Father is reviled and the images of saints are called idols, and when you no longer dread the Turkish peril that threatens all Christendom! At the eleventh hour you stir up dissension and conflict, and it seems you will not repent until the hoofs of the Turkish hordes clatter along your streets and their priests cry the name of the false prophet from the towers of the city churches!"

One or two weavers started to their feet and said to Sebastian, "This Michael Pelzfuss is poisoned with monkish mumbo jumbo and disdains the clear words of the Bible, which every honest man can understand. Shall we not open his eyes with our fists and kick the papistry from his belly, and so save his immortal soul before he can bring discord into our evangelical brotherhood?"

But Sebastian defended me and I returned home unmolested, though greatly troubled in spirit by all that I had heard. The next day, Sebastian visited me, heedless of the prejudice against our house, in the hope of overcoming my misgivings. Barbara listened silently, looking at us each in turn with her yellow-green eyes.

But I opposed Sebastian, and insisted, "Holy Church has stood fast throughout fifteen centuries and is glorious with the blood of the saints and martyrs. Pope Adrian is a stern, devout man who desires nothing better than to purify the Church and drive the money-changers from the temple. Yet the Church is lost if every shoemaker and blacksmith's apprentice reads the Bible in his own way and interprets it according to his ignorance."

Sebastian said, "The holy apostles also were ignorant fishermen, and God permitted His only begotten Son to be born on earth as the child of a common carpenter. Church and University have only complicated the simple message of the Scriptures."

"Sebastian," I persisted, "if men lose faith in Holy Church and the Sacraments, they will lose faith in everything else, and the result will be sin and perdition and the fall of Christendom. Even now there are those who shamelessly violate the days of fasting, who blaspheme against holy things, and defend their vices with texts from the Bible. The mean and miserly profess evangelism to dodge the tithes. Weavers demand the dissolution of the monasteries because the weavers' guild has become poor. Mercenaries carry the Bible in their knapsacks as their warrant for the plundering of churches and the raping of nuns. The Bible is a terrible weapon in the hands of an ignorant man if he seeks in it not his salvation but the gratification of his lusts. Believe me, Sebastian, Satan is the most diligent of Bible readers!"

Sebastian surveyed me, and his brow was pure and steadfast above the shaded, wide-set eyes.

"Michael, God gave man a beautiful land to live in, and power over all the beasts of the field, the fowls of the air, and the fish of the streams. With the blood of His only Son He redeemed mankind. He is no respecter of persons. This, and this alone, is the true teaching. Yet the peasant must toil like a slave for his lord, and the work of the craftsman enriches no one but the great merchant. The peasant is put in irons and left to languish in the castle dungeon if he so much as nips a fish from the river for his sick wife. The weaver loses his daily bread and is driven from the city if in his hunger he shakes his fist at the great weaving shops of the monasteries. This cannot be the will

157

of God. Therefore the Bible must be our weapon when God's Kingdom is founded on earth."

I sat staring at Sebastian. But now I saw him not as a friend but as a beautiful, deadly wild beast with a silky-smooth coat. His doublet was trimmed with silver buttons and the soft fur collar of the velvet cape brushed his cheek at every vigorous nod with which he emphasized his words. To him, the sin, suffering, and redemption of mankind were alien concepts; he sought in the Bible not the way to the Kingdom but a change in temporal affairs.

I said, "Erasmus laid the egg, Luther hatched it, and now Zwingli is crowing like a full-grown cock. But you have struck a spark and kindled a torch that may set the whole barnyard in a blaze. Why do you do this, and what is it that really torments your heart? You lack nothing that man may justly desire in this life. You're young and healthy, you come from a good home, and all doors stand open to you."

He avoided my eye, blushed crimson, and replied, "There are some doors that will not open to me, though I beat my knuckles raw upon them. But soon we shall open them with gunpowder, and no one will despise me then."

Barbara intervened here, and said gaily, "Sebastian, you need not smash the world to pieces for the sake of your lovesickness. Buy a well-tried love philtre, and a Bible will not be necessary. Your longing will be stilled and your soul will be at peace for a gold coin or two."

Sebastian leaped up and roared in a voice that quivered with hatred, "You witch, you jade, you evil-eyed creature! We've suffered enough on your account here in Memmingen, and your oath of purgation won't serve you much longer! You'll be burned at the stake one fine day and so atone for all your wickedness."

I hardly think that Barbara had meant to say anything malicious, but when Sebastian reviled her thus she rose, her green eyes sparkling with fury. Her cheeks turned suddenly so white that the freckles showed up like brown spots. For an instant she stared intently at Sebastian, then controlling herself she left the room without a word. Sebastian at once repented of his outburst and made the sign of the cross several times. Enraged at his violence, I derided him.

"If you would follow Our Lord according to the unequivocal precepts of Scripture, you should go and sell all you have and give the money to the poor—for you if anyone are the rich young man, and St. Francis did no less."

Then Sebastian turned pale, and said, "You're right, Michael, though

158

I don't intend to make the same mistake as St. Francis and seek Heaven beyond the grave. No, I will seek it here on earth. I will force the monasteries and the rich to share their wealth among the poor, and content themselves with as much as I myself possess."

With these words he cast the fine velvet cloak to the floor and trampled upon it, and tore the silver buttons wildly from his doublet. Flinging them about the room, he shouted, "Henceforth my clothes shall be those of a poor apprentice. I will earn my bread by the labor of my hands and be content with the same fare as the poorest boy in my father's house, begging no favors from any man."

When he had torn his fine clothes to rags, shedding scalding tears meanwhile, he dashed from the room and out of the house before I could utter a word of farewell. I concluded that he suffered some secret grief that he was too proud to disclose.

Barbara returned, still pale. She picked up the velvet cloak from the floor and brushed it, and gathered together the silver buttons, saying in a bitter tone, "It's easy for Sebastian to talk; he's a rich man's son and no one dare lift a finger against him. Were you to speak and behave as he does, you'd be driven from the city. Yet nothing ails Sebastian, save that a lady of high birth has disdained him because he comes of burgher stock. And his father is not so rich that he can buy himself an earl's coronet from the Emperor, as Jacob Fugger did."

I was struck by a new note in her voice, and asked, "Would you like me to talk as he does and preach the overthrow of the world?"

For the first time she avoided my eyes, and suddenly I saw her haggard and ugly, with high cheekbones and a freckled complexion.

"If you had faith, Michael, you wouldn't ask my advice," she answered. "But you have none, although you know that the Church is often cruel, the priests idle, and the monks avaricious and ignorant. Holy water and wax can be used for ill purposes as well as for good ones. Perhaps you are like that, Michael, and I too, though you may not know it. But my woman's reason tells me that the world cannot be altered—that there will always be rich and poor, powerful and oppressed, just as there are wise men and fools, strong and weak, whole and sick. So I neither love men nor wish them well. They wish me none, as you could hear from Sebastian's words. You're the only one I love, Michael. Let us live obscurely and arouse no ill will by betraying that we are both molded from enchanted wax."

But I forgot her enigmatic words when she looked at me again, her green eyes shining with tenderness. She was suddenly beautiful. I drew her to me, and desire swept over me like a wave. We found joy together though it was broad day. I told myself that though the world we lived in might be a foundering ship, I had not been born to save it, nor was I willing to bore a hole in the bottom. Not quite a full year was left to run before the planets were to meet in the Sign of the Fish.

6

So my friendship for Sebastian cooled. But he kept his word and lived thenceforth like a poor boy in his father's house, eating at the apprentices' table. In the evenings he read the Bible and wrote long pamphlets concerning Christian freedom, of which he contrived to get one or two printed. I had no wish to see him again, for the councilors were suspicious of him. He was earning himself a bad name, and even his own father mourned over his stubbornness and was inclined to believe he had been bewitched. I myself did not find the change in him so very abrupt, for he had undergone a long period of maturing, but his father, unable to see into his son's heart, could only note and lament the outward change. And indeed not many weeks had passed before Sebastian was as slovenly, haggard, and fiery eyed as any wandering preacher.

At about this time the tax-assessor to the council was overtaken by the calamity that Barbara had foretold. He tripped on the stair as he tried to crawl to his lodging, and broke his right arm, so that for a long time he was incapable of wielding a pen. With the approval of the council, he appointed me his assistant and shared his salary with me. This meant that he could abandon work altogether, though for the sake of appearances he would show himself from time to time at the town hall to give me his instructions. It was an arrangement that suited us both. Somehow or other his arm would not heal, and he explained to me that the left arm was just the one he needed for turning up the bottom of his tankard.

When the drink went to his head he would say to me, "I know what I know, Michael, and you can't pull the wool over my eyes! You young fox! I know whose arts I have to thank for my fall on the stair. But I bear you no grudge, since my life is the pleasanter for it. Nevertheless, you'd be wise to tell the red-haired Barbara that your temporal welfare depends entirely on me, since as a stranger and her husband you could never secure a post by yourself. Therefore my death, so far

160

from profiting you, would prove your undoing. So don't waste your time wagging your tail at the councilors. Put your trust in me and remember to tell your wife what I have said."

He talked in mysteries, and his message to Barbara I put down to intoxication.

I was mortally weary of the gunsmith's silent house and the low rooms in which I seemed to sense a continual lurking dread. I well knew that the taciturn gunsmith and above all his sullen son wished both me and Barbara at the world's end; and I disliked the sight of the mother, who suffered from dropsy and was almost entirely bedridden. If I sought the favor of the council it was not to injure my friend and protector the assessor, but because there were two small rooms in the basement of the town hall in which I hoped we might be allowed to set up housekeeping on our own. And in the course of time one of the councilors, whom I had always been officious to serve, gave me leave to take possession of these cellar rooms, providing the present tenants would move out. At Barbara's bidding I called on these people, a bailiff and his pox-eaten wife, and offered them a gold piece to go. The wife, whose vocabulary was large, poured forth a stream of abuse, but the bailiff was already mournfully putting their effects together, and bade her be silent and not draw misfortune upon them by cursing me.

It was in this way that Barbara and I acquired our first and only home, and for a year we lived there like little mice, hiding from the approaching storm and from the ill will of our fellows. In the evenings, when the town hall was empty, we cleaned its great echoing rooms, swept the stone floors, and scrubbed the stairs. In the dim light of winter mornings I lit fires on the great hearths, and during the day I carried out my clerkly duties quietly and unobtrusively without a cross word to anyone. Our patron, the tippling assessor, burdened us with his presence each dinnertime. Barbara did her best to please him, and I fetched a huge jug of the strongest ale for him every day from the tavern. Our guest was well aware of his own advantage, and certainly bore us no malice, but the longer he sought truth at the bottom of his tankard, the more crabbed, peevish, and sly he became. His knowing hints and allusions often brought tears to Barbara's eyes, and she would bite her lip and flush.

But why speak of what was disagreeable? We were very happy together and throughout that time I wished for nothing better. To our eyes, those walls glistening with damp were hung with brilliant tapestries; the dim light of the rape-oil lamp became the effulgence of a many-branched candlestick; and at night I seemed to take Barbara in my arms on a silken couch beneath the radiance of many wax tapers. She was lovelier to me than a queen, though heavy toil had reddened and coarsened her hands, and her life in half-dark rooms had turned her cheeks yet paler than before.

Often she would urge me to seek the company of friends, or of books, for she felt I was not born to live such a life forever and that fate had greater tasks in store for me. But a strangeness had grown up between me and Sebastian, and the councilors would have been far from content to see me frequenting his fanatical and heretical followers. Instead, I began to study Greek once more, although without the enthusiasm of my student years.

Barbara seldom left the shelter of our cellar, and then only after dark, as if she were afraid of meeting people and wanted them to forget her existence. This strange timidity of hers affected me also, so that at times I was afflicted with a painful dread of life in general. I preferred to think that things were best as they were and that any change could bring only misfortune with it. And with a clear conscience I can take my oath before God and all His saints that not once during the time we spent in our queer home did I see Barbara do anything suspicious, or anything that might have suggested witchcraft. If ever she had busied herself with deeds of darkness, I firmly believe that after our marriage she renounced such matters and wished to free herself from all that was evil.

As for the dog, it appeared in our home in a very natural manner. We saw it playing one day in the courtyard and no owner came to claim it. It was no more than a puppy—a black, shaggy little ball of the breed commonly carried by camp followers. The short legs of these little dogs grow weary on long marches, but they are useful in camp, for they guard their masters' sleep and discourage the approach of cutpurses.

Later in the day the dog began whining with hunger outside the door and I brought it in to Barbara, who gave it food and let it out again. But no one came to fetch it, and I felt sorry for the helpless little beast. Moreover, I thought it might be company for Barbara, who was alone in those murky rooms all day.

So we adopted the dog, and Barbara, stroking its soft black coat gently as it slept in her lap, spoke these words, "Your name shall be Azrael. May you be as mighty a dog as Azrael is an angel, for your coat makes you a true mandrake-hound. You shall make Michael and me so rich that we will leave this unfriendly city for the warm countries of the south. Make haste and grow, little Azrael, and seek the mandragora for us, though it should cost you your life, and we'll dress the plant in baby's clothes and sell it for many times its weight in gold, if we do not rather keep it, that we may prosper in all we do and grow rich quickly without having to stir a finger."

She smiled to herself. Still stroking the animal with her thin hand, she bent her wide green glance upon me and said, "Don't be dismayed at my words, Michael. I'm only joking. But I believe I know a place deep in the forest where a man was once hanged, and a plant grows there that might be a true mandrake. There's mortal danger in uprooting it, but I should feel no fear if you were with me—and then we should lack for nothing all our days. A black dog can pull it up for us. It may die in so doing, but we shall be unharmed if we stop our ears with wax; for when a mandrake is uprooted it utters a shriek so hideous that whoever hears it may fall dead or go raving mad."

"Barbara," I said, "don't call the dog that. Azrael is too weighty a name for the little beast. And I wish it no harm. I saw a mandrake once among the treasures of a relic-dealer in Paris, but it's very rare, and cheats have brought it into disrepute by carving common roots into human form and selling them for fabulous prices as true mandrakes."

Once or twice after this we spoke jestingly of mandrakes, wondering what we should do if we found one and survived its uprooting; but we soon forgot the matter. We began to love the little dog that was our companion and faithful friend. Its name soon took the form of Rael, and I fancy I quite forgot the magic word of which it was an abbreviation.

We were very happy, and yet sometimes at night I was tormented by an unspeakable oppression that stifled my very breathing. Barbara felt it too, and would come to me and press her face against my neck. On such nights we lay silent in our bed in close embrace, as if secretly we feared to lose one another. Yet when I think of it now, it seems as if these were the best of all our hours, when we came as near to each other as two people can come, though we spoke not a word.

So the year passed. Others besides ourselves held the future in dread, yet the great planets met together in February and nothing noteworthy occurred. Spring shimmered green about the city and sunbeams danced on the pewterer's wares in the market place. I was still young and I forgot my forebodings. I enjoyed my earthly bliss, mean, wretched, and mingled with wormwood though it was. But these swiftly speeding weeks of spring carried with them the last of my happiness. So with the spring of 1524 I will bring this book to an end, and will begin the sixth—the bitterest book of all.

BOOK 6.

Faggots in the Market Place

I

I HAVE seen many strange and unaccountable things in the course of my life, and I would not positively deny that there is such a thing as witchcraft. I have not forgotten certain childhood experiences in Mistress Pirjo's cabin. Moreover, there is too much corroborative evidence from several different countries to allow of disbelief by any thoughtful man. Perhaps the soundest proof of all is that even Doctor Luther, the archheretic, shares the Pope's views on this matter. Yet opinions may differ on the best mode of inquiry, judgment, and punishment, and to my last breath I shall maintain that the methods employed by Holy Church are wrong and horrible, though I should myself end at the stake for this conviction.

Further, I believe that much that is generally accounted witchcraft is no more than an expression of the eternal human desire to find a short cut—a desire, dormant in all of us, that awakens with mental suffering. Therefore in my opinion it merits neither condemnation nor punishment; certainly not the cruel penalties imposed by the Church. For the supposed short cut is an illusion, and illusions are no more deserving of punishment than are dreams.

But Barbara was no illusion. So it is easy to deride me for my heretical ideas, to mock me, and say that I myself am the best proof of the existence of witchcraft, since Barbara could cast her spell upon me, ugly, red haired, and freckled though she was.

Later I perceived that Holy Church required her death to demonstrate its power. But she died not as a martyr but as a witch, for the exercise of black arts. And this I declare to be a crying injustice and a disgrace to the Church, though I now feel no desire to accuse the Church, but will confine myself to saying that it had bad servants. Yet it is hard for me to blame Father Angelo, whom I knew, for I am sure that in fulfilling his heavy task he acted in good faith.

I have not been able to discover whether the affair was planned in the Curia or merely at the court of the Prince-Bishop, but I do believe that the Church as a whole was desirous of making an example, because of the heretical preachers whose utterances were becoming more and more outrageous. Sebastian's doctrine on the justice of God was on everyone's lips, and evangelical heresy was already so widespread that no one dared attempt to condemn the guilty, for this would have meant the arrest and execution of half the inhabitants of the diocese, and consequently open riots. But to condemn witchcraft was the recognized right and duty of the Church, as the most bigoted heretic would have admitted. So the Prince-Bishop and his judges, and perhaps also the wealthy upper class in the city, came to the cold-blooded conclusion that the smell of scorching flesh would have a wholesome effect on the disquieted populace. It was my wife Barbara who fell victim to this astute plan, but its success was not great enough to justify the means. Even now, looking impartially upon the matter, I cannot admit that those gentlemen were very farseeing. I bear them as savage and as bitter a hatred as ever, persuaded though they doubtless were that they were acting rightly and in the best interests of Holy Church.

2

It was I who admitted the gray-clad, rat-faced man to the presence of the council, unaware of his reputation. He spoke kindly to me and patted me on the shoulder as he turned his head ceaselessly this way and that, his cruel little eyes glancing everywhere, as if in constant search. Outwardly he was insignificant, and I could not understand why the councilors received him with such respect and at once ordered all doors to be closed, in order to engage him in a secret conference from which even I was excluded. It was not long before the doors were once more opened and the man approached me, attended by two councilors, who avoided my eye in some embarrassment.

"Your name is Michael Pelzfuss, is it not?" he inquired amiably. "I am Master Fuchs from the head of this diocese, and I should like to meet your wife Barbara. I have a word to say to her. Be good enough to show me the way."

Still unsuspecting, so deceptive was his friendly manner, I would have hurried on ahead to warn Barbara of the visit; but he gripped my arm and would not let me go. Thus I was compelled to bring him and the two councilors to our rooms unannounced, though I was ashamed of our poverty and would have preferred Barbara to change her dress before receiving them.

It was a bright spring day, and after the dark cellar stair the rooms seemed filled with the sunshine that streamed down through the little windows under the ceiling. Barbara was stirring something in the stewpot when we came in. She looked up, surprised.

"Is that you, Michael?"

Then her eyes fell on the stranger and she gave a great start. Her hand, still holding the spoon, sank, and she took a step backward. Her face whitened to a transparency that showed up the ugly yellow-brown freckles on her cheekbones.

The stranger regarded her searchingly with his cruel little eyes. Then he smiled, baring two yellow rat's teeth.

Turning to the councilors, he said, "That will do. We can go."

The gentlemen were taken aback, and one of them, with a pitying look at me, asked, "Will you not search the rooms, Master Fuchs?"

"That will do," he repeated, with a kick at Rael, who had innocently hurried forward to greet him. Then he turned to go. The councilors followed him in silence, and with a deep bow I closed the door behind them. Then I looked at Barbara in astonishment.

"What is this?"

She stood with the spoon in her hand, gazing into the distance, and did not answer for some time. The soup boiled over into the fire unnoticed, and Rael began to whine softly as if sensing her distress. Barbara bent down absently to stroke him.

"I must go away, Michael," she said. "The less you know of this affair the better. My one comfort is that they can do you no harm. But whatever happens—even if we should never meet again—I beg you to believe no ill of me, dearest Michael. I have always loved you, and you only, and ever shall."

167

My heart shrank at her words.

"Who was the man?" I asked.

"Fuchs, the Bishop's commissary," she answered, as if the name explained everything. But noting my blank look, she smiled slightly and at once seemed beautiful to me.

"I forgot you were a stranger, Michael, although of course that was how you came to marry me. Master Fuchs is the Bishop's witch hunter. He boasts that he can smell them out a mile off, and his mere glance is enough to condemn. I've already been forced to take the oath of purgation on his account, but at that time I lived in my father's house and was protected by his good name and by his guild. Now there is no one to protect me, and so I must go."

The full meaning of her words flashed upon me. Our isolation, my forebodings, Sebastian's words—all fitted together to form one clear conviction.

"You're right, Barbara. We must fly. Perhaps we may reach some town in the Confederation if we cross the forests and mountains on foot. And if we follow the Rhine we can pass over it to the French shore."

"Would you really come with me? Even if I was a witch and our flight convicted you as another?"

"Of course," I returned impatiently. "And you're not a witch, so let us talk no more nonsense but pack up as many of our possessions as we can carry and set off after dark."

"I love you, Michael," said Barbara. She kissed me gently, and her lips melted into mine. "But you're stubborn. I know I can't prevent your coming with me, though it should bring disaster on you, so let us plan our flight cleverly without arousing suspicion. Above all, you must attend to your work as usual while I prepare for our journey. But lest something unforeseen should happen and force us to make our escape separately, let us agree to meet in the wood outside the town where my uncle lives, at the place where I first found you."

She must have known as she said this that flight was hopeless. Her only thought was to keep me out of the affair and in safety. When late that afternoon I was bending over my copy, there came the sound of uproar from the market place. I rushed out with death in my heart to see Master Fuchs leading Barbara at the end of a rope. Her hands were bound behind her and two guards were warding off the howling mob, which was throwing mud and dung.

Master Fuchs waved a little bundle above his head in triumph, crying, "I caught her as she was making her escape—and why was she escaping? No innocent person flies from me."

"Witch, hag, warlock!" screeched the people, and they thrust aside the lances of the guards that they might kick and strike and spit upon my wife Barbara. Blood was already running from her nose and mouth. By frantic efforts I forced my way through to her. It was now my turn to seize Master Fuchs by the arm.

"Let her go, Master Fuchs," I sobbed. "She's my wife, and I her husband should know that she is no witch."

"Away, Michael, away!" cried Barbara, tearing at her bonds as if she would have thrust me from her.

But the mob now turned their attention to me and yelled, "The stranger, the stranger! Arrest him, Master Fuchs! He's as bad as she is."

Master Fuchs smiled self-consciously and raised his hand as a sign that he wished to address the people. The tumult died down and some cried, "Hear him, hear him!"

When Master Fuchs had obtained silence he spoke up and said, "I can well understand your agitation, good people, but it is not for you to revile and maltreat this woman. The Holy Inquisition shall make fair inquiry and judge her according to her deserts. If she is found to have been the cause of calamity and suffering among you, rest assured that her own sufferings will have been a thousand times worse before she rides to hell in the fiery carriage of her master. Know, good people, that Father Angelo the Dominican has recently arrived at the seat of the Prince-Bishop, bearing full papal authority for the trial of witches, both male and female, who have wrought so much iniquity in the diocese of recent years."

Suddenly a powerful voice rang out over the market place: "To hell with Pope and monks!"

In an instant all had joined in this cry, and they invoked perdition on Pope and monks as savagely as they had just cried out on Barbara.

A ragged, long-haired fellow whom I had never seen climbed upon the pewterer's stall, where with fiery eyes and arms waving like flails he roared at the top of his voice, "Hand over the witch to us, Master Fuchs, and down with Pope and monks! We can burn our witches without their help. Fetch faggots, good people, and let us purge the evil from our midst!"

Master Fuchs looked thoughtful and gave me a furtive glance. Suddenly he called an order to the men-at-arms and began dragging Barbara toward the town hall. With the help of the guards I contrived to hold off the surging rabble, push Barbara inside, and lock the heavy door, which well withstood the blows thundered on it from without. I knelt on the floor beside the swooning Barbara, unfastened the rope that bound her wrists, and wiped the blood and dirt from her face. My tears fell upon her cheek and roused her, and she opened her eyes.

"Age is telling upon you, Master Fuchs!" exclaimed one of the lesser councilors with some irony. "I cannot discern in your handling of this affair any of the matchless dexterity for which you're famous. It may cost you dear."

Master Fuchs laughed coolly.

"You're right," he assented. "There will be some unpleasantness when the good Prince-Bishop and Father Angelo come to hear of it. The city may not come off very cheaply, either. Listen!"

At that instant came the crash of the first broken windowpane, and a stone clattered across the floor. Outside, the mob was demanding in rhythmic roars the handing over of the witch for them to burn.

"Was it Satan himself who put it into your head to fly in broad daylight, hag?" asked Master Fuchs, with a light kick at the prostrate Barbara. "I meant to fetch you after dark, for I know all the tricks."

But he said this without marked malevolence; his air was rather one of curiosity, as if he had met with something new in his business. Two costly panes of stained glass were shivered to pieces and the councilors wrung their hands. Master Fuchs remained impassive.

"The times are bad," he observed. "Would it not be best for one of you gentlemen to go out onto the gallery and pacify the people? Tell them I have taken the witch out by the backdoor and that we're now galloping away from the city in the witch cart. Then tonight we shall be able to take our departure unmolested."

But none of those worthies betrayed eagerness to step out before the people amid the showering stones. The ironical gentleman, whom I knew to be secretly Lutheran in his leanings, turned pale and said abruptly, "Master Fuchs, hand her over to them. We must not encroach on Memmingen's rights as a free city. Barbara Pelzfuss was born and bred here, and cannot be removed without the consent of the council."

"In such a case as this the jurisdiction of a city council—of the Emperor himself—is subordinate to that of the Church," replied Master Fuchs. "In any case, if you remember, I have the council's written authority in my pocket. This morning you yourselves were agreed that she should be handed over to me. Rest assured that Father Angelo will be more than willing to return her to you in due course for you to carry out her sentence. But it is for the Holy Inquisition to try her. That is the kernel of the matter, as men of sense like yourselves should understand."

The gentlemen of the council, after some debate, agreed that Master Fuchs had spoken wisely. But none of them would venture onto the gallery, and they began pushing one another forward. Master Fuchs regarded them contemptuously for a time, then turned to where I was still sitting on the floor with Barbara's head in my lap.

"Michael Pelzfuss!" said he. "While there's life there's hope. Before long the mob will break in, and you know what will happen to your wife then. But in the hands of the Holy Inquisition she will be entirely safe until proof of her guilt has been established by means of evidence and her own confession. The trial may last several months, and I assure you that Father Angelo is a devout and righteous man of whom no one can speak evil. It is for that reason that he has been chosen to bear the heavy and most solemn responsibilities of an Inquisitor. Run up onto the gallery, Michael Pelzfuss, and tell them that I have taken your wife away."

At a loss how to act, I raised Barbara's head. She opened her green eyes and whispered, "Dearest Michael, plunge your knife into my heart. I shall die in your arms and feel no pain."

But I was a coward, an abject coward, and I clutched at the straw of hope that seemed to lie in Master Fuchs's false words.

"You're no witch," I whispered in her ear. "I will save you. Holy Church cannot pronounce a wrongful judgment. I myself will speak with Father Angelo."

She responded with a faint shake of her head and tried to cling to me, but tearing myself from her arms I rushed upstairs to the floor above, wrenched open the door of the outer gallery and ran out, shrieking and gesticulating.

"Seize him, good people! He has taken my wife out by the back way. Save her from the power of the Inquisition—save her, for they have not yet reached the city gate!"

I yelled and waved my arms until the uproar died down and they could hear what I said. When the first of them began running down the side street, the rest followed—a howling, unthinking mass. Soon the market place was empty of all save hats, staves, logs, and stones.

On my return to the lower floor, I was bidden to make out the customary account for services rendered to the city:

"To hunting down one witch at the statutory rate . . 7 gulden."

Master Fuchs signed the receipt with many ornate flourishes and the treasurer reluctantly counted the seven gold pieces into his hand. Slipping them into the purse at his belt, the commissary turned to me. "We must fill in the time until midnight," he remarked, "for it would scarcely be advisable to travel earlier. Luckily I left the witch cart at a stable outside the city so as not to attract attention. There is nothing to prevent our spending the evening in your rooms, and your wife Barbara may prepare supper for us. No doubt you will wish to accompany her as far as the prison. I have no objection to this, for I mean to take an armed escort. And Father Angelo will certainly want to interrogate you without delay."

Leaving the councilors to wring their hands and discuss the matter of the broken windows, we went down the cellar stair to our modest dwelling, which was as safe as any part of the town hall. Rael ran up to us whimpering with joy, and when Master Fuchs had sat down he took the dog into his lap and stroked it. He had ordered the men-at-arms to stand guard outside the door, and Barbara made enough soup for them as well. It was a good soup, for we had no reason to be sparing of our supplies. Master Fuchs said grace devoutly and ate enough for two, but my throat was constricted and I could not swallow many spoonfuls. I looked round at our little home, and never before had it seemed so dear, so cherished, and so safe as during those last hours before our journey to the realms of horror.

When the watchmen had cried the hour of midnight, we crept cautiously from the courtyard and along the same alley by which Barbara had sought to escape. No one molested us, and the council had given secret orders to the guard at the cattle gate to let us pass without delay or question. Soon we were rattling over the deeply rutted road in the witch cart toward the city of the Prince-Bishop. It was a fragrant spring night. We sat in the straw on the floor of the cart, Master Fuchs holding Rael in his lap and pinching the dog's ear thoughtfully from time to time. If Barbara had been well and strong, we might have attempted to escape into the darkness, despite the bars of the cart, which surrounded us like a cage. But she was giddy and could not have run far. Moreover, I was beguiled by the hope that Father Angelo, whose piety and justice Master Fuchs had praised, would be convinced of Barbara's innocence and soon release her, although indeed I had heard much evil of witch trials. And an attempted escape would have furnished very damaging evidence against her.

The night was dark, the wind sighed, the glowworms glimmered eerily in the grass, and the muffled thud of the horse's hoofs on the road before us seemed a presage of death. It was a night for witches. I sought to bring order to my thoughts and ask myself whether in my heart I believed in Barbara's innocence. She rested her head in my arms and gripped my knees convulsively; now and then her whole body was shaken by a deep sob.

To free myself from all doubts, I put my lips to her ear and whispered, "Barbara!" When she stirred I whispered again, "Barbara! If you're indeed a witch you can save yourself now."

But she only sobbed and clutched my knees yet more fiercely. And I saw that she could not be a witch, nor in league with the devil, for surely the devil would have taken care of his own.

3

The sun was rising as we drew near the city, and I doubt whether I have ever seen the world so young and fair as it was that morning. The snow-capped peaks in the distance rose above the horizon like blue clouds, the grass of the valleys was freshly green, and the river whirled its white-flecked waters over the smooth gray stones of its bed. The vineyards were golden-brown, budding foliage hung pale green veils over the black boughs of ash and lime, and before us rose the spires of the Prince-Bishop's city. Here and there the projecting upper stories of houses hung like swallows' nests above the city wall, and the thin, clear voice of the monastery bell was calling the brothers to prayer.

The watchman at the gate recognized Master Fuchs and allowed the cart to pass through the archway. Servant girls and artisans who were early astir paused to gape at the yellow-painted cart. Before long we had a little following of girls, apprentices, and children. The weary horse clopped at walking pace through the narrow streets until we reached the prison tower adjoining the Bishop's palace. Here Master Fuchs roused the jailer and gave Barbara into his charge. Then to my astonishment he seized Rael by the scruff of the neck and lifted him into his arms so that the dog yelped with pain.

"I'll take care of this," he said. "Father Angelo must decide whether it will be needed merely as a witness, or whether it's to be charged with witchcraft also."

Rael tried to struggle free and whined piteously to Barbara, who was still standing in the doorway. The frightful stench of the prison wafted out into the fresh morning air as the stunted jailer paused to stare malignantly at Barbara, and to debate with Master Fuchs the manner in which she was to be secured. I gave him a whole gulden and begged him to be liberal in the matter of her food and drink. But I was not allowed to enter that dark tower. Master Fuchs alone accompanied the jailer, still carrying the wretched dog. They cuffed Barbara in before them and the heavy door closed.

Some time later the door swung ponderously open again, and Master Fuchs came out into the daylight, wiping his hands on the skirt of his gray coat.

"You need have no fear," he said to the jailer. "Father Angelo will give you holy water and wax, and so long as you don't look the witch in the eyes, and remember your prayers, no evil can touch you. She's now harmless."

"What have you done to my wife, Master Fuchs?" I cried, horror-stricken.

"We put her in the stocks," he answered, "and then I examined her, as I am in duty bound to do, to assure myself that she had no accursed talisman concealed among her clothes or on her person which might endanger this good man and his family."

I stared at his eyes, his face, and his cruel hands, and was filled with boundless horror and disgust. But nothing was to be gained by angering him.

Mastering my feelings, I said humbly, "Dear Master Fuchs, I am an inexperienced youth and know nothing of trials. Tell me what I should do for my wife. And to save time let us meanwhile taste a cup of mulled spiced wine at some nearby tavern, to warm ourselves after our wearisome journey."

"A timely suggestion, Michael Pelzfuss," he returned. "Let us then go and drain a goblet together, and at the same time I can present my reckoning for the journey."

He rubbed his nose and looked me up and down, estimating my means.

"You're not wealthy," he went on, "and I will be moderate in my demands. But that is best discussed with wine before us."

174

At the gate of the courtyard I ventured to ask him, "What have you done with the dog, Master Fuchs?"

"It is fettered and bound in its own cell," he replied. "Don't be uneasy, Michael, for it has water, and the jailer's children will bring it bones and bread. It's a friendly little creature and I wish it no harm, though it was my duty to imprison it."

We continued our walk, and in a little while he added, "I'm very fond of animals, especially birds. At home I have many beautiful birds in cages."

We entered a pleasant tavern, where I ordered hot spiced wine, fresh-baked pastry, and fritters. Master Fuchs was still counting on his fingers as we sipped our morning drink, and said at last that in consideration of my youth and poverty he would be content with two and a half gulden. I knew he was robbing me, but that was his right and I stood in desperate need of his good graces. I knew that I should have to bear the cost of the trial and the witnesses' fees, whether or not Barbara was acquitted, but I cared nothing for the expense and only hoped that my money would suffice.

In answer to the questions with which I plied him, he told me that this time there could be no question of canonical purgation.

"You must try to understand the position, Michael," he said patiently. "Witchcraft is *crimen exceptum,* like *lèse-majesté,* high treason, and coining, but is of a far more horrible nature. The judge in such a trial must be armed with special powers, for he has to battle not only with the witch but with Satan himself, the father of lies, who stands unseen behind the accused to blind the eyes of the judge, confuse the memory of the witnesses, and expose all those present to great perils. It is evident, therefore, that the names of witnesses and informers must at times be kept secret, and that special methods must be used to extort a confession. All means are permissible so long as they tend to throw light on the matter and reveal the truth. If you consider the matter fairly and honestly, Michael, you must admit that this is only right."

I willingly assented, but maintained that Barbara was innocent. I, her husband, should surely know this better than anyone. And I added that the devil would have had an excellent opportunity to help Barbara escape the previous night if she had indeed been in league with him.

"I thought of that at the time, and was extremely uneasy," replied Master Fuchs. "But the devil is infinitely more cunning than we can suppose, and no doubt he felt it advantageous to array her in the robe of innocence and give her into the power of the court. For this reason

I presume that Satan has taught her certain tricks that will enable her to harden herself, though I have not been able to discover any unholy instruments on her. However, the Holy Inquisition has at its disposal expedients that my oath binds me to conceal from you."

"I hope at least that she will not be subjected to torments beyond the endurance of a tender woman," I said, frozen with terror at the thought. But Master Fuchs reassured me with kindly words.

"Nothing of that kind will happen, and in any case it is by no means certain that she will be put to the question. But if it should go so far, the examiners are not permitted to cause bodily injury to the accused. On the contrary, it has been laid down in unequivocal terms that the examination must not be such as to cause lasting harm. Nor may it exceed the strength of the accused. Of course it has happened now and then that Satan himself has killed a witch when he has seen that her resistance was weakening, but there's no harm in that, since such a death furnishes conclusive proof that witchcraft existed. The same applies to any death occurring in prison."

The good spiced wine burned my throat like gall when I heard these words, yet I ordered another cup for him. He went on to give me many examples of the devil's activities among his followers in prison. He told me of a twelve-year-old girl who had been got with child by the Evil One in her cell, and who confessed to nightly traffic with him. Both she and her mother were burned at the stake.

"Master Fuchs," I said, "I perceive that with the devil all things are possible. But your stories frighten me and I should be glad to meet Father Angelo as soon as may be, that I may lay the whole matter before him and appeal to his justice."

Master Fuchs most kindly arranged this for me, and that same afternoon I called upon Father Angelo in his austere cell in the monastery of the Black Friars.

4

My anguish was very great, but when I stepped within the walls of the cloister and in its silence breathed the familiar smell of incense and sweaty tunics, and walked along the cold stone corridor behind the lay brother, my riven heart was eased.

"This is the house of God," I thought. "It is hallowed by centuries of prayer, mortification, and devout contemplation. There are good monks and bad monks, but the house of God stands as a pledge that no evil shall befall Barbara."

When I entered the cell, Father Angelo rose from his knees before the image of the Crucified. Throwing myself at his feet, I kissed the hem of his black habit. He wore no sandals and I could see from his veined, gnarled feet that he went barefoot all the year round. Despite this his feet were very clean, and when I raised my eyes I saw that his face also was clean and radiant. It was thin from fasting and devotion, and goodness shone from it as he stooped to raise me.

"Do not kneel to me, Michael Pelzfuss," said he, "but to God and His saints only. Revere in me not the man, but the eternal and unshakable justice of the Church, which condemns the guilty and frees the innocent. Be seated, my son. Be comforted, and tell me all that lies upon your conscience, for thus you will best help yourself and your wife."

There were such kindness and consolation in his words that I wept, being weak after the long agony of fear, fasting, and sleeplessness. He soothed me, and bade me sit on a low stool beside his chair, and his compassionate voice melted the dams of my soul. I described my whole life, owned that I was of illegitimate birth, and told of my earnest desire to serve the Church. I showed him my crumpled diploma from Paris University, and declared that the hard blows of fate had brought me to repent of my sins and had inspired me to make a pilgrimage to the Holy Sepulcher of our Savior; but that on the way I had been attacked and robbed and left to perish in the forest.

"It was Barbara Büchsenmeister who found me in this terrible plight, and it seemed that God in His mysterious way had led her to me," I continued. "Barbara was kind and tender. She nursed me back to health and clad me, for I had not so much as a shirt to my back. My heart turned toward her and we married, that we might live together until the end of our days. We led a frugal, hardworking life and did no harm to anyone. Only the malice of our fellows, which has tormented Barbara since her childhood because of her appearance, has given rise to this terrible suspicion of which she's now the victim. But I her husband know her best, and by God Himself and the holy Sacraments I swear that she is innocent of the hideous crime with which she is charged!"

Father Angelo sat serene and motionless in his chair, regarding me with clear, searching eyes. He rested his beautiful, slender hands on the arms and encouraged me with brief questions whenever I hesitated, and I told him all that had happened to me, truthfully and without reserve. When I had ended, he sat quietly for a long time, still staring at me with those clear eyes.

At length with a deep sigh he said, "Michael Pelzfuss, I believe what you tell me and I desire to think well of you, since to atone for your sins you were on your way to the Holy Land when the witch found you and drew you into her power. But you lack experience and you fail to understand the terrible nature of the matter with which we're now concerned. Nevertheless, with God's help, I trust we may bring all to a happy conclusion, and I must therefore ask you a few questions."

He stiffened then and sat like a rock. The gentle eyes were bent upon me suddenly with the cold, hard look of a judge.

"Michael Pelzfuss," he began, "do you believe in witches and witchcraft?"

Making the sign of the cross I answered, "God forbid that I should doubt anything that the Church teaches, for I'm no heretic. Of course there are witches, but my wife Barbara is innocent."

He said, "Do you believe then that the witches whom Holy Church has condemned were guilty, and that they suffered no more than their just punishment for a most hideous sin?"

I lowered my eyes and pondered, but was compelled at last to answer in a low voice, "I must believe it, for Holy Church is incapable of error."

But something stirred in the secret depths of my mind, and I could not meet his gaze when I replied.

He sank back in his chair and his clear eyes were warm once more.

"Michael, my son, you have the true faith and are no heretic. Therefore you must believe also that justice and only justice will be done. The hunting down of witches is a hard and terrible task, which puts the spiritual powers of the judges to the test. In my weakness I have groaned a thousand times at the dread work with which the Holy Father has entrusted me. Satan searches out my infirmity and only by constant prayer and bodily mortification can I overcome the doubts that he whispers in my ear. Pray therefore also, Michael—pray for the sake of your own heart—pray that I may vanquish my weakness and like a true judge disclose the wiles of Satan when I inquire into this evil case."

His appeal bore witness to so deep an agony of soul, so pure a stead-

178

fastness, that my own fear shrank and seemed a petty thing beside the spiritual anguish of this holy man.

"Father Angelo," I said meekly, "with my whole heart I will pray that God may help you to discover the truth. And I will pray also for my own poor soul. Yet my most burning prayers shall be for my wife Barbara, that no evil may befall her."

Father Angelo responded with a slight shake of the head.

"Michael, my son, with God's help I will discover the truth. But never before have I been faced with so difficult a task, for I must both convict the witch by conclusive proof and at the same time save your blinded soul from doubt, so that in full reliance on the justice of Holy Church you may devoutly acknowledge that truth has prevailed, confessing this not with your lips alone but from the bottom of your heart."

Then he put many keen questions to me, about how Barbara had found me, how she had nursed me during my illness, and the manner of our marriage. He also asked about our dog, and wished to know how the assessor had broken his arm, from which I saw that he was very fully informed about us. But I answered all his questions freely and candidly and never contradicted myself when he worded them in different ways.

At last he asked, "Did you both go regularly to Mass and confession, and receive the Holy Sacrament together?"

I was compelled to admit that we had somewhat neglected our religious duties, but only because Barbara suffered from the hostility of others and was afraid to show herself in public. I assured him that we had never forgotten our prayers and had observed all fast days.

I added, "I deeply repent of our negligence and see that we ought to have defied the malice of the people and been more diligent in fulfilling our Christian duties, as indeed we desired to do."

"The innocent neither fear nor avoid their fellows," said Father Angelo. "Witches have good reason for abstaining from hearing Mass, and that she has neglected the Sacraments is even weightier proof. Nevertheless Satan is so wily that I should have regarded it as an equally grave circumstance if she had been a diligent churchgoer and communicant."

"My wife is not a witch," I declared, for I could find nothing else to say.

"You married Barbara Büchsenmeister. Is she then beautiful in your eyes?"

"I find her so," I answered.

At the thought of her in the stocks amid the filth and stench of the prison tower, I wept and cried out, "Father Angelo, in my eyes she is the loveliest of women and I love her more than anything in the world!"

Father Angelo started violently and crossed himself.

"It is enough," he said. "From now on you must devote yourself to ceaseless prayer, mortification, and penance. By no other means can I free you from the power of Satan. I have not yet seen the witch Barbara, but I know that she is ugly. She is older than you and the best marriage years were behind her when she met you. From now on you must not set foot outside the monastery walls. I will put you under the supervision of the Prior, so that you may pray and do penance until all witnesses are assembled and the trial can begin."

"Father!" I shrieked, falling on my knees before him. "I desire no better than to pray and mortify the flesh, but give me leave to visit my wife in prison and comfort her in her loneliness, for my heart aches at the thought of her dreadful plight."

My prayers left him unmoved, and indeed my obstinacy had begun to cause him some vexation. Therefore I held my peace and he took me to the Prior. At compline they put a candle in my hand, pressed consecrated salt into my mouth while the monks sang to drive the devil out of me, and Father Angelo and other good fathers offered up burning prayers for my salvation. This exhausting ceremony quieted me so far as to let me sink into a deathlike stupor. Yet three hours later I was shaken and roused by the monks and taken to attend the Night Office.

This treatment was continued day in and day out, and the constant vigils and penitential diet kept me in a merciful daze. Yet now and then my mind would be lit by a flash of consciousness, and when I remembered Barbara and her life in that prison it was as if someone had thrust a knife into my breast. I cried out in my agony, beseeching the brothers to chastise me with knotted ropes and with thorns, that my bodily hurts might deaden the pains I suffered on my beloved's account. And the good monks flogged me until my back was raw to drive the devil from my body.

Almost two months went by, and summer blossomed about the city of the Prince-Bishop. But I knew nothing of summer, for a bare cell was my dwelling place, a stone floor my bed, and my only path the vaulted passage to the church. Little by little the turmoil in my mind subsided, and when the good Prior saw that I was healed of my trouble he allowed a relaxation of discipline. My own clothes were restored to me, I was given nourishing food, and after a few days my brain cleared and I was myself again. From this I deduced that the trial was shortly to begin, and I was filled with a great impatience.

One day I asked the Prior for leave to get my hair cut in the town, and on obtaining it went straight to the prison. I dared not accost the porter, but I entered the courtyard so that at least I might behold the massive tower in which Barbara lay. I was shedding tears at the sight of it when all at once I saw Barbara's father the gunsmith walking from the door of the Bishop's palace to the gate. I ran after him and greeted him as heartily as I might, and although he displayed no pleasure at seeing me, he had been drinking wine and wanted someone to talk to. So after some hesitation he invited me to a tavern. Once seated on the wooden bench, he grew voluble and began at great length to lament the evils of the time in general and their effect on his own trade in particular.

At last my impatience got the better of me, and having interrupted him with hasty agreement and sympathy with his difficulties, I asked, "But have you no news of your daughter Barbara, my dear father?"

He looked askance at me and began to snigger.

"I've given my evidence and set my mark against my name," he said. "So at last I'm rid of her, with a full guarantee that neither I nor my family shall meet with any further troubles or unpleasantness on her account. Our reputation is now clear and nothing can be laid to our charge. Never have I known a more blessed day, and it's worth another tankard; for now my son can begin life anew and all the nightmare years lie behind us."

"Have you borne witness against your own daughter?" I exclaimed aghast. "Can you so detest your own flesh and blood? Then indeed the world is even madder than I thought!"

He thumped his tankard on the table for it to be refilled, and said, "I bear you no grudge, Michael, but did I not pay you fifty gulden at your wedding to take the witch away from our good city? Yet you chose to stay among us, and you must take the consequences. I've washed my hands of the matter, and so have my wife and son. You ask whether I hate my daughter. Well, now that those damned green eyes of hers can stare at me no longer, let me tell you that I have hated her ever since she was born. I believe she's no daughter of mine, for that matter, but some devil's spawn bred upon my poor wife by an incubus."

I stared at him, at his sullen looks and moist, tipsy eyes. Starting up from the table, I flung my ale into the crass face and rushed from the tavern, slamming the door after me.

But soon my fury had spent itself. My impotent rage could not help Barbara, and I would be wiser to keep a civil tongue in my head if I hoped to serve her. So I put on humility again and returned quietly to the monastery. No sooner had I entered my cell than Father Angelo sent for me. He was sitting with a thick pile of papers in front of him.

"Steel your heart to bear the truth, Michael my son," he said kindly. "The trial opens today and you must be strong. To prepare you for what must be endured I shall lay before you the collected evidence, though this step is not in accordance with proper legal practice. I do it for your soul's sake. Know then that your wife Barbara is a witch."

I had expected this and made no reply, but only bowed my head and made the sign of the cross to please him. Then I said quietly, "May I see her at the trial?"

Father Angelo sighed.

"We cannot prevent it, and for your soul's sake it is well that you should be present. But when you have read these sworn depositions I believe you will feel no further doubts. Afterward I shall ask you to sign your own statement, which has been taken down at my dictation by the secretary to the Inquisitorial Court."

He handed me the papers and I began to read them attentively, although at times I could not repress an ejaculation of anger or amazement. But I restrained myself and kept my eyes lowered so that Father Angelo might not observe their expression. His searching gaze rested unwaveringly upon me, and conviction had turned to stone that handsome thought-lined face.

I will mention only a few of those depositions. One laid by the parents of a former suitor of Barbara's described how she had quarreled violently with the boy in a meadow outside the town. She had made gestures at the sky, whereupon a tremendous thunderstorm broke and the lad was struck by lightning, although he had taken shelter under a tree while Barbara was standing in the open field. Witnesses were of the opinion that with the devil's help she had guided the lightning to strike down their son, and had made use of her own name, since St. Barbara protects men from lightning.

A woman declared that the milk in her breasts had dried up after a dispute with Barbara. My friend the assessor testified that Barbara had used witchcraft to make him stumble on the stair and break his right arm, which was necessary to his work. This she did to obtain his post for me. She had further lured him to dine with her every day in order to prevent the arm from healing. The bailiff stated that we had driven him and his wife from their comfortable dwelling in order to take possession of it ourselves, and stressed that they would never have moved out if they had not been afraid that Barbara would do them some harm by sorcery. The councilors told how from her childhood up Barbara had been a reputed witch, and that she had already been required to take the oath of purgation. Her father testified that once when Barbara had entered his workshop the smelting furnace cracked with a fearful explosion the same day, causing great damage.

Such were the testimonies that I read with the bitterest indignation; yet with each one my heart sank further. The last of the papers was unsigned, and I began reading it without at once realizing that it contained my own evidence.

I, Michael Pelzfuss, or Michael de Finlandia, baccalaureate at the University of Paris, told how Barbara in some mysterious way had found me beaten and robbed in a wood, and that only the Evil One himself could have led her to the hiding place where the ruffians had left me for dead. In the course of my illness Barbara had given me bitter potions to drink, of whose composition I was ignorant. Undoubtedly they were brewed according to some magic formula, for not long afterward I became enamored of Barbara despite her ugliness, and married her. Throughout our marriage she continued to cast her spells upon me so that I still fancied her the loveliest of all women. But now that the truth had been revealed to me, I renounced her and all works of the devil, and acknowledged that only by witchcraft could I have been induced to marry her.

When I had read this terrible document I raised my eyes and said in a firm voice, "Father Angelo, I will never sign this statement, for it is not true."

He made a movement of impatience, but controlling himself he asked in a conciliatory tone, "Are not those the words you spoke to me? Can you not see that it was her witchcraft that bound you to her? For no man in his senses could say that she is the loveliest woman in the world."

But notwithstanding all his attempts to persuade me, I refused to sign the testimony. At last he allowed me to rewrite it, and I told how Barbara had found me in the wood and nursed me back to health, that I had married her of my own free will and now loved her more than anyone in the world. But when I would have added how during our marriage I had never once seen anything that might hint at sorcery he forbade me, saying that it was not for me to decide whether or not Barbara was guilty, but for the judges, who would draw their own conclusions from the collected evidence, including my own. All too late I saw that he meant to use my evidence against Barbara. Yet because his will was stronger than mine, and because I hoped to be present at the trial and prevent him from twisting my words, I signed the paper and he took it back. He was calm once more, and there was beauty and compassion in his face when he looked at me.

"Believe me, Michael," he said, "I too am but a man, and the task that has been laid upon my shoulders seems often heavier than I can bear. Yet my weakness must be overcome or I cannot faithfully serve the Church. In such a case as this, even pity is a cruel weapon wielded by the devil himself, to tempt me to save his followers."

"I do not believe that my wife is a witch, whatever charges may be brought against her," I said.

Father Angelo leaned his head on his hands, sighed deeply, and sent up a silent prayer.

"Michael," he said, "I am weak. Since my childhood the sight of tears has caused me suffering, and the pain of others makes me ill. Because of this very failing I have been chosen for this work, so that by vanquishing my human infirmities I may glorify God. His Church stands and will ever stand, Michael. Its pillars and roof will ever shelter us. Earth's dross will pass away, but Holy Church endures."

His words crushed me, for they told me that Holy Church, with all the weight of its traditions and its great and venerable Fathers, was hostile to Barbara. She stood alone, without one to defend her. Even I, her husband, had signed a statement that was to be a weapon in the hands of her enemies.

5

The Court assembled in the prison tower of the Bishop's palace, in a bare room dimly lit by arrow slits in the massive walls. As I awaited the reverend fathers I peered through these narrow openings and marveled to see that outside the city it was summer, that the trees were in full foliage and all the land green; for the tower room stood high above the city walls and commanded a magnificent view as far as the cloudlike Alps.

Father Angelo, president of the tribunal, was supported by two other Dominicans, one of whom read out the charge. Master Fuchs was prosecutor. No other people were allowed to attend. When Barbara had been brought in, the guards and even the jailer had to remain outside the closed door.

Barbara had been washed and her hair combed, and she was clad in a coarse, clean smock—her only garment. I had dreaded this meeting, and had pictured to myself the horrors and suffering of her imprisonment, but I saw no outward sign of ill-usage and was reassured by her appearance. Nevertheless she had grown noticeably thinner, and there was a scar at the corner of her mouth; she now appeared to me of a startling ugliness. Her hair was rust colored and dull, and as with screwed-up, blinking eyes she tried to grow accustomed to the light I saw the yellow freckles that covered her face. I think it was some time before she could see anything, for now and then she would rub her eyes as if they smarted.

The examination lasted for more than two hours. To Father Angelo's charge of witchcraft and alliance with the devil, Barbara made quiet denial. Then the secretary read out in a monotonous voice the several testimonies, and to the Inquisitor's questions Barbara answered sometimes yes and sometimes no. I was relieved to find her still quick witted and resolute, for she gave affirmative answers to all that had really happened and could be proved, such as her quarrel with her suitor and with the young mother, the cracking of the furnace, and the breaking of the assessor's arm. But she denied positively having been in any way concerned with these calamities. Her presence and her convincing demeanor had their effect on me so that my secret doubts were dispelled and I honestly believed in her innocence.

By the time my deposition was read out, her eyes had at last accustomed themselves to the light, and she discerned me sitting in my corner. Once more those green eyes were bent upon me. Her thin face lit up and she was suddenly beautiful in my eyes, so that my heart was filled with rapture.

When all the evidence had been read out and the members of the tribunal had discussed each point in turn, Father Angelo, in a cold, stern voice, pronounced these words, "Witch Barbara! In the light of these indisputable and mutually supporting testimonies, the Court of the Holy Inquisition finds you guilty of witchcraft in each and all of the aforementioned cases, which have caused great harm and distress to innocent people. Since there can be no witchcraft without alliance with the devil, the Court considers this further charge likewise fully proven. Will you therefore freely acknowledge your guilt, or will you continue to place your trust in Satan and persist in your denial?"

"I am not a witch," exclaimed Barbara, "and I am not in league with the devil, whatever people may say behind my back. Ever since I was a child people have hated me because I am ugly and unlike them."

"When invited in plain terms to make voluntary confession, the witch stubbornly denied the charge," dictated Father Angelo, "but acknowledged that since her childhood she had been different from other people."

He turned again to Barbara.

"Both during your imprisonment and now before this tribunal I have done all I could to persuade you to make voluntary confession," he said. "Yet you remain obstinate. Therefore this Court will adjourn for two hours, after which the trial will continue, in accordance with Inquisitorial practice, with torture. Do not think, my daughter, that the devil your confederate can help you then! Confess, and spare us this painful duty which neither you nor we shall enjoy."

"But I am not a witch," wailed Barbara, and broke into weeping. Father Angelo ignored her tears, and summoned the jailer to take her back to her cell.

"Father Angelo," I pleaded, "let me speak to my wife and persuade her that it is best for her to confess if she is guilty, for I cannot endure the thought of her suffering."

"That is impossible, Michael," he returned impatiently. "She would only bewitch you again, as your own good sense must tell you."

He bade me go to the Prince-Bishop's kitchen and get something to eat, but I had no appetite, and for two long hours I paced about the courtyard. I tried to bribe the jailer to let me see Barbara, but greedy though he was he dared not imperil his own skin by disobeying Father Angelo's express commands. However, in return for the money I offered, he promised to give her a good meal.

When the venerable fathers returned flushed with wine from the Prince-Bishop's apartments, wiping their mouths and conversing eagerly together, I approached Father Angelo once again, and implored him to let me be present at the next stage of the trial.

This time he was more amenable and said, "I foresaw your request and debated the point with the Prince-Bishop. Such a thing has never been allowed before, but this is a most unusual case and I hardly think you can be released from the spell she has put upon you unless you hear the confession from her own lips. Therefore, by favor of the Prince-Bishop, you may attend, but only on condition that neither by word nor gesture do you interfere with the inquiry, but remain quietly in your place. Also you must take the customary oath neither to hate nor to bear malice toward any there present, nor to tempt, suborn, or bribe anyone to take revenge on your behalf, but to resign yourself to what takes place."

We returned to the tower room, where I took the oath as administered by Father Angelo. Then we went in single file downstairs to the torture chamber, which was windowless and had a vaulted roof. The place was lit by two torches, which revealed the executioner and his assistant in readiness. They were handsomely dressed in red, in the manner prescribed for those of their trade, although when torturing they were not permitted to shed blood or inflict lasting injury. As I looked about me in this cellar I tried to find comfort in the thought that none of those hideous pincers and thumbscrews would be used; but a ladder resting on trestles, a rope hanging from a wheel in the roof, and heavy stone weights were enough to put me in a cold sweat. The good fathers sat down where they chose, complaining at the miserable accommodation.

Barbara was then brought in, terror-stricken and trembling, but when at Father Angelo's order the executioner explained in what manner his instruments were used, she still denied in meek and pleading tones that she was guilty, and said she could not confess to something she had not done. Father Angelo merely sighed and told Master Fuchs to begin his examination.

For this the executioners removed Barbara's smock. She was naked. They threw her down and bound her hard by hands and feet to the ladder. She had grown very thin, but the carefully washed body was white, and the only visible signs of her imprisonment were the dark rings the stocks had left on ankles and wrists. She groaned once or twice when they cut her hair to the roots, and left not the smallest wisp upon her. Then Master Fuchs stepped forward and began to examine narrowly every inch of her skin and every bodily orifice for some devilish talisman which might render her insensible to pain. Father Angelo, from modesty, preferred not to watch this process, but conversed in low tones with the other dignitaries. I did not feel that

187

this treatment, brutal and shameful though it was, was unendurable, for I blessed every moment that spared Barbara real agony.

"Many a witch has boasted that she can remain quite insensible if only she may retain a tiny rag of clothing," remarked Master Fuchs. "But if this one is not quite powerless, then I am no longer fit to hold office."

He retired, and the good fathers approached Barbara's naked body, intoning loud prayers. They sprinkled her with holy water and pressed consecrated salt into her mouth. The ceremony of purification increased the executioners' caution; they had already crossed themselves furtively while binding Barbara's limbs. I could see that even the good fathers feared her in this murky, torch-lit cellar, and the sight filled me with despair, for it showed that they acted in good faith and were convinced of her guilt.

Father Angelo bade Master Fuchs apply the needle test. He took a long, sharp needle and began seeking an insensitive witch-stigma on Barbara's body. The good fathers leaned forward curiously to observe this proceeding, and every time she cried out and the blood flowed they heaved deep sighs. Master Fuchs tested minutely every tiny mole and even the nipples of her breasts, so that she screamed with pain. At last he found a large birthmark on one hip which did not bleed when he pricked it, nor did it seem to give her any pain. Without doubt this was the stigma that the devil had set upon her as a sign that she was of his followers. I was greatly shocked and disconcerted, remembering how in moments of passion I had kissed this mark, which I believed to be a mole.

The secretary committed to the record the result of the needle test, which had revealed a horseshoe-shaped insensitive patch on the witch's skin an inch above the right hipbone. Father Angelo ordered Barbara's release from the ladder, and she was then weighed. No one was surprised to learn that she was a good ten pounds lighter than was normal for a woman of her height and build. It merely confirmed the general belief in her guilt, since witches weigh less than other people, and float in water.

Father Angelo, having allowed Barbara to put her smock on again, invited her once more to confess. But she stood with drooping head and made no answer, whereupon Father Angelo with evident repugnance ordered the man to do his duty. He seized her while his assistant bound her hands behind her back. The rope that hung from the wheel was then fastened to her wrists and she was drawn up under the roof

188

and left suspended there, the joints of her shoulders most unnaturally wrenched. The executioner then released the rope and let her fall, but checked her before she reached the floor, thus wringing from her a heart-rending shriek as her arms threatened to be torn from their sockets.

"Michael!" she screamed. "Michael!"

The sweat was pouring down my face and I raised my hand to touch Father Angelo. But by the light of the torches I saw him staring at Barbara with distorted features, great beads of sweat glistening on his pure, lofty forehead. He suffered as I did at this ghastly sight, and my hand sank powerless. When the executioner had repeated the process a few times, he lowered Barbara to the floor, where she lay with her face against the stones. Father Angelo asked her relentlessly whether she would now confess.

Barbara moaned, cried aloud to the Mother of God for succor, and said, "What have I to confess? I don't know what to say. For God's sake torture me no longer, noble gentlemen!"

Father Angelo, exasperated, nodded at the man, who now brought forward a twenty-pound stone weight. Having bound Barbara's feet together, he attached this weight to her toes. Now when she was again drawn up she shrieked most fearfully, her shoulders cracking and her toes stretching and stretching. At the first drop the shoulders were dislocated so that she remained hanging with her backward-twisted arms stretched vertically above her head. She uttered a fearful cry that died away in a low, continual moaning, causing my body to jerk and start as if in convulsions. Father Angelo asked in a hard voice whether she would confess now, but when she tried to speak she lost consciousness. She was then lowered and the executioner rubbed her temples with a rag dipped in vinegar, and moistened her lips with brandy.

Master Fuchs said eagerly, "Reverend Father, do you note that she has not shed a single tear? Witches cannot weep, and that is the third test."

The fact was noted in the record. Barbara came to her senses, moaning softly, but when Father Angelo bent over her to extract a confession she seemed to have lost the power of speech and could only move her head.

To hasten the business, Father Angelo ordered the executioner to increase the weight, but added, "Gag her, for she deafens us with her howling, and it is needless to make this examination so trying for the reverend fathers and myself."

The man pushed a hollow, pear-shaped, wooden gag between Barbara's jaws; this kept her mouth open and distended her cheeks, but did not restrict her breathing. When he had increased the weight by nearly double, he hauled her up again with the help of his fellow, made fast the rope, and stood by to wait.

Silence prevailed for a time in the torture chamber. Nothing was to be heard but the crackling of the torches and the soft whisper of the sand running through the secretary's hourglass. Barbara's moaning had ceased, but her gasping raised and lowered her bosom. I saw her slender toes hideously stretched, and her shoulders began to swell and turn black and blue about the joints. The executioner fetched a mug of ale from a niche in the wall, drank from it, and offered it to his assistant. One of the Dominicans began murmuring prayers and slipping the brown beads of his rosary through his fingers. At last I could no longer control myself. I broke into violent weeping, dashed forward to Barbara, and tried to take the burden of those terrible weights.

"Confess, Barbara, confess!" I pleaded in my cowardice. "Confess for the sake of our love, for I can bear no more."

Her green eyes opened and she stared dully down at me, but her look had no effect on me now, and I felt only the ghastly horror of this torment when I lifted her thin legs in my arms.

Father Angelo came up to me and loosened my grasp so that Barbara's twitching body sank again, to hang by its racked shoulder joints.

"Do you confess, witch?" he asked, with a blow of his fist on her breast. "If you do not, you will drag your husband Michael with you to perdition!"

Then Barbara moved her head to show that she wished to speak. The executioner stepped onto the ladder to pull the gag from her mouth. The corners of her lips were cracked and threads of blood trickled down her chin.

"Perhaps I am a witch," she gasped, "but let Michael alone. He knows nothing about me."

With a sigh of relief, Father Angelo ordered the executioner to release the rope until the weights rested on the floor, making it easier for Barbara to speak. Then she was questioned on each separate deposition; she acknowledged them all to be justified.

Father Angelo dictated for the record, "Question: Do you admit that you commanded the lightning to strike your betrothed? Answer: Yes. Question: Do you admit that by means of spells and sorcery you broke the assessor's arm? Answer: Yes."

190

I shall not repeat all the questions and answers, but I should mention that from her own mouth I heard that guided by Satan she had found me in the wood and that by means of a magic draught had compelled me to become her husband. At this point Father Angelo gave me a sideways glance and no doubt caught a gleam of doubt in my horror-stricken eyes, for he altered the phrasing of his final question.

"Of what was the draught composed with which you cast the spell upon him?"

Barbara hesitated and her dull glance strayed, but at last she gasped, "Holy water, ergot, and the juice of henbane."

At this I was forced to believe that she had bewitched me.

In a voice that was barely audible she added, "Forgive me, Michael!"

Next Father Angelo asked, "Do you acknowledge that you have given food and shelter to the devil in the shape of a black dog, which you used in your diabolical arts?"

Barbara's eyes flew open and she exclaimed, "No! Rael is an ordinary little dog and has done nothing wrong."

"We shall see. Now consider and weigh your words carefully, witch, for I must know when, where, and how you entered into your pact with the devil. Further, I must know when, where, and how he set his mark on your body, how often you have had sexual intercourse with him, and in what shape or shapes he then appeared. Answer these questions and you shall be left in peace. When you have abjured the devil and all his works, Holy Church will receive you back into the fold, forgive you your sins, and save your immortal soul from the fires of hell. Answer, witch!"

But Barbara was silent and only stared at Father Angelo in astonished bewilderment. This annoyed him and he repeated his questions, to which Barbara returned merely a firm denial of any pact with the devil, with a plea for mercy because she did not know what he meant. Once more the torturer hauled her up, and I had to press my hands over my ears because of the ghastly shrieks that were forced from her.

"She shall hang there until her memory clears," said Father Angelo angrily. "In the meantime we can examine the dog."

Father Angelo too held his hands to his ears and hastened up the stair. All followed him except the executioner's assistant, who, terrified, was left alone with Barbara and the jug of ale.

My head cleared in the fresh air and light of the tower room, and I shivered with cold as my sweat-drenched clothes hung to my skin.

The jailer brought wine, of which we all stood in great need. Father Angelo, emptying his goblet, sank back in a comfortable chair with a sigh of relief.

"Bring in the dog, Master Fuchs," he ordered.

But when Master Fuchs returned dragging the reluctant Rael on a leash, I hardly recognized my own animal. The gleaming black coat had been shaved off, and all the gray, naked skin was covered with festering sores. Rael caught my scent and struggled yelping and whining toward me. Master Fuchs allowed him to jump into my lap, where he sat quivering and whining, licking my face and then pressing his muzzle against my shoulder while I shed bitter tears onto his wounds. The little dog at least was innocent, I knew.

"This dog is named Rael," observed Master Fuchs, "which is undoubtedly a singular and heathenish name. Also it can perform many tricks. Yet the same can be said of the performing dogs in the market. I have, as my duty prescribed, examined the animal to the best of my ability and tried to make it speak, since if it were an incarnation of the devil it could certainly do so. I've whipped the dog several times a day and burned feathers dipped in sulphur on its back, but without eliciting any sound that could be taken as human speech. The needle test also gave only negative results."

Father Angelo surveyed the dog with repugnance and held his nose, for the poor creature's sores smelled evilly. He soon wearied of the discussion that followed and ordered the executioner to continue the examination, for he was not so fond of animals as was Master Fuchs. A cruel thrashing followed, which I was compelled to witness through my tears. At last cold common sense told me that though Barbara had been tortured into confession, yet not the most agonizing martyrdom could bring that wretched little dog to speak.

"Father Angelo!" I cried, "you'll never force that dog to talk, though you should torture it to death. And my wife is already condemned."

Master Fuchs concurred.

"All my experience pleads the dog's innocence. It will be better to use it merely as a witness against the witch, and afterward set it free."

Father Angelo and the other members agreed with this view, and Master Fuchs fetched a bowl of water which Rael greedily lapped up. The executioner took the leash.

Refreshed by the water, the dog raised its eyes to Father Angelo as he addressed it formally, saying, "Dog, whoever you may be! The Court of the Holy Inquisition calls upon you to give evidence. I would remind you of the rights and duties of a witness, and order you to state whether or not there is a witch in this room, and if so, to indicate the same."

The executioner unfastened the leash whereupon Rael with a low growl rushed at Master Fuchs and bit him in the calf. Master Fuchs howled and kicked the dog across the floor, but Rael returned to the attack, and his victim was hard put to it to defend himself until the executioner had tethered the animal once more. I cannot deny that this unexpected incident made a deep impression on all of us. The executioner crossed himself and stared strangely at Master Fuchs, who was rubbing his leg and swearing, and reviling the dog for its ingratitude to the man who had spoken up for it and saved its life.

To Father Angelo he said, "This testimony is worthless, and for the sake of my good name I ask that it may be omitted from the record. The creature bears malice because my duty obliged me to torture it. I demand that the test be made again in the presence of the witch, who shall be lowered to the floor so that the dog may catch her scent."

The worthy fathers debated this among themselves and were of the opinion that Master Fuchs had spoken wisely. No mention of this incident was made in the record. Nevertheless Father Angelo cast furtive glances at him when we had returned to the cellar and the executioner had lowered Barbara to the floor. At once the dog began whining, and when Father Angelo had once more charged it to give its evidence irrespective of kinship, friendship, or enmity, it dashed forward joyfully to Barbara and began licking her neck, hands, and face. A note was accordingly made to the effect that the dog of its own free will had denounced its mistress as a witch. The charge against it was at once withdrawn and the dog was acquitted.

Rael's eager tenderness had to some extent roused Barbara from her swoon. She opened her eyes and moaned. But I was at the end of my endurance. All went black, and I knew nothing more until I came to my senses in the tower room, to find the executioner's assistant rubbing my limbs and pouring brandy down my throat.

"What has happened?" I asked feebly.

"The witch has confessed everything," answered the man. "The third degree was too much for her, and she abjured the devil. She said that twice a year she flew to the Brocken on a fire-rake and there lay with the devil, who sometimes appeared like a black goat and sometimes like a white-faced man. It gave me the cold shivers to hear her. And then Master Fuchs sent me up here to bring you around, so I've missed a lot of it."

A little later Father Angelo came up to the tower room. There was sweat on his forehead and he was trembling with excitement.

"The witch has confessed, Michael! When she was only twelve she gave herself to the devil and received his mark. Her teacher was a certain witch who was burned ten years ago. Remember, Michael, if ever there has been the faintest doubt of the possibility of a pact with Satan, the unanimity of the evidence collected from different countries —the similarity of its smallest details—proves beyond question the existence of such pacts. This confession is another link in the chain which for centuries our Holy Church has been forging round the devil's kingdom."

"Good God in heaven!" I cried. "Are you still torturing her? Has she not confessed enough?"

He looked at me as if in doubt of my sanity.

"Obviously she must give the names of her confederates," said he. "This is the most difficult stage of all examinations, and I fear she will have to undergo the fourth and fifth degrees before all the required information has seeped from her. But we're ready to continue all night, if need be. For if we leave off now and wait until tomorrow, she may recant, as witches often do when they've drawn fresh strength from Satan during the night. I believe in your innocence, Michael, but of course we must question her about you, and also learn from her the names of all those she recognized at the Witches' Sabbaths on the Brocken. It will take time and patience."

At these words I fainted again and remained in a merciful swoon until late that night. I awoke to find Father Angelo standing over me with a torch.

"Wake up, my son! All is over. We have fought a splendid battle, and have won. You've been found innocent of any offense, and if you like you may see your wife to bid her farewell. She can do you no further harm. The Court has shown her mercy because of her full confession and repentence. So in handing her over to the secular arm we shall stipulate that her neck must be broken before she is burned, so that she may be spared the agony of fire."

He went, and I staggered weak-kneed down the steep stair with Rael under my arm and re-entered the cellar—that cellar which I see in nightmares to this day. For if bodily suffering is great under torture, the mental suffering of him who must look on helplessly at the torment of one dear to him is perhaps even more hideous.

A fire was burning on the open hearth of the torture chamber, and the executioner with practiced hand was tending Barbara, while with kindly words he sought to comfort her. For she wept softly, ceaselessly, inconsolably, though he had reset her shoulder joints and had bound them with pain-soothing vinegar compresses. The jailer was also present, and giving him money I asked for food and strong wine and more water for the dog.

Barbara's eyes half-opened and I felt her heart beating wildly against her ribs. When I gently caressed her racked ankles and toes, she started in agony. Presently the jailer reappeared, bringing supper in two steaming earthenware bowls. He also carried a pewter jug of wine under his arm, which so rejoiced the heart of the executioner that he called me a noble gentleman and thanked me for bearing him no ill will.

"I've sworn an oath not to take revenge," I told him, "and you're in no way to blame for what has happened. You do your duty by your masters—and I see you have a kind heart, for you're working as carefully and gently as a doctor to repair the ravages you have made. Eat and drink, friend. You've done a hard day's work that can certainly have given you no pleasure. Then leave us alone."

I tried to feed Barbara, but she could only drink a bowl of soup and a little wine. But Rael ate with a good appetite until his lean sides swelled, and he was so happy to be with us again that he kept interrupting his meal to run and lick Barbara's hand or nudge my knee.

When the executioner had ended his meal, he suggested with some diffidence and much belching that since I was there I might find it convenient to pay him his fee. He talked volubly of his poverty and his large family, but dared not look me in the eye when he claimed four gulden, of which one would go to his assistant.

To be rid of him I gave him five, which put the poor wretch beside himself with delight. He knelt and kissed my hand and called blessings upon myself and Barbara. Moreover, he left me his salves and medicines, and told me what to do for her when the fever began to rise. He assured me also that if, as he hoped, he was given the task of carrying out Barbara's sentence, he would sever her neck so quickly and deftly that she would hardly notice it. Just as he was leaving us, I remembered that I had not seen Master Fuchs since I had come out of my swoon, and being in dread lest he should come and take Barbara from me and put her in the stocks for the night, I asked what had become of him.

Rubbing his broad palms together in embarrassment, the executioner at last confided in a whisper that Master Fuchs was under arrest and was now in the stocks in the dungeon beneath the tower.

"It was like this," he explained. "We'd started on the fifth degree and I was thinking that all my skill was to be in vain, when the witch —I mean this noble lady—began giving the names of her confederates. She continued to deny that you had had any share whatsoever in the crime, sir. Instead, she said that several times both at Christmas and on Midsummer's Eve she had seen Master Fuchs on the Brocken; and it seems he must have been specially favored by Satan, for he allotted tasks to the other witches and also celebrated the Black Mass. She then swore in the names of all the saints that Master Fuchs was the greatest witch ever seen in German lands. Therefore, despite some misgivings and Master Fuchs's oaths and protestations, Father Angelo arrested him and put him in the stocks. This clever little dog, you remember, had already accused him. And when he'd been taken away, the scales seemed to fall from our eyes and we remembered all sorts of queer little things about Master Fuchs's behavior during past years, and I don't doubt that Father Angelo will be able to collect abundant evidence against him. It also explains how Master Fuchs came to know so much about witchcraft."

This story so amazed and bewildered me that I fancied I must be going out of my mind. How could he, a tireless witchhunter of twenty years' standing, be guilty of this crime? But the executioner merely shrugged his shoulders and replied that the devil's guile was beyond human understanding.

6

At last Barbara and I were alone together and I felt a mournful relief, although the air of the vault was foul with sweat and suffering, and the hideous instruments about us still spoke of Barbara's long hours of martyrdom. A good fire burned on the hearth and I had spread my cloak upon the floor for her, and now held her shaven head between my hands. Her widely opened eyes gleamed in the firelight and I could feel that her fever had begun to rise.

In a little while she said, "Michael, I don't believe in God any more." I crossed myself and told her not to say such terrible things, but to be quiet and think of her soul's salvation now that the Church had forgiven her—now that she was soon to die. She began laughing, softly at first, then shrilly and discordantly, until her emaciated body seemed convulsed.

"So even you believe I'm a witch, and in league with the devil! Then why do you hold me in your arms and comfort me?"

It was long before I could think of a logical reply. At last I said candidly, "I don't know. Perhaps because in the days of our happiness I held you thus, and now in this evil hour I long to hide you in my arms, although from your own lips I have heard that you're a witch."

The grave eyes that she bent upon me were bright with fever.

"You won't believe me, Michael, but I love you and have loved only you since first I saw you. Don't think too badly of me now that I'm to die and we shall never see one another again. But what oaths are holy enough to cleanse me in your eyes? None. I can only swear that as truly as I no longer believe in God or Holy Church or the Sacraments, I am no witch nor have I ever been in league with the devil, though I have sinned and played with things that should not be played with. I learned about evil herbs and their uses from old women and charcoal burners. I wished harm to the assessor for your sake—perhaps I wished harm to others also, when I was angry with them—and my malice seems to have been stronger than other people's. That is all my sorcery amounts to. One thing I desired with all my heart and will and strength, and that was that you should love me. And you did. But there was no sorcery in it. This I swear."

There was such earnestness in her words and look that I was compelled to believe her.

"I believe you, Barbara," I told her. "But that you should drag an innocent man down to perdition, and die with that sin upon your conscience! If what you say is true, then you never saw Master Fuchs on the Brocken, and you've borne false witness against him. And from what I've seen here tonight Father Angelo is sure to force a confession from him which will be perjury, and will damn his soul to hell."

Barbara uttered a low laugh and touched my cheek with the palm of her hand.

"You're a great simpleton, Michael. But I've always known that, and perhaps that's why I love you. If you'd undergone all the pains of hell here on earth, as I have, you wouldn't talk such nonsense. Father Angelo would not have released me while there was a spark of life left in me to suffer agony unless I'd given the name of some fellow criminal. I named Master Fuchs not only from private revenge but because I remembered the scores of wretches he has sent to the stake, and the hundreds of innocent people he has beggared by requiring them to take the oath of purgation. Master Fuchs dug his own pit. But perhaps you think I should have put an end to my suffering by naming you as my accomplice, for that was the other confession that Father Angelo was most anxious to extract from me!"

I had forgotten that, and cold sweat broke out on me at the thought of what might have happened if Barbara had not loved me so dearly.

"Forgive my stupidity," I said humbly. "You're good and loyal and wiser than I am. That you could endure such agonies rather than name me! In your place I must have betrayed you."

Barbara smiled then and kissed my hand with lips that were hot and dry.

"Why talk foolishness? The sands are running out. Be good to me, Michael, as you were in the days of our happiness. Hold me tightly, for the fever is merciful and I shall not mind the pain; and I'm frightened of the dark...."

7

My soul was filled with a melancholy peace when next day I called upon Father Angelo. My anguish was dulled, for I felt that whatever happened to Barbara now could only be good in comparison with what she had been through. And there is a limit to what man can feel and suffer. That limit passed, the agony bursts the confines of the soul and flows out into a wide, still sea, and then the suffering is over.

In no other way can I account for my calmness that bright morning. I was resigned even to Barbara's death, and the knowledge that neither worldly power and wealth, nor even the Emperor's command, could avert her fate once Holy Church had her in its hands only confirmed my peace of mind.

But Father Angelo was anything but calm. He was pacing to and fro in the Prince-Bishop's study, haggard from sleeplessness and anxiety. When we had spoken a little of Barbara, his own troubles and his weariness overwhelmed him once more.

Bursting into tears, he said, "Michael, Michael, I am lost! My zeal for the Church has been my undoing. Master Fuchs, my trusted colleague, a witch! At first I could not believe it, and thought it some hallucination sent by the devil—some infirmity of my brain—but my eyes are opened. I see now the full import of this most frightful affair."

"But then why was Master Fuchs so vigorous in the persecution of witches? Why did he betray them? One could as readily suspect the Prince-Bishop himself. Master Fuchs is his devoted servant."

Father Angelo wiped the sweat from his forehead, blew his nose in his wide sleeve, and with a nervous glance about him said, "Master Fuchs, as the devil's lieutenant, was no doubt charged with the immediate pursuit and arrest of all witches who for some reason had offended his satanic majesty. After this I shall not dare to trust anyone. Even your reference to His Highness alarms me, for last night his behavior to me was by no means such as befits a Prince of the Church."

I asked diffidently if Master Fuchs could be convicted on the strength of Barbara's accusation alone, and he reminded me that this had been supported by the dog's behavior. Moreover, a nocturnal search at Master Fuchs's house had revealed all too plainly the existence of further evidence. A woolen doll had been found there, worn from much use. Also a bright-colored bird in a cage, which talked like a man, swore, and shrieked "A stoup of ale, a stoup of ale!" until one of the searchers, an ignorant man-at-arms, wrung its neck.

"But His Highness the Prince-Bishop is very greatly displeased with me," he went on. "Chiefly because I neglected to exact an oath of silence from all who were present at the time. Soon the whole diocese will be buzzing with the news that Master Fuchs has been convicted of witchcraft. The Bishop says this will bring incalculable shame and disgrace upon the Church, and foment heretical disturbance; and at last he threatened to report me to the Curia. In the end I had no choice but to remind him of the authority vested in me by the Holy Father himself. This fortunately sobered him and he said no more."

Father Angelo was now striding back and forth across the room, wringing his hands.

"Michael, my son, you know I seek only the truth, and if Master Fuchs is indeed a witch then he must be burned as such, irrespective of temporal conditions and events—although I can see that as things are today it will do the Church more harm than good. The Church has always to exercise a certain diplomacy in dealing with temporal matters, but that is something that concerns the papal legates. I can only follow the dictates of my conscience, wherever they may lead me. Let some astute legate unravel the tangle I have made, and I will return to the peace of the cloister and labor there like the humblest lay brother until my life's end."

With some hesitation I asked him whether he thought confession under torture was worth all its attendant trouble and suffering.

This halted him in his march, and staring at me as if I were not quite right in the head, he asked, "Michael, do you believe in God?"

I crossed myself and declared my faith.

"Then you must see how terrible a sin it would be to let a soul fall into the seething caldrons of hell if by means of bodily suffering— which is as nothing in comparison—it may be won for heaven. In submitting poor wretches to the pains of the Inquisition, my heavy task is lightened by the conviction that I am doing them the best service one man may do another."

I pitied him in his honest distress, and felt no hatred for him because I saw that he acted in good faith.

I asked him whether I might see Barbara again before her execution, but he forbade this positively, saying, "I believe in your honesty and worthy motives, Michael Pelzfuss, but your wife must no longer be distracted by worldly thoughts. She must spend what time remains to her in prayer and in acts of contrition. The date of the execution depends on the Prince-Bishop alone, who must decide whether to proclaim it all over the diocese or only in your own town, so that people may gather round the pyre and witness to their edification the unshakable power of the Church, and meditate on the state of their own souls."

To my question about the total costs, he replied, "The sum shall be as moderate as possible. I myself claim nothing but your prayers, though you may if you wish bestow in my name some lasting memento to the monastery. The two other members of the tribunal must be paid their statutory fee, and I fear that the secretary's account may be somewhat high, since he used much ink and paper for his record. However, I shall try to deduct some part of the expenses from Master Fuchs's estate. Then there is the verdict to pay for, and the signature of the Emperor's deputy, but apart from that I fancy there will be no other outlay than for your wife's board and lodging at the prison up to the day of execution, and of course the price of a load of the best birchwood. At a sober estimate, I believe twenty-five gulden should suffice."

Knowing from this that I had enough money to discharge all debts, I sighed with relief and in my gratitude I kissed the hem of his habit. It would have been most repugnant to me to beg help from Barbara's

200

father. Once more I sought permission to visit my wife, and was refused. Then I asked whether I might speak to Master Fuchs. Father Angelo was taken aback at this request, but after some reflection he approved of the idea, as it might lead to a voluntary confession. Just before I left, he seized me by the arm.

His features were distorted in a horrible grimace and the sweat stood on his forehead as he said hoarsely, "Wait! A thought has struck me—whether of God or the devil I do not know—but I see a chance of saving the Church from open disgrace. It occurred to me that we might introduce a length of rope or a knife into the prison. . . . If he were to do away with himself, it would both prove his guilt and stifle scandal. I quake to think where the road I have begun to tread will lead me! Yet if Master Fuchs at the devil's instigation should commit suicide before tomorrow, you will have earned seven gulden, Michael."

I promised to do what I could in the good cause, and Father Angelo gave me the rope from about his waist and a small, sharp penknife from the Bishop's writing table.

On coming out into the courtyard I found that I was very hungry, and so before returning to the prison I stepped into the Bishop's kitchen, where at a courteous word from me a pretty maidservant brought me bread and cheese and half a cold partridge, and a tankard of frothing ale. Then I crossed the courtyard. In response to my knocking, the jailer opened the iron-studded door, and taking up a horn lantern he led the way down to Master Fuchs through the stinking darkness of the prison.

8

We clambered and stumbled over heaps of filth, and now and then I heard rats jumping away and splashing into the pools. It was perhaps as well that the lantern dispelled so little of the darkness, for even as it was the place appalled me, and coming in from the fresh air I feared suffocation from its most ghastly stench.

At last the jailer raised his lantern and I beheld Master Fuchs sitting on the ground with his arms and legs extended and clamped into the small holes of the stocks. Being thus helpless, he had befouled himself and sat in his own pool. But I felt no great pity for him when I remembered that Barbara had sat alone in the dark for weeks, in the same rigid discomfort. Indeed, the thought made me tremble so much that I could barely control my voice.

"Is that you, Michael Pelzfuss?" he demanded angrily. "Have you come to mock me in my degradation? Is this morning or evening? Dig my purse out of my belt and get me some food and drink, for I'm famished, though I never thought I could swallow a morsel, so great has been my bitterness and my righteous indignation."

On the authority of Father Angelo I ordered the jailer to release the commissary's hands. The man murmured somewhat, but turned the rusty screws. Together we raised the upper beam of the stocks to allow the prisoner to withdraw his hands. He rubbed his wrists, ejaculated a couple of coarse oaths, and showed us how rats had nibbled his fingertips during the night. They were so raw that he could not undo the close-drawn string of his purse.

Having helped him and sent the jailer after food and ale, I said, "Matters are serious, Master Fuchs. Terrible testimonies are being collected against you. You're said to be the devil's steward and chief priest, and nothing can save you from the stake."

He crossed himself with a somber curse and said, "It's what I feared, and I suppose I must swallow the devil's brew with a good grace. But upon my soul I'm curious to know what proof has been established against me."

"*Pro primo,*" I said, "there is my dog's evidence."

"And that's my thanks for trying to save its life! I do believe the animal's possessed, after all."

"*Pro secundo,* there is my wife's evidence, extracted under the fifth degree, as you're aware."

To this he made no reply, but pushed the end of his beard into his mouth and began feverishly chewing it.

"*Pro tertio,* there has been found, carefully hidden in your house, a human effigy of wool, which had evidently been used for devilish purposes."

"That was a doll—a doll belonging to my little daughter who died of smallpox. My youngest and dearest daughter—her name was Margaretha—I kept it in memory—" his voice was stifled by weeping.

"Furthermore, there was found in your house a demon in the shape of a talking bird which is said to have demanded a stoup of ale from the Bishop's men-at-arms, one of whom was frightened and wrung its neck. Of this there are many witnesses."

Master Fuchs wept yet more bitterly and said in a broken voice, "My beautiful parrot! Have the ruffians killed it? I bought it from a wandering Spaniard who said he had conquered a city in Columbus's

202

Indies with some fellow called Cortez—there were pyramids, he said, and a million people with feathers on their heads. . . . But I have other birds, Michael. Who will feed them and give them water now?"

"I can do that for you. But you must see that all this evidence will gather volume like an avalanche and crush you beneath it. Father Angelo begs you to make voluntary confession, so that he need not torture you unduly."

Master Fuchs reflected for some time, sighed heavily, and said at last, "Fetch me pen, ink, and paper. I know the fate in store for me; I know that it's inevitable. Yet I shall find consolation in calling to mind every soul who has ever harmed me. They are many, Michael, for the life of a bishop's commissary is no bed of roses. I will now make a note of everyone who has struck me, cheated me in business or with loaded dice, emptied his tankard in my face, or otherwise made himself objectionable. Above all, I shall remember His Highness the Prince-Bishop, who has so basely abandoned me to my fate, and many other ecclesiastical dignitaries who have laid hands upon my rightful share of witches' property. I have much to recollect, Michael Pelzfuss, and therefore require pen and paper. Being no longer young, I cannot altogether rely upon my memory, and I do not mean to omit anyone."

"Jesus, Mary!" I cried. "Do you mean you will accuse the Prince-Bishop himself of being in league with the devil?"

"Certainly. But first I shall inform against Father Angelo, since it is he who in a mean and dastardly fashion has brought this disaster upon me."

I gasped, and pressed hands to forehead in an attempt to regain my wits. I now saw the full implications of this affair. I saw that Father Angelo had dislodged a boulder whose career he could not halt—the beginning of a landslide that would overwhelm and bury the last remnant of the Church's authority in a land already seething with evangelistic ideas. It was clear that this frightful scandal must be averted at all costs, and that Father Angelo's inspiration at the eleventh hour might yet save everything.

At this point the jailer returned with food and drink, and Master Fuchs ate with a good appetite. Deep draughts of the strong ale refreshed his memory, and he slapped his forehead now and then as he recalled some hitherto forgotten name.

When he had eaten his fill, I laid my trembling hand on his shoulder and said, "Master Fuchs, what will you give me in return for a painless release—an escape from torture and the stake—so that as a repentant sinner you may commend your soul to God's mercy?"

He answered soberly, "Michael Pelzfuss, for such a service I would bless you to my last breath. You have little to thank me for—although your wife is most certainly a witch and has taken a more frightful revenge upon me than could well have been imagined. But perhaps my blessing is not worth very much, so I will tell you that under a loose brick in my cellar floor you'll find a purse containing almost seventy gold pieces, some of them good Rhenish gulden and Venetian ducats. For your sake I hope that the Bishop's ruffians have not discovered this hiding place—and if you see anything else at home for which you could find a use, take it for good measure. But if they have already affixed the episcopal seal to my door, be careful, or you may be charged with theft. Promise me to care for my birds and either give them away to good children or set them free, as you think best."

He spoke ever more earnestly, and seemed to fear that I was tormenting him with false hopes out of revenge for the evil he had done me. He told of a splendid harquebus he had, of the new Imperial pattern, which I might take if I pleased; also some silver drinking cups and a Latin Bible. But I was afraid of getting into serious trouble for taking what was now Church property, and he was at some pains to overcome my misgivings. He promised to furnish me with written authority to remove goods from his house up to the value of fifty gulden, and gave me also much prudent advice.

His offers did not greatly elate me, however, for worldly possessions seemed but vanity to me now that Barbara was to die. Yet reason told me that time would pass and I should soon be in need of money. So I thanked him, and with the writing materials that I carried at my belt he made out the promised authority. I gave him Father Angelo's rope and the Bishop's knife, telling him he could choose the manner of his death—he might hang or he might sever the veins of his wrists. He had until morning to decide.

Master Fuchs grasped the rope in one hand and the knife in the other.

"You've given me a hard nut to crack, Michael!" he exclaimed. "I don't know which to choose. Ordinary hanging is impossible, for my feet are fixed in the stocks. Nor is the slow chill of bleeding to death very attractive. If I might have a bucket of hot water in which to hold my hands while I cut the veins it would not be so bad—but as you

204

say I have plenty of time to consider the matter, and this will serve to pass the time until cockcrow."

I was on the point of leaving him to his musings when in sudden fear he detained me. His fortitude had trickled away and I saw only a dirty, frightened old man whose beard quivered as he talked.

"Suicide is a mortal sin, Michael. But the torture awaiting me is comparable with the pains of hell, as I who have so often witnessed it should know. Say that you believe God will forgive me if I take my own life because of my human frailty—say that Christ has redeemed even me with His blood, as He has all other poor sinners!"

I replied that I believed in the justice of God, since it was hard to imagine life without it, and added that Christ had died on the cross as much for him as for anyone. Master Fuchs was relieved.

"And indeed," he said, "my share of worldly happiness has been small enough since I lost all my children by smallpox in the same week. And if as you say I shall escape hell and win my way from purgatory to the brightness of heaven it will be like throwing a double six. Pray for me, Michael, when I'm dead, and have a Mass said for my soul. You can afford it now."

To come out into the fresh air of the courtyard was like emerging from the underworld into paradise. The jailer unlocked the door for me, and I was most happy to learn from him that Barbara was sleeping and that the swelling about her joints was already partly reduced, thanks to the executioner's most excellent ointments. I gave him another gulden, which brought tears of gratitude to his eyes. But he seemed dismayed when I ordered him to procure a bucket of hot water for Master Fuchs, as he desired to wash. This the man considered damning proof of Master Fuchs's guilt, washing being unnatural and unhealthful. I would not argue with him over this, as it was a much debated question on which even the learned were disagreed. I repeated my order sternly and hastened to Father Angelo, whom I found at his devotions in the Bishop's study.

He broke off, and rising from his knees greeted me in an agony of anxiety and impatience. It seemed as well to keep him in salutary uncertainty, so I said that before the following morning I hoped to have persuaded Master Fuchs to see reason and leave this world of his own accord, thereby declaring his guilt.

"He is indeed a dangerous witch," I said, "and I tremble to think of the revelations he may make when put to the question. Half Germany may be in a tumult if his confessions are put on record."

"Michael," said Father Angelo, "if you will do your best in this for Holy Church and for me, I swear that I will make a barefoot pilgrimage to Rome, there to lay all before the Holy Father and accept the punishment which the Church ordains for me. This man must be removed."

I showed him Master Fuchs's authority to collect certain property from his house, but he demurred. It was a matter for the Prince-Bishop to approve, and His Highness was at present indisposed as a result of this crisis. Only after much argument could I persuade him to beg an audience for me. He went at last, and through the thickness of several walls I could hear His Highness bellowing for me to present myself immediately. When I entered his room and approached the bed, he thrust the curtains aside and protruded his face, purple with rage.

"Master Fuchs was the best witch commissary in all the German states, and added considerably to the revenues of this diocese!" he roared. "He was indispensable, were he a thousand times the servant of Satan. If we can clear up this matter for fifty gulden, then let us do it. Give me a quill!"

I hastened to dip my pen in my inkhorn and handed it to him. Hissing with fury, he scrawled his signature on Master Fuchs's authority and bellowed at the secretary to take five gulden from me for the seal. When I would have kissed his hand, he dealt me a stinging box on the ear.

"See that everything this filthy-booted fellow takes is valued in the presence of a notary," he said. "And whatever the value may be in excess of fifty gulden he is to pay into my coffers against a receipt. An inventory of Fuchs's effects must be drawn up without delay. And now you may all betake yourselves to the nethermost pit, and leave me to get some rest and to pray God to relieve Holy Church of such a blockhead as Father Angelo!"

The secretary would not accept the five gulden, but begged to accompany me to the commissary's house in order to make the inventory. He was a pleasant young man with hungry eyes, and he seemed inclined to further my interests. We conversed amicably as we went our way, and halted at a tavern for a cup of wine before proceeding to Master Fuchs's little dwelling, whose gables were squeezed between two great merchants' houses. We sent the Bishop's guard away to drink ale at our expense, and entered. From the rooms above came the twittering of birds, and there in the embrasures of the windows hung many cages made of twigs or of gilded wire, in which the birds hopped cheerfully from perch to perch. All else in the house was upside down. The bedclothes had been tossed into a heap on the floor, the bolsters had been ripped up, and the locks of coffers had been forced. The Bishop's secretary shook his head at the devastation, and began absent-mindedly to finger a silver tankard that had caught his eye.

I announced that I would fetch seed and water for the birds, and mentioned as I went that Master Fuchs had promised me a Latin Bible. Whereupon the secretary said eagerly that he would begin looking for it. I went down to the cellar with a candle and soon found the loose brick and the heavy purse beneath it. With a sigh of relief I took it and returned to the kitchen, where I discovered many varieties of birdseed, each in its little box.

The most beautiful of the birds I gave to two well-dressed little children whom I heard laughing in the street. They clapped their hands for joy and promised to take good care of them. The rest I set free from the upper window, though they seemed shy of their liberty and I had to shake the cages before they would fly.

The silver tankard had vanished from the shelf, but I observed a corresponding bulge in the secretary's gown. For this reason I made no bones about collecting two small silver goblets and a worn wine cup engraved with armorial bearings. Next, avoiding one another's eyes, we began examining the commissary's wardrobe, which was of the finest. At last the secretary took the bull by the horns and pointed out that if all these splendid garments, to say nothing of a valuable collection of pewter, were to be listed in the inventory, we should at once be suspected of having stolen something. Master Fuchs, he added, had lived a very solitary life because of his sinister profession, and it was therefore impossible that anyone should know the extent or quality of his possessions. The Bishop's guards who had already turned the place upside down had every reason to keep silence, since the money-box had been forced. Not a coin was to be seen anywhere, nor were there any candlesticks, which must certainly have been of silver. He further mentioned a Jew of his acquaintance who would be willing to turn much of this into ready money and could hold his tongue, avaricious and ill natured though he was.

I approved of his good sense, and so it was with certain reservations that we drew up the inventory, in which my inheritance to the value of fifty gulden was duly noted. This comprised the silver vessels I have mentioned, a woolen gown, the Latin Bible, and the big harquebus and rest. With this went bullet bag, powder measure, and silver-plated powderhorn, also a belt with wooden cups by which powder charges could be parceled out beforehand in the modern manner. Thus the gun could be quickly loaded seventeen times in succession. Over and above these listed items, I took a costly fur cloak. For some other garments, the pewter, the feather bed, and a couple of handsome chairs, the Jew whom we had summoned paid us seventy-two gulden, though only after much tearing of his hair and invocations to Abraham. Of this money I received half, and so of a sudden became a well-to-do man.

By our joint efforts we succeeded in compiling a respectable and convincing inventory. Nothing was lacking which a man of solitary habits would require, nor did anyone ever question its accuracy. This and the bargaining with the Jew took us until evening, when we returned together, firm friends, to the Bishop's palace. Here the secretary invited me to an excellent dinner, thanked me for my tact and fine feelings, and offered me lodging for the night, also any girl among the Bishop's servants whom I might fancy. I thanked him, saying that lodging alone would suffice me. Having assuaged my hunger, I left him to the girl who had served us. Rather drunk, I hastened to the prison with a basket of pears and peaches and grapes which I had taken from the table for Barbara, and went at once to tell Master Fuchs that I had attended to his birds.

Master Fuchs had provided himself with most brilliant illumination, and did not blush for the eight wax candles that were burning about him. Four were stuck with melted wax on the upper beam of the stocks; the other four were disposed among the dishes and on the rim of the bucket. He had enjoyed a copious meal and was as drunk as a lord; his hiccups were so violent that they sounded worse than oaths. I suggested he should drink no more ale, as the hiccups disturbed our conversation. He readily took my advice and we drank wine together from a pewter mug.

When the bottom of this mug became visible, I ventured to remind him tactfully that morning was near and that the cock would soon be heard crowing from the courtyard. He thanked me for calling this troublesome matter to his attention, but in his exalted mood he explained that he dared not commit the mortal sin of suicide, and indeed was rather looking forward to the vexation he would cause at his trial, and to seeing the Bishop's long face when accused of being in league with the devil.

I was in despair. All my efforts seemed to have been brought to nought by the commissary's drunkenness. For a long while I spoke persuasively of the last great service which he could do the Church to crown his twenty years and more of faithful work on its behalf, and of the possibility of saving his immortal soul and even shortening his time in purgatory. My words had some effect but, maudlin now, he moaned that he had not the courage, and that rope and knife were equally repugnant to him.

"But if you really want me to die, Michael," he added slyly, "do the business for me. No one will ever know. They'll think I took my own life, and only Almighty God will see that I am not guilty of suicide."

His proposal shocked me at first, but I was by now uncommonly drunk, and the astonishing dialectical eloquence of wine persuaded me that his request was no more than reasonable. He put his hands in the water and I severed the veins of his wrists; he shrank and cried out, and then the pain was over. He thanked me, and when I had raised the tankard to his lips for a last draught, he asked me to leave him to pray among his candles. And so I bade him farewell.

9

For many days I felt ill and forsaken of God and man, for though I did not grieve inordinately over Barbara's fate, knowing that death would come as a release after her sufferings, yet I missed her unspeakably and would have given anything to be with her during those last days. But Father Angelo was adamant. He and the other fathers who were preparing Barbara for death were her only company. All I could do for her was to send good food, cakes, sweetmeats, and wine, which the jailer carried to her at night after the monks had returned to their monastery. I did not write to her, as she could not read; but I hoped that the delicacies I sent, though she might have no stomach for them, would show that I thought of her and loved her.

I now lodged at the Black Swan, to which my baggage had been taken, including my share of Master Fuchs's possessions. The greater part of my money—in all about a hundred gulden—I had invested with the agent of the great house of Fugger. I had not long to wait, for the Memmingen city council sent word that the Prince-Bishop himself, together with the Emperor's deputy, must be responsible for Barbara's execution, there being in Memmingen so much resentment against the Church that the council dared not proceed with any ceremonial witih burning. In the future, Memmingen would exercise its privilege as a free city and deal with its own witches without alien intervention. Thenceforth the Bishop's commissary would have no business there.

His Highness, angered by this, decreed that Barbara's execution should take place with religious ceremonial on the following Sunday after High Mass, in the Cathedral square, as a public example and warning. On Saturday I watched from my window the stacking of the birchwood and the building of the scaffold. On Sunday morning I was allowed to visit Barbara in her cell, but only in the presence of Father Angelo and the two other members of the tribunal. I could do no more than embrace her and mingle my tears with hers.

"Michael, my dearest, you remember what I told you?" she asked.

"I remember," I answered, but at that moment Father Angelo separated us, saying that we should rather rejoice than mourn, since Holy Church had taken Barbara back into its bosom and was the surety for her eternal bliss. They sent me away, and while monks sang psalms in the courtyard Father Angelo heard Barbara's confession and gave her absolution. He then administered the Viaticum and Extreme Unction, the Cathedral bells began ringing, and she was led out under the open sky.

It was now autumn. Fruit trees were laden, and the blue heavens were boundless and filled with light. Barbara and her black following of monks looked somehow small and shrunken to my eyes, as if I were beholding them from a distance or from above. I wept no longer, but followed meekly in the rear of the procession. Barbara, with uncovered shaven head and wearing the coarse garment of the penitent, leaned upon Father Angelo as she walked the short distance from the courtyard to the Cathedral square. The monks sang very beautifully in harmony, and a great crowd of people had collected, among them country folk from the outlying districts who stood in fear and silence; for the Bishop's cavalry and foot soldiers had surrounded the market place to prevent hostile demonstrations.

The people liked to see witches burned, but the robes of the priests aroused their resentment, and a murmur ran through the crowd when the canons of the Cathedral emerged from the doorway led by the Prince-Bishop, who was arrayed in gorgeous blue and red vestments, with precious stones sparkling in his crosier and pectoral cross.

Holy Church in all its majesty was in attendance to witness Barbara's execution beneath the mighty towers of the Cathedral. But she mounted the scaffold alone. I was near enough to distinguish the features of her pale little face, and to note that she staggered, giddy from the unwonted fresh air and the walk from the prison. I fancy she was in a daze and hardly knew what was taking place. Yet she looked out over the crowd as if seeking something. I raised both arms above my head and she saw me, smiled, and nodded slightly, and for the last time I saw the green eyes, now more beautiful than ever before. She was again the loveliest of women to me. In a wave of fathomless anguish I realized that I should never hold her in my arms again.

But this moment was short. The executioner stepped up onto the platform behind her, bound her hands, and bade her kneel at the block. The Prince-Bishop tried to signal to him, but the fellow seemed stricken blind and deaf. At one blow he severed Barbara's head from her body so that she was spared all suffering; thus the good man fulfilled his promise. The intention had been for her to stand waiting while charge and sentence were read out to all present, but the executioner had spared her this ordeal, for which I was deeply thankful to him, and paid him more than he asked.

The belated herald hastened up the steps and read out a very long and monotonous proclamation, while Barbara's blood dripped down on the stones of the market place.

Hatred filled my heart—hatred so keen, so cold, that it inflicted its wound upon myself. I did not hate Father Angelo, nor the black-clad monks, nor the Prince-Bishop in his splendor. No, for the blame was not theirs; they were blind servants. Blame lay with Holy Church for its cruel abuse of power. The Pope alone was guilty of Barbara's suffering and death. While the herald read out the proclamation, I pushed my way forward to the scaffold and cupped my hands beneath the last drops of Barbara's blood. And I swore in my heart a terrible oath that I would fight the Pope's power to my last breath, and would allow myself no rest until Clement VII had been driven from the Papal Throne and had become a homeless, defenseless fugitive, while the might of Rome lay beaten to the ground.

I know not whether it was God or Satan who put that oath into my mind. Never before had I nursed such thoughts. Yet I believe it was from God, for He allowed me to perform it, and my desire was to be made reality before three years had passed.

But I could not know that then, and I felt alone and impotent in my hatred when the executioner heaved Barbara's body onto the pyre and rolled the head between her knees. The fire caught the birchwood, the smoke billowed out, and the smell that presently reached me bereft me of strength. I fell to my knees upon the stones and buried my face in my hands.

BOOK 7.

The Twelve Articles

I

HAVING discharged my debts to the Bishop and the council and paid the executioner his fees, I was ready to leave the city, and I hoped never to behold its spires again. I fetched my dog from the jailer, who had been looking after it, and hired a carter to drive us and my traveling chest to Memmingen.

My poor dog was wild with joy to see me. The jailer told me it had lain faithfully at my wife's feet during her fever until the good fathers drove it away. Barbara had treated its sores with the executioner's healing ointments and it was already well on the way to recovery. A new coat was growing from the shaven skin, but it was gray, not black; and the animal was still so weak that it preferred to lie in my lap rather than run by the roadside sniffing at all the good smells. When I held the poor beast in my arms I felt that Barbara was near, and so we comforted one another in our misery.

But in my sorrow and loneliness I yearned for some friend with whom I could speak freely and find consolation. For the first time in many months I remembered Andy, who had entered the Emperor's service and had gone to the wars in Italy. Although his term of service had long elapsed, he had not returned. He, if anyone, would have eased me, for he spoke my native language. He was a foolish fellow, though, and without me to guide him would no doubt have run headlong into the jaws of death.

As soon as I reached Memmingen I went to seek out Sebastian Lotzer. But I found only his father, who was deeply concerned for him; and he did not spurn me, even though my wife had been burned as a witch.

"We live in evil times, Michael Pelzfuss," he said, "and as you know the peasants in many districts are banding together against their overlords. They have even sacked monasteries and convents. The speech and behavior of my misguided son brought such disgrace upon me that I was compelled to show him the door. All I know of him is that he went out among the villages with Luther's heretical Bible under his arm and a beggar's staff in his hand, showering threats and abuse on his old father. The times are topsy-turvy. You've always been a decent, well-mannered young man, Michael Pelzfuss, but I cannot understand what possesses the youth of today that they should seek the overthrow of good order. Ever since the days of heathendom, our forefathers have toiled to build up our excellent social structure, in which everyone has his place. The son succeeds to his father's trade; laws, customs, and guild rules regulate a man's life from the cradle to the grave; and Holy Church cares for our poor souls. Everything has its price. Peasants pay tax and tithe and do their field service, even sins are assessed at rates laid down by the Church—the very stuff and cut of our clothes are determined for each according to his rank and standing by our sumptuary laws. No one during his whole life need feel the smallest uncertainty on any point. And now a few hotheads must try to wreck all."

I observed that the world was by no means as good a place as Master Lotzer seemed to think, and that I had already witnessed all too much violence, agony, poverty, and despair.

He agreed, but added, "A man-made order is of course faulty and imperfect, even though its foundations be divine, and we cannot avoid a certain unrest from time to time, any more than we can escape sickness and death. But such disturbance is a little thing compared with the blessings our great social order brings us. There can be no greater madness than to undermine the Church with false doctrines, for the Church is our foundation. If that falls, all falls, and the Day of Judgment is at hand."

I did not want to quarrel with Master Lotzer, but only to prolong the conversation, because I was lonely and forsaken and his room was

213

a snug, safe place in that raw, autumn weather. So we spoke for some time of these matters until I could not in decency stay longer, and then I bade him farewell.

The bailiff and his wife had moved back into the cellar of the town hall, and were using our bed and our other few sticks of furniture. But I would not reproach them; I had no heart to reproach anyone, and out of the kindness of their hearts they housed me for the night. It gave me a pang to see how Rael rejoiced at being in our old home again, and how he searched eagerly for Barbara until he was tired and fell asleep beside me.

I resolved to leave Memmingen. My chest I entrusted to the care of the bailiff, who promised to be answerable for it, being grateful to me for not causing him or his wife any unpleasantness. But as I was going through my effects before locking the chest, I came upon a Venetian mirror that I had taken from the commissary's house. Looking into it, I saw that my hair was matted, my cheeks hollow, and my eyes staring, and thought it no wonder that people turned in the streets to gaze after me.

"Michael Furfoot," said I to my reflection, "who are you, what do you want, and whither are you bound?"

But my reflection made no answer. I spoke for it and said, "Michael Furfoot, you're a dishonored, baseborn weakling from far-away Åbo. You've brought nothing but disaster upon all who have loved you, and, deservedly or undeservedly, you are accursed. Your mother drowned herself because of your shameful birth, and if you go home only the gallows will bid you welcome, because you were gullible and served ambitious men and dreamed dreams of a united and powerful North. What is it you want, Michael Furfoot?"

Rael, sensing my despair, came and nosed at my arm, and the dog's compassion so moved me that I smashed the valuable mirror to splinters. Pressing my face to Rael's warm coat, I wept most bitterly, while he licked my ear and neck to comfort me.

"Where shall we go, little one?" I asked, and getting no response but a wondering stare, I answered my own question. "Let us seek your mistress, for I think she will give us good advice."

I had money, enough to enter some university and live frugally for two years or more. But that salt had lost its savor. Or I could have resumed my broken pilgrimage; but that was hazardous since the fall of Rhodes, and having sworn that rash oath at the scaffold I lacked the will to go.

214

I locked my chest and set out in search of Barbara, taking with me the clothes I stood up in, a change of linen, the Latin Bible, and Master Fuchs's gun. I little thought that I was not the only man to wander forth thus aimlessly during those late autumn days. Sebastian had gone in this way, and many forsook home, workshop, school, and plough without fully understanding the urge that drove them forth.

At first I went to the town where Barbara's uncle lived and where she had nursed me back to health, and thence to the woods and the place where she had found me. The ground was strewn with acorns, a wild pig grunted in the thicket, and the air was damp with autumn. There in the forest I called Barbara's name aloud. "Barbara, my love, my all—come back! You promised we should meet here whatever happened, and I have come to look for you—"

But only the echo answered my cries, and Rael whined uneasily and howled the grievous howl of death at hearing me call Barbara's name.

Nearby stood a disused charcoal-burner's hut, and there I settled in for the winter. I would walk into the town to buy food whenever I happened to think of it, but mostly I sat reading my Latin Bible. Sometimes a wildcat would slink up to the hut, climb a tree out of Rael's reach, and start down at us with glinting, yellow-green eyes; and I would call it Barbara. I think I went out of my mind that winter, for I heeded neither hunger nor cold. I let my beard grow and my clothes became sooty and ragged.

Snow fell from time to time, and I even heard wolves howling in the forest. Then the snow melted, the winds of spring began to blow, and white flowers budded in the glades. More peaceful now, I went for long walks, seeking Barbara no longer. It was then she came to me; I felt her nearness in the sigh of the wind, the softness of her lips on the petals of flowers, and I glimpsed her in the somber glow of sunset. Then I wept for joy, knowing I was whole again. Having put myself into as good a trim as I might, I returned to the habitations of men. By the middle of February I was once more in Memmingen.

2

I did not come alone. This region of Germany was in an uproar and armed bands of peasants were pouring along all the roads. Sebastian Lotzer was once more in his father's house and his followers controlled the city, the council now having no say in anything and making no decisions without first consulting Sebastian or his scatterbrained lieutenants. When I entered the furrier's house I found Sebastian unfolding a red and white silken banner on which the cross of St. Andrew was sewed.

He rushed to me with open arms saying, "You've come at the right moment, Michael Pelzfuss, for today we nail our flag to its staff that the world may be changed and God's justice prevail in Germany!"

No rags for Sebastian now! He was wearing a velvet doublet with silver buttons, as before, although his standing did not entitle him to it. He was very handsome in his fiery enthusiasm, and his wide-set eyes shone as he began to read and expound the twelve articles that he had formulated. On the basis of these and in reliance on God's justice, and with the help of artisans and peasants, he planned to found a new order. I was not his only listener; the room was full of civic dignitaries, well-to-do farmers, and members of Sebastian's evangelical circle. This is what he read:

"1. Every congregation to have the right to appoint and if necessary dismiss its priest, and the priest to preach the Word of God only, without human inventions.

"2. The priest's stipend to be paid from the greater corn tithes and the balance to be used for the benefit of the poor of the parish.

"3. Cattle tithes to be abolished, since the Lord God created cattle for the use of man.

"4. Serfdom to be abolished, being irreconcilable with the Word of God. Christ redeemed every man with His blood, be he prince or shepherd; therefore we are and will be free, and recognize no authority beyond what is reasonable and Christian.

"5. God created the beasts of the field, the birds of the air, and the fish of the streams for man's benefit. Therefore hunting, fishing, and fowling to be free to all.

"6. Forests to return to common ownership, that every man may take from them firewood and building timber according to his needs.

"7. Days of field service and tasks with which the overlords have increasingly burdened the peasants to be reduced to a reasonable minimum, as ordained by God and practiced by the Fathers.

"8. Honest men to be appointed to fix the rates payable on farms whose rents have risen unduly, so that peasants may not be forced to work for nothing; for according to the Word of God the laborer is worthy of his hire.

"9. In place of the present arbitrary administration of justice, the old

216

laws to be respected. Punishments no longer to vary with rank or favor, but to be the same for everyone.

"10. Fields and pasture land annexed by the lords to be restored to common ownership.

"11. Tenants' crushing death-duties to be abolished, and with them the shameful robbery of widows and orphans."

Sebastian broke off, and looking about him he said, "Most important of all the articles is the twelfth and last, for it is meant to show that we propose no violence or sedition, but acknowledge God's justice to be the basis not only of our rights but of our duties.

"12. If any can demonstrate from Holy Scripture that one or more of our articles be not in accordance with God's ordinance, that article or articles to be renounced by us. But by the same token, we reserve the right to incorporate further articles, should these be justified by the words of Scripture."

The peasants observed that this was all very fine, but how in God's name were the articles to be enforced? And what of all the written petitions that peasants from near and far had been allowed to present to their overlords on condition that they returned peaceably to their homes?

Sebastian answered, "Let me as your brother advise you not to resort to petty bargaining for the sake of temporary easement, for in this way you may bring misery on others more unfortunate and oppressed than yourselves. I have read hundreds of your complaints and petitions—thousands even—and at first I helped many a poor man to write them, until at last I saw that all such papers are worthless. Therefore we shall nail our flag to its staff and choose a captain, a lieutenant, and an ensign from among us, draw up the articles of war, and swear to obey them, thus ensuring discipline."

But the yokels were alarmed at this and murmured that it was one thing to present lawful petitions, but quite another to raise the standard of revolt. Peasants always came off worst in a tussle with the overlords.

But Sebastian said, "How shall it profit you, my poor friends, if one of you has his rent reduced, another be given back his pasture land, a third have the right to feed his swine in the forest, and a fourth catch fish on a Friday for his wife when she's breeding? All your complaints are embodied in these twelve articles, as you would see if you used your brains! Only by acknowledging God's justice as the basis of a new order can a lasting improvement be brought about in your private

217

conditions. This question is great enough to fight for, and never will poor men have fought in a better cause. If you truly believe in a just God, my friends, you must believe that He Himself fights for His justice—and in that battle you are His instruments!"

The peasants muttered doubtfully among themselves, scratching their ears and shifting from foot to foot. There was no hurry, they said, and it would be best to sleep on the matter, for once the standard was raised there could be no turning back. It would be well to hear what the good men of Baltringen thought, and those by the lake, and whether they too meant to raise their standard. Sebastian was exasperated by their sluggishness.

"Can't you get it into your thick skulls that *now* is the time?" he exclaimed. "The Emperor has started a campaign and has taken every mercenary in Germany, so the German princes have only their own few garrison troops to turn to. The French King is laying siege to Pavia in Italy with superior forces, and Frundsberg has crossed the Alps with his *landsknechts*. We shall soon hear that the Emperor has sustained as smashing a defeat as he did at Marignano. Every day that passes is time wasted, for the princes tremble in their strongholds and all the monks are burying their treasures. You cannot suppose the nobles would be so foolish as to listen to the peasants' demands if they were not driven to it by the weakness of their position! By receiving your petitions they bribe you to go home, and so gain time to confer among themselves and recruit men for their defense."

His words had their effect, and his rustic hearers agreed with one voice that there was reason in what he said. After some debate they decided to include the petitions of thirty-four villages in Sebastian's twelve articles, to raise their standard and present the articles to the Memmingen council, that the justice of God might be adopted as the basis for the new social order within the jurisdiction of the free city.

Some days later the armed peasants marched into the town with their red and white banner, headed by pipers and drummers and jubilantly followed by apprentices and all the poorer folk, while honest burghers closed their booths and workshops and barricaded their doors. A hundred spokesmen negotiated with the councilors in the great conference chamber of the town hall. Sebastian and the pastor of the city spoke on behalf of the peasants, proving by quotations from Scripture that each one of the twelve articles was justified. The council defended themselves tooth and nail and quoted Scripture in their turn, but the peasants drowned their feeble voices, nor were many of them sufficiently versed in Holy Writ. So the marvel came about: Memmingen council accepted the twelve articles without strife or bloodshed, both for the city and for its dependent villages. At this, tremendous rejoicing broke out in the market place. Many peasants tippled till they lay senseless in the gutters, and apprentices made speed to borrow guns and crossbows, since the pursuit of game was now free to all.

But Sebastian pulled a long face and said, "My banner's needless now, and there is nothing more for me to do here. But Memmingen is only a drop in the great ocean of this land, and I believe in the twelve articles. If I had money, they would be printed and distributed throughout all villages, towns, and principalities; but the peasants are poor and niggardly and my father will give me no money for such things."

The council's adoption of the twelve articles had made a deep impression on me and made me feel that to bring them to the knowledge of all men would be a good action. But before I had quite made up my mind, word came from the town of Baltringen, summoning Sebastian immediately, for news of the Memmingen articles had spread and the leader of the united peasant bands was desperate, being submerged by the petitions of his followers.

We rode to Baltringen without delay and our eyes widened with amazement on our arrival, for here was no child's play. A great number of peasants, armed with lances, cudgels, and spiked clubs, had gathered in Baltringen and the neighboring district. Some said five thousand, some ten, and not even their leaders knew the exact figure, for the fellows came and went, and visited their homes from time to time to fetch food. But their elected chief was negotiating with princes and bishops and had already persuaded them to receive the peasants' complaints. This man was a simple, pious artisan named Ulrich Schmid, who had no personal grievance. He enjoyed a reputation for eloquence, and the peasants who met together at the inn of his village to air their woes chose him for their leader because he knew his Bible. He himself hardly understood how he had landed in Baltringen with a following of ten thousand peasants, all of whom bombarded him with their claims.

He had taken up residence at the town hall, where the vagrant mercenaries and armed peasants who formed his bodyguard drank and diced and brawled about him. He welcomed Sebastian with tears of joy and at once appointed him his adjutant, with a helpless gesture at the letters and bundles of papers that encumbered his table and cupboards and lay in stacks upon the floor. These were all complaints from the peasants against their temporal and spiritual lords.

Sebastian began to study them at once, but soon gave up the hopeless task and said that all points were covered by his twelve articles. These he read aloud to Ulrich Schmid, who listened attentively, agreed to them, and said that without doubt Sebastian had been sent by God to bring order to his mind. Schmid at once gave orders for the drums to be sounded to summon the peasant leaders, to whom the articles were then read and expounded.

A week of discussion, prayer, and explanation had passed before the peasants clearly understood what was being laid before them. But Ulrich Schmid, simple though he was, clung tenaciously to whatever was made plain to him, and repeated it tirelessly until it had penetrated the thickest skull and brought conviction with it. Thus we continued until at last all the peasants were invoking God's justice and burning their own petitions. They carried Ulrich Schmid around their camps on the shafts of lances. But when Sebastian and I met once more we were so hoarse that we could scarcely whisper.

"For God's sake," I said, "let us have these articles printed!" I told him I had a hundred gulden in bills on the house of Fugger, and that if it was God's will to realize His justice on earth I would get the money back some time; whereas if it was not His will, then it would be a matter of indifference to me whether I did or not. Sebastian was overjoyed and promised by his faith in the living God and divine justice that I would be repaid. He sat down at once to draw up the articles in a definitive form, appending supporting texts to each. He also wrote a preface, "To the Christian Reader," stressing that the Gospel in no way justified violence or tumult and that its only teaching was that of peace, patience, and concord. Since by these articles the peasants did no more than express their desire that this teaching should come into force, he wrote, they could not be charged with sedition; on the contrary, to oppose their reasonable demands was to oppose God's own teaching.

I have always been inclined to put more faith in others than in myself, and if something is said to me clearly and persuasively and often enough I feel bound to believe it; in this I fancy I differ little from others. It is understandable, therefore, that I took fire from Sebastian's words and gladly surrendered my bills, which the printer accepted in payment, for I believed I was doing those ill-used peasants a service. Shortly afterward the articles were ready, and mounted messengers galloped off north, south, east, and west with copies still damp from the press. Some time later Doctor Luther in Wittenberg published a commentary on Sebastian's articles. He agreed that the peasants' demands were justified, but urged them to be reconciled with their masters and to avoid violence and bloodshed.

News of Doctor Luther's support, and of the countless peasants up and down the country who had banded together to turn his teaching into fact, now raised our people's hopes beyond all measure, although the princes sent warnings by Schmid's envoys and reminded him of the toad that puffed itself up until it burst. They asked scornfully whether Ulrich Schmid expected God Almighty to come down from heaven as arbitrator to pronounce upon these articles. But Schmid promised that within three weeks he would summon all the eminent Christian scholars in Germany, including Luther and Zwingli, to give their judgment.

By Sebastian's advice, Ulrich Schmid sought to form a Christian league of all the great peasant armies in the different principalities, and to induce them all to take God's justice as the solution to their problems. To this end a meeting was held at Memmingen to which even the lakeside men and the great Allgau band sent their delegates. But when Sebastian had read out his twelve articles violent dissension arose, for the men from the lake would by no means renounce their just and reasonable claims in favor of some vague principle called the Justice of God, which anyone could interpret as he chose.

However, food, drink, and tactful persuasion at last convinced the hotheads that their only hope of success lay in unity. The negotiations lasted until evening, when all the weary leaders voted for God's justice, with the proviso that each man should be allowed to interpret this for himself. They said bluntly that the articles were pure rubbish and entirely beside the question. Since their first aim must be to secure their position, a thirteenth article was demanded, by which all monasteries and castles should be captured and disarmed unless their owners consented to join the Christian league.

Sebastian said scornfully that such an article would be worthless, since it was impossible for them to breach those walls with their bare fists. Yet in this he was mistaken, for most of the castles opened their gates freely, and the pipers and taborers who had formerly entertained the guests at banquets now gaily joined the peasant armies and marched at their head with capering and mirth. The princes said bitterly that the German nobility was behaving like a pack of old women, and that it was easier to fight the peasants than to rouse their lord-ships into drawing their swords in defense of their ancient and hereditary rights.

I need speak no more of the dissensions and parleying that ended in the Christian league, except to mention that to please and mollify Sebastian, the three peasant armies adopted his red and white banner with the St. Andrew's cross upon it for their standard. The men from the lake shore, from Allgau, and from Baltringen swore to venture life, honor, and property, each for all and all for each. Their spirit of unity was strengthened by the news that Ulrich, the former Duke of Würt-temberg, had openly promised to support their cause. With the French King's money he had recruited a mercenary army in the Confederation, and was now marching into the Emperor's domains to win back his dukedom.

Only good news came in during those feverish days of spring, and when the twelve articles had been distributed among the people, Baltringen became the meeting place of the peasant delegates, where they communicated and debated their common claims. Southern Ger-many was in a ferment, and the only forces the princes and the Im-perial governors had been able to scrape together were now marching against Duke Ulrich. No wonder, then, that the peasants rejoiced and basked in the spring sunshine, and allowed the monasteries to offer them lavish hospitality. They had the fullest confidence in the competence of their leaders to handle the princes.

Thus precious days were wasted, until like a thunderclap came the news that the Emperor, instead of being defeated at Pavia by the French King as had been expected, had brought off the greatest vic-tory within the memory of man. The Swiss mercenaries in the pay of France had been annihilated, and His Most Christian Majesty had been taken prisoner. This news frightened all thoughtful men. Peas-ants began to talk of ploughing and the spring sowing, and the wisest slipped away home. But the greater number continued to rely upon the justice of God.

Ulrich Schmid and the other delegates journeyed humbly to Ulm to treat with the princes, who now sang a very different song. Their words were harsh. They demanded complete submission from the peasants, who were to disperse immediately to their homes and pay their dues in money and field service as before. Only then would their Highnesses set up a commission to examine the twelve articles and give their decision, which should be binding to both parties.

Ulrich Schmid had gone to Ulm in full reliance on God's justice; he returned thence a beaten, weary old man, and he avoided our eyes. In a mournful voice he confessed that the peasant spokesmen had agreed to these terms and had guaranteed their followers' acceptance of them.

Sebastian cried, "Are you out of your wits, Ulrich Schmid? Have you lost your faith? If we disperse now the justice of God is worthless and all our troubles will return to us sevenfold."

"I believe in God and that is my only comfort," answered Ulrich Schmid, "but you don't know everything and cannot judge of the matter as I can, for the princes and their Imperial advisers spoke very freely to me. They told me candidly that there was an end to their patience and that they could not continue to hold their mercenaries under arms indefinitely; they would be compelled to make war upon us and slay us all if we did not submit."

Then the officers cried out as one man and said, "You're a fool, Ulrich Schmid! The princes must have bribed you. They have no troops, and their general, Jürgen von Truchsess, is on the march somewhere in the Württemberg passes, where Duke Ulrich's Switzers are smashing his little force like a pea on an anvil."

Ulrich Schmid shook his head wearily.

"You don't know everything even yet. The Confederation, aghast at the Pavia defeat, has recalled its men from the Duke's army. Duke Ulrich is alone and forsaken and has fled into France, leaving even his cannon in pledge for his debts. Jürgen von Truchsess is now approaching by forced marches, and we would be wise to avoid bloodshed by scattering, and relying on the goodwill of the princes to which they pledged their honor."

The uproar that then broke out was so violent that the noise of it brought men running from all sides. The officers yelled abuse at Ulrich, calling him coward, milksop, and traitor. And when the result of his embassy became generally known, he was cuffed and buffeted nearly to death. At last he wept and said he desired no better than to live and die for the good cause, and rather than await the princes' attack on the camp he would draw a sword to fight for God's justice if somebody would show him how to handle one.

But he was already out of the game. The best and most experienced officers put their heads together among their followers, and planned what was next to be done. To them came all the vagabonds, mercenaries thirsting for loot, and revengeful peasants who had had enough

223

of peaceful measures. Much has been told of bloody deeds committed by the peasant hordes from the moment their standard was raised, but I who was with them can affirm that those from Baltringen at least had been guilty of no great violence before this day in March. Not until that night was Schemmeringen castle burned, and as far as I know that was the first, although the peasant movement had been active for six months. The blame for it can be laid entirely at the princes' door. It was they who began the war and not the peasants. The peasants desired only peace and the justice of God.

Yet it seemed as if the peasants had only been awaiting a sign, for no sooner was Schemmeringen blazing to the sky than castles and monasteries were aflame as far as the eye could see. The rebels sought private revenge for the wrongs they had endured; many a cruel governor ran the gauntlet between their spears; many a nobleman fought hand to hand with them and was slain.

Even the more temperate among the peasants who had stood by Ulrich Schmid were seduced by the sight of their drunken comrades driving home cartloads of plunder from castle and monastery, and hordes of looters swept the country as far as the Danube valley.

Sebastian returned white faced from one of these raids and said, "I never thought to find myself in the company of marauding criminals. If fellows of this sort are to bring God's justice to the world, then I can no longer believe in a just God."

"What will you do?" I asked him.

He replied, "I will go back to my father in Memmingen, and these ruffians may administer their twelve articles as they choose. I have fought long enough against my father's will, and the Bible bids us honor our parents. If my good father still wishes me to study law, I think I shall obey him and enter Bologna University, since the war in Italy is over."

"It's easy enough for you to talk like that!" I retorted. "You can retire in good order to a home and a rich father. But where are my hundred gulden?"

"You gave them to the printer of your own accord! I see you're like all these others and think of nothing but stuffing your purse and your belly—and you needn't look so sour and find fault with me for going! This rabble can do nothing. At one time they had honest farmers of good standing for their leaders, and they listened to educated, intelligent men like myself. But now they follow shoemakers, tailors, thieves, ruffians, and masterless mercenaries who for two kreutzers would sell their own mothers and trample the articles under-foot. I advise you to fly too, while you may, for no good can come of this."

Then I laughed aloud, and surveying his handsome face and brown eyes and the soiled velvet doublet with its silver buttons I was ashamed of belonging to the human race—ashamed of having regarded this fellow as my friend when he was nothing but the spoiled son of a rich man—a boy accustomed to being cock of the walk and seeing others obey his whims.

And so I answered, "No, Sebastian, I shall not run away. Where should I go, for that matter? My only resources are a little dog and this good gun. Foreigner though I am, I come of a steadfast race; and if I was once a traitor, once is enough. Henceforth I shall howl with the wolves, having bleated lamblike at your heels too long. Wolves may bring about a new order, but you've shown me that sheep never will."

Thus our ways parted and our friendship was broken. Sebastian left the camp for his home, and I soon heard the reason for his change of heart. A dispute had arisen over his command of the troop; the veteran soldiers had wearied of him and had told him to hold his tongue and not meddle with matters he did not understand. But when he refused to be quiet, they struck him on the mouth and drove him forth with the butts of their lances. So he refused to consort any longer with robbers, and predicted a bad end for them.

When Sebastian had gone, I in my turn wearied of Ulrich Schmid, who was indeed a tedious, tearful fellow, and I joined Jürgen Knopf, leader of the Allgau men.

3

This Jürgen Knopf was a spindly man, whose big head wobbled on a skinny neck as if it were full of water. But there was no water on his brain; he knew exactly what he wanted and his attack on the Prince-Bishop's seat was no haphazard raid. He picked out his best men and took with him a few field pieces that he had captured in neighboring castles, and enough powder and shot to breach His High-ness's walls.

"I know that prison tower all too well," he said as we rode together, "and was once nearly hanged there. The peasants of this diocese have fought for their rights these hundred years and have lost everything.

But this present Bishop is worse than any we have had. He thinks nothing of half throttling a man with his own hands, and having him flogged within an inch of his life. Now for a change I mean to get *him* by the throat. That will be the happiest day of my life; after that I care not what happens to me."

Then, inclining his heavy head over one shoulder, he said with a sly smile, "I may tell you in confidence, Michael Pelzfuss, that I have sent messengers into Thuringia and Bohemia, and the best horse in all this region is on the way with my right-hand man to Pavia and Milan to speak to Frundsberg's *landsknechts*. They're our kinsfolk and countrymen and should be told of what is going forward here. If they come to join us, the princes have spoken their last word. But much money will be needed to pay these men, and that money I mean to take from the Bishop.

"Ulrich Schmid is a blockhead," he went on. "He cannot see that as matters stand today, only murder, violence, and plunder can weld our forces together. Nothing is more binding than joint crime, for then there is no going back, and only torture and the gallows await the man who throws down his arms and appeals to the princes' clemency."

There was no doubt a certain truth in what he said, although conscience told me that murder, arson, and theft were hardly the best means of securing God's justice on earth.

I realized that I was keeping questionable company. But we were now drawing near to the city, and at the sight of those all too familiar towers rising into the blue of the March sky my heart burned within me and I ceased to disdain my companions, reflecting that God might after all employ unlikely instruments for His vengeance. A year had passed since Barbara and I had entered this city in the yellow-painted witch cart.

A shot or two was fired from the walls, and little white puffs of smoke hung in the haze. But Jürgen Knopf had laid his plans well, for the apprentices and poorer townspeople started a timely rioting in the market place, thus striking terror into the hearts of the council, who themselves bore no very tender love for the Prince-Bishop. The councilors ordered the gates to be opened to us before we had fired a shot; they repudiated His Highness and even presented us with several culverins with which to besiege his palace. But to our sorrow we learned that the prelate had left the city and had sought refuge in a fortress at the top of a neighboring hill, taking his own treasure with him and also the most precious possessions of the monastery.

But good Jürgen Knopf was not cast down by this. "One thing at a time," he said, and marched at the head of his troops to the cloister that I knew so well. Here ensued a scene of savage destruction, robbery, gluttony, drunkenness, and debauch such as I had never before witnessed. First, all the ale and winecasks were rolled out of the cellars into the cloister garth, and when the invaders had taken the edge off their thirst they surged into the church and threw the gold-embroidered copes and altarcloths about the floor. The precious reliquary was broken open. Women kicked the holy bones along in front of them, and the most enterprising of the men wrenched off the gold and silver work and hammered it flat. Meanwhile others armed with nets emptied the fishponds. The most exquisite wooden carvings and images were chopped up for firewood and soon the great carp were boiling in holy-water stoups and fonts that had been carried out to the court. But the dry wood burned away like tinder, and reeling men stormed the monastery library to drag forth precious books and manuscripts and countless rolls of parchment from the archives to feed their fires.

When a certain white-haired old monk saw what was happening to these rare writings, he was so enraged that he tore a crucifix from the wall and attacked the marauders, tears pouring down his cheeks, and smote them, calling on all the saints for aid. Some of these men he succeeded in repelling, for they were good-natured enough at heart and did not want to hurt him, though they laughed at his holy zeal. But when Jürgen Knopf heard of it he dashed into the library and with a blow of his sword on the old fellow's head felled him to the ground in a pool of his own blood. After that none hindered the drunken soldiers from breaking the chains that secured the books to the desks. The brothers either fled or officiously proffered their services, professing secret belief in Luther's doctrines and the firm intention of leaving the monastery and taking wives at the earliest opportunity.

The debauchery and senseless destruction revolted me, and I could not howl with these wolves. I paced the cloisters and moved restlessly from campfire to campfire. The town drabs had swarmed in for their share of the booty. Some stripped themselves naked, arrayed themselves in copes and dalmatics, and pranced about to the sound of pipe and tabor. The noise and confusion were indescribable.

Sitting apart by a small fire was a grave old peasant. He was examining the illuminations in an ancient missal, and because he was quiet and not very drunk I sat down beside him. His fire had spared part of a carved wooden Virgin whose sweet, innocent face, formed by the skilled hands of some artist a hundred or two hundred years before, gazed at me reproachfully with its charred eye.

For hundreds of years this monastery had amassed and cherished its treasures. Man's hope of forgiveness and redemption had set the finest sculptors, painters, silversmiths, weavers, and embroiderers to work to adorn the holy place. And in one night, by a mob of ignorant, passion-swayed peasants, all was destroyed. I could find no explanation save that the Church had grown worldly, and that God desired to bring mankind back to its primitive, simple faith in the Redemption through the blood of Christ alone, without the mediation of avaricious priests and monks, or of vain images and relics. But when I beheld the filthy behavior of these peasants I could not but feel that the Lord might have chosen better apostles.

The peasant beside me began tearing the pictures out of his missal, saying, "I'm a simple, illiterate man, and all books save the Bible are superfluous and better burnt. But these paintings are beautiful and I shall take them home to the children, so that they too may have pictures to look at, like the children of princes."

He folded them carefully and put them into the purse at his belt, then threw the missal into the dying fire, and kicked the wooden face of the Virgin in after it.

"Let us sleep, in the name of God," he said. Then he crossed himself and lay back upon the ground, pillowing his head upon the bag that held his few bits of food and his spoils.

Next day the Bishop's palace was entered and plundered with very little resistance. Indeed the guards were soon glad enough to join the peasants, fearing that with the Bishop's livery on their backs they would never escape with their lives through the turbulent countryside, even if they could get out of the city.

Jürgen Knopf, incensed at finding the coffers empty and the most valuable objects removed, said, "Now at all costs we must attack that raven's nest and capture it, for we can never hope to win over our kinsfolk from the Emperor's army unless we can pay them handsomely."

He mustered his forces and had his artillery dragged to the crest of the hill. The gunners chose the weakest point in the walls and started a heavy bombardment. Despite their formidable appearance these walls

228

were of soft stone, and crumbled easily. But the Bishop's gunners and crossbowmen answered our fire. When the assailants heard the whine of bullets and saw the dust fly up from the furrows ploughed in the ground, they became somewhat hesitant and were inclined to abandon this wasps' nest for more profitable hunting grounds.

I stood among the other handgunners, drove my rest into the earth, loaded, and fired several shots, although my weapon kicked so violently that I thought my shoulder would be dislocated. Undismayed by the rain of bullets, the Prince-Bishop himself appeared upon the ramparts in armor as bright as silver. He stamped and roared and called down such fearful curses that we seemed to smell sulphur. We failed to hit him, though both cannon and harquebuses fired at least ten shots between them. Jürgen Knopf was well pleased at the Prince-Bishop's wrath, saying it was a sign that he was in a tight place.

He then sent some of His Highness's men-at-arms and lackeys up to the castle to convey his demand for immediate surrender; the besiegers, he declared, were only the advance guard. Ten thousand pikemen and heavy siege-cannon from the Confederation were on their way. He bade the heralds say also that Frundsberg had joined the peasants, the princes had fled, and the troops of Jürgen von Truchsess had been beaten to the last man. If the castle were not promptly surrendered, Jürgen Knopf could not answer for the lives of the defenders, for the enraged peasants would certainly take such cruel vengeance that not a man would be spared.

The messengers did their errand well, for that night mutiny broke out within the castle. We heard a tumult and some shots, and the drawbridge fell with a fearful crash. The mutineers had succeeded in damaging the chains so that it could not be raised again. Yet the Bishop managed to restore order, and next morning a number of bodies were thrown out into the ditch.

The lowered drawbridge had exposed the gate, however, and the master gunners tried to direct their fire upon it. But it was set far back under the archway, and outworks prevented us from moving our guns into more advantageous positions.

Jürgen Knopf muttered, "If only there were a brave man among us to nail a petard to that door, the fortress would be ours today. I'll give a thousand gulden of the Bishop's money to the one who will fix a petard there and fire it—and a thousand gulden is more than any of you have ever seen in your lives. The thing would be done before you could say a Credo. Here is the chance of your lives, good friends and valiant soldiers!"

But the veterans shook their heads and said laughing, "A thousand gulden is of no use to a dead man, as you well know, Jürgen Knopf, you old fox!"

During this discussion I had been tending a peasant whose right leg had been torn off at the thigh by a cannon ball. But his face was already bluish gray and I knew that he was dying, so I left him and joined the soldiers.

"What is a petard?" I asked them.

"Imagine an iron caldron," said they, "although of course much stronger than an ordinary caldron. You fill it with gunpowder and fasten a sturdy oak plank across the top by the handles. This board has a hole at each end, through which stout nails are driven into the door so that the petard is firmly fixed to it. Then you light the fuse and the door is blown to pieces."

I went up to Jürgen Knopf.

"Will you truly pay me a thousand gulden of the Bishop's money if I blow in that door?"

He looked askance at me, wagging his great head to and fro, but swore by the Holy Blood to keep that promise if I would fix the petard to the door and light the fuse. The veteran soldiers flocked about me and vied with one another in praising my courage, but I could see that they thought me mad and were persuaded that I would never come back for my reward. But I had my own reasons for making the attempt. When that burly peasant sighed his last in my arms and plucked at his breast with his calloused hands, I had a sort of revelation. I was weary of life after my many sorrows and the conflicting thoughts that had assailed me by the campfires in the monastery garden. I was weary of myself, and seemed to have found here an opportunity of leaving God to decide my fate. If His justice had no existence, then it was a matter of indifference to me whether I lived or died, as I should then be of no more account than a soulless beast.

But I was exceedingly frightened. The whine of every ball made me jump, and the sweat broke out on my throat and back when I so much as looked at the castle gateway and the smoke billowing from the towers that flanked it.

When the gunners saw that I was in earnest, they ran to their wagons and fetched me a petard. They had brought three with them. The one they chose, which was exceedingly heavy, was really very simple in construction. The gunners measured out a short fuse that would burn for as long as one might say a rapid Paternoster, so as to give me time to get away before the explosion. Jürgen Knopf promised to keep his boldest men standing by with an iron-shod balk of timber, to rush forward instantly afterward and smash in what was left of the door.

A friendly mercenary began taking off his breastplate and cuisses for me to wear, that I might have some protection from enemy fire. But having felt the weight of the petard, I realized that that alone was almost more than I could carry. My only hope of safety lay in a desperate dash for the cover of the archway. I thrust a short sledge hammer and two great iron nails into my belt, took the smoldering match between my teeth, heaved up the petard, and ran down from the gun emplacements toward the gateway.

I had no more than a hundred and fifty paces or so to cover, yet to me, bent double by the weight I carried, the distance seemed long enough. Halfway there I was breathless, my pulse thudded in my temples, and from the walls above came a ceaseless crash of enemy fire as the defenders discharged at me every weapon they could bring to bear. Dust spurted up all round me, yet more than powder and ball I feared the bolts that hummed about me like hornets, for the crossbow is many times truer of aim than the harquebus.

But Jürgen Knopf and his men directed heavy fire at the ramparts to distract and disable the defenders, and to my own amazement I was able to reach the archway and creep into what I thought was safety. Just as I ran into the shadows, the men above poured down caldrons of molten lead, a few drops of which splashed up from the ground and burned my legs. But I did not even notice this until long afterward, so great was my terror, although those leaden drops scarred me for life.

On inspecting the door, I was aghast to see that there were arrow slits in the wall on either side. As I raised the petard to nail it to the door, the barrel of a harquebus was thrust out and pointed at me. Dropping the petard, I hurled myself against the wall beside the opening as the shot rang out. At that moment another barrel appeared at the opposite slit.

After jumping from side to side in a cold sweat, I wearied of the game and felt how mean-spirited I must be thus to seek escape from God's decree. Seizing my petard again, I nailed it to the door with thunderous blows of my hammer, without looking around. Fear lent such strength to my arm that the nails sank into the stout timbers like pins into butter. A shot from behind blew a hole the size of my fist in the door beside my head. I snatched the smoldering match from my mouth and kindled the fuse. As it crackled and sent sulphur fumes swirling about my head, I made the sign of the cross and dashed into the open.

I fancy that no one had expected me to come out alive, for I had run fifty yards before anyone fired at me. At that moment came a crash louder than that of any cannon, and Jürgen Knopf's brave men were hurtling toward me with the battering-ram slung between them, followed by a flock of pikemen and harquebusiers all howling with fright and fury. I had to turn about and speed like a deer back to the gateway to avoid being trampled underfoot. This I did very unwillingly, for it seemed to me I had earned some respite. Down from the gatehouse towers fell showers of molten lead and bubbling pitch, and the fellows with the battering-ram uttered shrieks of fear and pain. But there was nothing for me to do but to run blindly at their head as if I were leading the assault, whereas in truth my only aim was to get out of their way.

The petard had smashed the ironbound timbers, and few blows of the battering-ram were needed to carry away the double doors and show us the courtyard like a bright patch at the end of the vaulted passage. Dropping their weapon with a yell of delight, the men poured through, and I with them. There was indeed nothing else to do with those sharp pikes at our heels. But no sooner had we reached the courtyard than we heard a tremendous crash behind us. A massive iron portcullis had fallen and caught us in a trap, barring our retreat and keeping us exposed to a rain of balls and bolts from every window overlooking the court. Behind us the pikemen thundered vainly against the grille, and of the score or so who had charged into the yard, ten had fallen in their own blood before one could say a blessing. Next moment the Bishop appeared, ordered his men to waste no more powder and ball, and roared to us to lay down our arms.

I had none to lay down, but I shouted my answer, "We have no intention of laying down our arms, my dear Lord Bishop. You must do that, to preserve your valuable life, for we're unwilling to raise our hand against the Lord's anointed. But I cannot long restrain these worthy men, who claim nothing more than that God's justice should be done. Your resistance has roused them to a frenzy of rage and you can hear them roaring like wild beasts behind me."

The good Prince-Bishop stamped his foot and bellowed, "I'll give you God's justice! You shall hang, every man of you! But who are you, fellow? I seem to know your face."

I saw that the Bishop was afraid, else he would not have deigned to bandy words with me.

Boldly I shouted back, "I am Michael Pelzfuss, and you know I could not mean you harm, good Bishop! Therefore I hurried in ahead of these desperate men to save your life if I might. Put an end to this savage bloodshed, most reverend sir, and by all that's holy I swear that you shall depart in peace without a hair of your head being harmed."

The other poor wretches who were still alive in that yard voiced their agreement, and promised that he and his servants should depart with their personal effects. My impudence certainly gave the Bishop some misgivings, and while he stood irresolute his guards began muttering that the terms were reasonable and that they had no wish to tackle Frundsberg if he had indeed joined the peasants.

To cut a long story short, His Highness surrendered as soon as Jürgen Knopf ratified the terms we had made. Knopf was furious at being thus deprived of his personal revenge upon the Bishop, but the men who stood pressed against the portcullis were as glad as I was to get off with their lives, for two or three cannon fired from the courtyard through the grille would have annihilated every man.

Thus Jürgen captured the fortress, and with it enormous booty. The personal effects of the Bishop he assessed at only ten silver cups, two hundred minted gulden, and two horses, on one of which was loaded the prelate's feather bed and bedclothes. When His Highness learned of this interpretation of our terms he was speechless with fury and could only gasp for breath. Indeed, his face took on so livid a color that his surgeon felt it prudent to bleed him on the spot, which he did with the help of two stout fellows to hold His Highness down. He was then hoisted into the saddle and allowed to ride away followed by his troops, whose baggage, women, and children brought up the rear in wagons. Pipes played, drums rolled, and the peasants' culverins fired salvos of joy. In the opinion of the Bishop's men-at-arms, the affair had been concluded with honor to both sides.

I have no idea of the amount of money and other treasure Jürgen Knopf seized, for he allowed only two of his most trusted men to accompany him to the strong room under the keep. When his followers began to murmur, he distributed three gulden to each man, which corresponded to the retaining fee of a mercenary, while those who had

233

entered the courtyard and yet lived received six. This pacified the men and they went off to eat and sleep, but I approached Jürgen Knopf and demanded the thousand gulden he had promised me.

He avoided my eye and sighed, "Michael Pelzfuss, I fear that you like everyone else greatly overestimate the Bishop's wealth, and you must remember that more than thirty thousand gulden are necessary to pay ten thousand mercenaries. Therefore I cannot just now pay you the whole sum in ready money. In recognition of your courage, you shall have thirty-five gulden now and a written undertaking to pay the balance, which I shall do as soon as the new order is in force and God's justice prevails upon the earth."

Exasperated by this reply and by the burns on my legs, from which I now suffered agony, I reviled him for a perjurer and blackguard and demanded at least half the money at once. After much abusive and embittered argument I extracted a hundred gulden from him, of which half were underweight, and the written promise of nine hundred more, accompanied by an exhortation to trust in God. I never knew what became of all the Bishop's treasure, for Jürgen Knopf could have spent only a fraction of it on the hiring of mercenaries, and when he came to be beheaded it had vanished without trace. However, a bird in the hand is worth two in the bush, as good Mother Pirjo used to tell me, and in token of his good intentions Knopf gave me a fairly sound horse from the Bishop's stable. At daybreak, while the white stars of the summer night were yet shining, I rode back to Baltringen with news of our great victory and of the Bishop's shameful flight.

4

But my news brought no great joy to Ulrich Schmid, whose faith was weakening. Violence bred only violence, he said, and Jürgen Knopf would perish by the sword that he had taken. Wearying of Ulrich Schmid, I returned to my lodging, stabled my horse, and limped on my singed legs up the narrow stair to the little attic room that I had been fortunate enough to keep for myself alone. My landlady, the worthy widow of a spice merchant, to whose care I had entrusted my dog, had promised to admit no one to my room uninvited. My indignation may be imagined, therefore, when on entering I found a strange mercenary sprawling on my bed, mouth agape and snoring. He wore bright colored slashed breeches and his doublet was open, revealing a hairy chest. Even in sleep one hand gripped the hilt of his sword and the other clutched his purse. My dog was curled up on the man's stomach and never even rose to greet me, but merely wagged its tail and blinked at me as if to say that it was not seemly to disturb the warrior's repose. I did not recognize the man, although there seemed something familiar about that broad, stupid countenance, and in my displeasure I shook him roughly to rouse him. As he woke he spoke in many tongues, gave the order to fire, and swore in Spanish.

But when at last he came to himself he sat up on the edge of the bed, looked at me, and said, "Michael Furfoot, my brother! So you're alive. Why are you limping like an old woman with bad legs?"

My eyes became clear and I recognized Andy, whom I had so sorely missed and given up for dead. I cried for joy and embraced him, and he gave me the old bear hug that winded me and nearly cracked my ribs. He had grown in height and breadth, and his whole person had taken on something of the rough brutality of the mercenary, but he surveyed me as of old with his sleepy gray eyes, and his hair was on end as usual. He spoke Finnish haltingly and mixed with many foreign words; nor was I fluent, for it was many years since I had spoken my own tongue.

"God be praised that you're back safe with me again!" I cried. "Now I can take care of you and keep you out of any more mischief —and I have money, so you need lack for nothing. How you have got along all this time without me I cannot imagine."

But Andy shook his heavy purse proudly and said, "I've not come back a pauper. When I heard of all the troubles in Germany I left the Emperor's camp at once to find you, for my three years' service was up and the Emperor owed me more than I owed him. There can never have been a more penniless Emperor than this one! He owes money not only to every king and prince in Europe, but also to the meanest pikeman and muleteer in his army. Still, I have been lucky and can't complain. I'm glad I heard of the troubles here before I drank up all my money. I came because I knew that a pious scatterbrain like yourself would be getting well seethed in the caldron— and now I can snatch you out of it."

"You're as big a fool as you look, Andy," I retorted. "You understand nothing of it. The poor peasants and artisans of this country have risen as one man to build a new order on the basis of twelve excellent articles which I won't bother to repeat to you now. You haven't the wit to understand them. I will only assure you that they are admirable; I myself helped to draft them. God's justice is to be

235

made a reality in this world, by force if need be, and I am glad you're here to support the good cause."

Andy yawned and scratched his ear.

"Well, you're a scholar, and you're learned in these theological matters. All I saw as I came through the countryside in search of you was that this new order seems to have taken the bit between its teeth. Many who say they're fighting for it are anything but good men. A devil's brood. I would rather take you back with me to Italy, where the trees bear golden fruit."

No doubt he meant well, and I smiled pityingly and said, "Let us not quarrel. Let us rather tell of our adventures. I am anxious to hear all you have done and how you contrived to prosper so. And I will tell you of my misfortunes, that you may understand that I am not the man I was when we parted."

But at the word "prosper" Andy looked grave and said, "In every cup there is a drop of wormwood, and by this I don't mean hardship, privations, cold, hunger, fever, and wounds. These are inseparable from the Emperor's service. I mean something else, which I shall speak of later. But you need not tell me of your troubles; I heard them all as I came from Memmingen to Baltringen in search of you. I know about your wife and I share your grief, though without surprise. Anyone but an innocent like yourself could see that she was a witch. I've heard also that you've become an admirer of Luther's teachings and an agitator. So you have nothing new to tell me and had better let me talk, as I have many instructive things to say. It will be as well, perhaps, to have some refreshment, for my tale will take until evening."

Thus reminded of my duties as host, I hastened downstairs, forgetful of my weariness, and found the spice merchant's widow in the back kitchen taking newly baked bread from the oven. She was in a state of high indignation and was clucking like a hen.

"Master Michael, sir, I don't wish to think ill of your friend, who pays for what he drinks and is pleasant spoken. But I cannot allow him to bring his foreign slut into my respectable house. She speaks in a heathen tongue, she's insolent, she wears clothes above her station and feathers on her head instead of the two-horned red cap she deserves. There must be an end to this shame, and I hope your friend will soon have the good sense to kick the trollop out."

Astonished at these observations, I called Andy down and questioned him. He crossed himself devoutly and said, "I would as soon handle

236

a sack of wild cats, and have no wish to discuss her just now and spoil my dinner. It is she who is the drop of wormwood in my cup."

He emptied a tankard of ale in two gulps and asked for more.

"Yet one should not cast aspersions on wormwood," he added. "The Italians brew a strong drink of wine and wormwood which has cured many of stomach cramps and ague."

I urged him to control his craving for ale and wine and reminded him of its evil consequences, but he contradicted me flatly.

"It's plain you've never been on a real campaign," he said. "A good soldier never drinks water, but spends his last farthing on wine or ale if necessary. I've seen all too many fellows waste away and die from drinking ditchwater. My sergeant trusted neither lakes, pools, nor rivers; but if you must drink water, he said, drink it hot, with herbs infused in it. I pass this good advice on to you, Michael, since you seem to be going asoldiering, and such throngs have gathered in the city that pestilence will soon appear among us and weed out the water drinkers."

He said this very solemnly, and I felt bound to believe him, for he knew more of such matters than I did. So I drank ale and wine with my dinner, and we were soon very merry together, thumping one another on the back and joking with the spice merchant's widow. She was most liberal and was forever setting fresh dishes on the table and crossing herself in admiration at Andy's capacity. When he had taken the edge off his hunger, he began his tale.

"May God bless our good hostess and reward her pains! I was weary of olives and donkey-steaks. First I must say a word about world politics, for you, Michael, know more of heavenly affairs than earthly ones. But I have been forced to learn something of them, for a soldier must know in whose cause he sells his sword and risks his neck. For that reason there's no place like the campfire circle of an evening for gossip about emperors and kings and their doings, and I've learned many profitable lessons from such talks."

He emptied a tall wine cup, which was entirely hidden in his massive paw, and begged our hostess to fetch him a larger one.

He then went on, "Well, as you may remember, I took service with the Emperor, thinking I was doing something clever, as our good sovereign Charles V is the greatest ruler in the world and reckons among his dominions Austria and Naples and Spain and the Netherlands, to mention only a few, and besides that he is Emperor of Germany and India and America beyond the oceans. And if all the tales of the New World were true, he would be the wealthiest man in the world. But he suffers from a chronic shortage of money. This proves that the Spaniards who bring those tales from the New World are the biggest liars ever seen. There is no other prince to be compared with him, except possibly Francis of France—whom I know well, as I helped to capture him at Pavia—and Henry VIII of England who has made money by the wool trade."

Here he emptied another tankard, wiped his mouth, and continued, "The German princes are not worth mentioning, for here earls and princes and bishops and free cities spring up everywhere like mushrooms in mold. The Archduke Ferdinand, brother to the Emperor, is the only notable one. The great Sultan Suleiman of Turkey is a chapter in himself, and I'll say no more of him except to mention that evil tongues speak of an alliance between him and the King of France against the Emperor."

This aroused my indignation and I broke in, "As erstwhile student of the University of Paris—a city whose peer may be sought in vain the world over—and friend to France, let me say once and for all that such talk is false and wicked. We should not add to the burden of a noble, chivalrous King who has so manfully opposed the Emperor—opposed him because it was surely never God's intention that one man should obtain dominion over all the world."

Andy crashed his fist on the table with a delighted roar.

"You've hit the nail on the head, Michael—and that's why the two are like cat and dog, and have never agreed since they competed for the Imperial crown. France is the wealthiest, most powerful state in Europe and the only obstacle to the Emperor's spreading power. But now I must go on to explain affairs in Italy. There is a country that will tolerate no overlord. The Emperor and the King of France have never ceased fighting for the Dukedom of Milan and the fertile province of Lombardy, whence I've now come. Venice, Milan's neighbor, plays the greatest part in Italy today because of her possessions—though we must not forget the Pope, who is a Medici and therefore controls both Rome and Florence. Furthermore, we have the kingdom of Naples, which belongs to the Emperor but which, by some hereditary title, is claimed by the King of France."

"This is all going round and round in my head," I protested. "Tell us what you yourself have heard and seen. I have only one thing to say—both Emperor and King are acting criminally in making war upon one another, since all their problems of inheritance could be resolved by law with justice to both parties."

. Andy laughed heartily.

"The problems of their inheritance and of the alliances and settlements of their ancestors are so involved that not the devil himself could straighten them out, and many learned lawyers have puzzled themselves silly over them, and turned monk. Emperors and kings recognize no right but that of might; he who can afford the greatest number of pikemen, harquebusiers, cavalry, and artillery wins his case. The Dukedom of Milan was the official pretext for the war, and it was in the French King's possession when I and other brave men crossed the Alps and chased the French into Provence, plundering, raping, and murdering as we went. For our leader was the Duke of Bourbon, Constable of France, who was furious with King Francis and wanted to do him as much harm as possible."

The spice merchant's widow crossed herself and declared that she could not believe such crimes of Andy. I asked how it was possible for the Constable of France to side with the Emperor against his own King.

Andy, somewhat embarrassed by the widow's remark, cracked a bone between his teeth and gave the marrow to Rael.

Then in an attempt to excuse himself he said, "Looting is all part of the soldier's trade, and I never killed anyone for pleasure, as the Spaniards do. And as for rape, I would only say that the women ran toward us rather than away from us. As regards the Constable of France, he betrayed his own King and joined the Emperor so that under his protection he might carve out a kingdom for himself on French soil. However, this Duke of Bourbon led us to such purpose that we melted away like butter in the sun, and when we'd been besieging Marseilles for some time I found myself compelled to leave my beautiful culverins in the hands of the French and toil back to Italy with many others. The King of France, against all expectations, had contrived to raise a huge army and was now racing neck and neck with us over the Alps to Milan."

Andy grew excited, thumped the table again, turned his tankard upside down, and said, "But I wanted to tell you of the battle of Pavia, and now God help me to come to the point, for that was a battle worth talking of. Wiser fellows than I have said that it decided the destiny of Europe and secured the Imperial power for hundreds— even thousands—of years. The Emperor, they say, has only to make

239

the King of France his vassal, set forth with him against the Turks, and win back Constantinople, which to our shame has lain under the yoke of the infidel for a generation. But to come back to Pavia. We, the ragged, starving remnants of the Emperor's army, crawled back over the Alps like a pack of beggars, or like motherless lambs. We were mocked by everyone, and down in Rome they hung a notice on a certain stone which they call *pasquino,* where they write up dirt: *"Lost, Stolen, or Strayed: The Imperial Army. Finder handsomely rewarded."* But they shall eat their gibes yet. One shouldn't strike a man when he's down, and an honest soldier's misfortune may not be his fault, as we see from the French King's sad fate."

I begged him to come to the battle of Pavia, of which I was most eager to hear a truthful account, but he retorted in some irritation, "How you do rush at things, Michael! All this is part of the story. A good artist never paints the Holy Family all starkly by itself. No, he fills in a rich background of fertile valleys, vineyards, waterfalls, and cities. I've seen fine painters at work in Italy and I know what I'm talking about. You will never understand this battle unless I tell you all that led up to it.

"Well, we trudged across Lombardy, hungry, penniless, and ragged, to seek shelter in Milan, longing to have stout walls about us again. But the plague had swept Milan; all the beds in the abandoned houses were infected, the population had shrunk to a third of its number, and above all there was nothing left to steal, for the Emperor's garrison troops had seen to that. So we left the place hastily by the east gate as the French marched in by the west. All this was very discouraging for the Duke of Bourbon.

"He thanked us for our faithful service and bade us a sad farewell, having urgent business elsewhere. In the walled city of Pavia he left five thousand German *landsknechts* and a couple of hundred Spanish harquebusiers who still trusted to the Emperor's promises; for he wanted to keep at least some part of the Dukedom in his master's name. But I and many others declined with thanks, and we spent a weary winter in Lombardy, to the despair of the inhabitants.

"Meanwhile the French King laid siege to Pavia, which was a harder nut to crack than he expected. Yet he was so bent on its capture that he even tried to divert the course of the river, so as to attack the city wall at its weakest point. But the waters rose with the autumn rains and swept away all his works, and the sappers with them, rest their souls. Three months he wasted outside Pavia, and his forces were so

240

numerous that he sent a part of them to occupy Naples and save time. But at the beginning of February the Duke of Bourbon returned from Germany with ten thousand *landsknechts* under Frundsberg's command. Thus he and the Emperor's general, the Marquis of Pescara, and de Lannoy, the Viceroy of Naples, were able to form us into something resembling an army. We marched to Pavia and began in our turn to besiege the besieger, the French King, whose troops had dug themselves in behind impregnable field-works, from where they made long noses at us and commented unfavorably upon our fighting prowess and our origins, and so forth.

"We were indeed in a very ticklish situation, for from the hills the French campfires were seen to form an unbroken ring round Pavia. I fancy the Imperial forces had never been in such a fix. It was only a matter of time before the city must surrender. The men had not been paid for six months, and when I tell you that they had already eaten all the donkeys, dogs, and cats in the place, even you will realize that they had good reason to feel downcast.

"For two weeks we hung about the beleaguered city while the Emperor's officers disputed among themselves as to what was to be done. At long last they determined to trust to luck and break by night into the park of Mirabello."

"A park?" I exclaimed. "What can a park have to do with the battle of Pavia?"

"Am I telling this story or are you?" he retorted sharply. "This park, which belonged to the Duke of Milan, was very large and bounded by a wall. It lay immediately outside the wall of the city. There was not so much as a stag or a peacock left in it, for the French had eaten up every living thing. The Marquis of Pescara decided that under cover of night we should muster all our forces north of this walled park, break into it, and take the French by surprise."

Andy raised his eyes reflectively to the ceiling, then looked admiringly at his huge hands, shook his head, and went on, "Pescara addressed the Spaniards, and Frundsberg spoke to us Germans. He told us that in all the world we owned but the plot of ground we stood on, that next day our bread would be finished, and that the impoverished Emperor could not pay us our wages. At these words many men wept and we felt again like motherless lambs. But he put heart into us by saying that the French King's camp was full of wine, meat, and bread, and bursting coffers, and that there awaiting us

241

were the most eminent gentlemen of France, whose ransoms would make their captors rich men.

"It was a windy, overcast February night, and one I shall not forget. Never have I sweated as I sweated then with my crowbar at the high wall of Mirabello park! We had been ordered to wear white shirts, or at least white rags tied round our arms, so that we might know our own men in the darkness and in the confusion of the assault. But this was easier said than done, for our shirts were tattered and far from white. We did the best we could, and achieved one rag per man—with a little goodwill one might say one white rag. However, the precaution proved needless and an utter waste of our precious linen, for the wall was stouter than we thought and day was dawning before we struggled into the park. But the enemy alarm had sounded long since, and we came face to face with the French army drawn up in impeccable formation, ready for battle. And there was King Francis himself in armor inlaid with gold, mounted on a white horse at the head of his steel-clad knights. They had even had time to drag their field-pieces into position, and we received a fiery kiss of welcome. The French gunners used balls chained together, which is against all decent tradition in warfare. Arms and legs whirled in the air like autumn leaves at the first volley, and our advance guard had to wear the bloody sark and take cover in the thickets."

"But was this a miracle from God?" I asked. "I cannot understand how your little force could overcome the most invincible army in Europe."

Andy answered after some reflection, "I cannot think that God had much to do with the battle of Pavia, since His Most Christian Majesty of France was fighting His Imperial and Catholic Majesty, with the Holy Father backing both. That is, if I have rightly understood the politics of the matter. I give the credit to the consummate generalship of Pescara and our own valor. However, at that moment we were very far from victory. When the Imperial cavalry charged with leveled lances, the flower of French chivalry uttered a tremendous shout. The King set spurs to his charger, and the proudest cavalry in the world swept forward like a stormcloud with lightnings of gold and silver, and the ground beneath them rumbled and shook like thunder. They cut our horsemen to pieces. King Francis drove his spear through an Italian prince whose name I forget, and he perished beneath the horses' hoofs. The King fancied the battle was over, and truth to tell so did we as we charged him with our pikes, Frundsberg running beside us, panting and exhorting. Frundsberg knew as well as we did that a line of clumsy pikemen has little chance against armored cavalry—and now the Switzers were advancing on our other flank. Their haste was the greater since they loathed the Germans and wanted to share the honors of victory with the French. This was the decisive moment of the battle, I believe, although we knew nothing of it then. We hung back to say a last prayer and to commend our souls to God, until the pressure behind us became too great and we were forced forward— as was, of course, the intention. It is to insure this necessary pressure that pikemen are drawn up for the attack in squares ten men deep."

So deeply absorbed was I in Andy's account that I almost forgot to breathe, and the widow crossed herself and exclaimed in horror and dismay. Andy began arranging crusts, bones, and knives upon the table, moving and rearranging them as he continued his story.

"This carving knife is King Francis and his cavalry. This juicy bone is the Swiss force now charging. But this bit of liver is the black Italian troops, who are mad with rage, and they dash in front of the Swiss to share their laurels, because they think the war's being fought over Italy and they want to have their say. They mask the French guns, thus, and the French King's seneschal jumps up and down in a frenzy, tearing the plumes from his helmet, thus. Our own advance troops have retreated to this crack here. But now this wine cup—bang, bang!— here comes the world's finest general, Pescara. He reconnoiters the field, gathers up our scattered cavalry, and sends his Spanish harquebusiers, fifteen hundred of them, against the King's mounted knights. They creep forward from bush to bush on either flank, so. A few hundred Germans armed with the Emperor's new handguns creep after them. Now those well-drilled Spaniards have planted their rests—they load, fire, and reload with amazing speed. Each man can loose as many as five shots in fifteen minutes! Smoke swirls round the bushes, shots crash out, and the heavy balls pierce the French armor as if it were paper. One ball will go through two men and two big horses. The like has never been known. The riders tumble right and left and their huge chargers rear up and fall, screaming."

"Poor creatures," cried the widow tearfully. "Horses are dear, and it would have been better to harness them to the plough or sell them than to ride them to their death in that wanton, cruel way."

Andy went on unheeding.

"The dismounted riders crawled about on all fours trying to get to their feet, but they were weighed down by their heavy armor. The others wheeled about and tore panic-stricken from the field. Look, the carving knife rushes toward the bone—the flying cavalry trample the Swiss under foot and stir them into a screaming mass. At the same moment we clash with the Italians—here we are, this steak-beater—here am I and here's Frundsberg, roaring. We have a good press behind us, but the Italians fight like wild boars. Frundsberg strikes down their leader, I swing my two-handed sword, cleave the spear shafts, and clear a way for our pikes. But the Italians won't yield, and we have to cut them down to the last man before we can come at the Swiss. There goes the liver to the dog. Won't he eat it? Just sniffs at it! Plague on him.

"Well, as I say, the Switzers have got under the feet of the French cavalry and they can't stand against us—no pressure behind them—they turn and fly! For the first time in history men of the Confederation show their backs to the enemy. The King of France raises his golden visor to see better. 'Mon Dieu, mon Dieu!' he yells. 'What's the meaning of this?' But the Swiss don't stop to explain. And look—from this little summer palace of Mirabello, Pescara sends a detachment to turn the French flank, when all of a sudden a fearful crashing and thundering in their rear! This wooden platter is the city of Pavia, and the Spaniard Leuva, commandant of the beleaguered forces, leads his men out to the attack. They're mad with hunger and lust for plunder—they make mincemeat of the French rearguard and the flying Swiss. None of our men have seen such a massacre. The clear streams of the park run red and the frosty air is full of steam, as at a pig-killing."

"Jesus, Mary! That reminds me," cried the widow. "I forgot to bring you the pork sausages I put to warm in the oven."

She hurried off to fetch them. Andy bit into one absently, and with staring eyes and a full mouth he continued his story.

"Even now King Francis might save himself; he has his horse. But no; he has seen victory turned into the most smashing defeat of all time, and he's blind with rage. This pattern of French chivalry cannot endure the shame of flight. The noblest blood of France flows about him and he will fall sword in hand. He sets spurs to his horse, storms in among the lances—and his noble charger falls under him. Howling, swearing, and cuffing, we hurl ourselves upon him, for never has a mercenary taken a more valuable prisoner. Being strong, I throw the Spaniards aside like so many gloves, and manage to grasp one of the King's legs, that at least I may snatch a spur as a memento. The rest tear the armor off him, for it's worth tens of thousands of ducats.

"We would have rent him in pieces in our greed had not de Lannoy, the Viceroy of Naples, spurred forward and belabored us with the flat of his sword. We give way, and King Francis sits up and wipes the blood from his face, for he's wounded in the face and in one hand, and no wonder. We call our names and claim our share of the prize, but de Lannoy wrenches the King's sword from the hands of a Spaniard, returns it to His Majesty, kneels, and requests him to surrender to the Emperor. The Duke of Bourbon also gallops up, but King Francis spits blood in his face, crying 'Traitor!' and surrenders his sword to de Lannoy. Well, in two hours all is over. Twenty thousand men lie dead in that park, Frenchmen and Germans, Switzers and Spaniards, lords and bumpkins, knights in gilded armor and rough pikemen, higgledy-piggledy together. Our booty is enormous, our victory yet greater. We yell, sing, loot, and wallow to our hearts' content, and in our joy we forget the pain of our wounds."

Andy drew a deep breath, swept aside knives, cups, and bones to show that the battle was over, and let down his breeches to display a well-healed stab in his great thigh. The widow, agreeably impressed, felt the thigh and said admiringly that it was like iron.

But Andy pulled up his breeches again and went on, "We had so many prisoners that we released about four thousand Swiss and French rather than feed them, for they were poor and we could have got nothing for them. But we captured many noble gentlemen too, and I can't complain of my winnings. We never got a farthing for the King, however, for thousands were ready to swear by the Virgin to having been the first to lay hands upon him, and so de Lannoy told us all to go to hell; *he* had captured the King, and all present could bear witness that it was to him the royal prisoner had given up his sword."

"We know what gentlemen are," put in the widow. "As well grasp a hedgehog as seek justice from one of them. A fistful of prickles is all you get."

Andy swallowed a stoup of wine, looked at me gravely, and said, "Michael, my brother, I have talked high politics with you and told you of the battle of Pavia, in which thirty thousand well-equipped, seasoned soldiers led by brilliant generals engaged an army of thirty-five thousand. I told you this to show that in comparison with high politics and regular warfare this senseless peasant rising is a mere cobweb on the wall. An experienced leader will mow down those peasants as a sickle mows corn. This battle has rendered the Emperor

245

all-powerful—and he does not love Lutherans. He has sworn to uproot heresy in Germany, and then, with the help of a united Christendom, to conquer the Turks. From the bottom of my heart I implore you to see reason. Let's get out of here while we may and seek other and better markets."

His words gave me much to think about, and yet I did not consider him fit to be my counselor. Also, I was somewhat drunk, having consumed more wine than necessary in my joy at meeting him again.

So I retorted, "You're still the same poor simpleton, Andy. You may be able to wield a two-handed broadsword, but controversy is beyond you. And your spoils are nothing to boast about; anyone can slip his hand into his neighbor's purse. You must learn that the justice of God is more than the rights of kings; and although the twelve articles are a human conception and therefore faulty and imperfect, yet they are based on the Word of God and no power on earth can prevent their realization, for the Lord will smite His adversaries as Samson smote the Philistines with the jawbone of an ass. And remember that the peasants are better armed than Samson was. They have spears like soldiers, and armor, and even guns—"

But Andy, skeptical and puffed up with his experiences, replied, "I may be a dunce beside you, but common sense tells me that God is on the side of the Catholic Emperor and in no way favors heretical peasants. I seem to have heard too that the Bible bids us obey those who are set in authority over us. And I believe it is also written that one should render unto God that which is God's and to the Emperor that which is the Emperor's. As I see it, the life, honor, and estate of a private man are the Emperor's, while his soul is God's."

Before I could make any crushing retort, the door opened to admit a light-footed woman with red cheeks and smiling mouth. She wore a ragged dress and a hat with a trailing feather, and as she entered she crooned a melancholy little song:

> "Monsieur de la Palice est mort,
> Mort devant Pavie.
> Un quart d'heure avant sa mort
> Il était encore en vie."

The spice-merchant's widow snorted with indignation and said, "There she is, the nasty trull that Master Andrew brought from Italy. Take a stick to her, Master Michael, and send her packing from my decent house!"

246

But when I heard the woman's voice and beheld her features, I sprang up and crossed myself as if the Evil One himself were before me; for as I live, there stood—slightly unsteady but very real—Madam Genevieve of the relic-dealer's house in Paris. At the sight of me she cried out for joy, threw her arms about my neck, and kissed me on both cheeks before I could shake her off.

All the bounce was out of Andy. He seemed to shrink where he sat, and he said to me pleadingly:

"Forgive me, Michael! I couldn't help it. She has stuck to me like a burr all the way from Pavia. She has made my life such a burden that I hope you'll take her off my hands. I seem to remember that you were once rather sweet on her and that she's in your debt for certain matters."

I was thunderstruck and speechless. Madam Genevieve seated herself in a somewhat frivolous attitude, pulled the front of her dress down in a revealing manner, and gazed at me as if she had been a dog and I a piece of meat.

She continued humming her tune until I came to my senses and said angrily, "God help us all! I've heard more than enough of Pavia to last me a lifetime—and if you've brought this noble lady as part of your spoils all the way from Pavia, Andy, you're stupider even than I thought, and you're very far from having done me a service."

Madame Genevieve seemed to think that I was finding fault with her song, and she said in injured tones, "Monsieur de la Palice was a better man than either of you! The French made up that song about him after the battle. He was surrounded by a hundred Spaniards and fought alone to his last breath, though his eyes were dim and one arm was off at the shoulder, and there was a gaping wound in his thigh."

I tried to silence her, that I might collect my thoughts, but I might as well have tried to stay a mill wheel.

"I, if anyone, can vouch for his manhood, for he was pleased to favor me, and in the morning he gave me twenty gold pieces in a beautifully embroidered silken purse. And believe me or not, the King of France himself has kissed my hand—and other parts—for he was a gallant knight who found camp life tedious."

She continued long in the same vein, and made it clear that she had had unusual success in her chosen profession.

"In chivalry, liberality, and the arts of love, none can compare with the French knights," she went on. "And God knows it was the mercenaries alone who brought misfortune upon me, for they robbed me of clothes, beauty-box, ointments, and all the possessions which were the fruits of my industry in the French King's camp, and which I had collected in order to secure for myself and my children a life free from anxiety."

"Jesus, Mary!" I cried, ignoring Andy's warning grimaces. "Have you children, my dear Madam Genevieve?"

Andy broke in.

"Michael, my dear brother, I beg you not to believe all this woman tells you. She says she has a boy and a girl lodged with foster parents in Tours. She says the boy is nearly five years old—and although I don't believe it, she has bound me to her by insisting that he's my son."

"It's impossible to be mistaken," said Madam Genevieve. "I knew it as soon as he was born. He's the image of Andy, and I had all the trouble in the world to persuade my first protector that *he* was the child's father. You remember him, Master Michael, do you not? However, he was convinced at last, and after much argument he recognized the child as his bastard. The boy is now under the protection of a noble family, though his father—his legal father I mean, of course—was a waster and a boor. Peace to his memory. He perished at Pavia like so many others, being luckily drowned while seeking flight across the river, thus avoiding the open shame of cowardice. I have named my son André Florian, that he might bear the names of both his fathers, legal and natural. Many's the time I've remembered with regret Andy's tenderness when in the arms of feebler and less pleasing lovers, until at last God's providence led him to rescue me from the violence of the Spaniards at Pavia."

Madam Genevieve spoke so gently and persuasively and the glance she sent Andy from her violet eyes was so devoted that I could not doubt her, and began to feel that Andy had acted rightly in taking his son's mother under his protection, notwithstanding all the trouble and expense it would cost us.

But Andy said, "Do you believe her, Michael? If so, it's your duty to shoulder your share of the heavy burden of paternity, since the boy is really half yours and should be called André Michel Florian!"

At this I exclaimed in the greatest astonishment and indignation that I had never so much as touched Madam Genevieve, though in my youthful folly I had not lacked the will; that her falseness had saved me, for which I now thanked God, seeing the dilemma into which she had brought Andy. But Andy, regarding me mockingly with his honest but somewhat fuddled eyes, pointed out that she owed *me* the

248

debt for which he on my behalf had accepted payment on account, and that I was therefore at least equally responsible for the child. This I could not deny, and I was filled with impotent rage. Madam Genevieve interpreted my silence as assent, and continued the woeful story of her adventures. Of how after the battle she took refuge in the monastery cell that her protector had secured for her, and arrayed herself in all her finery in the hope that some noble lord would come and offer her his protection. Of how, instead, her retreat was invaded first by a filthy, bloody rabble who robbed her of everything, even her clothes, and then by Spaniards who, finding nothing else to take, robbed her violently and successively of her honor.

She wept at the memory of her ill-usage, and when at last she had concluded her recital she added, "You must understand, Michael, that a woman's success depends on her clothes, her aids to beauty, and the dressing of her hair. The loss of the money did not so much distress me, for I could soon have earned as much again if only I had had the clothes and other effects to enable me to find some high-ranking protector in the Emperor's camp. Without them I was no better than the meanest drab. But by the mercy of Providence I found my son's father, who rescued me from these straits, though he has not yet procured me the wardrobe I require in order to regain my former standing and provide honorably for my children."

Andy vowed he would never throw away his hard-won ducats on fallals for her, were she a thousand times the mother of his son, but I realized that we would not be quit of Madam Genevieve until we had furnished her with the effects necessary to her profession. I told her therefore that the peasants were looting castles in every direction and that their women were flaunting silks and velvets and furs, and I had no doubt that we could obtain suitable garments for her at a moderate price. But meanwhile, I told her, I was weary and the burns on my legs were painful.

"Let us sleep," I said, "and hope that tomorrow may prove a better counselor than today."

Madam Genevieve's eyes gleamed, and entirely misunderstanding my allusion to bedtime she flung her arms about me, offered to help me to bed if my legs were unsteady, and to dress my burns. The widow firmly refused to lend her her own bed, and predicted a bad end for us all. So we climbed to the attic and shared my couch, Madam Genevieve in the middle. Andy was asleep and snoring as soon as his head touched the pillow; whereupon Madam Genevieve embraced me affectionately and whispered in my ear. But I resisted her seductions, being all too weary, and fell asleep with her soft arms about my neck.

5

Not until the next day was I made very forcibly aware of the evening's intemperance. However, a morning draught of ale cleared my head to some extent and I dragged myself to call on Ulrich Schmid. His captains reported that a peasant army numbering five thousand was on the march to Leipheim on the Danube, there being many wealthy monasteries and castles in that region. I announced that I too would ride there without delay, for I was convinced that the sooner we were rid of Madam Genevieve the better. Ulrich Schmid applauded my decision and urged me in God's name to bid the peasants join the main force as soon as possible, for the Swabian General Jürgen von Truchsess was approaching by forced marches, slaying, beheading, blinding, and burning the men of many scattered parties. The Leipheim bands would be wise to hurry.

So we set off to Leipheim. The road was furrowed by spring rains, wild flowers gleamed in the meadows, and the fresh air was filled with the scent of limes, although the month of April had barely begun. We thought of our poor homeland, which at this time of year was still icebound, with its gray cabins half buried in snowdrifts, and we were melancholy. Andy told me that among the German mercenaries he had met with a Danish lieutenant who in his time had served under King Christian. This man told him that the King had long since lost crown and lands to his uncle the Duke of Holstein and had fled to the Netherlands, to seek protection with his brother-in-law the Emperor. In a weak moment the Swedish nobles had chosen Gustaf for their king— Gustaf of the Vasa line, who had so vigorously stirred up Sweden and Finland against their lawful monarch.

We beguiled the way with lively talk, and Madam Genevieve entertained us with many unedifying stories of the French court and of the French King's habits. When we reached the little town of Leipheim we found that the peasants had pitched camp on the surrounding slopes, and there the all too familiar confusion, drunkenness, and debauchery prevailed. Trade was brisk in the market place of the town, but the Jews who had swarmed hither from all directions like flies to a dunghill had already laden their barrows with the most valuable wares, which they had bought for a song from thirsty peasants and for which they now demanded shameful prices. We turned our backs on the market and wandered about the neighboring camp, from sheep-fold to byre, from thatched hovel to shed; for peasants had quartered themselves in all these places. They willingly displayed their booty, and when I came upon any of their leaders, or at any rate those among them who shouted loudest, I gave them Ulrich Schmid's advice to return to Baltringen and present their claims in peaceful negotiation with the princes' general, who was on his way to teach the peasants manners. But these people were besotted by their own strength and their many successes, and said that they believed neither in negotiation nor in generals, and least of all in Ulrich Schmid, who was an old woman.

While we were conversing in this way, Madam Genevieve discov-ered a chestful of splendid attire—silks, velvets, fur-trimmed capes, lace, and feathers. It contained also a box of ointments and face paint, and silver-handled mirrors, brushes, combs, tongs, and spatulas, and was no doubt the property of some distinguished lady who had packed them for flight. Madam Genevieve wound her arms around my neck— and would have done the same to Andy if he had let her—begging us to buy the chest with all its contents, for it was exactly what she needed. She told us playfully that we should never recognize her when she had put on the new clothes and had painted her face, and she tripped about us so lightly and charmingly, as is the way of Frenchwomen, that what with this and the spring sunshine and the green slopes dotted with flowers my youthful memories revived, and I asked the ensign what he would take for the box.

The negotiations that ensued were long and, on his side, voluble. He meant the things for his wife, he said, and could not think of taking less than a thousand gulden. Even the Jews had offered him a hundred and fifty. Madam Genevieve pleaded with me and wept, and I was so distracted that at last I offered sixty, whereupon he closed the lid of the chest with a bang and said he would not hear another word of the matter.

Andy meanwhile had been gazing toward the hills and the valley of the Danube. The river had overflowed its banks and half-encircled the little town in its foaming loop.

"I see horsemen approaching," he said. "They wear armor and carry lances, and they seem in a great hurry. They look to me more like princes' men than peasants, their mounts are in such good condition."

The ensign turned aside, blew his nose in his fingers, and said,

"There are many of us and I don't even know all my own men. These people have no doubt come from the other side of the Danube to join us."

We looked down the valley and watched the riders charge full-tilt at some peasants who were driving wagons laden with grain. The riders transfixed them and trampled them underfoot. We heard faint cries and saw two of the draught-horses shy and overturn their load. Yet at that distance and through the haze the whole incident had the air of a dream, and we could not believe that we had seen aright.

But Andy pointed to a second group of horsemen approaching the city along another road.

"I have some little experience of warfare," he said, "and it seems to me high time to sound the alarm, for if I'm not greatly mistaken these are von Truchsess's patrols sent forward to reconnoitre. The main body cannot be far behind or they would never have ventured a skirmish under our very noses."

The peasant officer laughed heartily at Andy, but at that moment the church bells began to ring. Peasants poured from every gateway like bees at swarming time and rushed up the hill, tripping over their lances as they came. Both troops of horse halted to survey the field, then wheeling suddenly they set off at a gallop.

On our hilltop the drums began to roll, and out from shed and store-house crawled the peasants, rubbing the sleep from their eyes.

The ensign had turned pale, but trying to put a good face on it he said, "If those were indeed the prince's men, they were but few and with God's help we shall beat them in open combat. Yet perhaps it would be prudent to fortify our position here. I beg you, sir, as a distinguished officer, to give us your advice. Our traditional method is to surround ourselves with a ring of carts, but we would gladly consider newer methods if you have knowledge of such from your glorious campaigns."

Pikemen were now to be seen marching along the valley, moving with precision and flanked by cavalry.

"Did you say sixty gulden, noble sir? Add ten to that and the chest is yours."

Madam Genevieve, unmoved by the horsemen and the waving forest of spears along the valley, jumped for joy like a young girl and begged me to shake hands on the bargain. But Andy restrained me.

"Better postpone your deal until a more convenient moment. We seem to have landed in one of the less agreeable kinds of wasps' nest.

252

Von Truchsess appears to be an able general—although of course not to be compared with the Marquis of Pescara—and I'll wager that he means to tie us up in this loop of the Danube before half the sand can run through an hourglass. Here come teams of oxen dragging culverins, and I will now take my leave, being a stranger with no business here."

The peasants were dragging their carts into a ring, driving stakes into the ground and stretching ropes between them. I saw that they were also bringing two small cannon into position and that there were handgunners among them.

At this I rejoiced, and said to Andy, "Go your way if you please, Andy, and if your conscience will allow you. But the place for me and my good gun is here among these stout fellows who seem ready to fight for God's justice."

Madam Genevieve flatly refused to go anywhere without the chest and gave point to her words by flinging herself over the lid and clinging to it with both hands. The peasant owner—after a hasty glance into the valley, where companies of pikemen were breaking into smaller detachments and encircling the hill in faultless order—observed hastily that worldly vanity meant nothing to him; his only jewel was the Word of God, and he would therefore be content with thirty gulden. This advantageous bargain and the obstinacy of Madam Genevieve blinded me, and I rapidly counted out the money without even pausing to sort out the fullweights from the underweights.

But Andy said, "Michael, I beg you for the sake of our long friendship, come with me. I may be stupid, but experience tells me that this is our last chance. Since Madam Genevieve is stubborn, I'll agree to take the chest, but we must leave at once."

But my faith in the victory of right over wrong made me deaf to the voice of reason. I fancy my exploit with the petard had gone to my head; moreover, I had never yet seen the peasants meet with defeat.

I answered scornfully, "Run away, Andy! Row across the Danube to safety. I'll fetch you when we've beaten the princes' troops—and next time you boast of your wars I'll believe as much of it as I care to."

Andy glanced about him, made the sign of the cross, and said, "Too late. We've wasted time in chattering. I'll stay by you, since I came all the way from Italy to save you from just such a calamity."

There was no time to say more, for captains, ensigns, and sergeants, wearing cocks' feathers in their caps in token of their rank, were running to and fro like headless hens and cuffing their men into position.

There were about thirty harquebusiers among the five thousand defenders. I joined them when the cavalry began riding up the slope, drove my rest into the ground, and although my heart was fluttering like a leaf I primed, loaded, and fired. When the horsemen saw the flashes from our weapons, they turned aside to let the foot soldiers through and to surround the hill.

The pikemen advanced uphill with a short, firm step, and their supporting artillery opened the bombardment. The wagons forming our defenses were smashed and overturned, and our forces were thrown into great disorder. When the first rank of the pikemen had reached our palisades, Andy told me to fire into the thick of them, and he brandished his two-handed sword. But it was useless. Confronted by the long, vicious pikes, the peasants were seized with sudden misgivings as to the justice of their cause, and having no pressure behind them they turned and took to their heels downhill toward the town, between the squares of infantry.

At this stampede Andy laughed and said, "Now will you believe me, Michael? Come, we must make a dash for it."

We needed no second bidding, but set off in a headlong career, Andy clearing our path with his broadsword and I with the butt of my gun. Our horses had vanished and Madam Genevieve shrieked and wrung her hands and besought us to save her chest of valuables, but Andy smote her on the mouth and dragged her onward. We charged through the struggling throng of fugitives and somehow kept together. I hung onto Andy's leather belt and he hauled Madam Genevieve along now by the arm, now by the hair, still carving a bloody lane through the mass of peasants or between the murderous, slashing, clubbing pikemen. At least two thousand fleeing peasants met their death on those slopes.

Andy led us without pause through the town of Leipheim and out on the other side. Not until we reached the riverbank did he halt to regain his breath and to survey the swirling green floodwaters. Peasants who had followed us and who in their panic hurled themselves into the river were swallowed up and borne away downstream, heads whirling and arms tossing.

While Andy was getting his breath back, the mob thinned out. He caught sight of some men a little way along the bank who were carrying a stranded boat down to the water's edge. He dragged us toward them, shouting to them to wait for us. But they had no intention of waiting, and as soon as they had launched their craft they hurled themselves higgledy-piggledy into it. Down sank the boat into the mud and would not budge.

Andy seized the sternpost, and putting forth his colossal strength he dragged boat and men to land. He spoke fairly to these fugitives and offered to buy the boat, but all the reply he got was a knife slash over the hand. Unperturbed, he remarked that if they preferred violence to honest dealing he was their man. Then with the flat of his sword he felled the fellow who had wounded him, gave me his sword to hold, waded into the water, and began throwing the rest out over his shoulder into the river. The eddying waters carried them away, but one slenderly built fellow begged for mercy and asked to come with us over the Danube. There was room for four in the boat and Andy ordered us aboard without delay, for people were streaming from the city gate and enemy cavalry was approaching. He grabbed Madam Genevieve by the hair, for she had refused to entrust her life to such a leaky old cockleshell. I crouched on the bottom to load my gun, and the stranger seized the oars.

We were not an instant too soon, for Andy had to strike at several peasants who were trying to climb aboard. Only by ceaseless blows of his sword was he able to free himself, push out the boat, and scramble over the side. Many waded out into deep water and tried to grasp the gunwale; we would certainly have capsized had not Andy severed their fingers. Then the current carried us away. The little stranger began to row bravely toward the opposite shore and Andy helped with the steering oar, though once or twice we spun round like a cork in a whirlpool and our hearts were in our mouths. But Andy was not happy.

Staring glumly before him, he muttered a short prayer and said, "May I be forgiven my cruelty on the bank, for I did ill in cutting off the hands and fingers of innocent men. Yet the boat could not carry more than four, and is it not better that four should be saved than that all should drown?"

Our wretched craft was tossed like a nutshell on the seething flood, and leaked so badly that when at last we touched the shore we were soaked to the waist. No sooner did I feel dry land beneath my feet than I was seized with a wild lust for revenge. I had contrived to keep my powder dry, and despite Andy's protests we made our way upstream along the bank and joined a group that was standing opposite the river gate of the town, staring at the drowned and drowning as

255

they swept past, and at the fearful massacre that had begun on the other side.

Pikemen and cuirassiers had surrounded a mass of peasants numbering many thousands and were putting them to death. At a little distance a general in glittering armor bestrode a black charger. From his waving plumes and the standard fluttering before him I knew that this must be Jürgen von Truchsess. He had raised his visor and I could plainly see his curly beard and lean, dark features as he looked on complacently at the slaughter that his men were achieving in so masterly a manner. But the gentlemen of his suite were urging him to put an end to this pointless killing, no doubt reminding him that peasants did not grow on trees and that they were necessary for ploughing and sowing.

At last von Truchsess ordered the trumpets to sound and summoned the provost marshal in order to administer justice in a lawful manner. He shouted so loud that the breeze carried his voice over to us. When I heard him call the executioner, I drove my rest into the ground and primed my gun, despite the idlers beside me who begged me not to fire and who took to their heels panic-stricken. Even Andy said it was unnecessary to poke a stick into a wasps' nest. I laid fresh powder in the pan, kindled the match, fastened it to the trigger, aimed, and fired. But I never hit Jürgen von Truchsess. My fine gun burst in two with a crack; no doubt water had got into the barrel on our way over, and it was God's miracle that neither I nor the bystanders were hurt by the sharp splinters, though the powder peppered my face.

Our little companion began preaching with great energy, and saying this was a proof that the Swabian peasants had fallen a prey to false doctrine. This observation made a certain impression on me, since I was much shocked at the destruction of my good weapon in my very hands. So I asked him who he was and why he thought the Swabian peasants had gone astray although they held by Luther and were fighting for God's justice and the twelve articles. The stranger told me he was the least and humblest in the land, one Jacob the Tailor from the good city of Mühlhausen in Thuringia. He had brought letters and messages from his master and preceptor to the people of this region, with the praiseworthy object of rousing them to resist their overlords and to join the company of God's elect. Jacob had intended to journey farther, but in Leipheim they had only laughed at him and spat on his letters, and were now receiving their well-deserved punishment; for God is not mocked.

And a punishment it was. The executioner stood ready. The men-at-arms dragged forward the peasant leaders, and a priest whom we had seen mounted on a donkey among the peasant defenders. The soldiers had no great trouble, for defeat had humbled the peasants, who now vied with one another in pointing out their leaders and in helping them forward out of the press with eager punches in the back. Heads rolled before the hoofs of the black horse, among them that of the priest.

Jacob rejoiced. "Luther is no holy prophet," he said, "but rather a wolf in sheep's clothing. God's true spokesman is my master and teacher, who has come out of the wilderness, like St. John the Baptist, to preach the congregation of God's elect, and the millenium. As for me, I have no further business in these parts and I shall return to my master. The pikemen seem to be seeking a raft to cross over to us."

He was right, and we hastened away, the tailor acting as our guide. Every step took us farther from Baltringen, where I had left Rael in the care of the widow. But Baltringen was far away, and both the Danube and the enemy lay between. It was evident that I could be of no more service to Ulrich Schmid, and indeed he was beheaded less than a week afterward. His army was dispersed without a blow being struck, and the peasants returned to their own charred doorsteps—all that remained of their homes after von Truchsess's visit. But this I did not hear until much later.

We panted beside the little tailor over soggy headlands, along ditches, and through thickets, to avoid molestation. Madam Genevieve wept bitterly and unceasingly, reviling us because we had not saved her chest and because she was now poorer than before, having lost her shoes in the mud.

The many omens, our singular escape, and the bursting of my gun had made me thoughtful, and I feared that some divine intention lay behind these things. So I examined the tailor about his faith.

He held forth throughout our journey as fast as he could draw breath, and said among other things, "My master is Thomas Müntzer, who is now founding a community of the elect in Mühlhausen, after doing the same in many other places, including the Confederation, although he has been driven out of all of them and cruelly persecuted for his faith. He's not yet thirty-five, nevertheless he has studied at many learned universities and speaks Greek and Hebrew and knows the Bible by heart. In his youth he was considered the most studious of all the scholars in Germany. But God gave him no peace, and he could never remain long in one place. He became teacher, preacher, and confessor at many convents, until God's word came to him through an ignorant weaver who had received divine grace. Thenceforth my master renounced all his scholarly degrees and titles and became God's servant, and the messenger of the gospel of the Cross."

As he paused for breath I remarked that Luther also bore the message of the Cross. But this angered him, and he went on, "Luther chose the easy way. But faith alone will not admit us to the company of the blessed. Man must bear the cross that God has laid upon him— bear it until heart and soul are humbled and until all that is left is man, stripped of vanity and pride. And into that man God breathes His holy breath and he is made one with the blessed, and God speaks through his mouth. Since the way is hard, the number of the chosen is small, but they are the salt of the earth and the Lord shall deliver the ungodly into their hand. I see in our present deliverance a sign from heaven—a pointing finger toward you also as the chosen of God. Therefore I urge you to come with me to Mühlhausen and become my master's disciples. You're both strong fellows and of bigger build than I am, and I'm afraid to travel alone in these turbulent times, especially at night. God must have sent you to be my companions and protectors."

Evening drew on, and Andy decided we were now at a safe distance from Leipheim. So in the heart of a forest we flung ourselves down exhausted. We divided among us a piece of bread that Andy found in his wallet and a cheese that the tailor brought from his beggar's sack. We had a mouthful each, and we even contrived to kindle a fire and dry our clothes. Then we lay down side by side to keep one another warm through the chill night.

Next morning we had to decide whither we should go, for it is hard to wander aimlessly. Andy was for returning to France, but when we had come out onto the road again and had a clear view of the surrounding country, the roar of cannon and the thick columns of smoke above the western horizon caused him to change his mind, and he thought it wiser to continue with Jacob the tailor.

On we wandered, like the children of Israel in the wilderness, for by day our steps were guided by clouds of smoke and by night by pillars of fire from burning castles and manors. Soon we were able to eat our fill again, and I swallowed enough fat mutton to last me all my life. I felt I never wanted to behold another sheep, for there were very great flocks in Thuringia at that time. We found fine clothes for Madam Genevieve, and she no longer looked like a tattered camp-follower when after a fortnight's uneventful trudging we arrived at the good town of Mühlhausen.

258

BOOK 8.

The Rainbow Banner

I

MÜHLHAUSEN was a large town, one of the largest in Germany, for it had a population of more than seven thousand, more than could be housed within the walls. The poorer people had spread into five outer suburbs; thus Mühlhausen was twice as big as Leipzig, for instance, or Dresden, which were accounted big cities.

The streets were thronged when we arrived. I saw many broken doors and shutters, and at every corner men stood in groups arguing about divine grace, the Gospel, the manner of administering the Sacraments, and the cross that must be borne by rich and poor alike. Overcrowded though the city was, money and fair words obtained us lodging at an inn. Jacob the tailor was in haste to return to his wife, but he urged us to attend evening service at the church when we had eaten, so that he could present us to Thomas Müntzer and to his military commander, Heinrich Pfeiffer.

I invited Madam Genevieve and Andy to come with me, but Andy declared that he was weary and unwilling to cause scandal by falling asleep in church, while Madam Genevieve expressed a desire to wash herself and put on the clothes we had procured for her on the way. So I was reluctantly compelled to go alone. But when I arrived I could scarcely enter, the church was so packed.

Above the altar hung a huge banner—thirty yards of heavy white silk bearing across it a rainbow, and the legend in Latin: THE WORD OF GOD IS ETERNAL. But I forgot this banner in my eagerness to behold Thomas Müntzer. My first impression of him was one of insignificance, however. He was a head shorter than I, his nose and mouth were flabby, his chin small, and his cheeks sallow like those of a bilious person or a foreigner—an appearance enhanced by his almond-shaped eyes. In some strange way his face reminded me of a startled pig, especially while he was preaching.

Yet when he began to speak I forgot his appearance, and was held spellbound by his eyes alone, which glowed with singular fire. I have never heard so intense, so irresistible a sermon as that preached by Thomas Müntzer. His whole being was aflame with such unassailable conviction that one could indeed believe that the Holy Spirit dwelled in him. He uttered no mad yells as those ragamuffins did who for years had tramped the countryside expounding the new faith. At all times, whether he raised or lowered his voice, every syllable could be clearly heard in the remotest corners of the church.

First he reminded the congregation of what he himself had endured and of the cross that had borne him to the ground, thus freeing him to receive and reveal the word of the Lord. It was not he who now preached, he said modestly, but God who spoke through him and made known His will to the people; no one need now grope in ignorance or seek guidance in the Bible. Every man who turned a deaf ear or who derided Müntzer and his followers, or who in any other way offended those who had leagued themselves to fulfill God's purpose, made himself Satan's martyr and would be his own executioner; for the Day of the Lord was coming when all the ungodly should perish.

To see and hear Thomas Müntzer was to believe him, though I cannot explain his power. After an hour's repetition of the same phrases, he began upon a fresh theme. God had revealed His purpose to him in four principles. First, the word of God might be expounded freely and without restriction by everyone, but the tongues of the unrighteous must be silenced. Second, timber, fish, fowl, and game, meadows and pasturelands should be free to all. Third, the nobility must tear down their fortresses and castles, renounce their titles, and give honor to God alone. Fourth, and this was something new to me, the nobles should in return enjoy the use of estates belonging to the Church, and all those domains which lack of money had forced them to pledge in security for loans should be freely restored to them.

At this last point a murmur of astonishment filled the church, but Thomas Müntzer thumped both fists on the pulpit, and standing on tiptoe he cried that the Lord in His mercy willed that the princes should submit to Him freely and of their own accord, and not be goaded into bloodshed.

After developing these principles for some two hours, he worked himself into a frenzy of enthusiasm and called upon all present to subdue their hearts and rally humbly about his standard in a league of perpetual union with the divine will. In this league all possessions were held in common, and every member must submit himself in blind obedience to the will of God as it was revealed from time to time through Thomas Müntzer. If he said "Strike!" it was their duty to strike. If he said "Bide your time" they must be content to do so. They must be cunning as serpents and harmless as doves against the day when God would empty the vials of His wrath over the unrighteous. But God chose His own servants, wherefore none could join His league without trial, and during that testing time a man must show his faith and subdue his own desires, that he might be found a vessel fit for God's purpose.

As Müntzer spoke there was much sighing among his congregation. Many good men shed tears and said that the conditions were hard and that Luther brought men less painfully to a state of bliss. But those who were saved silenced the doubtful and fainthearted. Müntzer raised his voice and cried that this was no time for wailing and gnashing of teeth but rather for rejoicing, for the Lord would deliver the unrighteous into the hands of His servants and share out their riches among them—riches that were the sweat and blood of the poor. Let everyone now steel himself against the wiles of Satan, join the ranks of the faithful, and with them assume the stewardship of the Kingdom of God, which in all its glory was soon to arise upon the earth.

He came down from the pulpit, wiped the sweat from his brow, and stood listening to the joyful acclamations of the people, his dark, slanting eyes surveying them somberly.

He raised his hand repeatedly but in vain to gain silence for Colonel Pfeiffer, who was far from pleased at the prolonged applause. But the sullenness of this man melted as he climbed into the pulpit, and he smiled jovially at the people's shouts of greeting and at their laughter. He was evidently a favorite with them and of a broad humor, for he entertained them in their own coarse vein, his beery face radiant with good-fellowship. I will not repeat what he said, as it was insignificant

261

and expressed in terms unbefitting a decent man, though Luther himself was not always above lewd speech. I soon gathered that his aim was to lead the faithful in a crusade against the neighboring towns, and he declared that the troops of the princes were nothing to be afraid of, for they were divided among themselves and paralyzed with fear.

His good-humored assurance came as a relief after the steely discourse of Thomas Müntzer. More and more of the congregation joined with him and shouted that they would march forth beneath his standard. Yet I noted that this joyful tumult was in no way pleasing to Müntzer, who once or twice made as if to pluck Pfeiffer down from the pulpit. When the speech was over and the people were pouring from the church, determined to embark the very next day on a profitable and not too arduous campaign, Thomas Müntzer seized the commander by the collar and dragged him to the sacristy. As the congregation thinned I caught sight of Jacob the tailor, who seemed to be looking for me, and I made my way to him. Relieved to see that Madam Genevieve had not come, he led me to his master, who wished to question me about the battle of Leipheim, from which the four of us had so miraculously escaped.

So I came face to face with Thomas Müntzer. He did not offer me his hand, but only stared at me with his slanting, wrathful eyes. My knees shook as I remembered my sins and wondered how I could have displeased him, but I soon saw that his rage was directed at Pfeiffer, who stood shamefacedly apart, thumbing the edge of his sword. Throughout our interview Thomas Müntzer hit on ever more telling abuse, which he slung at Pfeiffer from the corner of his mouth without taking his eyes off me. This made our conversation somewhat confusing.

I told him all I knew of events in Baltringen and elsewhere, and gave it as my opinion that von Truchsess would easily quell the Swabian peasants without loss to himself, as at Leipheim.

My account of these dark and bloody events did not depress Thomas Müntzer. Indeed, he seemed the calmer for it, and said, "You speak rightly and sagely, Michael Pelzfuss. God has certainly endowed you with the gift of reason. The peasant leaders of Swabia are as wild boars in the Lord's vineyard. They have not the faith, and have driven Jacob the tailor forth with mocking. But what is to become of the Lord's vineyard if these ravening beasts surround me also, and seduce my faithful ones into seizing my sacred standard and rushing forth with it on ill-fated adventures? My task is to weld this league into a weapon for the Lord's hand, but my advisers are of Satan and they plot how to destroy my work and stuff their own bellies and purses. Sheathe your sword, Pfeiffer, you tainted of the devil!"

But now Pfeiffer was angry. He thrust his sword back into the scabbard and said, "Pox on you, Thomas Müntzer! What are you and I but two poor devils, equal in the sight of God? Remember, you've been driven from this town once already. Mühlhausen is more mine than yours, and my womenfolk have stitched as diligently as yours at our banner. I shall carry it where I please. Langensalza has given me so much trouble that I shall not let it slip through my fingers now, when its people have read the signs of the times and beg my help. Your cowardice shall not prevent us from raising the standard, and if there were a grain of manhood in you, you would see that our band will grow like an avalanche if we march now. If we stay, it will melt away to nothing. And if anyone lifts a finger to help us once we're brought to our knees before the princes' executioners, I'll eat my weight in dung."

They wrangled on in coarser and coarser terms until I knew not what to think of them. At last Pfeiffer roared that at dawn he would sound the assembly. Then it would be seen whom the faithful would follow, Pfeiffer or Müntzer. He then strode away, banging the door resoundingly behind him.

Müntzer, now tearful and trembling, said that the day that showed him Heinrich Pfeiffer swinging from the gallows would be one of rejoicing for him and for the Lord. The little tailor put an arm round his shoulders, comforted him, and said that all would turn out well for God's inscrutable purposes. Let him but steel himself to follow his standard and their foes would fall like grain under hail. I too did my best to cheer him, and he begged me earnestly to join his band, that he might have at least one sensible adviser and an envoy who would convey to the princes the letters that God moved him to write, for at least once a week he was favored with some divine message that his courage might be sustained.

The thought of being his messenger afforded me little delight, despite his assurances as to my safety, and I returned to the inn after dark in a gloomy frame of mind. Müntzer's sermon had made a deep impression on me, certainly, yet afterward I had seen him to be a weak, perplexed mortal like the rest of us. I breathed in the cool night air and raised my eyes toward the stars. As I surveyed that sparkling canopy I saw myself as another lonely spark in the night, blown by

God's mighty breath for some unsearchable purpose over the seething caldron that was Germany.

My sorrow hung more heavily upon me than it had for many months past, and I remembered the childish oath I had sworn when the blood of my wife Barbara poured warm over my hands. I seemed to see Holy Church rising in majesty before me to the very stars. For fifteen centuries it had so risen from an ocean of sin. Cleansed by the blood of martyrs, illuminated by the glory of the saints, it had offered through its Holy Sacraments the one way to salvation for all poor souls. Who was I, wretched worm, to loosen the smallest stone in that great structure, though I should ally myself a thousand times with wild prophets of the new doctrine and seek to found God's kingdom upon earth?

Forsaken of God and feeble of faith was I beneath the stars of that spring night. My heart was sick and my thoughts stood out starkly, mercilessly. I could not endure the naked conviction that I was but a man. I lowered my eyes and hastened to the warmth and light and simple companionship of the inn. Man's place is among men, and death alone can numb his incurable woe.

2

I see now that our campaign was as wild and senseless as a drunkard's meandering from tavern to tavern. When we came to Langensalza, it appeared that the inhabitants had dealt unaided with their own authorities and did not desire our interference in their private affairs. So we continued on our way, and without fear, for at our approach the nobles fled. We lacked for nothing, for the flocks and fishponds of the monasteries supplied us. Müntzer won new adherents daily from the towns and villages we passed, and they brought with them cartloads of booty from previous raids—clothing, arms, grain, and pork. Müntzer received them on horseback, greeted them as brothers in Christ, and allowed them to share their plunder with us. Our force grew like an avalanche, as Pfeiffer had predicted, and Madam Genevieve had no reason to complain, for in that fine April weather our march must have seemed to her like a joyous party of pleasure.

Müntzer's confidence increased daily, and daily he preached from the saddle beneath the rainbow banner. But when he learned that Doctor Luther himself, incensed at Müntzer's fame, had come to Weimar to urge dukes and margraves to take arms against him,

Müntzer summoned me and said, "This Doctor Luther of whom we hear so much, and whom the trusting people have come to look up to as to their God, has at last shown himself in his true colors. He has been weighed and found wanting. His day is done and his own deeds stand in judgment upon him, for he has allied himself with the most malignant, the most bloodthirsty of all tyrants, the Margrave of Mansfeld, who drove me from my congregation and made me a beggar. Luther preaches against me and warns the people not to rally to my standard. For this he shall pay dearly. But first he must be prevented from turning John of Weimar against me. I must warn Duke John of Luther's detestable intrigues and urge him to listen to God rather than to man. You must ride to Weimar, Michael Pelzfuss, and hand my letter personally to the Duke. Bring his reply to me wherever I may be—for I am led now not by my own will but by my ever growing army, as God shall direct."

He showed me the word of warning that he had scrawled to Duke John, and the little I saw of it did not greatly incline me to bring it to the notice of a powerful lord. But Müntzer rebuked me for my little faith and swore that I should be in no danger, for he held many hostages among his followers who would be put to death instantly should so much as a hair of my head be harmed.

There was nothing for it but to choose the best horse and to entreat Andy to come with me through that turbulent countryside. I assured Madam Genevieve that we could hardly be absent for more than four days, and in well-chosen words commended her to the care of Jacob the tailor. But Madam Genevieve replied haughtily that she did not need a tailor to look after her, and I perceived that I no longer enjoyed her full favor.

We mounted our horses, Andy and I, and set forth. We avoided towns and populous districts as far as we might, and on the afternoon of the second day we were in Weimar, where many armed horsemen were assembled. I saw no reason to mention who had sent me. So when I reached the castle I explained to the officer of the watch that I bore an urgent secret dispatch for His Grace. In proof of my good faith I gave him three gulden, which impressed him greatly. He at once admitted us to the courtyard and summoned grooms to water and rub down our horses. The Duke was evidently awaiting news, for it was not long before we were taken into the castle between two guards. We were then relieved of our weapons, including even my table knife, from which I deduced that Duke John was a suspicious man.

Andy, who professed no eagerness to gape at dukes and suchlike, chose to remain near our weapons and if possible get himself a meal. A white-haired chamberlain escorted me to the Duke's study, where I awaited the arrival of His Grace.

He appeared wearing a shabby velvet cap and a stained doublet. He seemed nervous, and asked me mildly who I was and why I had seen fit to disturb an old man instead of handing my letter to a servant. I could only fall on my knees before him, beseech his goodwill, and acknowledge that I was the bearer of a letter from Thomas Müntzer.

The good old man crossed himself and opened the letter gingerly as if afraid it might burn his fingers. Having spelled his way laboriously through it, he sank into his armchair with a sigh.

"Who am I, poor mortal, to be aware of God's purpose? Everyone seems to know better than I—everyone overwhelms me with advice! My beloved brother the Elector lies at the point of death, and I have always relied upon his judgment. His subjects have named him Frederick the Wise. When he heard of the peasant revolt he summoned his failing strength to write to me and advise me to avoid the use of force. Who knows, he said, whether these poor wretches have not some reason for what they do? Both spiritual and temporal authorities have oppressed them, chiefly by preventing the dissemination of the Word of God. We can but beseech the Almighty to forgive us our sins, and place all our trust in Him. Thus did my dear brother the Elector write. But according to the most recent reports he is near his end. Soon I must hoist the black flag on the tower and, as the new Elector, assume responsibility for the fate of his domains."

He fell silent, wagging his trembling head, and I addressed him with respect.

"May I venture to take that as your answer? May I take back word to him who sent me that the good Duke wishes him no ill and does not mean to use force against the peasants?"

He exclaimed hastily, "No, no! For God's sake never let it be known that I spoke thus! Doctor Luther is at present my guest, and he is a stern and fiery servant of the Lord. Were he to learn of it he would deafen me once again with his fulminations, and it is more than I can bear. I have already mustered my forces, and my cousin Duke George has promised to ride out from Leipzig to meet the peasants. Many others have offered me their aid so that I can no longer alter my decision, even if I wanted to. It will be best to let Doctor Luther give you all necessary information. For myself, greet Thomas Müntzer and

266

bid him pray for me, if indeed he is a true servant of the Lord. Urge him to lay down his arms and flee to some other country, or I fear he will meet with disaster and drag many with him into the jaws of death."

Duke John rose hurriedly, gave me his hand to kiss, and went out of the room, leaving Müntzer's letter open on the table for Doctor Luther to read. And as I awaited the coming of the great man whose fame in a few years had spread far and wide throughout Germany and into distant countries, I trembled. I dreaded this encounter more than I had dreaded my audience with the Duke.

Yet my fear was groundless. The great teacher, wearing doctor's cap and gown, entered with some freshly written pages in his ink-stained hands, waving them to and fro to dry them. There was also an ink smudge on his face. It seemed that he had interrupted some urgent work to speak to me, for he was still glancing over the lines he had written, and laughing a little to himself, though the laughter boded no good. I had leisure to observe him for a moment or two and found him no longer the thin, thought-burdened, prematurely aged monk who had revolted against papal and imperial power, and whose face was familiar from countless portraits. No, this was a stout, powerfully built man in the prime of life, with a rocklike jaw and rosy cheeks.

"You poor boy!" he said. "Do you know the diabolical trap into which you have fallen? You have a pure, innocent face and cannot be to blame for your error, which must be laid to the account of the gust from hell now blowing over Germany."

He caught sight of Müntzer's letter on the table, picked it up, and read a few lines. Then, quivering all over with rage, he tore it into a thousand pieces and stamped upon it.

His terrible black eyes pinned me to the wall as he said, "Evil has shown itself in its true colors and none need hope for mercy. The day of wrath is at hand, for the peasants have refused to listen to me and continue to put the Holy Gospel to their own base uses. A Christian must submit to violence and injustice and not seek vengeance by twisting the word of God. He must rather turn the other cheek, that he may receive a heavenly reward for his long suffering. Have I not warned you, you stiff-necked miscreants, you agitators and robbers? Have I not said that I must look upon you as enemies because you seek to oppose and debase my evangel more abominably than ever Pope or Emperor did? I will have no pity; I speak my mind—I have written it, that it may be known throughout Germany. Give ear, young man, give ear, and bear this message to your master as His Grace's answer!"

He sat down at the Duke's writing table, wrapped his gown about his knees, and began to read in a loud voice the pamphlet he had written in condemnation of the murdering, marauding peasants. He had written it in such haste that he could not always decipher his own hand, and sat hunched over the paper, breaking off now and then to mutter over some correction, strike out a line, and write in another, or, like a practiced proofreader, make a cross in the margin and insert the amendment there. These continual interruptions were troublesome to his listener, but I could remain in no uncertainty as to the argument. Since the peasants had revolted against their lawful and divinely appointed masters, since they had sacked castles and monasteries and then masqueraded in the mantle of the Gospel, calling one another brothers in Christ, they were trebly deserving of death, both of soul and body. The time of grace was past; the day of wrath and of the sword was come.

He read his main point through twice, that it might be etched into my memory; first slowly, with pen poised as if half willing to modify its tone, then quickly and harshly and with relish.

"Smite, strangle, or stab them, therefore, as opportunity may offer, openly or in secret, bearing in mind that there is nothing more poisonous or abominable than a rebellious person; he must be destroyed as a mad dog is destroyed. Crush him or he will crush you, and the nation with you."

I perceived that this open letter was addressed to the German nobility, and his vindictive words so grieved me that I would willingly have died. In that hour I saw no burning castles, plundered monasteries, or naked corpses; I thought only of the simple, pious men who had labored all their days without being able to put by so much as a few poor gulden, and who now in their childlike faith in the word of God believed that His Kingdom would come, and by their efforts.

Forgetting my fear, I flung myself at the Doctor's feet, seized his gown, and said through my tears, "Learned Doctor Luther, I'm but a poor sinner, but believe me, these people are not all mad dogs. Most of them are simple, God-fearing men who seek the institution of divine justice on earth. They believed in you and trusted you as if you had been God Himself. You gave them the Bible in their own tongue, and you cannot desert them now that the princes are preparing to march against them. Try at least to mediate—try at least to forgive them, if you refuse to make common cause with them in founding a new and everlasting order in Germany. For not even princes can withstand your strength and your spiritual stature!"

But he disdained my hand and drew aside the skirts of his gown as if I had been one of the mad dogs he wrote of, and he answered heatedly, "I am not accountable to you or to anyone else in this world, but to Almighty God alone and my own conscience. I will not permit a rabid mob to smash my Gospel to pieces. I will fight them tooth and nail to the end, as I have fought Pope and Emperor."

I perceived that Doctor Luther was already so great in his own eyes that he could not tolerate competitors either in learning or in doctrine, and regarded everyone who touched his articles of faith as a forger and counterfeiter. He dissociated himself from the peasants because they had interpreted his teaching so freely as to distort it. No doubt he felt he had more to gain from the princes' favor, and desired to exculpate himself in their eyes by means of this open letter, which would constitute their strongest weapon, so great was his reputation in Germany.

Full of bitter desperation I rose, looked him boldly in the face, and said, "I am still a young man and, compared with you, uneducated. My opinion will count for less than a grain of dust in the scales of time in which your words and actions will be weighed. Yet your talk of 'my Gospel' jars my ears, for by heaven it is not your Gospel alone but the Gospel of every poor man. And this I have always thought to be the basis of your teaching. The clear word of God speaks against you, and you yourself are by no means given to turning the other cheek! Moreover, for a long time you hid from the Emperor's wrath when all Germany was calling for you, and now it seems you will skulk again—and behind the princes, to flatter them."

This was no way for me to speak to the great man, and he was right to deal me a stinging blow on the cheek.

Yet so great was my resentment that I felt no pain, and with tears of rage and humiliation in my eyes I said, "Strike me if you will! The ink on your fingers is the blood of the innocent and it drips from every letter in your pamphlet. Why should you not gain the princes' favor, Doctor Luther, and make them bishops of their own provinces as you have promised? They can interpret your Gospel better than ignorant peasants. You are bound to win if you bribe the nobles with Church lands; and then you can build stouter, loftier walls about your Gospel, so that it is no longer the free fire of God, and a danger, but well fenced in by the bastions of your will. How keen will be your satisfaction when your letter is read aloud in every church in Germany, and when the Catholic princes—who hitherto have held you in greater detestation than the devil himself—do your bidding in slaughtering their bondsmen! But in the sight of God your immortal soul will be sick indeed."

Doctor Luther listened, white with fury, yet it seemed as if my words had bereft him of strength, for he did not touch me again. He stared at me profoundly as if to sound my soul, and then began talking to himself.

"It may be true. I may have been freer and happier in my faith when alone I defied the stake and the Emperor, than I am now when the plots and wiles of Satan hem me in on every side. But can you, you pale and angry youth, be the voice of conscience? No, no—you are but Satan's latest hallucination come to muddy my clear thoughts. Away with you, tempter, back to the devil's arsehole whence you came!"

I felt that he was ill at ease, and it is certain that he found himself in a very painful dilemma, now that he had allowed himself to be snared by the princes and had become their instrument. Yet I felt no compassion. I shouted at him, and through me shouted thousands upon thousands of disillusioned and despairing people.

"Be of good cheer, Doctor Luther! Your victory is assured, and now that you have allied yourself with the princes no one can withstand them or bring them to their senses. But blood shall cry out from the ground and bear witness to your crimes. Those who have blessed the name of Luther shall from this day curse you and call upon God to punish you. The voice of the fatherless and the widows shall mount to you from their ruined dwellings. Woe to you if you walk alone at night or venture upon the highroad without an armed escort! For every peasant who escapes from the mill that you have set in motion will believe he performs an act pleasing to God in taking your life. This hatred you must bear until the day of your death, Doctor Luther, and you may be sure the people will no longer believe what you teach. Rather will they stop up ears and eyes, and turn again to the shadows from which you once raised them for a moment's glimpse of hope and the bright flame of the Gospel."

He was once more cool and controlled, and stood before me like a massive rock.

When I had done he shook his head, smiled drily, and said, "I know that language. Do you think I have never been cursed before? Because of my Gospel I am probably the most bitterly execrated man in Christendom, and your feeble tongue cannot compete with that of Rome. Go back to your teacher with my greeting, and take this piece of advice for yourself. Remember that today's enemy may be tomorrow's friend, and vice versa. Germans have blessed my name enough, and more than enough. Let them now curse it for a while. It will not be long before they come to bless it again."

His somber eyes were upon me and his jaw was like iron. I was not the man to stir his conviction by a hair, and feeling abashed and small I withdrew backward to the door and went out, leaving him alone in his loneliness.

3

The white-haired chamberlain had been standing with his ear pressed to the door, and was not at all disconcerted at being caught in the act.

"My hearing is not what it was, my dear young sir," he said, "and it's no sin in me to listen, because a man with good ears can hear the Doctor's voice through many walls and doors when he is roused. But you're a brave man, Master Pelzfuss, to shout back, and I believe even the Duke will laugh in his sleeve when he hears of it. These are no laughing times, however, and I'm deeply grieved at all the evil which is coming to pass in the world, for I too am the son of a peasant, despite the high position I have attained. My lord Duke is assailed on all sides—yet one should not revile Doctor Luther, for he is a pious man and the most scholarly in all Germany, and like my master he desires only the country's good. What of you, Master Pelzfuss?"

I told him that I too desired only the best and was full of sorrow because of the fate in store for the peasants. Drawing me to a window, he pointed through the green glass at armed riders, and at pikemen drilling with the precision of a clock.

Then rattling his purse thoughtfully he remarked, "We live in troublous times and there's a lack of ready money at the ducal court. Moreover, I have grandchildren to whom I wish to bequeath a modest legacy. Now I hear that you bestowed a considerable sum on some lieutenant or other at the gate, and I can only deplore such waste of good money. I too have a purse, and could give you much useful advice."

I answered hastily that I was a poor man and that I could make no use of his advice, however good it might be. Luther had already put in his word, and fresh troops were entering the courtyard in a constant stream. My only course was to return instantly to Müntzer and urge him to prepare for battle without delay.

The chamberlain agreed that this was so, but added, "They had almost better disperse and return to their homes, were it not for the suffering that would result if the princes, meeting no resistance, were free to roam up and down the countryside and exact their toll from the peasants' backs. The men of the lakeshore in Swabia did well to make their stand on an impregnable crag, so that von Truchsess dared not engage them in battle. The princes' forces are not so very large, and it would be an easy matter for one who knows to give numbers and routes, so long as he was sure of a fair return for his trouble."

He shot me a sideways glance from beneath the grayish tufts of his eyebrows. I could see he knew what he was talking about, although it was hard to believe in his honesty, since he was Duke John's right-hand man. I asked what he thought would be a fair return, but he spread out his hands and said he would be content with what I could offer. He then led me through a maze of passages to a distant room, where a table was spread with bread, cheese, meat, and a pitcher of ale. Having unrolled a finely colored map, he indicated to me the assembly points of the princes' troops.

"The good Duke John is to mobilize on the seventh of May," he said, "and there are not many days to go. The peasants' most dangerous enemy, however, is His Grace's cousin, Duke George of Saxony, whose domains have suffered most from Müntzer's raids. He is to leave Leipzig any day now, but I hardly think he can muster more than a thousand horse and two companies of pikemen, and these will include the Mansfeld forces who are to join him in the course of his march. That dashing young Margrave, Philip of Hesse, has promised to hasten to his support from the other direction with fourteen hundred horse and as many foot. The Duke of Brunswick may possibly accompany him. In any event, the princes mean to advance in three strong wedges from east, south, and west, and if they succeed in uniting before the decisive struggle, their strength will be formidable. But there's many a slip betwixt cup and lip, and the peasants' position is not altogether hopeless if they will only consent to negotiate and come to some agreement."

I ate the bread and cheese and washed it down with the Duke's good ale, looking now at the map and now at the lively eyes and bushy eyebrows of the old man.

"If this information is correct, all the gold in the world would not

272

equal it in value," I said, "for gold cannot buy a man's freedom once he is dead. But as I told you before, I am poor and cannot afford more than let us say ten gulden. But you shall ever be remembered in my prayers."

I took ten gulden from my purse and tried not to let the rest jingle, but the old man seemed less deaf than he had claimed to be.

He grabbed the money with a sneer and stretched forth his hand again, saying, "This is no time to be niggardly, my dear sir, and I would not wish so noble and handsome a youth to come to any harm. If you would round off this gift somewhat I might find it in my power to procure you a safe-conduct signed by Duke John. Such a document would afford you security for your life, honor, and property should matters take an ill turn and deliver you into the princes' hands. Remember, such men are cruel in their wrath. I believe Duke John has taken a fancy to your frank, innocent face and would certainly furnish you with a pass if I approached him on your behalf."

It seemed to me that such a paper, though it might save me from the princes, could as easily be a source of danger if found upon me by the peasants, who would take me for their lordships' spy. So after some reflection I replied that the document would have little value for me, but that he should have another five gulden if he could procure it. He entreated me to increase the sum by a trifle, but in vain, and at length with a snigger he left the room as if to make his request to the Duke. He returned immediately, however, with the promised safe-conduct signed and sealed, certifying that Michael Pelzfuss de Finlandia was in the Duke's service and under his protection, and requiring all concerned to support and assist him in the fulfillment of his task.

I perceived at once that the old man had tricked me, that for some reason this paper had been prepared beforehand, and that it had been in his possession for some time. It could only be with the goodwill of his master, therefore, that he had disclosed the princes' plans, and the Duke evidently meant to make use of me in some scheme of his own. This awoke in me the uncomfortable suspicion that he must also have provided a suitable sum of journey money as inducement. I had been duped by the chamberlain, like a peasant at his first horse fair. But what was the Duke's purpose, and what were the tasks allotted me? I swallowed my indignation as best I might, praised the old man's cunning, and asked him what message he bore from His Grace. The better I understood this, the better I could serve him.

273

The old chamberlain looked grave, patted my cheek with his paper-dry hand, and said, "You take the matter very handsomely, young man. And indeed money runs in as readily as out, whereas good counsel is precious indeed. The information I have given you is as correct as can be hoped for in these explosive times. The Duke's chief desire is to still the storm as his brother advised, and he is doing his best to prevent the peasants from meeting with an overwhelmingly superior force. But if they harden their hearts and choose to fight, he will let them have their way. And if the princes want to teach them a lesson, well and good. Whichever way it goes, he hopes for such severe losses on both sides as will promote a compromise."

"I can make neither head nor tail of this," I said. "How can His Grace so betray his kinsfolk and peers?"

"Who knows? Perhaps Duke John would be glad to see the corners rubbed off a presumptuous lordling or two before taking the field himself with his great force. But whatever happens you may be sure he will come off best in this slippery game. He can afford to wait."

Such cold calculation seemed to me almost sinful. But I believed only half of what the old man told me, and as I could get no more out of him I bade him a frigid farewell.

Andy was sitting on the edge of a horse trough, surrounded by armor-clad horsemen and mercenaries who leaned on their lances and now and then burst into roars of laughter. As I drew near I heard that he was speaking of the great battle of Pavia and his own exploits there, but when he saw me pushing angrily through the cluster of listeners he gave a glance around and drew his horse toward him. Putting one arm beneath its chest and the other beneath its rump, he lifted the poor brute off the ground. This feat of strength drew a roar of amazement from the soldiers, who readily made way for him as he began placidly walking toward the gateway with the horse helpless in his grip. I untethered my own mount and walked after him across the courtyard. At the gate, Andy set his animal upon its legs, patted its neck, and climbed into the saddle—he was not even breathless—and we rode side by side out of the fortress, waving farewell to the soldiers.

I could only think that Andy was the worse for drink, for in no other circumstances did he ever show off his strength. In general he was a modest soul.

I would not even speak to him until we had passed through the city gates, but once safely out upon the highroad I said bitterly, "I blush for you, Andy. There was I in the clutches of Doctor Luther—in deadly peril—defending our cause tooth and nail, while you were befuddling yourself among our adversaries and were not ashamed to torment a wretched animal before my very eyes."

He remained silent, and his silence so exasperated me that I renewed my reproaches in more acrimonious terms. Only then did he stare at me and say, "But for me we should now be food for crows in Weimar castle courtyard."

It was an explanation I wanted to hear, I told him, not the babblings of a drunkard.

"I've not been drinking, Michael. Though why you should be so severe when you reek of ale a horse's length away is more than I know. But when I was sitting on that horse trough I was in as tight a place as St. Peter was when he sat by the fire in the high priest's house. There was no end to the questions they asked me: who was I, whence did I come, wasn't I one of the Mühlhausen murderers, and hadn't I ridden in with the pale young fellow who was soon to be brought out for hanging? I had all my work cut out to see that they didn't steal our horses, and I could think of nothing to do but tell of Pavia, for that I know by heart and lying doesn't come easy to me. They were muttering together about starting a brawl at the gateway and killing us as we rode away. I've no notion why they wished to do this—unless you'd been talking foolishly up there in the castle. So I lifted up the horse to frighten them and the trick got us through the gate. But we came near hearing the cock crow for the last time, and if you, my lord and master, had delayed much longer, I might have denied you when you came, and said 'I know not the man!'"

Andy's story made me very thoughtful, and I wondered whether it could have been the Duke's intention to have me slain at the gate with his safe-conduct on me, so that he could not be blamed for my death. But this seemed to me an unnecessarily devious plan, even for the good Duke, and I concluded that there were those about his court who guessed at his duplicity and who, seeing me taken into his chamberlain's confidence, felt it best to intercept me before I could pass on my secrets to the peasants. Two or three other possibilities occurred to me and set my head buzzing like a beehive. So I resolved to depart from my previous intention and lay the whole matter before Andy.

"Forgive my ugly suspicions," I said. "I see now that you acted very resourcefully. But what would you give to have Duke John's safe-conduct in your pocket, signed and sealed, to save you should we fight and lose and see our banner dragged in the mire?"

275

"We shall fight, that's certain, and I know from the drill of those troops how the battle will go. They have artillery, too. Be very sure your banner will be dragged in the mire, and no doubt a ducal pass will come in handy. But something tells me that you've been wasting money and hope to make up half your loss from me."

His words offended me the more since I had indeed thought to share expenses in a practical manner.

"How can you think so ill of me, my dear Andy!" I said. "Have we not always shared everything together? In Weimar I succeeded in obtaining much valuable information which I meant to confide to you if you would contribute at least five gulden toward my heavy expenses."

"May heaven forgive your avarice," said Andy, but he began to loosen the strings of his purse. "Let this be the last time. And you must swear that if in spite of everything we come out of this alive, you will trust to me hereafter and follow my advice—and perhaps let me save you and carry you off to some happier country—without arguing and jibbing and appealing to Holy Writ."

This was a bitter pill, and for a long time we rode side by side in silence through the darkening May evening and the heavy fragrance of the woods. But five gulden is five gulden and would now be easily earned, since I had already made up my mind to tell Andy all I knew and if necessary share with him the protection of the safe-conduct. The sweet melancholy of that twilight among the green Thuringian hills, now tinged with the glow of sunset, softened my mood.

"As you will, Andy," I said at last. "It has ever been my hope that men, who all have an equal share in the Redemption, should live peaceably together and that none should be either too rich or too poor. I have believed it possible, and that is why I marched forth under the rainbow banner. But should my faith prove false, then all things will be indifferent to me and I will go where you will."

Andy said, "I understand your sadness, Michael. When I was a little fellow I used to run through the woods chasing the rainbow, but it glided away from me and melted just when I thought I had it fast. Now you seek to grasp your rainbow—but believe me, you'll never reach it here on earth. But there's much else in this world that is good and pleasant. We live in a time of great change—a time made for young men, Michael, and the wide green earth opens its arms to us. Italy pleased me, and I should not wonder if there was some smiling valley there with vineyards and a crenelated tower that a strong man might win for himself. Stranger things have happened, and men who began as ignorant mercenaries have died field marshals, attended to their graves by knights in gilded armor and five hundred chanting monks. Such stories have been told me as true. I listened to them shivering and hungry beside the campfire, and warmed myself with them when I felt an outcast in a bleak world, like a young raven fallen from its nest."

I think Andy would not have revealed such thoughts to me if the evening had not been so clear and so magically beautiful. He forgot himself and his stupidity, and like a child slipped into the world of fantasy. I had not the heart to wound him, though inwardly I laughed bitterly enough at his daydreams.

"It's true that blacksmith's boys have become kings," I said, "and one climbed onto the papal throne. But I wonder which of us is clutching at the rainbow now—you or I?"

Andy answered gently, "Michael, a man can achieve whatever he desires, if his will be strong enough and his health good. Anything in *this* world, I mean—not rainbows in the sky. When I was sure of this, I set out to find you, for I wanted to share my coming success with you. Also I need you because you can read, and because you'll no doubt see to it that in my quest of this world's blessings I may not too rashly endanger my soul. Loss of salvation would be too great a price to pay even for an earl's coronet. This is my only reason for giving you the five gulden."

He stretched forth his arm, and in the gathering darkness the form beside me seemed to loom larger so that I was filled with a strange uncertainty. Leaning over, I tried to distinguish his features.

"Is it you, Andy, or another?" I faltered, and cold shivers ran down my back.

But my fears melted when I felt Andy's warm fist in mine, and the five good pieces. We rode on in silence until at a burned-out farmstead we found an empty byre. Here we stabled our horses and lay down to rest, for we were weary.

When we had ridden another two days past ruined, smoldering manor houses and through the dense clouds of flies that swarmed about the stiffened corpses, we had had enough of traveling in the wake of Müntzer and resolved to head straight for Mühlhausen, whither his army must sooner or later return.

We had not passed beyond the eastern outskirts of the city when we saw the rainbow banner flying in the fresh breeze, and beneath it the mounted figure of Thomas Müntzer, whose head drooped and whose face was yellower than ever. The band of the faithful seemed to have dwindled in a marked degree and I counted only about three hundred men. First came a score of mercenaries bearing harquebuses on their shoulders, and the rest trudged behind, their spears waving like corn in the wind. But the faces of this little band glowed with fervor, and they were singing Müntzer's battlesong—"Come down to us, O Holy Spirit, Come!"—at the top of their voices.

We reined in our weary horses and waited for the standard to draw level with us. I said, "What in heaven's name can have happened? Where is Pfeiffer?"

We were not long left in doubt, for when Müntzer saw us he brought his mount to a stop with a clumsy tug at the reins, and gave the order to halt. He delivered to me a violent and ill-tempered reprimand for my delay, but I returned a soft answer and asked whither we were bound, why our company had dwindled, and where Pfeiffer was.

Mention of this name still further infuriated him, and he declared that Pfeiffer had been but one more devil's snare about his path; that at last he had squared accounts with him and had cast him off, for Satan to claim. Müntzer was on the way to Frankenhausen with his few remaining adherents—the fruitful grain from which the tares had now been cast out and which should bring forth a hundred—and a thousandfold. Frankenhausen had accepted his four articles, and six thousand sturdy peasants were waiting for him to come and found the Eternal Kingdom, the Christian order, and the German form of worship. Never before had such a great army been seen in Thuringia. He saw in this the finger of God, and was therefore on his way to them, leaving Mühlhausen to its own iniquity.

From this I perceived that he and Pfeiffer had broken with one another for good and that Pfeiffer had driven him out and taken possession of the town. I rode up beside him and questioned him cautiously about Madam Genevieve, but he replied that he had expelled all harlots from among his followers, on whom he had now imposed perfect chastity, that cleansed in body and in soul they might prepare and dedicate themselves for the battle. I therefore bade Andy return to

Mühlhausen, find Madam Genevieve, and bring her secretly to Frankenhausen.

Andy sulked at this, but turned and rode back as I asked. I continued beside Thomas Müntzer and told him of my expedition to Weimar—or as much of it as he could hear without excessive rage. I said that Luther had turned against the peasants and was inciting the princes to a general massacre, but that there was still a chance of compromise. Also that the good Duke John begged Müntzer as a true messenger of the Lord to pray for him that he might arrive at a wise decision.

But my words threw Müntzer into a great passion, and he refused even to consider negotiation with the princes until they had renounced their titles and destroyed their castles. With only two or three of the faithful beside him he could with God's help overcome an army of a hundred thousand men. He spoke of the new order and of the divine truth that had been revealed to him that very morning—a truth that rendered his four points superfluous and condensed God's purpose into three short words. He spoke also of his past, as a man does who feels the approach of death.

"Men are blinded and deafened by their temporal concerns," he said. "They hear without hearing, they see without seeing. We must bow beneath the burden of the cross until we are emptied of hope, desire, and affections—emptied even of disappointment—and are as a blown egg. Only then can we receive the word of God. It may issue from the lips of the unworthy, from the lips of the learned or of the ignorant, from the lips of babes or idiots, from the lips even of one who does not understand his own message."

I trembled to hear him, for I knew that he spoke truly and that I myself had experience of what he said. Even now I must believe that there was something holy about the man.

Next day, wearied from our long march, we arrived at Frankenhausen. The two captains of the peasant army there, of whom one was a burgher and the other a nobleman who had lost all his possessions, came out to meet us and saluted Thomas Müntzer and his banner with respect. I rejoiced to see no signs of disorder anywhere, although a good six thousand peasants were encamped in and about the city. These serious, sturdy men were now drawn up in even ranks behind their leaders, seemingly imbued with zeal and determination. It was the most comforting sight I had seen in all these months of confusion. Infected by Müntzer's conviction, I felt that all attempts at negotiation would be absurd, and I repented of my misgivings.

It was Friday afternoon and, regardless of the arduous journey he had made, Thomas Müntzer at once addressed his new followers with such fervor that many kneeled and hailed him as the messenger of God. The time for mediation was past, he said; let the righteous steel their hearts and minds, and dedicate themselves by prayer and fasting as champions of the Lord.

When he had been speaking for some time and had worked himself into a passion, he called me to him that he might dictate a letter to the Margrave of Mansfeld, who had already shown himself the sworn enemy of God by driving His messenger in a shameful manner from the town of Allstedt. This is what I wrote at his bidding:

"I, Thomas Müntzer, erstwhile preacher in the town of Allstedt, adjure you in the name of the living God to cease your tyranny. You have begun to slay and to torture Christian people. You have compared the Christian faith to childish prattle. Carrion! Who has set you up to govern a people redeemed by the precious Blood? I charge you to prove before the congregation of the faithful that you are worthy to be called Christian. If you do not come I shall proclaim you outlaw, and he who slays you will perform an act pleasing to God. For authority is given us from above, wherefore I say: Sanctioned by the living, everlasting God we shall hurl you from your throne by force unless you submit. For you are of no service to Christianity but rather a running sore in the body of God's Elect, wherefore your lair must be purged and razed to the ground, saith the Lord!"

Müntzer read this letter aloud to the assembled peasants, who nodded and agreed that the Margrave of Mansfeld was a pitiless master and deserved a hard fate. But not content with this, Müntzer ordered three of the Margrave's servants who had been taken prisoner to be led forward. One of them was of noble blood, another was a priest, and the third a simple youth who stared in bewilderment at the men by whom he was confronted. At the top of his voice Müntzer demanded whether the servants of so ungodly a master were not a thousandfold deserving of death, and whether their death would not prove to Mansfeld that Müntzer was in earnest? And the peasants, wrought to a frenzy by his sermon, shook their lances and shouted that these men's lives were indeed forfeit. Müntzer ordered their immediate execution.

280

Thus blood was shed of set purpose for the first time beneath the rainbow banner.

But when he saw the blood spurt and the bodies jerk convulsively on the ground before him, Müntzer himself looked aghast and his face turned yellower than usual. He quickly mastered himself, however, and resumed his preaching until his features glowed with ecstasy and his voice was borne over the whole valley like the wind of God. The four articles, he said, were but the first step on the way to the eternal Kingdom, where there should be neither rich nor poor, princes nor burghers, peasants nor apprentices, but only the liegemen of God. And God had now revealed His truth in three simple words, which Müntzer would declare to them when the time was ripe.

The peasants in Frankenhausen had been given plenty to think about that night, but wandering at Müntzer's orders from one camp to another I heard nothing but praise of him as a true vessel of grace.

5

Next day weeping fugitives brought us news that Duke George and the Mansfeld lords were on the march. But the runaways drew comfort from our large numbers, which they said far exceeded those of the Duke's men, despite the horsemen Cardinal Albrecht had sent to his aid.

This Albrecht had once unlawfully purchased from the Pope two bishoprics and the archbishopric of Mainz—with Fugger's money—though he had not even attained the canonical age. As security for the loan, he had allowed the house of Fugger to traffic in indulgences within his domains—a practice that Luther opposed when he nailed his ninety-five points to the church door in Wittenberg. Sparks from those hammerblows had kindled a conflagration that was now laying waste a great part of Germany, and it was doubtless for this reason that His Eminence felt it his duty to quench the flames in blood. But the most astounding feature of it all was that he now reckoned Luther among his brothers-in-arms—Luther, whom he held in greater detestation than the devil himself. The world was unhinged indeed, and it was hard to believe that only seven and a half years had passed since Luther struck those fateful blows.

The peasant captains, having interrogated the fugitives, now drilled their troops, while handgunners made haste to cast leaden balls for their weapons. Cheerful, ordered activity prevailed in town and camp, and it was evident that this was to be no planless struggle.

But in the afternoon Müntzer interrupted these preparations, which he considered superfluous since he had the Lord on his side, and summoned the men to hear another sermon. He spoke of the little band of God's faithful, and invited others to join it and receive the new baptism. A large number of peasants stepped forward reverently. Bidding them strip, he took them to a pool at the foot of the city wall and with his own hands pressed them beneath the surface of the water, though it was but May and the water very cold. At the sight of their shivering, spluttering comrades, many would-be candidates hastily resumed their clothes and hid behind the sergeants. But Müntzer blessed those who had received baptism and embodied them as a special guard about the standard, and this they regarded as a high honor.

I began to fret at Andy's delay. Somehow in that overcrowded city I had contrived to find a lodging for the two of us and for Madam Genevieve. It was in a bakery, and although bread for the peasant army was baked in our room all day, at night it was spacious and warm, if floury. I needed Andy's advice in military matters, for I had been on no campaign save the flight from Leipheim, which had shed little glory on me or on anyone else. Yet I was now very sensible of my responsibilities, for if God had perhaps endowed me with more intelligence and learning than these simple captains, He had thereby made it incumbent upon me to use them to the full in His holy cause.

I tried to call to mind what Andy had taught me, and remembered his account of the havoc wrought among the French cavalry at Pavia by the Emperor's harquebuses. From this I concluded that pike drill was less important than the overhauling of all the handguns, falconets, culverins, and other pieces that the peasants had dragged from captured castles and had abandoned higgledy-piggledy in the muddy courtyard of the town hall.

The burgher captain received my suggestion without enthusiasm, observing that guns were dangerous and unreliable weapons that often caused more damage to their users than to the enemy. The other officer regarded me pityingly and said that I could use my peashooters if I wished. His plan was to build a stout ring of wagons to halt the cavalry.

At this I protested indignantly, but I was interrupted by Müntzer, who said, "The Lord is our stoutest shield and mightier than the armor of our enemies. In Him do we trust!"

282

I assented, but observed that He could hardly be expected to drag us to victory by the hair if we would not raise a finger to help ourselves. In the end I was given permission to act as I thought best.

I began by inspecting the cannon, at least five of which appeared to me sound. To serve them, I should need twenty-five strong men, also draught animals, harness, ammunition, wadding, matches, and a good many other things. I toiled all day and far into the night in procuring these necessities, and set women to sewing bags for the powder charges. By midnight all was done. I was dead tired, and having arranged for my men to relieve each other on guard lest our animals be stolen, I rolled myself in some flour sacks, asked God's blessing, and fell asleep.

I seemed hardly to have closed my eyes when I was roused by a roll of drums and an appalling crash. Then I found that someone was shaking me and telling me to get up. There was a great hole in the bakery wall through which I could see that it was still dark outside, but I was choking with the dust of fallen masonry, and bricks were still tumbling about me. I asked what in God's name had happened.

"The war has started," said Andy placidly, for it was he. "I rode in one jump ahead of the Hessian cavalry. But I never knew they carried cannon on their horses; that's something new in my experience. I was on the point of rousing you when that ball came through the wall, and I have St. Barbara to thank that it didn't take my head with it."

From without came the shouts of men, the neighing of horses, the cries of women, and the thud of running feet. Drums were sounding, and a church bell began clanging for dear life.

I thought my last hour had come and tried to crawl into the oven, but Andy grabbed me by the arm and said reassuringly, "The horsemen were not many. I fancy they were only scouts sent on in advance of the main force, and they would hardly venture to storm a city. However, I took the liberty of giving the alarm, as I felt it was unfair for you all to be sleeping so sweetly when I've been riding hell-for-leather through the night to help you, with death at my heels."

We went out into the courtyard, where my gunners were running hither and thither like crazy hens, shouting "To arms, to arms!" One of them confessed to me shamefacedly that it was he who in the heat of the moment had fired off the gun. I was so enraged that I struck him on both cheeks and swore to have him hanged. But Andy interrupted me. No harm had been done, he said; the man had been guilty of nothing but zeal, and it was now time to drag our artillery into position.

The city was in a turmoil. I bade Andy order the gunners to take up their stations, as his voice was more powerful than mine. He shouted and the men stood instantly to their guns. He then inspected each piece with care and told me I had set them in as good order as could be expected of me. He thought they would make a good loud bang, though they compared unfavorably with the improved weapons used by the Imperial army.

I saw that he was jealous because I had five guns under my command while he had nothing but his broadsword, so I clapped him on the shoulder and said, "The grapes are sour, Andy! But never mind—I hereby appoint you master gunner. You shall direct the fire as you will, provided you obey my orders, for I bear the ultimate responsibility."

But Andy, expressing no gratitude, merely muttered to himself and followed me with dragging steps to the market place. Day was now dawning, there were lights in the houses, and the good citizens were stowing their possessions into boxes and bundles ready for flight, although they had no idea where to go. Armed peasants dashed hither and thither about the streets, without purpose. Drums and church bell were now silent, and only a persistent trumpet in the market place was sounding the assembly.

Müntzer and the burgher captain stood by the church door, and the little market square before them was crammed with peasants. The officer was saying that strange riders had come from the west, some approaching as far as the town, but Müntzer retorted that this was nonsense because the enemy was expected from the east. No one could come from the west without first subduing Erfurt and Mühlhausen. Müntzer was shivering despite his costly fur gown, but his courage increased with the growing light and he began preaching to keep himself warm. His sermon was soon interrupted, however, by the arrival of the other officer, the nobleman, who galloped up to the church door, swung himself from the saddle, and reported that enemy horses had ridden in at dawn to attack and scatter the peasants encamped west of the city. The peasants had retired in disorder and had taken refuge in the town. Many had fallen. Handgunners on the city walls had opened fire and the attacking force had retired into the woods, but who and how many they were it was impossible to say, for estimates varied from ten to a thousand.

Andy stepped forward and remarked that the peasants were not very good at counting, since to his certain knowledge the party numbered only twenty. Their main force could not be far behind, he said; they were the Margrave of Hesse's men, as he well knew, for they had been at his heels all night and were free with their tongues.

This report made an impression on the captains, but they were loath to believe it. During the discussion that followed, a sentinel from the city gate came running with news of a mounted force numbering some two hundred that was approaching slowly from the west. The command was at once given for the troops and baggage train to leave the city in good order by the eastern gate and to form a defensive ring of wagons outside the city.

Their order was far from good, however, for in their eagerness to escape from the narrow alleys the drivers flogged their teams until sleds and carts were locked together, and at the gate the press was so fierce that many ribs were broken. I hardly know how we should have got the guns away if Andy had not taken command and, wandering in a leisurely fashion through the mob, roared unceasingly that in war there was never any hurry and that he who hastened slowly arrived first.

The wagon stockade was built on a flat-topped mound a gunshot from the town. While the carts were still lumbering in an endless stream from the gate, we dug our emplacements, strengthened the lashings, and directed the culverins southward, whence the cavalry attack was expected. While Andy was seeing to the heavy guns I mustered the harquebusiers and stationed them in line under cover of the wagons, bidding them keep their weapons in readiness and their matches burning, but not to fire until they could see the features in the riders' faces.

The enemy had made an encircling movement about the city and now came suddenly into sight. The drivers who had not yet reached us promptly abandoned their teams and fled toward our stronghold, and the soldiers marching beside them lost their heads and ran too. This was too tempting a spectacle for the horsemen. We heard the notes of a trumpet; the riders closed up, lowered their lances, and charged to cut off the fugitives and mow them down.

At the sound of thundering hoofs and jingling harness the fleeing men threw down their weapons and turned northward along the wall of the city with the cavalry at their heels. The gates were shut against them, despite their hammering and their piteous cries for admission. But at that instant came the roar of our first cannon, followed by the four others, and great smoke clouds billowed up before us. A yell burst from two thousand throats as some of the horses were seen to fall and the rest to be thrown into confusion. The harquebusiers could contain themselves no longer and loosed off a ragged volley. Some of the horsemen were unseated, and the rest wheeled and fled as hastily as they had charged. Several riderless horses were left galloping about the field.

"Victory, victory!" howled the peasants, and the erstwhile fugitives turned back to pick up their weapons, plunder the dead, and slay the wounded. Men poured out from our fort to share the booty, despite roars of command to stand fast, while others shouted and laughed and embraced each other till all bedlam seemed to have broken loose. The enemy might now have captured our position without trouble, for only the most steadfast gunners remained at their posts and reloaded.

When at last order was restored, Andy wiped the sweat from his face and said to me, "Old Nick himself couldn't fight a battle with these clods!"

Yet he seemed far from displeased, and settled himself comfortably on a gun sled to superintend the reloading of our pieces and the neat stacking of cannon balls.

"Given a year, or even a month," he went on, "I could turn these fellows into gunners. What have they been doing these last three weeks? In that time I could have cast four demi-cannon of the new pattern, and eight smaller pieces—all from the bronze scrap they took from the castles. Ay, and made wheels, carriages, wedges, and all, and trained men to handle them! But there's neither head nor tail to this war, and they needn't fancy they've won any victory, for all their screeching."

He followed up these remarks with a short lecture on artillery in modern warfare, and ended, "With a score of mobile guns and trained men to serve them, we need have feared no cavalry in the world. But our cannon are few, our gunners raw, and all the rest of the men half-wits. Let them cheer. They'll sing another song presently."

But I had been infected by the general jubilation, and even Müntzer crept out from a cart whither he had hastened in order to say his prayers, and bade us all kneel and thank God for the great victory. Rejoicing peasants flocked in with the weapons, clothes, and armor of the slain, and seemed quite to forget their contemptible flight. The colors and badges of these trophies were those of Hesse, and they proved to us that the princes were approaching Frankenhausen from two directions, to surround us. One of the captains sternly reprimanded the peasants for having thoughtlessly slain these men before they had been interrogated, for they could have furnished valuable information.

286

But this difficulty was solved by a peasant who was going to visit his home and lay in a stock of provisions. He lived in the neighborhood, and undertook to find out how many men the Margrave was bringing against Frankenhausen.

A council of war was then held, and a very friendly and peaceful one it was in that spring sunshine when all was triumph. Andy was summoned to give his advice, but consented only after much persuasion. Quoting the Marquis of Pescara as his authority, he urged that we should take up our position on some eminence that would be difficult of access and yet afford a way of retreat to the defenders. The hillock we at present occupied was too low to give us a view westward over the city.

"I can see a steep crag to the north," he said, "which would give us a wide view of the valley on three sides, and beyond it are dense forests where the six thousand of us could vanish like a needle in a haystack. Cavalry could not follow us there. I see also a narrow gully running up the crag from the direction of the town. We could clear a road for the wagons there, and it would be sheltered from enemy fire. I suggest that we make our way thither at once, build a stockade at the summit, and dig in our guns. For that, I'm sure, is what the Marquis of Pescara would have done."

The captains surveyed the hill and acknowledged the good sense of what he said, and after some further discussion the plan was carried out.

Müntzer planted the rainbow banner at the summit, and, exhilarated by the view and the fresh breeze, he named the place the Hill of Battle. The peasants, greatly comforted by the sheltering woods in their rear, went to work with a will, felling trees, sharpening stakes, and building the stockade, while Andy saw to the placing of the guns. When he had thoroughly inspected the position, he remarked that unless the princes had very superior forces they would not even attempt to capture the fort and would rather consent to negotiate. So he thought it safe to return to the town, as Müntzer and many others had done, and look for a few more serviceable guns. We walked together down the sheltered valley where ox sleds and carts had already cleared a passable road, and only now did I think of asking Andy what he had done with Madam Genevieve.

He answered, "The mother of our son is a wanton, frivolous creature. We might go to hell for all she cared, she said; she had no mind to keep company with wastrels and go to war and lose all her belong-

287

ings. She had settled down with a wealthy brewer and sleeps soft in his wife's bed, for he has sent his family away and stays behind to look after the brewery."

I asked him whether he thought this man would protect Madam Genevieve's good name, which was really our duty as the fathers of her son. But Andy said that indeed the brewer had time for nothing else and had even let the ale turn sour.

When we reached our lodging in Frankenhausen, Andy brought out a bundle that he had tossed into a corner that morning. He opened it and showed me a fine velvet doublet, a plumed cap, and a pair of close-fitting breeches, and told me he had bought them for me cheaply in Mühlhausen, so that if necessary I could dress in a manner befitting my position—when making use of Duke John's safe-conduct, for example. He had paid only one gulden and two schillings for the clothes, which were in fairly good condition, and I was delighted with them, being accustomed to but the plain dress of a scholar.

However, I had but little money left after paying my gunners their hire, and as I hardly expected to find a use for the suit, which was forbidden to one of my order, I vanquished the temptation.

Andy rolled the clothes up again and stowed them under the kneading trough, saying, "As you will. But remember, demand determines the value, and though today I was willing to sell them at cost price I might ask five gulden another time when you're in urgent need of the things, and so get back the money you wrung from me on the way from Weimar. However, that's your affair."

We then examined the cannon that lay derelict in front of the town hall, but Andy shook his head at them. So we went on to an alehouse, which we found crammed with people. Money and cajolery procured us a tankard of small beer and a piece of pork, and as we allayed the worst of our hunger we listened to what the peasants were saying. To hear them one might have thought they had routed a thousand armored cavalrymen with their bare fists, and the number of the enemy slain had already risen to two hundred. However, the main thing was that they were now confident of overcoming any number of the princes' troops, and after listening to them for some time we betook ourselves to the church to hear some real news.

The peasant who had gone to fetch provisions was back again, to everyone's amazement. He reported that his homestead was undamaged, though occupied by the enemy, and that his family and livestock had taken to the woods. The soldiers quartered in his house told him

288

they served Margrave Philip, with whom the Duke of Brunswick had allied himself. They were very proud of having ridden from Eisenach to Frankenhausen in a single night, and said they were only staying to breathe their horses and await the infantry before attacking and destroying the peasant forces. They knew he had come to spy on them, but cared nothing for it, for they were two thousand; and indeed, he said, he had seen the horses and they were many. He had then been brought before Margrave Philip, who was in radiant mood after his historic ride and who bade him tell the Frankenhausen men that he would spare them if they would hand over their arms, their standards, and their leaders, and disperse to their homes. Further, they must bind themselves to make good all the damage they had done to castles and manors.

"The gate of pardon stands open until my horses are rested," he had said. "Today I will only thrash you. Tomorrow I will slay you and your comrades."

The peasant, who pulled many grotesque faces as he talked, and seemed at once half-witted and sly, said he fancied that the Margrave was ignorant of Duke George's approach from the opposite direction and might therefore be open to a parley. But at this all present made loud objection, saying they would beat them first and talk afterward. Then the fellow looked grave. He was not much of a soldier, he told us; moreover his back was sore from the thrashing and the Margrave had indeed a great number of horses. By our favor, therefore, he would go quietly home again.

There was a great outcry at this and he was seized by many horny hands. Fortunately there were people from his village in the church who defended him from the general indignation, saying that he was simple. So he was allowed to depart in peace, though Müntzer called after him that the gate of mercy stood open to the princes also if they would knock humbly upon it and beg admittance to the company of the Elect.

6

By daybreak all were to be mustered on the Hill of Battle, and I think I have never known a gloomier Monday morning. Chill rain was falling and we were bad tempered from lack of sleep.

But our spirits rose with the sun, which drove away clouds and rain, except for a brief shower now and then. The soaking banner dried and floated out once more. Soon a lively activity prevailed as the men warmed themselves by strengthening the palisades and banking up the wagonwheels with earth. Our gunners had kept their powder dry during the night. They had also carved the choicest pieces from a horse that had fallen the previous day, which tasted not unpleasant when grilled over the embers. But soon we espied mounted patrols approaching from the east, some of whom ventured a little way up our slope, near enough to shout insults and threats. Not long afterward marching columns could be seen both to the east and to the west. At that distance in the broad valley they did not look so very formidable, but when the sun pierced the gray clouds it sparkled on spearpoint and breastplate. Andy, shading his eyes, observed, "They have artillery—heavy artillery. I can count up to sixteen in a team. If they have mobile cannon-royal it's high time for our master to call upon the Lord for aid, for our little toys can do nothing against those."

Immediately after this the drums sounded to summon the leaders to a council of war. To these men Müntzer announced that Duke George was approaching and that it was only right to convey to him a message of God's purpose. He then read out a letter the captains had written, to the effect that the peasants claimed only divine justice and desired to avoid needless bloodshed. A similar letter was to be sent to Margrave Philip, bidding him return home and stir up no more hatred among decent men. The leaders listened approvingly to these moderate words and chose four sturdy men as messengers.

The afternoon passed peacefully away. Margrave Philip's troops pitched their camp west of the city, out of range of our guns, while from the east came the joint forces of Duke George and the Mansfeld nobles, who took up their positions quietly on the eastern slopes of the hill. The two men who had been sent with Müntzer's message to the Duke returned crestfallen, and would not look at their comrades or answer their questions. To Müntzer and the leaders they reported that the Duke promised to consider the peasants' claims some time in the future, but only on condition that they laid down their arms immediately and dispersed. Müntzer must be handed over, with his closest associates. All others were assured, on the ducal honor, of safety to life and limb.

A loud murmur arose; men put their heads together and twitched at one another's sleeves. But Müntzer silenced them angrily. They would be mad to trust to the promises of this cruel man, for the Lord had hardened his heart as once he had hardened the heart of Pharaoh, and the Duke's army would go the way of Pharaoh's if only the peasants would trust in God.

During the prolonged dispute that followed, the opposing forces formed themselves into a wheel of which the hub was the Hill of Battle. These movements seemed planless at first, but then came a despairing cry from the north side of the stockade. Men were running up and down, waving their arms and pointing up at the lofty wooded heights. When we climbed onto the wagons we could plainly discern many glittering lances north of our stronghold. Our retreat had quickly and quietly been cut off, and team after team was dragging field pieces to the summit of every hill.

Uproar and lamentation broke out. Fists were shaken, men tore each other's hair, and demanded negotiation while a chance of pardon yet remained. Many cried out for Müntzer to be handed over on condition that he should be allowed to defend the four articles of his faith in public disputation. Bloodshed threatened, for the band of God's faithful flocked to their standard, crying death and destruction upon those martyrs of Satan who to save their own skins would betray and forsake the messenger of God.

Throughout this commotion Müntzer stood on a wagon beneath the rainbow banner, his yellow-gray face lifted to the sky and both hands pressed against his breast. He was wearing his long fur gown, which lent him dignity and height, and no doubt his serenity was given him from above, for when he raised his arms the whole camp fell silent and even the agitators began whispering "Hear him, hear him!" The stillness was intense and all that could be heard was the snap of the heavy silk banner in the breeze. The five brilliant colors of the rainbow glowed above Müntzer's sallow face, and beneath them was seen the sacred legend: VERBUM DOMINI MANET IN ÆTERNUM.

He spoke quietly at first, yet his voice was borne like a wind from the Lord over the six thousand upturned faces, and all heard and understood his words.

"The time of trial is at hand. The hour has come for the Lord to pluck forth the ungodly and to confront each man with his final choice. Let who will depart, for the Lord will suffer no waverers and cowards in His chosen band. But remember the fate awaiting those who lay down their arms and fall defenseless into the hands of those bloody men. The rest who stay by me will fight like men, and in the light of victory they shall behold the setting up of God's Kingdom on earth.

He will turn aside the cannon balls, and the armor of the Holy Ghost shall be our shield against lance and glaive."

A sudden childish smile broke over his face as he went on.

"I will not refuse negotiation if the Duke will send his most learned scholars to engage in controversy with me on the theme of divine justice, and will be willing to abide by the four articles whose excellence I shall prove in disputation. But this he will not do. God's justice is all the justice you can hope for here below, but because of the hardened hearts of these princes you must win it sword in hand."

He raised his voice, and in a kind of ecstasy cried out, "But in what does divine justice consist? I have proclaimed it in four articles, but now the time has come to draw aside the last veil that you may behold that justice revealed most brilliantly, most gloriously, in three words: *Omnia sunt communia!*"

He drew himself to his full height, and stretching up his arms to heaven, he shouted as loudly as he could, *"Omnia sunt communia,* all is in common! This, the will of God, is proclaimed through my mouth, and in these three words is all His justice comprehended. Lands, fields, pastures, forests, birds, beasts, and fish—all are owned by us in common. Cattle, houses, castles, corn bins, ploughs, tools—each one of us owns all and no one owns anything. There are neither rich nor poor, neither high nor low, and no man has more than his neighbor, for all is held in common."

The peasants stared at him with eyes like saucers, and I also was thunderstruck, for I realized that he proclaimed the Kingdom of God indeed, and that the minds of ordinary men would refuse such a message. No one dared utter a sound.

He lowered his hands, and the power of him brought six thousand men to their knees in prayer. Only the graceless Andy remained sitting on a powder keg, chewing a bit of horseflesh.

Six thousand men knelt, filled with a fervent faith in God and God's messenger, and Müntzer prayed aloud, saying, "My God, my God Who hast revealed Thyself to me, send us a sign from heaven to put the unbelievers to shame. Give us a sign that we may believe and no longer fear the raging of the unrighteous."

Involuntarily I raised my eyes, as did many. Black clouds hung over the Duke's camp, but our own lay in dazzling sunshine. From the west came a flash, then a bang, and the next instant a cannon ball sped over our heads like a bird with humming wings. The throng quaked together, but the ball passed harmlessly by.

Andy spat, pushed off his cap, and scratched his head until his hair stood up like a yellow brush.

He stared at me and said, "Holy Mary! Am I to believe that this man is telling the truth? How are we to own everything in common? We should all be milking each other's cows—and may I be damned if I'll share out my hard-earned money with the rest of the world. There wouldn't be enough to go around and I should be left with nothing."

I said that all would be made clear in due course, and that rather than puzzle our heads about it now we should rejoice that even enemy cannon balls were turned aside. But this Andy would not believe.

"Poppycock!" he said. "You ought to know sighting shots when you see them. The gunners send the first one beyond the target and the second short of it, and then they train all their artillery on a point between the two, fire all together, and score a hit."

We had not long to wait. Several successive flashes in the west sent eight whining balls into our midst. Heart-rending shrieks mingled with the crash of broken wagons. Shafts, wheels, limbs, heads, and entrails spun in the air. Many who were unscathed fancied they were hurt, being drenched in the blood of others, and they cried out on Müntzer for a liar. The tightly packed throng swayed this way and that in a desperate attempt to find cover, and men threw themselves in heaps into the nearest hollows. Flashes in the east brought two more balls into the thick of the mass, and others sang overhead.

"For God's sake, Andy, fire!" I shouted. He smiled slightly, but to please me and stiffen the courage of the gunners he took a match and put it to the touchhole. The gun roared and the smoke billowed up, but to my mortification I saw the ball strike the ground and rebound once or twice far short of the Duke's troops.

Andy ordered a prompt reloading, and turning again to me he said, "That's as far as our cannon will carry, and the enemy can shoot us to pieces at their leisure before storming our position. While we're waiting, it will be as well to dig some trenches to shelter in. But when horse and foot launch their assault in close order I shall have five forceful words to say to them—ten if we're quick."

Müntzer strove to hearten his terrified men, and the band of the chosen sang a battle hymn that mingled with the cannon's roar, but the destruction continued. The clumsy earthen parapet was leveled and the palisades were knocked into whirling pieces above the heaps of the maimed. At last the hymn was silenced by the deathsong of the flying iron, and one idea prevailed: to run!

The men threw down their weapons, shook their fists at Müntzer, knocked down their officers, and kicked them. Müntzer was a false prophet; they would not share their fields and cattle with anyone; they demanded only their own, in defense of which they had gone to war. The first rush of men from the stockade down the sheltered gully was followed pell-mell by the rest. They overturned their own wagons for better speed, and those who fell were trampled mercilessly underfoot by their stronger comrades.

At that moment trumpets sounded from all the surrounding hills. The cavalry in the valley advanced and the refreshed and rested pikemen began a formidable charge. Yet the rainbow banner still floated above us and Müntzer on his cart wrung his hands among the faithful few who stayed by him.

"Now for some quick thinking," said Andy. "I would rather drink the executioner's cup than be stuck like a pig among this cowardly riffraff. From now on I will fight only in the service of kings and emperors. They understand the business, and a good general gives a man at least the chance of dying with his face to the enemy."

He roared at the gunners, who were attempting to slip away from their posts, and then said, "Say your prayers quickly, Michael, while I look about me. If we can muster a score of level-headed fellows we may have the luck to break through and hide in the woods."

Then it was that I saw the rainbow banner droop and fall to the ground, to be trampled in the dirt by the panic flight of the chosen. Müntzer was first, tripping over his fur gown, his face distorted with terror. At this sight I lost my head and fled also, faster than anyone, and my speed may have saved my life. For at that instant there came an appalling explosion behind me and the whole stockade was engulfed in a cloud of black smoke. I fancy that some gunner in his haste had tossed his burning match into an open powder keg. But I did not stop to consider the matter; the din lent wings to my feet and I sped on faster than before.

Not until I had neared the lower end of the track did I pause for breath, and there a ghastly sight met my eyes. From one side charged the Margrave's savage horsemen, and from the other, down the steep slopes, rushed the Duke's footsoldiers, howling the names of Jesus and the Virgin. Between them they slashed, stabbed, and bore down the packed mass of fugitives and trampled their blood into the mire.

Just then I heard five cannon shots from the hill above. As I was looking about me, rigid with terror, for a way of escape, I beheld a black and sooty form descending in an equable manner from the fort. I fancied it was the Evil One himself and was in no way surprised, for here if anywhere was the place for him. But the specter gripped me by the collar and dealt me two stinging blows on the cheek, and so I came to my senses and saw that it was Andy. He was black from head to foot, and forelock, beard, and eyebrows had been singed away. I asked him why he struck me, as I had the Duke's safe-conduct in my pouch and could come to no harm.

Andy pointed to the bloody turmoil in the valley, and said amiably, "Don't let me stop you! Your passport will make an excellent shield. They'll kill you first and read the letter afterward—if they can read, that is. I'm glad I was able to fire off my cannon, though I didn't stay to spike them, as a gunner should."

Some of the faithful had turned and were running up the path again, their hands over their eyes.

Andy drew his sword, stood in the way and cried, "Today, good men, each of us must make his final choice, as your master Müntzer said. Choose therefore whether you will die by my sword or the enemy's. If you're wise you'll pick up some of these scattered weapons and follow me, for a loyal soldier doesn't leave his leader in the lurch, and I seem to see the fur mantle flapping about down there in the thick of the struggle. Well begun is half done, and I will lead you. Brother Michael, take up a sword or a pike and follow me."

The men would not obey him and tried to buffet him aside with fists and elbows. Then Andy raised his broadsword in both hands and clove the foremost to the waist at one stroke, so that brains and blood showered far and wide. This caused the rest to change their minds, and they bent to look for some suitable weapon among the many discarded clubs, pikes, and wolf-spears on the ground. They cursed him, but swore to follow.

Andy, wasting no more words, set off downhill, calling over his shoulder, "Bring up the rear, Michael, and make a hole in anyone who tries to turn back."

So we dashed down into the infernal mill whose grist was human flesh. We stumbled over heaps of corpses and saw blood flowing in streams down the steep, rain-scoured slopes.

But our little band grew until we were nearly fifty, for Andy gathered in all the sobbing wretches who, slipping and sliding in the blood and slime, were seeking to escape. He had only to show his sword for them to obey, and we who had been the first to follow gained courage

295

and pressed the newcomers between our ranks to prevent their flight. Our speed increased with the steepness of the slope, and we pushed as best we might, to give Andy the needful support. So compact, so speedy was our rush, so ruthless was Andy in hewing down friend and foe before him, that we made headway through the inferno, and indeed many preferred to allow our party, solid and bristling with blades, to pass by in order to resume their former combat behind us.

Like a prickly ball we rolled out of the hollow way, and in passing, Andy seized Müntzer by the fur collar, dragged him to his feet, and threw him behind into our midst. I remember little of what followed. Then suddenly the walls of the city loomed over us. We squeezed through the gateway and popped out on the other side like a cork from a bottle. No sooner had we space about us than our party scattered as by magic to take shelter in attics and cellars. Andy and I were left alone, staring after them. I had not even had time to reckon how many of us had fallen, though I fancy they must have been few if any, and I could have had no better lesson in how a resourceful man can get the better of even the most desperate situation.

Andy was a terrifying sight, black and bloody from head to foot, but I hugged him and wept tears of joy.

"We're safe!" I cried. "Henceforth we will travel everywhere together, you in front and I to guard your rear."

But Andy answered, "You hug too soon, brother, for the business is not yet over. Let us first visit our good bakery, for it's getting somewhat noisy and the threshing we saw may soon be continued in the streets."

We hastened to our lodging, therefore, and Andy, closing the door behind us, remarked, "Well, what say you, Michael? What will you give now for a neat suit of clothes?"

I glanced down at the clothes I wore and realized that in my present filthy and bloodstained condition I would instill no confidence, brandish my safe-conduct as I might. So I told him sulkily that I would give him one gulden and two schillings for the suit. But Andy turned a deaf ear to this offer, and seating himself on the kneading trough so that I could not come at the bundle, he began to wash the soot and blood from his face, swearing because the gunpowder had skinned it here and there. By good luck the women had brought several buckets of water to the bakery to mix their dough, so that I too was able to wash my face and hands and comb my hair. To mollify Andy, I offered him the comb, but he seemed to think he had no need of it; indeed his hair had been so severely singed that it was almost as pitiful to see as

296

was his face. I offered him two, three, and at last five gulden for the clothes, but his only answer was a wicked laugh. Throwing his burned and bloody rags into a corner, he stood up naked save for his linen drawers. He picked up his sword and said he would be off to get himself a better outfit and leave me to think the matter over, though I begged him not to leave me. Through the hole the cannon ball had made in the wall I saw him striding sword in hand across the square.

I hesitated no longer, but drew the bundle forth, undressed with trembling hands, pulled on the fine breeches, and buttoned up the velvet doublet. Ruff and buttons alone were worth more than two gulden, I saw; and when I had set the velvet cap with its fine-fronded stork's feather on my head I could contain myself no longer and admired my reflection in the bucket. Red shoes that fitted perfectly completed the array, which I was confident would save my life, and I resolved to pay Andy whatever he asked.

I had been long and impatiently awaiting his return when at last he appeared in the baggy breeches and pied leather jerkin of a mercenary. He carried helmet and breastplate in his hand, and under his arm was a shoulder of mutton.

"The deal's concluded, I see," he remarked. "Help me into this harness."

I fastened the shoulder straps with trembling fingers. To my question about how he had acquired these things he replied with a disreputable story involving a mercenary whom he had slain and stripped and a woman whom he had thereby saved from rape. The woman, it seemed, was grateful to Andy; she invited him to continue the work which the vanquished mercenary had so promisingly begun, and requited him with two silver cups and the mutton.

I bade him keep his shameless brutalities to himself and inquired what I owed him for the clothes. He replied gently with another question.

"How much money have you left?"

Seventeen gulden and a little silver, I told him—a poor reward for all my striving on behalf of the heavenly Kingdom. He must show consideration for my poverty.

"As you say," he assented. "Give me seventeen gulden. The silver you may keep."

Nothing would move him, neither tears nor prayers, and when I heard the approaching noise of hoofbeats and clattering arms I was forced to hand over the sum he demanded, consoled only by the

297

thought of five unavowed gulden that I had stitched into the hem of my shirt.

The slaughter continued all that night, and I believe no more than about two hundred peasants survived. Huddled in our dark room we escaped detection, and when day broke Andy thought the city quiet enough for us to show ourselves, armed with the pass, so that no one would guess that we had been in hiding. We brushed the flour from our clothes and left the place openly, I mincing along as befitted a young lord, and Andy trudging after me with belted sword and a pike over his shoulder.

7

The little town of Frankenhausen was a sorry sight that May morning, although a cock in some barnyard attempted a halfhearted crowing, as if to say that while there was life there was hope. But the sound died hoarsely and doubtfully away. Countless flocks of crows wheeled overhead and darkened the sun with their heavy wings. Citizens who had something to fear or to hide sat trembling in attic and cellar, while others paraded their innocence in the market place, where the princes had been holding a review.

We came at the right moment. No one heeded us, for all eyes were turned on the conquerors, who were dispensing justice before the church. Near them, in a pool of dried blood, lay the mutilated body of a priest whom women had slain during the night. I had been wondering whether Müntzer had escaped, but I saw him now, small and bent, with his hands bound behind him. They had deprived him of the fur mantle that had made him seem so tall the day before, and his yellow face was soiled with blood and filth. Beside him stood the proud mercenary who had found him shamming sick in a cellar.

The princes were gorgeous indeed; they wore complete armor, their helmets were adorned with waving plumes, and their breastplates were inlaid with gold. Duke George was short and stout, and in his broad countenance I seemed to trace a family likeness to Duke John, and the same hint of peasant cunning. He had bound a black scarf about his helmet, by which I guessed that Frederick was dead and that John was now Elector—a circumstance that gave added value to my credentials. But of all the assembled nobles the one who held my attention and who seemed to exercise authority over the rest was Margrave Philip of Hesse, who with his men had achieved that incredible night march from his own domains to Frankenhausen. His face was thin and bony and his light blue eyes had the same cold and ruthless expression in them whether they were bent upon Müntzer or upon his fellow princes. There was a haughty smile upon his face.

These nobles plied Müntzer with questions about his doctrine, and he made quiet and humble answer until Ernst of Mansfeld, growing weary of him, struck him under the chin with his iron gauntlet. Nor could I marvel at this, remembering the letter that Müntzer had sent this cruel man only three days earlier. Thomas Müntzer spat out a little blood and raised his head, and was now moved to exclaim that he would demonstrate the truth of his teaching before the greatest scholars in Germany, including Luther himself. If by means of Scripture his beliefs could be proved false, then he would submit in all humility to their decision; but until this happened he would continue to regard himself as God's zealous servant and messenger.

The princes roared with laughter, but Duke George said angrily that Luther was as black a heretic as Müntzer. The Duke of Brunswick observed that Luther deserved death at the stake for all the uproar he had caused. Only the Margrave of Hesse disputed this; he spoke favorably though with irony of the man upon whose advice they were now acting, and proposed making him Pope of Germany. But Duke George forbade such talk in the hearing of the people, and Müntzer, raising his head once more, begged permission to take part in a public debate.

Duke George laid his hand gently on Müntzer's thin neck, stroked it with his finger tips, and said, "Why not give this stubborn man the disputation he demands? Let me beg Your Highnesses to leave him in my hands. I will take him immediately to Feldrungen, where no unseemly brawls can disturb his weighty discourse and where he shall defend his thesis before impartial witnesses and an executioner of proved integrity. No materials or instruments necessary to such a debate shall be lacking."

Laughter greeted this proposal, and Duke George himself laughed till he choked.

"I wish him well," he went on, "and for his soul's sake I will find him a worthy opponent to convince him of the efficacy of the Church's doctrine, without which there can be no salvation. And this is desirable also for the sake of the poor wretches whom he has led astray."

Müntzer stared aghast at the princes, his face distorted with immeasurable horror. He looked like some wretched badger in a trap. Kneeling, he prayed not to be delivered into the hands of his mortal enemy, but to be granted an honorable disputation. But not one word was spoken in his defense. Nor did I step forward and testify that Müntzer was in some way inspired, though God had mocked and destroyed him and six thousand simple men with him. I stirred not a finger in his defense, although I knew well enough the fate in store for him. Instead, I hid behind Andy, and they led Müntzer away weeping and crying out for help and looking in vain for someone to stand by him, in that town where only the day before he had been hailed as the messenger of God.

I have no wish to dwell longer on the unpleasant events in Frankenhausen, and will mention only that as soon as an opportunity offered I approached Margrave Philip, presented my letter, and told him of the praiseworthy task I had performed within the peasant army in seeking to induce its leaders to negotiate and avoid bloodshed. It was true that I had failed, I said, yet I ventured to beg his favor and his permission to accompany his troops to Mühlhausen.

I was bound to take this step, despite extreme alarm, for at any moment a citizen might have denounced me as one of Müntzer's worst fanatics. And I was wise to address myself to the Margrave, though Duke George was ruler of that region, for it flattered Philip's vanity and he told me graciously that I had done my work well, since the peasants' temporizing had given the troops time to surround the hill and cut off our retreat, thus relieving the country of another six thousand bandits. Not even Fugger's money would have sufficed to pay troops enough to clear that forest.

He talked for some time in this vein, and as he seemed pleased to have a listener I ventured to ask what Fugger's money had to do with the matter.

At this he stared and said, "How else could I have maintained sixteen hundred horse and as many foot? Without rich Jacob's money the German princes would have been helpless, and beggars would by now have been rulers. But the peasants interfere with Jacob's trade and so he finances our campaigns. Von Truchsess could not have recruited a single lance without Fugger's twelve thousand gulden. Fugger means to claim this from the Archduke Ferdinand in due course, for it was with Fugger's money that Ferdinand purchased the dukedom of Württemberg, from which Jacob had driven Duke Ulrich for his unpaid debts. Rich Jacob has the knack of getting his money back."

I stood before him with eyes respectfully downcast, stroking my

300

soft beard, which had grown long during the revolt and which I did not mean to shave off, as I was well satisfied with my new appearance.

Curiosity overcame my fear, and I asked, "Am I then to understand that all these poor fellows have been massacred just to please Jacob Fugger, and not because they were heretics?"

"That is a point worth considering," observed the Margrave. "The more I think about it the more inclined I feel to take Martin Luther under my protection as my chaplain. Somehow I must pay my debts, and there are many wealthy monasteries in my domains which, if I embrace the evangelical doctrine, I may seize. It is unbecoming a prince and margrave to run Jacob's errands—for the sole condition on which he would pay my men was that I should come straight to Frankenhausen. Between Leipzig and Erfurt he has a great copperworks where he brings the ore from his Hungarian mines. There's silver in this ore which, if extracted in Hungary, he would not be allowed to take out of the country. So he prefers to do his smelting here. You'll understand, therefore, young man, that Jacob was in a fever of anxiety and sent his steward to urge me to make a forced march, when he heard that six thousand rebellious peasants were in the neighborhood of his precious smeltingworks. Yet if you fancy he'll set this against what I owe him, you're greatly mistaken."

"Shall even the holy Word of God be trampled in the dirt for a little copper?" I exclaimed. For the first time his pale blue eyes rested on me searchingly as he said, "I hope for your sake that you're no disciple of Müntzer!"

He bent forward to peer at the letter, which I still held, and read my name.

"Michael Pelzfuss de Finlandia, I will give you a piece of advice which I myself am now taking to heart. In questions of faith, a man must choose the one most advantageous to him. You gain nothing by defending Müntzer's doctrines. Quite the contrary."

He dismissed me then and I went to look for Andy. We spent another night in the bakery, but now that by the Margrave's favor I was out of danger, I felt a great sickness. I took no pleasure in my fine clothes or my soft beard, and huddled shivering in a corner. My gloomy thoughts deprived me of appetite, and Andy began to fear that I had inadvertently drunk water.

I think my heart was sicker than my body, though Andy was generous enough to hire a wagoner to drive me to Mühlhausen under the protection of the Margrave's troops; and indeed I could scarcely have walked so far. I have but confused memories of the days that followed, though I know that after much hesitation Elector John allied himself with the other princes outside Mühlhausen, and the combined forces were thereafter so formidable that the braggart Pfeiffer never for a moment thought of opposing them. He flitted from Mühlhausen one fine night with a couple of hundred other rascals, but was caught and brought back in chains.

To avoid utter destruction, the town had to bind itself to pay the princes forty thousand gulden within five years. Walls and towers must be demolished; all artillery, all articles of gold and silver, as well as provisions, horses, and other draught animals must be surrendered immediately. Only then did the princes think fit to enter the city.

Andy and I walked unobtrusively in the procession and afterward went to the house of Eimer the brewer. This good man had just flung aside the peeled willow wand of submission and was washing the filth from his legs after crawling with his fellow citizens before the conquerors. Neither he nor Madam Genevieve recognized Andy without his hair or eyebrows, and with his face all burned. So Master Eimer cursed us and said there was nothing left in his house to steal since Pfeiffer's rabble had shared out among themselves in a Christian manner all they could carry away. But then Madam Genevieve's eyes were opened and she made haste to make much of my brother Andy—until she caught sight of me. She looked long at my face and my new clothes, then fell into my arms and kissed me rapturously. Her unexpected tenderness overwhelmed me, and I was glad to press my head against her white, perfumed neck and shed bitter tears. She spoke sweet words of comfort and told me that she could never have guessed how slim and attractive I could look in fine clothes and a beard.

The brewer seemed only moderately pleased at our coming and at Madam Genevieve's welcome of me. But she had great influence over him and when I had shown him the Elector's safe-conduct Master Eimer perceived at once that we could be of use to him. He was a big, black-eyed fellow of fifty, with only a few flecks of gray in hair and beard. His eyebrows also were black and bushy, and his ruddy face was covered with little blue veins. Once persuaded that he might trust us, he took us to the room above. This presented a very different sight from the ground floor, which he himself had stripped and damaged, to convince all intruders that there was nothing left to take. He served us with strong ale and good food, and let us sleep in a feather bed. I have much to tell of him, for he was no fool; but first I must speak of Müntzer's death.

During their stay in Mühlhausen the princes dispensed justice, and the inhabitants busily informed against one another to avoid suspicion. Thus on the day of execution fifty-four citizens had either to slip the noose over their heads or kneel at the block, according to their rank. The Margrave of Mansfeld brought Müntzer to Mühlhausen—or what was left of him after his disputation with a competent torturer. Thomas Müntzer was now a limping, shattered wreck, and even his voice was faint and broken when he made his confession.

He acknowledged that all his teachings had been false and that he now commended his soul to the Church, which alone could save it. The pious Duke George was moved to tears at Müntzer's perfect contrition and expressed his joy that the reclaimed heretic had partaken thankfully of the Sacrament. As I listened to Münzer's meek and voluble confession, my last hope was crushed. I could no longer believe that the Kingdom of Heaven would come on earth, for if God had spoken through Müntzer's mouth, surely He would have sustained him through the torture, unendurable though it was for any ordinary mortal.

Being of the priestly order, he was beheaded, but Pfeiffer was hanged. This swaggerer met his death with consummate impudence, and from the very ladder he delighted the soldiers with lewd and blasphemous jests. He set the noose about his own neck, the executioner jerked away the ladder, and so Pfeiffer danced his last jig. And that is all I have to tell of Thomas Müntzer and his rainbow banner. My new book shall treat of Madam Genevieve, Eimer the brewer, the Emperor Charles, and many instructive and edifying matters.

BOOK 9.

The Ungrateful Emperor

I

WHEN the princes had made an end of their justice and had squeezed all they could from the citizens, they went quickly away. Eimer the brewer asked what we meant to do next, and thinking he wished to be rid of us I spoke of my dog in Baltringen, and a chest in Memmingen which I could put to good use if it were still to be found. Whereupon Andy, reminding me stiffly of my promise to him, said that I must accompany him and Madam Genevieve to France, whither he had long undertaken to escort her, and there become acquainted with our son.

Eimer, clearing his throat in some embarrassment, asked Madam Genevieve whether she herself had anything to say to this, and as she remained silent he went on to explain that he had come to have a great regard for her and did not wish to lose her company. Though he was one of the richest burghers in Mühlhausen, he would soon be beggared by the high taxation if he stayed. That morning he had succeeded in selling his brewery, though for a meager sum because of present conditions, and now desired to shake the dust of the place from his feet. This was no sudden whim, he said, but a purpose that had been maturing within him for many years, and we were not to suppose he was acting thus because he was tied to any woman's apron strings. As for his wife, it was the brewery he had married, not the woman, who was a scold; and he had no children of his own. He had never ceased to regret the deal. Now he had a mind to visit Nürnberg, where he could realize some bills of exchange, and he invited us all to come with him, and thence escape either to Hungary, the Swiss Confederation, or Italy.

Andy was thunderstruck, and gazed in reproach at Madam Genevieve, who said hastily, "You shall ever be my son's father, dear André, and Michael too! But can I help it if this good man, who is still in the prime of life, has taken a fancy to me?"

"This is a most scandalous affair," I said, "and you will live to regret it bitterly, Master Eimer—so bitterly that you will wish you were dead. You do not know this wanton woman."

2

By the middle of June we had arrived in the rich and mighty city of Nürnberg, which was the most beautiful I had seen in Germany. We remained there for several days while Master Eimer settled his affairs, and found the place to be like an island in a sea of unrest. No one there knew anything of disturbances save through hearsay, and this, said Master Eimer, was because too many powerful interests were concentrated in the city and too many merchants lived there for any disorders to arise.

When he had visited Fugger's agent and had received payment on his bills, he said to me, "If you look at a map, Michael, you will note that the places that have suffered least are those where Fugger has an agency. And yet those shameless factors charge up to thirty per cent brokerage."

Nevertheless he rubbed his hands, and there was a smile on his moist lips that hinted at something shady in his dealings. He had a large acquaintance among the burghers, and to one of these, by name Anton Seldner, he introduced us. Eimer confided to Seldner his intention of settling in some other country and starting a brewery.

"You've come to the right man," said Seldner, "and I strongly advise you to go to Hungary. Numbers of German fugitives are making their way there every day, and they're all beer drinkers. But what is more to the purpose, my brother Martin now manages the Carpathian copper mines on behalf of the Crown, and if I give you a letter to him he may sell you the right to supply his miners."

"I remember your brother well, and I pity the Crown once he gets his hands on the mines. But how can he be there? Fugger owns all the copper in the world save in Sweden and Spain."

Seldner, laughing, clapped Eimer on the back and mocked him for a country cousin.

"Is it possible? Have you heard nothing of the greatest events of our time? Fugger's monopoly is broken and the Hungarian Crown has taken charge of the mines. There was a riot. Fugger's office in Buda was mobbed and robbed, and now the landed aristocracy have forbidden the exploitation of natural resources except by servants of the Crown."

Eimer tore his beard is agitation.

"Then the world is indeed upside down! What wonder that Fugger takes thirty per cent—but the thing is outrageous, for the Hungarians are undeveloped, uncivilized people and can never succeed without the knowledge and method of the Germans."

"They're capricious and warlike, and good herdsmen," said Seldner, "but they hate Germans and Jews, and no doubt Fugger has given them every reason for this. Certainly Jacob went too far this time, and he and his partners are said to have cheated the Crown of at least a million Hungarian gulden."

Master Seldner spoke in great detail of the enormities committed and the vast estates purchased by this hated firm, and ended, "But Fugger brought off his greatest coup last year. In the teeth of mounting hatred he bought a title for Thorza, one of the partners, and with it control of the Mint. The King is a child in business and flings his money about like most Hungarians. So to get more he authorized Thorza to alloy the silver coinage with three quarters of copper, instead of with one half as before."

Master Eimer broke out into violent curses, plunged his hand into his purse, and threw down on the table a fistful of coins stamped with a handsome coat of arms and the head of King Lewis.

"God!" he cried. "Now I understand why the fellow asked me if I would accept Hungarian silver, as he lacked other small change. How the devil was I to know that it had lost half its value?"

"Quite so," said Seldner. "But the Hungarians swore worse than you, having learned the art from the Turks. Well, certain merchants—I name no names—swept up all the old coins in their coffers, ran to the Mint, and had them melted down; each old coin made two of the new ones. The King was not a farthing the better for the new issue, but

306

some made a hundred-per-cent profit. Not content with this, however, the landed aristocracy, paying the old prices with the new money, bought up all available property in Hungary—herds of horses and cattle, flocks of sheep, and many other things. But when they tried to buy goods from foreign lands they found that prices had doubled. At this there was a fearful uproar and Fugger's agents came near to losing their lives."

I pondered long upon this remarkable story, and at last observed, "This much at any rate I understand: Jacob will not long tolerate the ill treatment of his agents or the loss of his mines. The young King will be put in the corner and the country will go downhill. So I feel no wish to settle there and start a brewery."

But Master Seldner said, "Hungary is a rich, fertile land of boundless plains and pastures, vast herds of horses, and so many sheep that no one can compute their number. There are also vineyards, and above all the Hungarian landowners understand nothing of business. They drink wine, listen to music, dance, hunt, and ride—when they're not busy with the Turks—and a clever man can prosper among them and grow as fat as a tick in no time. But they show no mercy to heretics, for their faith has been strengthened in battles with the infidel, and they tolerate no religious discussion, fearing that such talk might stir up the serfs against them, as by God we know it would."

He spoke well and temptingly of Hungary, declaring that Fugger's power was now so broken that it admitted of other enterprises. He himself would be glad to go there if only he could persuade the Nürnberg senate to give his brother their support, for the mines were too big a mouthful for one man.

3

At last the day came when Master Eimer's affairs were settled, and he announced his purpose of journeying at once to Venice, the biggest market in the world. There he could acquire a new identity by changing his name and dyeing his beard.

"To carry a large sum in cash on such a journey would be foolhardy," he said. "So I have invested my whole fortune in bills on the house of Bisani, on the Rialto. Madam Genevieve has promised to accompany me, and we shall travel with Fugger's mails for safety and speed. By all means come with us if you wish, but now it must be at your own charges, since I have no further need of your protection."

307

I was grieved at his words, having believed we were all to travel together into Swabia, where I would pick up my dog Rael, and thereafter through the Confederation to Lyons and on to Tours, to visit our son. Andy had already bought a present for him from a skilled toymaker in Nürnberg—a donkey that could move its legs. I could see that Master Eimer's plan was most distasteful to Madam Genevieve, who smiled sourly and said that she had had very different ideas. But Master Eimer promised to buy her yards of gold brocade in Venice, a mirror, and some of the famous glass. I could not afford to travel post with the others, so it was decided that Andy and I should make our way on foot through Swabia and the Confederation to Lombardy, and join the others in Venice late in the summer. Master Eimer bade us inquire for one Kaspar Rotbart at the Fondaco dei Tedeschi when we arrived, and then we would be sure of finding them.

When next I saw Madam Genevieve alone I upbraided her for her fickleness, but she defended herself warmly and said she had always yearned to see Venice. Certainly she had hoped that Master Eimer would bring his fortune out of Nürnberg in coin, yet good might come of this Venetian trip after all. She reminded me of the countless proofs she had given me of her true affection, and urged me to hasten to Venice and relieve her of Eimer, whom she accompanied only for the sake of her children's future.

Madam Genevieve had, as she said, favored me with frequent expressions of her regard. Indeed while Master Eimer was preoccupied with his affairs her attentions had been at times exhausting. The thought of my dear dog and of summer wayfaring also helped to make this parting easy, and in my foolishness I really believed she could not live without me.

Before they left us, Andy expressed a wish to invest his considerable savings in bills of exchange. But Eimer seemed so eager to act for him that he pretended to change his mind. No sooner had they gone, however, than Andy went straight to the house of Fugger and obtained in return for his money a note which he had only to present at the branches in Venice, Milan, or Genoa to receive its equivalent in specie. I warned Andy that he had jumped into the wrong barrel, and told him of events in Hungary; but he only whistled carelessly and said he would take the risk of payment being stopped, for the earth was as likely to start moving around the sun as rich Jacob to lose his money.

Then we set forth on our journey from Nürnberg to Baltringen. But it was not so merry a jaunt as I had hoped, for here and there from low mounds of earth bony hands protruded, and crows circled round the burned-out farmsteads. The haggard women and scared children whom we met would not speak to us, and in the villages that had been spared it was hard to buy food. Thrice we saw gibbets with bodies hanging from them whose tatters showed them to have been priests. And the peasants we encountered cursed Luther, whose only achievement had been to make princes and prelates more arrogant than before and the peasants a great deal hungrier.

So we made all the speed we could. In Baltringen we called on the worthy widow, who had long since given us up for dead. And no words can describe my dog's rapture at beholding me again. He leaped up at me, licked my hands, and tore madly round the room, knocking against tables and benches in his delight. His coat had grown thick and glossy and he was as fat as a pig. The widow told me she had fed him as well as she could; indeed she had grown so fond of Rael that she was loath to part with him.

I was saddened by this, and resolved to let Rael himself choose between a full dish in the warm chimney corner and the privations of a journey with me. When I left him on the threshold for the widow to lure indoors with a juicy bone, he yapped in farewell, licked her hand, seized the bone, and made off after us. Andy admitted that Rael was a sagacious and prudent dog, and had brought his own provisions.

So we came merrily to Memmingen, where I went straight to the town hall and down the steep, dark stair to my old home. The bailiff and his pox-eaten wife still dwelt there but were far from glad to see me, as they had hoped to possess themselves of my chest and indeed had made public proclamation that unless claimed within a year and a day it would be held forfeit. They lamented their poverty and the hard times, but when I opened my chest I found everything in good order.

Regretfully, I sold Master Fuchs's fur mantle and all the other things save for a little linen, some fine lace, and the silver goblet. Out of the money I received I bought a Mass for Master Fuchs's soul—though I now had little faith in such things—gave alms to the poor in the House of the Holy Ghost, and paid the bailiff for taking care of my chest. When finally I had discharged certain debts to Andy, there remained a good hundred gulden in my purse. It now seemed beneath my dignity to walk, and for the next part of our journey I hired a horse at every change-house. Andy walked with a hand on my stirrup, and when Rael grew weary I set him before me on the saddle. In this way we made better speed. In a few days we came to Lindau, where the

Emperor had his arsenal, and sailed thence across the great lake to Swiss territory and freedom.

We now set our faces toward the "great fence," and lofty ice-blue peaks towered above us on every side. This must indeed be the greatest fence God ever made. The sight of it took our breath away and filled us with dread, and it seemed to us impossible that poor mortals could cross such a barrier as this.

Yet to my amazement we did it, in company with some merchants, though at night we suffered bitterly from the cold. Terrible winds howled through the passes and we had often to help heave aside the boulders that had rolled down the slopes and blocked the road. Rael grew thin and could now run far without panting. I believe I have never breathed such pure, invigorating air. I well understood how it was that even the emperors had never subjugated this nation, though their possessions enclosed it on all sides. It is a land created for men of toughness and endurance, who fear neither giddy heights nor sudden death.

From the exhilarating air of the Alps we descended in a single day to the stifling heat of an Italian July. The little town where we spent the night stank of rotting greens and ordure. Its small, dark-skinned inhabitants gathered round the wagons shrieking, yelling, and waving their arms, which led me to fear a riot at any moment. But Andy reassured me by explaining that this was correct behavior in Italy. He also advised me to learn Italian as quickly as I could, as it was the language of commerce and more widely used than any in the world.

We took leave of the merchants, who were bound for Milan, and continued quietly on our way from Imperial territory to that of the mighty Venetian republic. July was half over, fierce heat prevailed, and in the fields about us the grain was turning gold. Often we slept in the middle of the day and walked in the mornings and evenings, or through the moonlit nights. Yet Andy assured me that I still knew nothing of real heat in Italy.

I now come to what was perhaps the most remarkable of all my adventures; and because of the slander and suspicion to which it later gave rise I must stress that Andy and I had sufficient money for our needs, and that the arms we bore were for self-defense, not assault and robbery, which it would never have entered our minds to commit. This explanation is necessary, for since I attained my present high position certain people have affirmed that it was because of this incident that I fled from Christendom; whereas the truth is that I did not leave until

310

two years later, and then only from the most excellent motives. Hitherto I have related everything as it happened, without seeking to hide my faults and errors; nor in this instance do I see any reason to lie.

Andy had some reason of his own for wanting to avoid the town of Breschia, and having made a detour by means of a bridle path we rejoined the highroad as evening was drawing on. Suddenly three shots rang out ahead of us, followed by shouts and the clash of weapons. A riderless horse bolted past us with tossing head and glaring eyes, and sent my dog scuttling to heel with his tail between his legs. I told Andy that this was no affair of ours and that we had better take to the woods, but he, having vainly tried to halt the runaway beast, said that he would do nothing of the kind so long as the highway swarmed with horses for which their riders seemed to have no further use. So, with our firearms in readiness, we crept along the road, Andy first, then myself to guard his rear, and the dog last, still with his tail between his legs.

Presently we came in sight of a band of robbers. One of them held two horses while the rest stripped clothes and purses from the lightly armed riders, both of whom were dead. Andy fired his harquebus, uttered a hideous howl, and rushed upon them brandishing his great sword. After the first shock of surprise they saw that we were only two and made ready to kill us, but I, praying God to let my unreliable wheel lock work and fire the priming, pushed the barrel of my weapon against the chest of one of them and pulled the trigger. The gun fired, the man fell, Andy accounted for another, and the rest leaped astride the two stolen horses and made off with their plunder. We won nothing from this little brush, which in itself was of small importance. But it so happened that my bowels were loosened by agitation, so that I was obliged to retire into the woods. Rael was with me, and after scampering among the trees he began to growl, and then uttered a sharp bark. He did not come at my call, and on going in search of him I found the body of a young man. Blood was still flowing from his wounds and his face was warm; I took him to be the rider of the third horse, which had bolted past us. No doubt he had fallen from his mount when he was hurt and had crept away to hide from the robbers.

When I opened his purse I gave a cry of joy, for there lay twenty Venetian ducats and a quantity of silver. I was still counting the money when Andy came to find me, having called in vain from the road, and he was filled with envy at the sight of the gold. The fine clothes of the young man tempted me, but I felt it best to leave the spot without delay. Andy turned the body onto its back in the hope of finding more, and took a gold pin from the shirt. And now we noticed a strange thing. Careless of his purse, the young man clutched to his breast, even in death, a long tube encased in leather.

"This shall be my constable's baton, for I see three golden lilies stamped upon it," said Andy, loosening the dead man's fingers. "That is, should the French King ever appoint me to the command of his army."

He thrust the case into his bosom as though it were his property, and we made haste to leave the woods, and continue southward on our journey. We walked as long as the moon was up, and at its setting we halted to eat and sleep beneath some trees near a spring. We dared not light a fire, being even then aware that discovery would lead to hanging; for who would have believed our story?

We awoke in brilliant sunshine and examined our spoils. The purse, which was embellished with gold thread and pearls, must alone have been worth two ducats, and while I jingled the good gold in it to vex Andy he unbuckled the strap from his red leather case and drew forth an iron cylinder with a keyhole in it.

The leather was stamped with the lilies of France and the French King's arms, and Andy said suddenly, "I know what this is! A dispatch case from the French court. I've seen such things before, and no one has the key to them but the Keeper of the Seal and His Majesty's ambassadors abroad."

This put me in a great fright, so that I dropped a coin and was a long time looking for it.

When I had found it I said, "Let us bury the thing at once and be off, for no one robs the royal mails with impunity, and those fellows little knew what they did when they meddled with a king's messenger."

But Andy was determined to discover what the tube might contain that was of such importance, and worked for a whole hour to force it open. Yet when he had done so he was disappointed, for instead of the gold he had hoped for he found only some sealed letters addressed to the French Queen Mother in Lyons. At this time the Queen was handling affairs of state on behalf of her imprisoned son. Andy tossed the papers aside with an oath. But now that the cylinder had been forced for good or ill, I was seized with a fatal curiosity, and a desire to learn something of the world's affairs. It was ill done, I admit, and my only defense is that I could have no notion of the formidable matters with which this act was to involve me. Once more let me emphasize that the letters came into my hands by a strange chance, and it was never my purpose to become possessed of them.

I broke the seals, then, and began to read the dispatches, which were written in French. The longest was from Count Alberto Pio, the French ambassador to the Curia in Rome, giving his secretary Sigismundo di Carpi instructions to put through certain negotiations in Venice and then to forward the letter to the Queen Mother. The second letter was from the said Sigismundo di Carpi, who stated that he had entrusted the dispatches to his own secretary, Sismondo Santi. He affirmed that the Signoria of the great republic was even now equipping an army and that he himself was hastening to the Confederation for the purpose of recruiting ten thousand soldiers. There was also a letter from the Signoria, which I could not read, as it was in Italian. All that remained, wrote Count Alberto Pio, was for the Queen to sign the treaty of alliance; when His Holiness Pope Clement VII had received this he would be ready to send his troops and those of Florence against the Kingdom of Naples.

It took me a little time to grasp the significance of this, for like the rest of the world I had lulled myself into a belief in lasting peace. But as I read I exclaimed aloud and prayed for help to understand. I soon saw that these letters would cost me my life were I to be taken in Venetian, Milanese, Florentine, Papal, or French territory, for they concerned nothing less than a tremendous conspiracy against the Emperor and world peace. Behind the alliance stood His Holiness Pope Clement VII, and it was apparently to be led by the Marquis of Pescara, commander-in-chief of the Imperial army in Milan. I soon felt that this burden was too heavy for one man to bear, and to Andy, who at the sight of my great agitation had begun to question me, I related the whole story.

"It has an evil sound," said Andy placidly. "The Emperor has disbanded his troops, having no money to pay them with. But in Milan the Marquis of Pescara still has authority, and Frundsberg can stamp ten thousand pikemen from the ground at any time."

"But you miss the kernel of the matter," I said. "Pescara has been secretly plotting against the Emperor, who has treated him badly and not rewarded him as he deserves. King Francis was snatched from his hands and taken to Spain. Moreover he is furious with de Lannoy, the Viceroy of Naples, and the Duke of Bourbon, who are both sitting at their ease in Spain guarding the spoils and making up to the Emperor.

The Pope has promised him the crown of Naples or of the Two Sicilies, once Naples is taken, and has sent him many doctors of theology and jurisprudence to draw up a statement proving that he may without loss of honor forsake the Emperor and ally himself with his enemies, despite his post as commander-in-chief of the Imperial troops."

"The devil!" exclaimed Andy, and was silent for a long time.

At last he said, "If this is true, the poor Emperor is sitting in a leaky boat and I pity him, for de Lannoy and Bourbon are no match for Pescara. But now let us light a fire and burn these papers as quickly as possible, so that we may forget all about them and pursue our journey with a clear conscience."

But greedy and ambitious plans were already weaving webs in my head, and I was intoxicated by the thought that in our hands lay the destiny of the world.

"God pity you, Andy! These are valuable papers, worth much money. Let us not be such blockheads as to burn them. Let us rather consider who would pay us the best price."

Andy said, "At the lions' banquet there's no room for rats. We have no business in so great a game, and can expect nothing but a violent death, no matter who we sell them to. The broken seals show that we know their contents. The Pope would burn us at the stake, Pescara would have us drawn and quartered, and the Queen Mother would no doubt hang us for robbing her mails."

"But Andy," I said reproachfully, "this is so great a matter that we must not consider our own skins. We must remember that world peace is in danger and that Providence has placed these papers in our hands that we may save it. The Emperor alone can remove this threat to his power, and we must convey the papers to him with all speed. If he pleases to give us a suitable reward, let us accept it humbly as a gift from God."

Andy, with his head in his hands, ruffled his hair and said, "The Emperor is so damnably poor that we should gain little by helping him. We shall be jumping into the wrong barrel, Michael, and taking a short cut to hell if we seek to prop up his tottering throne when even Pescara forsakes him—for the Marquis knows what he's doing."

But I was obstinate and said, "This good young Emperor seems chosen by God to restore order in a troubled world. Poor though he may be, he is not far from world domination, and when he perceives the Pope's treachery he will surely crush him and purify the Church. He has also sworn to uproot heresy in Germany, and I have nothing against that, for with my own eyes I have seen that it was not God's will to bring the Kingdom of Heaven on earth. Luther's day is over, and all Germany curses his name. And I cannot but feel that a certain oath that I swore at my wife's scaffold—an oath that I will not repeat even to you, for fear you should suspect me of madness—was perhaps a good oath, and will come to fulfillment."

Andy reminded me bitterly of my promise on the road from Weimar, but I absolved myself from this by paying him five gold ducats from Santi's purse. He protested that a promise was a promise and that I must travel his road, having already brought trouble enough upon us both.

But when he saw that I was unshakable in my purpose, he put the money into his purse with a sigh and said, "If I have well understood those letters, it seems that the Holy Father and the other Italian princes have had their fill of foreign rule, and claim Italy for the Italians. I don't wonder at this, having seen how the Imperial troops behaved in Milan and Lombardy. But who am I, an ignorant man, to argue with you? I must go with you, lest once again you run your head against a wall. Let us therefore turn and make all haste to Milan."

I looked at him aghast, for Milan, the headquarters of Pescara, was the last place we should visit. But Andy said it was the last place in which they would look for us.

4

We arrived in Milan at the end of July. The scanty Imperial troops were still laying siege to the castle, which Sforza, the only rightful Duke of Milan, was stubbornly defending. Andy met many Spanish and German mercenaries who had been his comrades at the siege of Marseilles, and for the sake of appearances he inquired about the chances of enlisting. But he was told that the Emperor could afford no more men and that those he had were obliged to find their own food. The population in this once wealthy city had been reduced to a third, and whole districts had been burned to the ground. Nevertheless, confidence in a lasting peace had stimulated trade. I went at once to Fugger's agent and wrote a letter to Madam Genevieve, informing her of the change in our plans.

I told her that, suddenly oppressed with our sins, Andy and I had resolved to make a pilgrimage to the monastery of Santa Maria de Compostela, in Spain; she was therefore not to wait for us but to continue her journey to Lyons, where we hoped to join her on our return. Failing this, we would take the toy donkey to our son in Tours and then come back to look for her in Venice.

It was clear that Madam Genevieve would fancy we had taken leave of our senses when she read this, yet I could not otherwise account to her for our actions. I sealed the letter, and handed it to the factor with a ducat and a half, requesting him to forward it to the address of Kaspar Rotbart, Via Fondaco dei Tedeschi, in Venice.

We had already begun to prepare for the journey to Genoa when we met with a sudden stroke of good fortune. News came to our ears that a certain Don Gastaldo, one of Pescara's lieutenants, was bound for the Emperor's court in Spain, and many homesick Spanish mercenaries were competing for a place among his attendants. Andy obtained an introduction to him through an officer whom he had known at Pavia, and when the young lieutenant, a devout man, learned of our purpose he was glad. He praised the miracle-working madonna of Compostela and readily gave us permission to join him, provided we traveled at our own expense and would go with him all the way to the Emperor's court.

We journeyed to Genoa in company with Don Gastaldo, and there he dismissed the remainder of his escort, save for two Spanish harquebusiers. It was clear that he was engaged on some important mission, for we went aboard a great galley whose oars rendered it independent of the wind. This vessel carried many cannon, and the captain placed a fine cabin at Don Gastaldo's disposal in the after part of the ship. One or other of us was posted night and day at the door of this room, with match burning, and when Don Gastaldo walked the deck to enjoy the fresh air an armed man walked at his heels. At the time these precautions seemed exaggerated, but later events proved that he had every reason to insist upon them.

The long banks of oars rose and fell in unison, which was a fair sight, and the winds being favorable our voyage was rapid indeed. I would gladly have spoken with the fettered oarsmen, but while rowing they must not be disturbed, and when they rested they were so exhausted that they lay with heaving ribs beneath their benches, like emaciated hounds. Also their deck stank, and the men whose task it was to flog the lazy to greater efforts warned me against going below among them. For these men were savage, hardened criminals, ravenous because of their meager diet. And certain stories I heard, though doubtless exaggerated, removed my desire to visit them, and I kept an eye on my dog as well.

After a fortnight's voyage we entered the port of Valencia, in Spain. But we had no time to see much of this great and colorful harbor, with its multitude of shipping, for Don Gastaldo was in haste to proceed. That same day we climbed into the saddle to begin the long and arduous journey to Madrid, in the neighborhood of which the King of France languished in prison. During the monotonous days that followed I saw more than enough of the arid yellow hills of Spain, the everlasting dust, and the wretched goatherds whose swarthy faces grimaced at us from the wayside.

In the river valleys there were indeed fertile tracts to be seen, and beautiful cities, but the Moorish aqueducts and palaces lay in ruins, and the fierce August heat had scorched even the richest soil to a yellow pallor. I must confess that this land of bare hills and plains frightened me, its wine smacked of the red dust of the roads and burned my mouth, and I could not understand why the two surly harquebusiers had so longed to return hither from the glory and good cheer of Italy.

The nearer we came to Madrid, the more clearly did I perceive the difficulties to be overcome before we could gain the ear of the Emperor. Affairs of state must take up all his time, and we learned that French envoys had arrived in July to negotiate the release of their King. I was in no way cheered by the howls of wolves among the hills, which brought Rael whimpering to my side at night as we lay in some miserable mud hovel, or by the smell of faggots burning before the church of a little town. We happened to pass this place at the moment when a Jew and a Moor were being burned. They were bound back to back at the same stake and wore headdresses on which devils were painted. Black-robed monks chanted and waved their crucifixes, and notwithstanding his haste Don Gastaldo halted here in order to attend the mournful ceremony. He told us that no other Christian country had such trouble with heretics as had Spain. Here the Holy Inquisition must fight both Jewish heresy and inherited, ingrained Mohammedanism. The smell of this smoke moved him profoundly, therefore, and brought back precious memories of his childhood.

We came to Madrid on one of the last days of August, weary and sick from our journey through blinding heat and dust. Don Gastaldo heard to his great delight that the Emperor had just arrived here from Toledo, and without pausing to brush the dust from his clothes or even remove his spurs he hastened to seek audience of His Majesty.

We never troubled our heads about what his errand might be. I admired him greatly, for though he had grown thin and hollow-eyed from the rigors of the journey he remained as lively and supple as a rapier. Andy told me that nowhere in the world were there soldiers of such toughness and endurance as the Spaniards.

As for us, we crawled stiff and sore into an inn, where in Latin, French, and Italian we ordered food and drink. The wine went to my head at once. Andy drank his from a bucket, and Rael under the table gnawed ravenously at a bone and growled at anyone who tried to stroke him. Soon a group of Spaniards had gathered about our table to gape at our eating and drinking, especially Andy's, crossing themselves and following every mouthful with their dark eyes.

Andy, feeling now in charity with all the world, said, "These poor scarecrows have their share in the Redemption, like us, and they cannot help their gloomy natures. Let us fill them up with wine and see if they can smile."

And so we did. But the rumor of free drinks flew round the town like lightning, and soon the place was so crammed that we could hardly lift our elbows, and the landlord was compelled to bar the door. But one little man climbed over the wall into the courtyard and joined us. He had bat's ears and lively eyes and spoke fair German and even Latin, so we welcomed him as a Christian. When the drinking was over we carried him to the room that the landlord had put at our disposal and laid him in bed between us. He had a poor head for wine.

Luck was with us, for this little fellow was to be of great service. When we woke next morning we partook cautiously of wine to clear our heads. Meanwhile he told us that he was the Sieur de Lannoy's barber and had attended his master from Toledo to Madrid. With this profession he combined that of pimp, and was ready with introductions to the best brothels in Madrid. But what with our exhaustion and my own wholesome dread of the French pox we did not feel inclined to avail ourselves of his services. Seeing that he was well disposed toward us, however, I asked how a poor man might gain audience with the Emperor. We were pilgrims from a distant land, I told him, and having accompanied a Spanish officer as far as Madrid I was most eager to meet the greatest ruler in the world, so that I could tell my children of it, if ever I had any.

The good barber surveyed me very searchingly and replied, "Our young sovereign has been forced to surround himself with a wall of hundreds—or even thousands—of people to keep off those who would

318

have audience of him. He is continually besieged by suppliants from every country—inventors, mathematicians, philosophers—who outdo one another in the lunacy of their projects. But one aim they all have in common: to get something from the Emperor. Then you must remember that he is in debt to merchants and princes throughout Christendom. There can be few to whom he owes nothing, no moment of the day when he is secure from suitors. I can well understand that despite his youth the Emperor is weary of mankind and a lover of solitude.

"Just now," he went on, "it is harder than ever to catch his ear, for French, English, Venetian, and Papal envoys—and of course the Duke of Bourbon and the Sieur de Lannoy—are prowling around him like so many black cats, spying upon him and pursuing their separate intrigues. France has offered a ransom of three million gold ducats for its King provided he may retain the Dukedom of Burgundy, which the Emperor covets. But the Emperor and the Duke of Bourbon insist on the surrender of the Dukedom, while the good Sieur de Lannoy would prefer to accept the ransom and win over the King as friend and ally. And in King Francis the Emperor has a prisoner as stubborn as himself. Is it any wonder, therefore, that His Imperial Majesty craves peace and leisure to ponder these weighty matters?"

The barber's remarks gave me much food for thought, and showed me that our errand was even more complicated than I had fancied, for were I to appeal to the wrong person this person would do all he could to prevent our audience. The papers in my possession clearly showed that the right course for the Emperor was to make peace on moderate terms, release King Francis, and so make a friend of him. For otherwise France would join the Italian alliance to set him free.

"But suppose," I said, "that someone could produce clear proof that a speedy peace with France is in the Emperor's best interests, and that by prolonging the dispute he destroys himself and his empire. Do you think that such a person could obtain an audience of him? And if so, to whom should he apply?"

The barber stiffened and looked at me with eyes as expressionless as hard-boiled eggs.

"Are you drunk?" he exclaimed. "Such a man should of course sell his secret to the French envoys. But above all he should not chatter of such things to a chance drinking companion. You must be very simple, Michael Pelzfuss. Much more of such talk and you'll find yourself in the dungeons of the Alcazar, or with the sword of one of Bourbon's men through your body."

Andy remarked, "This good brother of mine is a queer fellow who trips over his own tongue at times, having a weak head for wine. Nevertheless for safety's sake, dear drinking companion, I find myself reluctantly compelled to wring that skinny neck of yours."

The barber put a hand to his throat and grew sober at once. He glanced at the door, but Andy stood in his way.

Having cautiously poked at Andy's chest with his forefinger to remove him, the little fellow sighed and said, "It won't pay you to kill me, for if you really do possess such secret information, I am perhaps the one who can best serve you. I believe de Lannoy can obtain an audience for you behind Bourbon's back and may even pay you for it, for he dearly loves to steal a march on the Duke whenever he can."

And so it was that he brought us into the presence of de Lannoy and persuaded that gentleman to hear us while his beard was being trimmed and oiled and his hair curled. And when I had told as much as I dared, he was overjoyed at the opportunity of unmasking his rival Pescara and revealing him as a traitor.

"This is very great news," he said. "Leave the papers with me and I will see to it that they reach the Emperor's hands without delay. You may be assured of my favor and a fair reward."

Here Andy cleared his throat and nudged me.

Summoning my courage I said, "We're both poor men and money would not come amiss. But we undertook this long, arduous, and costly journey to show our loyalty to the Emperor, and therefore I cannot deliver these valuable papers into any hands but his. Let him give us what reward he thinks fit and from you we will ask nothing."

De Lannoy's face darkened.

"How am I to know that you're not common cheats and adventurers?" he demanded. "How am I to know that this is not one of the Duke of Bourbon's traps? And what hinders me from calling my servants and bidding them take those papers from you by force?"

Andy absently picked up a large silver vessel from the table and without effort squeezed it into a shapeless lump.

De Lannoy crossed himself, and I said, "Your honor, noble Sir, and your renown as prince of chivalry and the ablest general in Europe will not permit you to see harm done to such poor fellows as we are."

He was moved by this and by the fact that we sought no reward from him. Nevertheless I had to show him the letter concerning Pescara's alliance with the enemy and his promised reward—the crown of the Two Sicilies.

When he had read the letter he crossed himself many times and said that he could never have imagined so blackhearted and dastardly a betrayal. Yet I could see that inwardly he was gloating over the chance of harming his rival. He began to hope that the Emperor would send him at once to Milan to arrest and execute Pescara, and was willing to relinquish the honorable post of King's jailer in favor of so pleasing a task.

When he had departed to discover how best an early audience might be arranged, the little barber asked bitterly who was to reward him for his services. He was a poor man, he said, and would renounce all claim to a share of the Emperor's gift in return for a modest recognition now. This seemed to us a good enough bargain, and when we had haggled for some time he accepted fifteen ducats. I thought him simple indeed to sell his share so cheaply. But alas, we were simpler than he.

We now took up residence in the Viceroy's palace under his protection, which seemed the wisest course in a land so riddled with treachery and intrigue, and later that day de Lannoy told us that he had arranged a secret audience for us. The Emperor, on his return from hunting the next afternoon, was to complain of thirst and call in at de Lannoy's mansion for a draught of wine, while the company awaited him outside.

The Sieur de Lannoy condescended to invite me to his table that evening, as he had no other guests, and this was the greatest honor that had ever been done me. He had no doubt concluded from my appearance and manners that I was of noble birth, though for one reason or another I preferred not to acknowledge it, for there were many young noblemen at that time, especially in Germany, who being impoverished or under a cloud sought their fortunes in foreign lands.

He begged news from abroad, but I could tell him little save that Luther had married a runaway nun that summer; for so I had learned from Fugger's agent in Milan. At this my host crossed himself devoutly, saying that no better could be expected of him and that it set the crown upon his heresy. When he had drunk a handsome quantity of wine, he grew inquisitive and inquired about my lineage, because, he was pleased to say, my education, fine features, and clean hands proved that my origins could not have been obscure. I told him as much of my country as he could understand, and said that having been adviser on Finnish affairs to the unlucky King Christian II, I lost both position and fortune when he lost his crown. As for my birth, I was a bastard, I told him complacently, and thereby rose in his esteem. He said that the Emperor had a bastard daughter named Margaret, whom His Majesty dearly loved. She was to wed a son of the Duke of Ferrara. This son was born of the Duke's marriage to Lucrezia Borgia, herself a natural daughter of the Pope. The Duke of Ferrara had the best artillery in the world and plenty of money, and would be a valuable ally for the Emperor when he came to straighten out the complications in Italy.

De Lannoy mentioned that Pope Clement VII himself was an illegitimate son of the Medici whom the freedom-loving Florentines had slain in the church. His mother had been a poor peasant girl of the region, and the Medicis had been put to a great deal of trouble in hiring witnesses who would testify to a secret marriage.

"I would not offend you for the world," said my host delicately, "but how wrong it is, how sad a proof of the decay of the Church, that the Papal Throne should be occupied by a bastard—and one moreover who has the insolence to wear a beard! It would not surprise me if this Pope were to saw off the branch he sits on by conspiring against the Emperor, for it is to Imperial favor alone that he owes the Papal tiara."

5

Before the Sieur de Lannoy joined the hunting party he made such arrangements in his house as would let the Emperor's visit appear one of pure chance. He dismissed his servants for the day and kept only the most necessary guards on duty. Then, placing a carafe of wine in a porous cooler in his study, he bade Andy and me keep watch from a window, so that we might be ready to wait upon His Imperial Majesty immediately on his arrival. Toward evening we beheld a brilliant party riding along the narrow street, and people flocked to the windows and out into the road to see the Emperor ride by. He was mounted unpretentiously on a fine gray mule and wore a flat cap. As he drew near the Viceroy's house, we saw him complain of thirst, and dismount, assisted by de Lannoy. With a sign to the rest to wait for him, he entered, followed by a huge, clay-colored hound.

Here the catastrophes began. Unknown to us, an old woman had taken advantage of the emptiness of the house to scrub the entrance hall. The Emperor slipped on the wet floor and would have fallen had not de Lannoy seized his arm. The old crone was so thunderstruck at the sight of His Majesty that in her efforts to drop a curtsy she shot the dirty water from her pail all over his feet. De Lannoy in a rage gave her a violent kick, whereupon she shrieked to the Virgin, slapped him in the face with her dripping clout, and assured him that her ancestors had been fighting the Moors when his were still being hanged as horse thieves.

I had set the study door wide open, and while this scene was yet in progress the dreadful hound sprang past me and hurled itself on Rael. It was one of those savage, diabolically cunning brutes which Spaniards in the New World used for hunting Indians, and which they held in such respect as to allot each of them a man's share of all the plunder. In a fight for his life my good dog seized this monster by the ear and never let go, though the shaking of the great beast's head tossed him repeatedly into the air. Unthinkingly, I kicked the Emperor's hound, and it bit me in the leg, so that I howled as loudly as Rael. Thus it will be seen that my audience with the Emperor proceeded not altogether as planned, and that I merited his displeasure.

The Emperor shouted an order, drew his animal toward him, and began tenderly and wrathfully examining its torn ear. I gathered Rael into my arms, from which safe place he growled and snarled his defiance of all large Spanish hounds, and I left him to lick his wounded paw in a neighboring room. Then I returned limping to His Majesty's presence. It must be admitted that he was right to bring a bodyguard with him into a strange house, and this uncannily clever animal was better than any human guard. For now that its rage was abated it began roving up and down the room and sniffing at every corner to insure that no eavesdroppers stood hidden behind hangings or in the great cupboards.

The Emperor sat down at the writing table while de Lannoy, in despair over what had passed, poured wine into a golden cup. I had no time to fall on my knees, for hardly had I returned when His Imperial Majesty in very ungracious tones demanded to see the papers, which de Lannoy then respectfully handed to him.

He read calmly and attentively, without betraying the least agitation. Having finished the first one, he sipped fastidiously at the wine and ordered de Lannoy to dismiss his guests, with the excuse that he was slightly indisposed and would not detain them. De Lannoy was then to remain outside the door and guard against intruders. I could see that the Viceroy was far from pleased at this command, but he could only

323

obey, and soon I heard the hoofbeats of the departing company. Yet the Emperor had nothing to fear, for the great dog sat beside his chair with lolling tongue and seemed to ask no better than to bite me in the other leg.

The Emperor read the letters very thoroughly, and I had leisure to observe him. At the time of our meeting he was only twenty-five—two or three years older than myself. He was about my height, neither short nor tall. His dress was of a distinguished simplicity and was unadorned save for the Order of the Golden Fleece, which hung from a chain about his neck. His complexion was dull and his cold gray eyes had a secret, watchful look, for he hid them beneath their heavy lids as if to conceal his thoughts. His chin, sparsely bearded, protruded stubbornly. His ears lay flat to the head, and his forehead was low. Physically, he was without blemish. He carried himself well and had exceptionally fine legs, and he resembled all young men of good birth who since childhood have exercised themselves in the use of arms. His demeanor showed gravity, firmness, and a level head—showed also that all too early he had been compelled to shoulder an overwhelming burden from which he did not shrink. And although there was something hard and relentless about the Emperor Charles, I did not feel that he would deliberately wrong any of his subjects, and the longer I looked at him the deeper grew my respect.

When he had read all the letters he laid his white, shapely hand upon them, looked at me for the first time with that searching gaze of his in which I could detect something like repugnance, and said, "Do you imagine that all this is news to me?"

I was thunderstruck. I could only stammer that I had risked my life and endured great hardships to serve him by bringing this hideous treachery to light as speedily as I could.

His lip curled as he said, "You were not speedy enough, for I have known of it for two days. I owe you no explanation, but lest you should fancy I am trying to cheat you of the reward you no doubt expect, let me tell you that the Marquis of Pescara is the most faithful of my subjects, and feigned to join the conspirators in order to discover their plans. This has placed him in an extremely difficult and unpleasant position, and it should be held greatly to his credit that he set loyalty to me above his personal honor. As soon as he had collected all necessary information he sent his lieutenant, Don Gastaldo, to me with a letter of explanation. I tell you this, that the Marquis' reputation may not incur the slightest stain through malicious gossip. Yesterday I told the papal legate my opinion of the Pope and his devilish adviser Ghiberti. This should prove sufficient warning to the conspirators."

My hopes were utterly dashed, and I felt as empty as an eggshell. I had wasted my money, and my only reward was a bite in the leg.

The Emperor rested his head wearily in his hands and said, "I'll not deny that these papers have a certain value, in that they bear out the Marquis' words. But I must know how they fell into your hands, for that to me seems incredible."

I summoned fresh courage and told him as candidly and briefly as possible of the robbery we had witnessed near the town of Breschia. Nevertheless I became enmeshed in my own words when I sought to explain how we had come to force the lock and break the seals. The Emperor heard me out with patience, his cold gray eyes shaded by their heavy lids.

When I had finished he said, "Your story explains much that was obscure, and confirms my belief that there is no one in this world whom I can unreservedly trust. Frank though Pescara's letter seemed, your account shows that he had no choice but to reverse his tactics as soon as he knew that these dispatches had fallen into alien hands. He had to cover himself in case they fell into mine. It explains why he was suddenly in such haste to write to me, when for two months he had been in secret communication with our enemies without giving me the slightest hint of the matter, and also why the French envoys so obstinately refuse my terms."

He reflected for a time, and then continued to give free rein to his thoughts, as if he had been alone.

"I hardly think France will dare go to war with me so long as the King remains my prisoner. The French use these intrigues merely to force me into a peace unworthy of my position and my victory. In any case I can be sure that as soon as the Queen Mother hears that her mails have gone astray she will do as Pescara has done: reveal the plot to me and so threaten me with a war that she dare not embark upon. And I see once again how little all these plots are worth and how ready each man is to betray his confederates when he fancies he has anything to gain by it."

But having thus ruminated aloud, he remembered my existence and addressed me.

"I see you're waiting for your reward, and I don't deny your right to beg my favor, for in this ungodly age one must at times use dirty tools, even in high politics. Yet to recompense murder and theft would be to bring the blood of that young secretary, your victim, upon my own head. I must have time to consider how best to requite you for the service you have done. Meanwhile I see you're agog to sell the news of Pescara's disclosure to the French delegates, and I will not prevent you, for the matter cannot long remain a secret. I hope they will pay you well."

The Emperor thought me sharper than I was, for it had never occurred to me to sell my news to the French. But having had the hint, I saw that I might well turn an honest penny in this way. At the same time I trembled to note His Majesty's disbelief in our story and his conviction that we were common footpads who had murdered and robbed the French courier. No doubt he had seen too many questionable actions presented in a flattering light to believe good of any man. I fell on my knees before him and swore by the blood of Christ that I was innocent of murder or assault, and that although I relied on the Emperor's favor I could not accept any material token of it while he believed me guilty.

But with an impatient gesture he silenced me, as if to say he had heard enough sacred oaths in his time to know their value. His hound got to its feet, stretched, and yawned into my face—for kneeling brought my head on a level with the dog's. The Emperor also rose and promised that I should hear from him in due course. Nothing remained for me to do but to open the door for him with a deep bow. De Lannoy hastened to open the outer one, and while His Majesty paused to draw on his gloves the hound took the opportunity of lifting its leg against the doorpost. For the first and only time I saw a faint, sardonic smile flit over the Emperor's lips.

De Lannoy held his stirrup and would have attended him, but His Majesty waved a gracious dismissal and rode away accompanied only by his guards and his hound. De Lannoy slammed the door, and I have never heard a man swear as he swore then. Nor was he pleased to learn that our news was no news and that Pescara had forestalled us in betraying his confederates. Indeed he flew into so towering a passion that he ran at me, boxed my ears, and kicked my dog. Luckily the barber came to my aid before I sustained any grave injury, calmed his master with tactful speech, and led us from his sight, begging us not to be offended at de Lannoy's violence. Such outbursts of passion were characteristic of gentlemen; they were not obliged to control themselves as poor people were. When he had grown calmer, we would find him as well disposed toward us as before, and we would do well to accompany him to Toledo, for we had no other protector and our money was coming to an end.

Wine was our only remaining consolation. Very bitterly I told the barber all that had passed between me and the Emperor, while the little man practiced his arts upon me, washing, dressing, and binding my leg. But as I drank, my spirits rose little by little, and I was consoled by the Emperor's promise to remember me.

But Andy thought this a faint hope. Placidly he drank his wine, and said, "I fancy we've not seen the last of our mishaps, brother Michael. Fortune mocked us in sending us hither in Don Gastaldo's company. And Fortune I think has many more such pranks in store."

I told him the Emperor had nothing against our selling the news of the Marquis' treachery to the French—for treachery it was, though it was his fellow conspirators he had betrayed and not his sovereign. I asked the good barber the best way of setting about this.

Rubbing his nose thoughtfully, he said, "I don't doubt that I could arrange this affair, for thanks to barber colleagues, and to those other interests of mine, I know two of the French envoys. But let us not be hasty. If the Emperor is willing to frighten the French with the news, he can have nothing against our selling it also to the papal legate, to the delegates from the Venetian Signoria, from Florence, Mantua, Ferrara, and elsewhere. The price they will pay, however, will depend on the seller. My master, being a gentleman of rank, would command a hundred times more money than you could. We must find as many customers as possible before the affair becomes common knowledge."

The good barber agreed to content himself with ten per cent of what we received, and with his help we drew up a list of all the representatives in Toledo whom de Lannoy should approach. When the project had been explained to this gentleman he took us back into favor, but said that he could not engage in so degrading an undertaking for less than half the gifts. For gifts they must be, he said. He could not demean himself to ask for money, and when he came to dispose of the presents to the Jews he would be bound to sell at a loss. But the barber explained that all he need do was to engage each customer to strict secrecy, and then, on the pretext of a temporary embarrassment, request a substantial loan, for which the security would be a singularly valuable piece of information about Pescara.

In the end, Andy and I had to agree to divide the profits equally with de Lannoy, and moreover to deduct the barber's commission from

327

our half, leaving ourselves with twenty per cent each. Yet we were comforted by the thought of being spared all difficulties and dangers. As soon as it was generally known that Pescara himself had informed against his allies, the highway robbery would be forgotten and our life and honor would be safe. Till then, Andy and I were to remain quietly in Madrid while de Lannoy rode with all speed to Toledo, bearing with him our best wishes for his success.

6

Yet it was not long before we began to feel uneasy, for we heard not a word from the Sieur de Lannoy or his barber. We passed the time in devout prayers for His Most Christian Majesty of France, whose poor health and melancholy had been rumored abroad, and in gazing at the sun-baked plateau and the riverbed, where water lay in pools beneath the autumn drought. One day succeeded another in vain waiting, and we began to suspect that de Lannoy had shamefully cheated us.

Matters were not so bad as we feared, however, for when a fortnight had passed we received a summons to wait upon the Viceroy without delay. And so we rode to Toledo. I must acknowledge that the sight of this wealthy and most beautiful city, perched on its crag in a loop of the river, did much to raise my opinion of Spain. The Sieur de Lannoy dwelt here in a silent palace in whose colonnaded court fountains played among the ripening vines.

He received us graciously, saying, "I owe you an explanation, and I will be frank with you. The affair has not turned out so well as I had had hoped."

The barber handed him a paper, and I listened round-eyed as he read out names and sums, for he had done business with eighteen different envoys. The Venetian ambassador had paid most—three thousand gold ducats. The poorest return had been from the King of Hungary's representative, who could raise no more than ten. The papal legate had offered only two thousand, as he declared he had foreseen the whole affair. In all, de Lannoy had gathered in nine thousand one hundred and ten ducats, and admitted that he might have done worse. But then his face clouded.

"Much of my work has been rendered profitless and has caused anger, for despite the promise of secrecy exacted in each case, everyone hastened to sell the secret elsewhere. Thus the affair came shortly to the ears of the Emperor, who was prompt in borrowing eight thousand ducats of me to pay his Milanese troops their arrears. He said it was only fair that his enemies should thus indirectly finance his army, and gave me his word that I should be repaid. When this happens, therefore, you shall have your share, that is to say four thousand five hundred and five ducats, of which you must give my barber nine hundred and eleven."

This ingratitude and injustice brought the blood surging to my head, and I demanded at least our share of the eleven hundred ducats that remained to him.

But with a deep sigh he said, "This is what I feared. But as a nobleman I understand little of money matters, and being incensed that the Emperor should have borrowed the sum I had so painfully collected, at great hazard to my honor, I thought to try my luck with the dice. Most unfortunately I lost a thousand ducats. One hundred and ten are left to me, therefore, and if you insist on your own interpretation of what is due to you, I am willing to divide this sum in the agreed proportions."

I said bitterly that he had had no right to gamble with our money. Yet I did not prolong the heated argument that ensued, as nothing was to be gained by angering him. We divided the money, therefore; he kept fifty-five ducats, the barber received eleven, and Andy and I took the remainder, twenty-two ducats each. Andy was of the opinion that we might have come off worse, but days passed before I was able to overcome my indignation, and I reckoned over and over again both in my head and on paper that by rights we should have received eighteen hundred and twenty-two ducats each, and become rich men.

We now had no choice but to await recognition from the Emperor. I began to understand Pescara's feelings after Pavia, when in faraway Italy he waited vainly month after month for recognition of his incredible victory. Nearly two months passed before His Imperial Majesty was pleased to remember us.

I need say nothing of those two months, for the whole world knows how King Francis declined into a melancholy that threatened his life and therewith the Emperor's plans. Everyone will remember how his learned sister Margaret the Duchess—and later Queen—of Navarre journeyed from France to her brother's sickbed, bringing with her a flock of court beauties to raise his spirits and to beguile the hours he must spend in bed.

By the beginning of November the King was restored to health, and

329

his sister left Spain without having been able to bring him nearer freedom. But now King Francis, driven to extremes, threatened to abdicate in favor of his son, who was still a minor. When I heard this I bribed de Lannoy with the last of my ducats to remind the Emperor of his promise, for I saw that the outbreak of war was now only a question of time and after that I could have no hope of his favor.

The Emperor kept his word and granted me an audience in his own study. He asked my name and Andy's, and bade his secretary enter them on a completed document, to which the Imperial seal was appended.

"I have considered your case," he said, "and despite some qualms of conscience I have rewarded you—and more liberally than you can ever have expected—for it does not become the Emperor to remain indebted to murderers and thieves. I heard recently that a certain swineherd, by name Pizarro, is now equipping an expedition at Panama, in the New World. He believes he has found the way to the realm of El Dorado, whose paths are strewn with gold dust. He calls this country Biro or Peru. I cannot afford to send him the soldiers, ships, horses, and donkeys that he asks for; and indeed I'm weary of throwing money away on enterprises that come to nothing. Better one ship safely docked, laden with spices, than ten vessels full of precious stones which all unaccountably go to the bottom. I can help Pizarro in no other way than by sending you, and this document will secure you a free passage to Panama next spring. But for equipment—and above all you must take horses, which the wild Indians hold in great dread— you must be at your own charges."

He threw me a glance and evidently perceived the bitterness of my disappointment, for he hastened to add, "Read carefully the terms of this concession, for besides the free passage, it entitles you to greater privileges than even Grandees of Spain enjoy in this crowded Old World. It confers upon you the governorship of any province in Peru —such province to be determined by agreement between you and Pizarro. It gives you the right to occupy any territory you may win by the sword, on condition of converting the Indians to Christianity and teaching them to cultivate the soil, grow spices, and mine for gold and silver; and on condition of owning no more than four thousand Indian slaves at any one time. When you've made your conquest you shall send to Spain for a competent attorney to keep an eye upon your activities—in my interest and at your expense."

He went on to speak of taxes and tithes and royalties and possible future ennoblement for me and my heirs, and at last the secretary handed me the document. I could but drop on one knee and then retire from the Imperial presence, carrying in this worthless paper my only recompense. With tears of indignation burning in my eyes, I went straight to the tavern, where Andy and the little barber were waiting to share the spoils.

May I be forgiven. I spent my last silver coins in getting so drunk that I cursed the Emperor's avarice and ingratitude aloud. Nor was I the only one, for many friendly customers joined with me and agreed that it was easier to squeeze blood from a stone than money from the Emperor.

While I was raging and swearing and pounding the table in impotent rage, spilling wine on the precious paper, a Spaniard approached whose clothes were nothing to boast of but whose sword seemed of the best. He took up the document and spelled his way through it.

Then, regarding me with burning, hungry eyes, which seemed ever to have gazed at far horizons, he asked, "What will you take for this?"

"God pity me!" I said. "I have indeed strayed into the land of madmen. I want nothing for it."

He said, "My name is Simon Aguilar. Remember me in your prayers, for I may have need of them. I'll not conceal from you that in the right hands—and I think those hands may be mine—this paper may make its holder rich. And it will enable me to take my young brother, who may obtain release from prison on condition he sails for the New World. If he remains here, they will cut off his nose and ears, to the great disgrace of our family."

I said, "Take the paper, in God's name. It will cost you no more than the notary's seal and signature, by which the transfer is made legal."

Simon Aguilar embraced us both and promised to remember us when he became prince and grandee in the New World. When we had concluded the business in the presence of a notary, we took leave of the poor maniac and returned crestfallen to de Lannoy's house.

7

It seemed that our raging in the tavern had attracted attention and that we had been followed, for next morning, almost before we had had time to hold our aching heads under the fountain, a captain with a plumed hat approached us to ask whether we would take a cup of wine with him and discuss a profitable piece of business.

He led us not to a tavern but to a house that presented a blank side to the street, close against the city wall. He begged us to excuse this obscure retreat, and said he had reason to avoid observation. His name was Emilio Cavriano, from Mantua, and he had come to Spain in the service of the French King, bringing letters and gifts to cheer the royal prisoner. When he had set good wine before us, he asked whether our disgust with the Emperor was genuine and whether we were willing to enter the service of another, more liberal master.

I said I regretted having cursed the Emperor so openly, but Andy declared his readiness as an honest soldier to sell his sword and swear fealty to the highest bidder, so long as he was not asked to sail the seas to foreign lands but was allowed to fight like a Christian against good Christians. There was no question of fighting, or even fencing, said our host; loyalty, obedience, and horsemanship were the only requirements. In token of his good faith, he paid us each three ducats hire, and took an oath from us of a month's fealty to the French King.

Then he said, "This is so great a matter that oaths signify little, but if you betray me I am not the man to shrink from taking your lives, flee as you may. But the reward in store for you binds you faster to me than any oaths."

The plan was no less than that of helping King Francis to escape from the Alcazar and conveying him over the frontier into France. A man who risked his life for King Francis would be a rich man all his days—had not three million ducats been offered as ransom?—to say nothing of the honor and position which the King's favor would bring him.

The plan, briefly told, was this. Every evening a Negro entered the King's prison apartment to light a fire, now that the weather was turning cold, and being but a Negro his comings and goings were unheeded. His Majesty had only to blacken his face with soot and assume the well-known garment of this fellow, to leave the palace under cover of dusk whenever he pleased. The Negro had been bribed, and the escape would remain undiscovered until the following morning. Fresh horses awaited the fugitive at suitable points along the route, and not all the Spanish cavalry could overtake the best horseman in France once he had had a night's start of them.

Andy said, "If all is in readiness—the Negro bribed and the horses waiting—how do you need our help?"

332

Cavriano explained that many precious days had been wasted by the King in a final appeal to his captor to modify the peace terms. During this time the conspirators had suffered grave losses. One had been killed in a duel, another imprisoned for debt, a third had had his leg broken when thrown out of a brothel, and a fourth had talked too much and had had to be silenced with a dagger. It was therefore necessary for someone to ride once more along the escape route and ensure that all the horses were still at the agreed places; while for the flight itself the captain must have the support of as strong and valiant a man as possible, in case of some mishap that might necessitate the use of force.

It was agreed that I should ride to the frontier, await His Majesty on the riverbank opposite Bayonne, and row him across as soon as he arrived. Andy was to attend His Majesty from the Alcazar to the place where the first of the horses was waiting. Captain Cavriano gave me a map showing where the relays were stationed, also the necessary passwords, and twenty ducats—for which he would require strict account —in case any of his men had grown weary of waiting and had sold their horses for wine. If no message had been received from me, the ride would begin on the night of the full moon.

Next day we took leave of the Sieur de Lannoy, saying that at last we were to set forth on our pilgrimage to Santa Maria de Compostela, and he bade us farewell with evident relief.

Heavy with foreboding, I rode from stage to stage in constant dread of robbers and wolves. But fortune favored me and I arrived safely at the frontier, near the town of Bayonne, having spent no more than three ducats on the most necessary expenses. During the daytime I remained on the French shore, and at night rowed over in the sturdy boat I had hired, and lay hidden among the reeds. The moon had reached the full two nights before I arrived, as I had ridden at an easy pace for my dog's sake, and I expected the King within three or four days.

But alas for this enterprise also! Two days later, as I was standing on the French bank, I saw about ten men riding down to the ferry on the opposite side, shrieking and swearing and driving a string of horses in front of them. They brandished their weapons, sent the wretched excisemen flying, and forced the ferryman to take them across, towing the animals behind them. As the craft drew near the French bank, I recognized Andy, hastened to him, and asked in God's name what had happened and where the King was. He answered shortly that as far as he knew King Francis was still in his tower, unless he had been moved to a place of greater security.

Not until we had brought the horses a safe distance from the frontier and had ridden into the town of Bayonne did he explain that Captain Cavriano had been arrested and that the whole plot had been laid bare through the arrogance and touchiness of the French. One Montmorency, a gentleman of the King's suite, had given His Majesty's faithful valet a box on the ear because the man had inadvertently jostled him with his elbow. The valet, deeply offended, and prevented by his low birth from demanding satisfaction in a duel, had taken his revenge by disclosing the whole plot to the Emperor.

Fortunately for Andy, His Imperial Majesty had been unwilling to believe in so dishonorable a plan, and while Captain Cavriano was being interrogated, Andy quietly took his horse and made for the frontier. He did not know at which places the relays of horses were to wait, and so he halted at every village where suspicious-looking riders and mounts were to be seen and took them with him. In this way he rescued ten of the fourteen relays. It seemed unnecessary to let them fall into the Emperor's hands, he said.

Now that the fugitives had got their breath and had had a meal, there arose among them so violent a dispute over the horses that we had to withdraw into a neighboring wood to settle the matter. And I regret to say that settlement was not achieved without violence and loss of life. In the end, each man received two horses, except Andy, who took four.

I came tolerably well out of the affair, having saved seventeen ducats of my journey money and the three for my hire. And when I had sold my horses—one in Bayonne and the other in Lyons—I had in all forty-eight French gold ducats.

8

For it was to Lyons we went, by the shortest road, and we arrived in time to celebrate Our Lord's Nativity. The Queen Mother and all the French court were still in residence here, and the inns were crowded. But we sold our horses for a fair price, as I have mentioned, and when we had attended midnight Mass and eaten and drunk well, we began to consider whether Madam Genevieve might have arrived here from Venice in company with a certain Kaspar Rotbart. We inquired for them at many inns, but Lyons is a large city, and I think we would never have found her had not Andy, after two days' vain search, taken it into his head to visit a brothel and learn the names of the best and most famous courtesans.

I thought this most unsuitable, and insulting to Madam Genevieve's honor. Yet at the very first house we were told of an insolent, greedy woman lately arrived from Venice, who had set herself up in rivalry with the oldest and most respectable establishments in Lyons. She had brought Eastern girls and had rented a house by the city wall. And no complaints had availed, since she numbered the most eminent courtiers among her patrons and gave generously to the Church. The worthy matron to whom we spoke warned us against the place and frightened us with tales of shameful disease and of Oriental vices which no Christian could meddle with and preserve his soul.

We found the mysterious walled building without difficulty, and at our knock the door was opened by a Negro clad in red and gold. After a glance at our clothes, however, he refused us admittance and tried to shut the door in our faces. But Andy was stronger than he, and when he had given the insolent brute a tap on the nose we walked inside. Alarmed by the noise, Madam Genevieve herself came to meet us, lovelier and more splendidly dressed than ever. She displayed no great delight at our appearance, however, and scolded us for having broken her midday rest and for having struck her Negro. Nevertheless, she invited us to partake of wine and fruit in her room, which was adorned with soft rugs and Venetian mirrors.

"I never could have believed you would play me so base a trick and leave me with that brewer!" she complained. "I depended upon you to rid me of him. When Michael's letter came I wept bitterly and resolved never to trust a man again. After the brewer dyed his hair and beard and changed his name, he became ever more tediously enamored, and pestered me to go with him to Hungary. He made my life a burden to me. And then I had to consider my future, for though I am still an ornament to my establishment I am not so young as I was. And so I resolved that as soon as I could be rid of that ungrateful brewer I would renounce my frivolous ways and lay a firm foundation for my future."

Madam Genevieve sighed at the memory of her troubles, and went on, "Fortunately, he was at last obliged to cash those miserable bills in order to begin his journey to Hungary. When he had done this there was nothing for it but to enlist the aid of a gallant officer, who was on the point of embarking upon a long voyage. He craved distraction and companionship to soothe the pain of departure, and when he had heard my story he promised to help me. He filled Master Rotbart with drugged wine, and then, when we had spent an agreeable night together, he ordered his men to carry Rotbart aboard his galley and chain him to a bench while he slept. We laughed very merrily together at the thought of Master Rotbart's surprise when he came to be roused by the whiplash far out to sea."

"Dear Madam Genevieve," I said, "let us not laugh at Master Eimer's miserable fate, but rather pray for him; for the life of a galley slave is no theme for jesting."

"You should have cut his throat for me long since," retorted Madam Genevieve, "if only he had not tied up his money in those papers. But in this way I was able to inherit it, and without arousing suspicion, since everyone knew he was bound for Hungary and saw nothing strange in his disappearance. I bought three young and unblemished girls from a Turkish merchant, and some fine furniture, carpets, and mirrors, which I dispatched to Marseilles by sea. With these I furnished this house, where I receive only gentlemen of distinction who can pay ten ducats or more for a night."

Madam Genevieve clapped her hands, and immediately three young girls entered, whose faces were veiled and who wore transparent Oriental trousers. One of them was almost black, another brown, and the third and loveliest had an ashen skin with greenish lights in it. They touched forehead and breast with their finger tips and bowed low, ready to serve us.

Madam Genevieve said, "They need not wear those veils, for I have had them baptized and have taught them Christian prayers, hoping that this will be accounted to me for merit on the Last Day. But they're still shy in the presence of strange men, and reveal their bodies more readily than their faces. This has caused a great sensation, and many a gentleman has paid a ducat to see them unveil. Men's desires are strange, and nothing so much attracts them as what is unlawful and forbidden. Indeed I have learned a great deal about startling and unusual pleasures since I began to devote myself seriously to the profession, and I fancy I shall soon be able to satisfy the desires of even bishops and cardinals, which as a rule only Roman courtesans can do."

When at my request she had dismissed the girls, she went on to tell us that since settling here she had sent to Tours for her children, and lodged them in a neighboring village. She visited them daily and took them to Mass, and had engaged a priest to teach them to read and write. She spoke so naturally of her shameful profession that I could find nothing to say, though I was tormented by her faithlessness and my own jealousy. I bade Andy leave us alone together, and then accused her very bitterly, asking what had become of the love which with a thousand tender vows she had assured me of in Nürnberg. But she was warm in her own defense and said that that true love died when I left her in the lurch. I saw her then for what she was. I saw that she had meant only to lure me on to kill Master Eimer, and in disgust I pushed away her caressing hands. But when to appease me she offered me the post of pimp and Andy that of doorkeeper, my rage knew no bounds, and I cursed her and left her house.

Yet Andy prevailed upon me to visit the children in her company on the following day, for in truth I was curious to behold our son. And in this matter Madam Genevieve had not lied, for the boy had Andy's sleepy eyes and the same fair tuft on the top of his head. The girl also was very pretty with her round red cheeks, golden curls, and sparkling eyes, and Madame Genevieve predicted proudly that one day she would be a credit to her mother. She hugged me so hard with her plump little arms and played so charmingly with my dog that my heart melted toward her and I gave her a shining gold ducat, that she might not feel envious of her brother when Andy gave him the walking donkey he had faithfully carried with him from Nürnberg.

Thus Madam Genevieve contrived to bind me to her through her children, nor could I blame her too severely for working to secure their future in the only profession for which she was qualified.

9

Lyons was a wealthy city. The food and wine there were good and the time slipped rapidly away. We had no goal, and to us one place was as good as another.

One day Madame Genevieve happened to tell us in her candid way of a client of hers—an unhappy gentleman from the court—who was to go on a secret mission to Constantinople, or, as the Turks heathenishly called it, Stamboul. So troubled was he that not all her arts availed to distract him, for his predecessor had been slain by the savage mountain dwellers of Dalmatia, while on his way to Constantinople by land from Ragusa.

"What in God's name has the court of His Most Christian Majesty to do with Christendom's bitterest foe?" I marveled.

"As I understand it," remarked Madam Genevieve innocently, "the Queen, on behalf of King Francis, is inviting the Sultan to ally himself with France against the Emperor. Secret negotiations have been going on ever since the defeat of the French, and the Sultan has promised them his help."

I could never have conceived of so abominable, so hideous a thing. I felt cramped and confined in that perfumed, cushioned room. I felt as if all that remained in me of honor and decency were being slowly stifled. Without a word of farewell I rushed from the house and strode about the streets in great perturbation of spirits until late in the evening.

That night I said to Andy, "Let us rise at cockcrow and leave France as speedily as may be, for surely God's curse must fall upon this wicked land."

Andy said, "For once you are talking sense, Michael. Providence has blessed this country with wine too excellent for a poor wretch like me, and my money will soon be gone. I long for guns and an honest war that can bring a man fame, wealth, and even honor, if he chooses the winning side."

So once more we girded our loins and departed from that rich and decadent city. At its gates I shook the dust from my feet, dreading for the place the doom of Sodom and Gomorrha, which must surely overtake it when the cup of God's wrath was full. When we had walked for some time, we crossed the mighty Rhine and came to the fair town of Basel, upon whose steeps the new buildings of the University clung like swallows' nests. Behind them rose the lofty spires of the Cathedral. We put up at the Three Kings, near the ferry. I had soon taken so great a liking to this free and lively city that I resolved to enter the University and study there as long as my money lasted.

There were a great many printing houses in Basel, and in its bookshops learned men were to be met. The great Erasmus himself found refuge here, after his desk in Louvain University had been overturned by fanatical students because of his alleged heresy. The booksellers would allow even poor students to browse over the new volumes, and nowhere did news of the world's events arrive more swiftly, for this free city of the Confederation lay at the junction of the trade routes between France, the German principalities, and Italy.

During this eventful spring King Francis, finding the Emperor adamant and his own efforts vain, accepted the peace terms. He agreed to all the Emperor's demands and left his two sons as hostages and pledges for his good faith. And it surprised me not at all to learn that as soon as he had regained his freedom and had returned to French soil he broke all his promises, saying that they had been extorted under duress and were therefore valueless. He at once took up his residence in Cognac, where he received envoys from the Vatican, Venice, the other Italian states, and also England, and formed a Holy Alliance with the purpose of waging another war against the Emperor. By summer this war was in full swing, and the united armies marched on unhappy Milan, now governed, since the recent death of Pescara, by the Duke of Bourbon.

But Andy said that the Emperor's cause was now a lost one, and rather than join his army he would go into Hungary and fight the Turks. For there at least he would win salvation if he fell in battle, and handsome spoils if he survived. I encouraged him in this praiseworthy enterprise, for in this chaotic world a Christian must fight against Turks, and Turks only, to be sure of the justice of his cause. Although indeed the Sultan appeared to be fighting side by side with the Holy Father, and we learned that he had raised a great army to march into Hungary and hold the Imperial domains in the southeast, while the troops of his ally the Pope marched on Milan.

When Andy heard this he said, "Now the devil is loose indeed! God help me, even *I* could turn Lutheran when I think of Pope and Turk fighting as allies against Christians."

I warned him to keep such dangerous thoughts to himself, at any rate in Hungary, which fancied it was fighting the Turks on behalf of Holy Church and the Catholic faith. And so we took a mournful farewell of one another, and he lent me twenty ducats for my studies, thinking it needless to carry much money with him when, if fate prevented his return, it could be devoted to so worthy an object.

I gravely feared that this was the last I should ever see of him, for hideous stories were coming from Venice and Hungary about the inhuman cruelty of the Turks. Indeed, because of it the Church promised immediate entry into heaven for all who fell in battle against the infidel. And this was my best comfort when we parted.

My life might have glided smoothly on, bringing me honor and distinction in learning, if I had not once more encountered Doctor Paracelsus. But to tell of him and of my departure from Basel I must begin yet another book. And this book I hope will be the last concerning the wanderings of my youth, for writing has made me weary. But I still have to describe the fulfillment of my oath, and so I continue my story, though I ought now to dip my pen in blood and write upon black paper.

BOOK 10.

The Sack of Rome

I

DOCTOR PARACELSUS was at this time famous throughout Germany for his miraculous cures, and this was the reason for our unexpected meeting in the taproom of the Three Kings. Not that there was anything unexpected about finding him in a tavern, for he was at home in such places. The wonder was that he should be in Basel when his practice was in the good city of Strasburg, far to the north on a lower reach of the Rhine.

I knew him at once, although notwithstanding his youth his hair had thinned and his face was furrowed with care and travel and immoderate drinking. I ran up to greet and embrace him, but he received me in a most hostile manner and fumbled for his great sword, for which unfriendliness I reproached him. Then I spoke of the past, and of the Stockholm massacre where he had acquired that sword. I told him my name and reminded him that I was his former assistant and pupil.

He glared at me with befuddled eyes and said angrily, "One and twenty of my pupils have swung on the gallows where they belong, and not one has had loyalty enough to stay with me above three months. They spy out my secrets and slink away, to boast the world over of their studies with me, and to harm my reputation with their

340

imperfect knowledge. May the devil fly away with you if you're one of them."

But at last he remembered me and spoke more gently. He told me that Frobenius, the famous printer, had sent to Strasburg for him, having lost the use of one leg after a stroke. The incompetent physicians of Basel wished to amputate, with the help of a barber-surgeon, but Doctor Paracelsus believed he could cure him without an operation. However, before visiting his patient he desired to refresh himself with wine, for he had had a long and exhausting ride. We spent the evening together and afterward I had to help him to his room. There, having first thrashed about with his sword to drive off the elementals that were wont to attack him whenever he had drunk heavily, he threw himself fully clothed on his bed.

This encounter took place late in the summer, by which time my first enthusiasm for study had cooled. I was somewhat weary of poring over old folios in which university scholars placed more faith than they did in the evidence of their own senses. Hence my willingness to resume my studies with Doctor Paracelsus, although his morbid conceit, which had increased with the years, and his quarrelsomeness made him a very difficult companion.

I must acknowledge, however, that his behavior altered as by magic when he stood beside a sickbed. His face then was radiant with gentleness and spiritual force, and the mere touch of his hand brought relief to sufferers, whose confidence he quickly won. He cured the old printer's leg in a few weeks, and his reputation in Basel was established. Patients flocked to the door of his room at the inn. Frobenius the printer and the great Erasmus vied with one another in singing his praises among their numerous and influential acquaintances.

Erasmus Roterdamus himself became his patient, and when Doctor Paracelsus had thoroughly examined him he was satisfied that Erasmus suffered from tartarous disease. Variants of this disorder attacked liver, gall bladder, and kidneys, and could be the cause of cruel agonies. The Doctor boasted that he was the first physician to study these complaints, to find a cure for them, and to call them by their right names. He prescribed well for Erasmus, put him on a light diet, and forbade him to drink anything but red Burgundy.

As the Doctor's errand boy, I often had occasion to meet the great Erasmus, but I must confess that I was greatly disappointed at what I saw. He was a wizened little man who wore furs and cowered indoors even in summer; he was querulous with visitors and snapped at them to shut the door. He feared draughts like the plague, was fussy about his food, incessantly bewailed his bodily frailty, and saw in the correct interpretation of a Greek word a greater victory than those of kings upon the field of battle. The blue-tiled stove in his room burned constantly, and so intense was his fear of sickness and death that he even avoided his good host Frobenius as long as he was bedridden.

His greatest and indeed his only pleasure was to go downstairs to the clanking press, breathe the smell of printer's ink, finger the damp sheets, and make corrections on them with the pinpoint script of an old man. Frobenius was publishing his works in new and fuller editions, but Erasmus was singularly ungrateful and ready with complaints, although the printer lodged him in his own house and paid for the Burgundy and for all the delicacies that might delight his desiccated palate. Yet Erasmus wrote constantly to his patrons in every corner of Europe, complaining of poverty. It would have been hard to find a king, prince, or nobleman who had not time after time received his begging letters. For this reason purses stuffed with gold arrived at his lodging in a steady stream. No sensible man wished to incur his displeasure, for in his dialogues he was likely to castigate most cruelly any persons or views of which he disapproved. In his personal expenditure, however, he was niggardly.

When Doctor Paracelsus sent me for the third time to collect his fee, Erasmus made this proposal: "It would be a great loss to the world if your master's incomparable learning and his new conception of the laws of medicine were to be wasted because of his roving life. The post of physician to the town is at present vacant, and it carries with it the duty of lecturing at the University. I will undertake to exert all my influence, and that of Frobenius, to obtain for him this profitable appointment. If I succeed, I dare swear that no patient will ever have given his physician a more princely reward."

He regarded me with the thin smile of the aged, and added, "We know all too well the good Doctor's weaknesses, yet I don't doubt that once appointed to the Chair of Medicine at the University he will take trouble with his clothes and behavior, weed out his vocabulary, and model himself on decent people. We cannot allow so great a man to be lost to humanity for the sake of a few trifling faults. If this offer does not satisfy the good Doctor, I know nothing of human nature. In any event, I trust he will abstain from these distasteful reminders. After all, it is an honor for him to have the great Erasmus as his patient."

I bore this message to my master at the Three Kings, and so far from being angered as I had expected, he was delighted at the prospect of putting an end to his wanderings with a well-paid appointment, and of publicly expounding his new principles from a desk in the University.

"But don't imagine that I shall lecture in Latin," he said. "I mean to speak a language that all honest people understand. Anyone willing to read in the great book of Nature rather than wither away among mildewed parchments may be my pupil, though he should have passed none of the University examinations. Among other things, I shall teach the art of curing the French pox cheaply and infallibly by means of red mercury—and I laugh even now to think of the uproar this will cause among the apothecaries, and how Fugger will tear his hair when all the guaiacum bark he has ordered from America is thrown on the dustheap. Just as Luther once burned the Papal Bull of Excommunication, so shall I throw the works of Avicenna and Galen into the fire —and I think I shall do it next St. John's Day, when the midsummer bonfires are kindled and all the students assemble before dispersing for the summer vacation. Thus the news will be spread quickly throughout Germany. Ay, indeed, that is what I shall do, though I be called the Luther of Medicine for it, for like Luther I mean to stand by my actions."

I was at great pains to explain how fatal it would be for him to lecture in the vernacular. The first condition of scholarship was a perfect command of Latin, by which the learned of every nation could understand one another irrespective of language or origins. His University colleagues would use the innovation as a weapon against him and allege that his knowledge of Latin was insufficient for lecturing. I knew also that they would demand to see his diploma, and Doctor Paracelsus was strangely reserved on that subject, although he boasted of having studied at many universities in different countries, until he had wearied of the imperfect and pernicious teaching they had to offer. His attainments in Latin were indeed meager, as appeared when he attempted to dictate his thoughts to me in the evenings over a cup of wine. Usually he would relapse into German and leave me to translate his reflections as well as I could.

My forebodings were but too well justified. When Erasmus and Frobenius proposed to the city council that Doctor Paracelsus should be appointed, scholars, physicians, and apothecaries rose as one man and opposed the candidature. When challenged to produce his diploma, Doctor Paracelsus replied haughtily that he had long since

343

put it to its only fit use. Meanwhile the apothecaries sent word to Augsburg of the Doctor's condemnation of guaiacum as a remedy for the French pox, thus arousing the powerful enmity of Fugger. I will not enlarge upon the malicious tales that were put about, but it was said among many other things that he obtained both knowledge and nostrums from the Evil One; and his strange habits, his vituperation, and the language he used in drunken battles with elementals were such as to furnish ever fresh material for slander. He scorned to refute the rumors, in his measureless contempt for his adversaries and their superstitious ignorance.

I should be loath to belittle his genius and his phenomenal powers of healing, but it must be remembered that as the number of his enemies increased he took delight in frightening them. When in need of credit at the taverns he was all too ready to boast of his remarkable talents, which simple people believed to be of the devil.

Clearly his uncontrolled behavior and poisonous tongue did him ill service where the new appointment was concerned, and at last both Erasmus and Frobenius advised him to return to Strasburg and there await the council's decision, since his presence in Basel went far to defeat their efforts on his behalf.

Doctor Paracelsus himself was no doubt convinced of having done all he could to conciliate. He had neatened his appearance, lowered his voice, and modified his drinking, for in his heart he greatly desired the post and the opportunities it offered for defying the learned Faculty of Medicine. But he was easily offended and morbidly tender of his reputation, and in the end he grew so weary and discouraged that for the first time I saw him reduced to tears.

"They all hate me because I'm solitary and a German," he said, "and because I teach new principles. Yet my knowledge is of God. All that is perfect is of God; all imperfection is of the devil. I ask no more than to read in the great book of Nature, cure people of their diseases, and break through the web of lies and errors woven by the ancients and revered by scholars."

He would have ridden away that night, though it was now November and the cold, dark roads swarmed with brigands who liked nothing better than to cut the throats of lonely travelers. I persuaded him to postpone his journey until the morning, as I needed time to consider whether to go with him, stay in Basel, or travel south, which last I had long been tempted to do.

Ever since the autumn I had mourned Andy as dead, for reports had reached us from Hungary of an overwhelming victory won by the Turks, under the personal leadership of the Sultan, on the plains near Mohacs. Yet this terrible omen of blood and fire which lowered in the eastern sky failed to unite Christendom against the common foe. The war in Italy continued, and it seemed as if in spite of all the Emperor might yet be the victor.

The Sultan alone was the gainer by the holy league, being left to conquer Hungary undisturbed while Christendom plunged the dagger into its own breast. Events in Italy showed that Venice was looking solely to her own advantage, and seeking to secure her Lombardy frontiers, which were menaced by the presence of Imperial troops in the neighboring Dukedom of Milan. The Venetians had no other interest in the league than this. Indeed, an impartial observer might detect in their behavior a certain duplicity, a certain desire not to weaken Imperial power unduly; for the Emperor was the only worthy European adversary of the Turks who constituted the chief threat to Venetian possessions and commerce.

Such reports rang in my ears like challenging trumpets. In Germany, countless hordes of mercenaries were rallying to the standard of the famous Frundsberg, and were content with earnest-money and vague promises of pay in their eagerness to march against Rome and the papal power. It was clear that the Emperor was summoning all his forces to crush the Pope and that he did not hesitate to make use of heretical allies, for without His Majesty's knowledge and sanction Frundsberg would hardly have dared make such liberal promises to his troops. Might it not be God's will that I should perform my oath and see the Pope hurled from his throne? So when my master's return to Strasburg forced the decision upon me, I did not hestitate; I determined to furnish myself with certain necessary medicines, join the Imperial army in Milan as surgeon, and with it march on Rome.

At our parting Doctor Paracelsus was generous enough to give me eight pills of a miraculous drug called laudanum, which could alleviate the most agonizing pain. He also gave me other remedies and ointments containing red mercury for the treatment of the French pox. He imparted much sage advice concerning plague, and spoke for an hour or more on Italian fevers.

"On all big campaigns, far more men die by pox, plague, and fever than by lead and steel," he said. "I fancy you'll never make a good physician, Michael Pelzfuss, but many army surgeons have made fortunes with faultier and more dangerous knowledge than yours. Take care not to do more harm than good with your medicines, and wherever possible leave the healing forces of nature to effect the cure."

His parting words strengthened me in my resolve. I went with him to the banks of the swift-flowing Rhine and wept when he stepped aboard the ferry. I stood looking after him until he dwindled to a gray speck in the distance and vanished from my sight.

Doctor Paracelsus returned in the following year to Basel at the council's summons, and according to his promise he burned Galen's books in the midsummer bonfire. Yet in six months, as I later heard, he was flying for his life.

The company and teaching of this remarkable character had a stronger influence upon me than I realized at the time, and I readily acknowledge that in his sphere he was a genius and a man of perfect honesty, though he could never clearly formulate his teachings. He was as rugged and stern, no doubt, as the fir trees and crags of his native region, and he liked to call himself "peregrinus" and the "wild ass of the mountains." Yet I admired him more than I admired Erasmus, with his stove, his fretful scholarship, and his flattery of the great.

2

If after the blizzards of the Alpine passes I had hoped to find good cheer in Milan, I was never more mistaken, for there only chaos and famine prevailed. The Imperial troops were unruly and paid no heed to their officers, being many months in arrears with their wages, and it was now every man for himself. Hardly had the supply column with which I traveled passed through the city gates than it was attacked and plundered, and no doubt I too would have been robbed if I had not come as a physician. As it was, I had to carry Rael under my arm to protect him from the shaggy, wild-eyed men who would gladly have made a meal of him. Fortunately for me the town was full of sickness, and medical supplies were exhausted. I might have prospered, had not food been so dear that all my earnings went in a twinkling on bread, meat, and wine for myself and my dog.

When I arrived here shortly before Christmas I learned that Frundsberg had long since marched south with twelve thousand pikemen, and was now importuning the Duke of Bourbon to leave Milan and unite both armies under his command. The Dukedom was sucked dry, robbed of its last sack of grain, its last fowl, its last pig, and in all Milan there was not one door that had not been forced. Bourbon and his

346

officers melted down their plate, ornaments, and gold chains into coin, for distribution among the men, to prevent mutiny and to induce them to march; and though as a newcomer I could hope for a surgeon's share of this payment, yet I had no choice but to march with them. So I bought a scraggy donkey, loaded my belonging on its back, and moved off with the Duke's men at the end of January. So began for me the bloody, unforgettable year of 1527.

Meanwhile the troops of the holy league, led by the Duke of Urbino, had clashed with Frundsberg's men, it being no doubt the aim of the Italians to prevent the union of the Imperial armies. Nevertheless, having suffered some reverses, the Duke of Urbino retired to consider how best he could serve the Venetian cause. So it was that in February we met Frundsberg by the river Trebbia. On the very first evening, Germans and Spaniards were at one another's throats, and I had as many casualties to attend to as if it had been a regular battle. The fight arose from a dispute over whether Germans or Spaniards had more money owing them, and which would be paid first when the Emperor's funds arrived. It was a vain contention, for no money came, although our commander-in-chief contrived to raise a loan from the Duke of Ferrara, who was anxious to remove these marauding allies from his domains. But when after another fortnight we had left Ferrara behind us and were nearing Bologna, the men, weary of hunger and rain, called a halt once more and demanded the balance of their pay.

As I was in no way bound to the Spaniards in whose company I had left Milan, and spoke their language imperfectly, I had joined Frundsberg's Germans. And it was now that I had one of the greatest surprises of my life.

The Duke of Bourbon was so foolish as to pay only the Germans from the sum that Ferrara had lent him, and just when I was tethering my donkey to an olive tree before treating some of these men for the French pox, we were attacked by a flock of ragged, barefooted Spaniards who meant to rob me. My patients were in no condition to defend themselves, and besides they had let down their breeches for the medical examination, so that in the first shock of surprise they could not even run. I should have been lost had not their cries of distress brought a burly fellow rushing to our aid, brandishing his sword and uttering ferocious howls. The Spaniards fled, and when I turned to thank my rescuer I found that it was Andy. So certain had I been of his death that at first I took him for a ghost that my burning prayers had summoned from the realms of death.

But when Andy saw who I was, he thrust his sword back into its scabbard, pressed my hand hard between his own, and said, "Upon my soul, it's Michael! What in God's name are you doing among these wolves when you should be improving your mind in Basel?"

He sat down, took a juicy bone from his wallet, broke it in two, and crushed the pieces between his teeth, that Rael might lick out the marrow. His gnarled toes showed through the rents in his boots and there was little left of his sleeves, but his breastplate was polished and spotless and his sword in good order. I asked him how he had escaped alive from the battle of Mohacs and had found his way to this God-forsaken army, which all Italy was cursing.

He answered in his usual ingenuous way, "I escaped from Mohacs for the good reason that I was not in time for the battle. I have never met such haughty, hot-tempered nobles as those Hungarians, and I lost all desire to fight at their side. They disdain artillery and put their faith in armor and swift chargers. At Mohacs they rode straight at the hundreds of cannon which the Sultan had concealed behind his advance-guard. Reliable witnesses say that the Turks held their fire until the Hungarian cavalry were within a few paces of the cannons' mouth, and the first volley determined the battle. Not two hours had passed before the Sultan's army had mowed down the Christians, and that was the end of Hungary. Not many escaped to tell the tale."

I begged for more particulars, but Andy seemed unwilling to enlarge on his Hungarian experiences.

He said only, "I heard that whole villages fled from their lords' oppression and sought refuge in the Sultan's domains, for the Sultan does not persecute Christians as such and allows them to practice their religion freely. Yet at the same time he forbids extortion and injustice. This was one of the reasons for my unwillingness to fight for the King. And I hear that at least two of Hungary's most eminent men are already competing for the Sultan's favor, each in the hope of wearing the Hungarian crown as his humble vassal."

Andy refused to say another word about Hungary, and he took me forthwith to his camp. A score of pikemen had chosen him for their leader, and under the ragged tent that sheltered them from the spring rain they shared their meal with me. I was glad enough for his companionship, for that evening open mutiny broke out and the German pikemen had to don full armor and form squares to defend themselves against the raging Spaniards. These men had attacked their own of-

348

ficers and threatened to cut their pay from Bourbon's back; the Duke was forced to take refuge in Frundsberg's tent.

But when next morning the Spanish leaders had restored a measure of order among their men, the Germans in their turn began to feel sorry for themselves and to show one another their burst boots and ragged clothes. Toward noon they surrounded Frundsberg's tent and howled that they were being cheated and must have their pay without further delay.

I was standing in the thick of this yelling mob when Frundsberg stepped out, and for the first and only time I beheld the great general at whose very name men trembled. The sight of his bull-like frame and massive face silenced the men for a moment; one or two of them even began to cheer. Then the outcry broke forth again. The pikemen flung their ragged boots in the dirt before him, tore open their shirts to show their ribs, and demanded their money.

Frundsberg was unused to mutiny, and his broad face swelled and turned purple with rage. He roared so passionately that his voice failed him. He reminded the men of the articles of war that they had sworn to obey and threatened to let each one of them run the gauntlet. But this only exasperated them. They yelled that it ill became Frundsberg to appeal to those articles, which entitled them to regular payment with at most one month's delay. And suddenly the men nearest him lowered their pikes until Frundsberg's mighty frame was encircled with glittering points—no agreeable sight for a general who valued his dignity.

What wonder, then, that he was wrought to the extreme of passion! His eyes filled with tears, he lost the power of speech, gesticulated blindly, then staggered and fell headlong, though no one had so much as touched him. This greatly disconcerted the mutineers, who fell silent and slunk away, while a sudden deathly stillness descended upon the camp. Fortunately I had my lancet by me and was able to let a little blood from the inside of his elbow. But he had fallen victim to a stroke and could neither move nor speak, only glare helplessly with his bloodshot eyes. He was very pitiful to see. Later he was carried back to Ferrara to receive the necessary care, but he never fully recovered from the effects of this attack.

Gone then was the one leader who could keep discipline among the pikemen. His two colonels assumed command, and the Duke of Ferrara, seeing that further trouble threatened, remitted another fifteen thousand ducats. Thus the pikemen received a ducat each and made no more complaint, being shocked at the misfortune they had caused.

After this incident the Duke of Bourbon summoned his officers to a council, at which he bade them put heart into their men by describing to them the wealth that awaited them in Florence and Rome. A measure of order was restored in the camp and the troops were ready to resume their march, when as a climax to our misfortunes the Master of the Imperial Horse arrived from Rome with the news that the Sieur de Lannoy, the Viceroy of Naples, had by authority of the Emperor made peace with the Pope. I know not how many peace treaties had been signed that winter, but the Pope had broken his word more than once. Now however he had paid sixty thousand ducats according to the terms of the treaty, and the Master of the Horse had brought the money with him for distribution among the troops, who were then to be sent packing.

The first revolt had been violent enough, but I have never heard a worse tumult than that which arose when this news spread through the camp. Germans and Spaniards forgot their quarrel in face of the common threat to deprive them of the hoped-for plunder. They hailed one another as brothers-in-arms and formed a joint soldiers' council. This council waited upon the Duke of Bourbon, asked him what he meant to do, and declared that the army in any event would continue the campaign, whether under their old leaders or under new ones to be elected among themselves.

The Duke received the deputation cordially, and said that if the army had resolved to continue he would with God's help lead it to Rome, at the risk of incurring the Emperor's displeasure. His Majesty had not rewarded him according to his deserts, and when the French King broke the peace treaty the Duke lost all the benefits the Emperor had claimed on his behalf. Moreover, the Duke hated no one more than their Sieur de Lannoy, the Emperor's favorite, and saw no reason to respect a peace which that gentleman had been pleased to conclude. Indeed, he considered he would better serve the Imperial cause by defying it, since the Pope was prompt to break his word whenever he won any advantage.

The Duke of Ferrara furnished us with the necessary provisions, wagons, gunpowder, and a few light cannon, to be rid of us. At the end of March we struck camp and continued on our way. Once started, our army grew like an avalanche, for political refugees as well as bandits and every kind of criminal smelled booty and joined us.

But during the march that followed, many were to sink helpless in snowdrifts, and be devoured by wolves; many were to be slain by peasants and herdsmen whom the brutalities of the soldiers had driven to desperation. To avoid the Tuscan valleys, which were occupied by enemy troops, the Duke of Bourbon led us over the roughest passes of the Appenines, the spine of the Italian peninsula. Spring was late, snow was falling in the mountains, our provisions were running out, and there was nothing to steal. What wonder, then, that one and an-other thought of his mother and his home, and would have turned back if he could? But just when both bread and flour were exhausted, the Duke was able to point to a rich and fertile land spread out below us in the distance, where the mighty Arno poured its yellow-green flood through luxuriant valleys. The wealth of Florence and Rome lay in sight, and we charged down the mountains more like a ragged, savage band of robbers than a regular army.

So we reached the valley of the Arno. But now the Florentines be-came aware of approaching danger, and the Duke of Urbino cut short his siesta and came marching through Tuscany. I cannot say whether Urbino had really undertaken to defend Florence, but his mere ad-vance inclined Bourbon to prudence, and by the most arduous and painful forced marches he led us straight to Rome. The Pope had dis-banded his army and the Duke hoped to arrive before he could reor-ganize his defenses. We struggled forward toward that shining mirage, forgetful of hunger and privation, abandoning even our cannon. We urged on comrades and pack-animals alike, and the only thought in our heads was Rome, Rome!

Those febrile, strenuous days linger but mistily in my memory, but I recall that once as I staggered along leaning on my donkey's pack I seemed to see in those wan, haggard, forward-straining scarecrows, a pack of wolves. A week of forced marches brought our exhausted army to the gates of Rome. We had grown now from ten thousand to thirty thousand men, for the disbanded papal troops readily joined our army as we drew near the city.

At night during the short hours of repose the sound of hammers rang out about the campfires, where our men were building scaling ladders. And past us streamed unhappy fugitives with their sluggish, lumbering carts and their bursting bundles. On the fifth of May the Imperial army poured up the hill of Mario, and I beheld the proud walls, gates, spires, and roofs of the Holy City, golden in the sunset. I gazed out over the town to which for a thousand years Christendom had made pilgrimage in faith and penitence, and whose churches, altars, and shrines were adorned with gold and silver from every corner of the world.

I believe the same awe was felt by all of us as we halted to stare in breathless silence at the mirage that had suddenly become fact. I question whether Rome had ever appeared so magnificent in the eyes of a pilgrim, so overwhelming in its glory, as now when it blazed in the sunset like some golden treasure chest—now when we were to break it open and hurl a bygone era into darkness.

The Duke of Bourbon had reined in his horse at the summit of the hill, his armor flashing in the sun. After a moment's silence, a gasp and a roar burst from countless throats, and the Duke with blazing eyes shouted orders for the disposition of his troops for a dawn assault.

3

I doubt if any attacking army ever found itself in so wretched a plight as ours. One day's ration of bread remained to us, and the trained, disciplined troops of the alliance were slowly approaching to crush us against walls which, in the darkness of night, appeared impregnable. We had no artillery to breach them with, and the powder of the Spanish harquebusiers sufficed for no more than a round or two for each man, the greater part of it having been soaked and spoiled in the incessant rain. When I sat by the campfire and stared at the lofty ramparts, I felt it would be as easy to split rock with a wooden mallet as to storm these walls with pike and sword.

The Duke of Bourbon had summoned his officers to a council at the monastery of Sant'Onofrio, but meanwhile many soldiers' councils met about the campfires. These bodies had been growing in numbers and influence ever since Bologna, and at the present conclaves guards were posted to warn off intruders. The chief aim of the Spaniards was to insure the sack of the city, for they feared that through eleventh-hour negotiations the vast plunder would slip through their fingers. Among the Germans ripened a firm resolve not to let the Pope escape; he should surrender his wealth to them and then hang. They, like the Spaniards, feared lest their officers should snatch the fruits of victory from their hands. This mistrust increased as the night wore on, and both Spaniards and Germans determined to risk anything for spoils the like of which no army in Christendom had ever carried home. News of these secret meetings spread throughout the army, and there can have been few who remained quite ignorant of them. It was also learned that the Pope had excommunicated the Duke of Bourbon, thereby causing him very deep distress.

At daybreak, banks of fog rolled in from the surrounding marshes, and when the drums beat and the trumpets blew for the assault the walls of Rome were swathed in dense mist—a most fortunate circumstance for us, since it hid us from the defenders. Ladders were raised at two points, but the garrison repulsed both scaling parties with gunfire and hand-to-hand fighting, while from the citadel of Sant'Angelo came the boom of cannon.

Heedless of enemy fire, the Duke of Bourbon rode along our front wearing a billowing white cloak and glittering armor, by which he was easily recognized. His great eyes glowed in his emaciated face as he exhorted his men to the attack, puzzled and angered by their apathy. The Spaniards did no more than drive their rests into the ground and take aim at the walls, while the Germans huddled together, whispering and muttering.

Seeing this, the Duke dismounted in a fury near the wall of Campo Santo, where he induced the Germans to pick up their scaling ladders and then led the charge toward the base of the ramparts. Many ladders were raised at the same time into the mist that still hung above us, and not even eyewitnesses could say exactly what took place.

But as the Duke set his foot upon the lowest rung, several shots rang out both from besieged and besiegers, and the Duke fell headlong, shrieking, "Mother of God, I am dying!"

A leaden ball had pierced his hip and groin. The soldiers lifted him, and the Prince of Orange flung his cloak over him so that no one on the wall might shoot at him again. He was then carried to a chapel in a neighboring vineyard, where, in defiance of the ban, he received the Sacraments at the hands of his confessor. He lived but a few hours, but in the delirium of death he tore the bandage from his wounds and strove to rise, shouting in a terrible voice, "To Rome, to Rome!" The cry was borne through the open door of the chapel to the soldiers who were even then storming the walls.

Historians have written beautiful accounts of how the Imperial army rolled forward like a flood to avenge their general's death, but if truth be told, neither Spaniards nor Germans shook off their apathy until they were assured that his wound was mortal. Only then did they launch a vigorous assault, shouting rapturously to one another that there was now no one to hinder the sack of Rome. Many claimed the honor of having slain the Duke, among whom may be mentioned a certain lying goldsmith, Benvenuto Cellini by name, who directed the fire from the Castello Sant'Angelo. (After the disbanding of the papal troops the commandant of the citadel was obliged to man his guns with artists and other riffraff.) But I am convinced that it was some Spanish harquebusier, egged on by his comrades, who slew the Duke of Bourbon.

However this may be, Spaniards and Germans now outdid one another in the ardor of their assault. The Spaniards discovered in Cardinal Armellini's garden a house built against the city wall. An underground passage, hastily blocked up with rubble, led from the house into the city. While they were shoveling their way through, the German pikemen threw up scaling ladders in long rows by the Gate of the Holy Ghost. The first man to reach the top of the wall alive was a preacher named Nikolai, a weaver by trade, and the second was Andy, who mowed down the gunners with his great sword and at once trained the cannon inward against Sant'Angelo. When I saw the gates opening, the pikemen pouring in, and Andy dashing about unaided among his guns, I commended my wounded to the care of God and climbed up on the wall to help him.

Meanwhile before the Church of St. Peter the Swiss Papal Guard was being cut down to the last man. Nor did the Imperial troops content themselves with killing, but tossed burning brands into the houses so that smoke began mounting to the sky. They slew every horse or mule in sight, lest any use them to carry away private booty before the whole city was captured. The reduction of this quarter was quickly achieved.

The guns of Sant'Angelo were still thundering, making it difficult to approach the citadel, but none of our men troubled to remain and answer their fire, and Andy and I soon found ourselves alone upon the wall. The incessant lamentations of the multitude were borne up to us like the roar of the sea, and above it all could be heard the shrill, triumphant battle cries of *"España, España!"* and *"Imperio, Imperio!"*

I gave no further thought to the perils that threatened us, being infected with the universal madness. We rushed down from the wall and sped toward the citadel. The Spaniards meanwhile had stormed St. Peter's and the Germans the Vatican, and only afterward did we learn how at the last moment the Pope eluded us. He had spent the morning at his devotions in the Sistine Chapel, surrounded by cardinals and foreign ambassadors, and while the Germans were yet struggling to force the gates of the Vatican, His Holiness was hustled by his attendants to the covered corridor leading from the Vatican to the citadel.

Flocks of fugitives were now pouring over the Tiber bridges to seek shelter in the same place, and with them came the wretched inhabitants of the Borgo quarter, so that a most fearful press of people developed before the moat and drawbridge. Many women and children were trampled underfoot, and others fell into the water and were drowned. At this moment the Sant'Angelo garrison made a sudden sortie to collect provisions from the nearest houses, for the fortress was not victualed for a siege. The firing was discontinued for fear of injuring the citizens, and Andy and I found ourselves, together with many Spaniards and pikemen, in the very thick of this indescribable confusion.

It was thus we came to behold the flock of dignitaries as they rushed from the covered passage and buffeted their way across the bridge into the stronghold. At their head staggered a bowed and sobbing man over whose shoulders someone had flung the purple cloak of a bishop. We learned afterward that this helpless, weeping, broken fugitive was none other than the Pope himself. Thus was my goal achieved—a goal that had seemed remote enough when I swore my deadly oath and the blood of my wife Barbara coursed over my hands.

We had still not captured the walled quarter of Trastevere, on the same side of the river, and it was late in the afternoon before the citadel was entirely surrounded and the Imperial leaders were able to remarshal their forces in battle order. The old city on the farther bank was yet safe, but the people of Rome were so panic-stricken that few among them thought of defense. The greater number were concerned only with finding safe hiding places for their valuables. Wealthy fugitives sheltered within the massive walls of palaces, and many cardinals who numbered themselves among the Emperor's friends remained quietly at home, relying on their immunity. These dignitaries offered sanctuary to other persons of distinction. The foreign embassies were also thronged, while the poor, who had no powerful patrons, gathered up their belongings and crowded into the countless churches and monasteries of the city.

Even now the citizens had but an imperfect understanding of their situation, for when at a meeting of the city council a few bold spirits proposed the demolition of bridges over the Tiber, to secure the districts on the left bank, the councilors unanimously opposed so drastic a measure on the grounds that the bridges were beautiful and would be costly to rebuild. Thus God smote the citizens with blindness. At dusk

355

the trumpets once more sounded the attack and the Imperial troops marched in an orderly manner toward the Ponte Sisto, for it was evident that only the reduction of the whole city would assure us the victory.

At the last moment the troops were halted by the eighteen-year-old Margrave of Brandenburg, who was studying in Rome and who had now placed himself at the head of a civic delegation in an attempt to pacify his compatriots. But the bearded, filthy pikemen laughed in his face, drew him into their ranks, and scattered the solemn deputation with lowered pikes. A few young Roman noblemen had been able to muster a couple of hundred followers to hold the bridge until dark. They bore a banner with the legend *Pro Fide et Patria,* but the pikemen soon trampled it underfoot along with the bodies of the defenders, and marched across the bridge, to spread like an inundation over the defenseless district. I fancy some ten thousand lost their lives during that first day, of whom the greater part were unarmed fugitives.

When darkness fell, the army commanders sounded the assembly. The Spaniards camped in the Piazza Navona and the Germans in Campo di Fiore, where they built fires of doors and furniture, rolled winecasks from the cellars, and began to refresh themselves after their hard day's toil. Rome was ours, and as the number of our own dead was very small, we had every reason to rejoice. Yet the leaders desired to keep their troops together, for they feared surprise by the allied armies. And indeed signals blazed until late at night from the fortress of Sant'Angelo, where the Pope was waiting for his friends to come and rescue him.

The troops kept together until midnight, united by the common peril. Then, being drunk, they grew rowdy and discontented. By God, they said, they had not captured Rome sword in hand merely to sit shivering on its stones while officers disported themselves with gay Roman ladies on soft couches. The lines thinned out; one group after another slunk away into the dark streets, until the dying embers of the fires glowed in a deserted square. Only a gray cat remained to lap blood from a worn marble paving stone.

I had been busy with the wounded, and now as I sat with Andy in that silent place we heard the noise of doors being broken in, the shrieks of women, and the clang of hammers on ironbound chests.

Andy looked at me, crossed himself, and said, "Those are suspicious sounds. I fancy the Spaniards are stealing a march upon us honest Germans, though it was agreed that looting should not begin until daylight. I think we would be justified in seeing some of the sights, dark though it is. At least we might find a softer bed than this marble."

Neither he nor I knew our way about in Rome, and we wandered off at hazard, followed by three of Andy's pikemen who had lingered at their bivouac. Lights shone through the broken shutters of many houses, and we heard the shouts of drunken soldiers amusing themselves within. We turned down a side street which still lay in darkness, although from its farther end came a glow of torches and a sound of splintering wood. A round-cheeked man who had seen us coming opened his gate as we passed, and shielding the flame of a candle with his hand bade us welcome to his house. He had ever loved the Emperor, he said, and asked no better than to have the privilege of entertaining his brave soldiers—so long as there were not too many of them. He was a wine merchant; he had filled many flagons with his best wine this evening, and his wife had laid the table for the expected guests. He could see by our faces that we were decent men and we must take up our quarters there and make ourselves at home, since there were only five of us.

We could not but be touched by so cordial an invitation, and we promised to do our part by keeping out intruders, as indeed Andy had occasion to do in the course of the excellent meal we then enjoyed.

But when Andy's three pikemen had finished eating they wiped their mouths with the backs of their hands and suggested diffidently that it was time to come to the point, and to achieve the object for which they had marched on to Rome.

Andy turned to our host and said, "If you're a true and faithful servant of the Emperor, as you claim to be, pay us our arrears and send in your account to His Majesty."

The wine merchant pulled a long face, wiped the cold sweat from his forehead, and bewailed his poverty, but at last after much haggling he handed over twenty ducats. This came to only four ducats each, however, and the soldiers muttered that he was certainly richer than he pretended. Then, as Andy continued placidly drinking, the men began to break open drawers, cupboards, and chests and to toss the contents all over the floor, although both the merchant and his wife fell on their knees and begged them not to do so. They then eyed their hostess's plump curves and expressed a desire to celebrate the great victory by the enjoyment of feminine society. And when in a most unseemly manner they began to pinch and stroke her, she clung in terror to her husband, who pleaded with them in the name of the Virgin to leave his

357

wife alone; and he hastened to fetch two servant girls from their hiding place in the attic. These poor dark-eyed maidens wept and struggled, but in vain, and two of the men dragged them to the merchant's own bed while the third, awaiting his turn, went to the cellar after more wine.

Our host's behavior to these poor girls shocked me, and I said to him sternly, "Deceitful dog! I see by your face that you're cheating us and have hidden your money. We shall be forced to hang you for your treachery to the Emperor's loyal soldiers."

Andy agreed that hanging was the best reward for such a false man, and seizing him by the collar he bade me find a rope. Whether he was in earnest or not, the merchant believed him and promised to show us the hiding place if only his life and the honor of his wife might be spared.

We descended therefore to the cellar, where with trembling hands our host rolled aside a great cask and disclosed a little door. In the cellar beyond we found a young boy and a lovely girl barely fifteen years old, who pressed themselves against the mildewed wall in an agony of fear, thinking their last hour was come. There was also a quantity of silver vessels and candlesticks, and a large leather bag filled with gold ducats. The girl came out at our bidding, sobbing with fear, but Andy pushed the merchant inside and ordered him to hand out the valuables to his wife and daughter for them to carry upstairs. When we had assured ourselves that the moldy hole was empty, save for the food and water that had been left there for the children, Andy told the man that he and his son must be locked in for their own safety, and that his wife and daughter were at least as competent as he to do the honors of the house.

No sooner said than done. The door was shut and the cask rolled against it, despite the curses and lamentations of our prisoner. The girl wept as bitterly as he, but I comforted her as well as I could. When I stroked her hair and asked her name she told me she was called Giovanna, and begged that we would be merciful to her. Then, having returned to the supper table we spread our booty upon it and divided it honorably between us, so that Andy as leader took three eighths, I as surgeon two, and the pikemen an eighth each. The men were not envious, and in their delight over these unexpected riches they each gave a ducat to the maidservants, who dried their tears, smiled, drank wine with us, and taught the pikemen Italian.

So the night passed merrily away, and only once or twice did Andy have to rise and warn off soldiers who thundered at the door in hopes of robbing the house that we had taken under our protection. Andy talked politely and at length to our hostess, and persuaded her to drink a quantity of wine; and despite the loss of so many valuables she even smiled once or twice when his arms went around her. Giovanna was so young and beautiful that I could not take my eyes off her, and I stroked her soft hair and sought to dry her tears. Drunk though I was, I wished her no harm and was content to kiss and caress her. When she saw this she returned my kisses and we slept innocently in one another's arms.

Next morning when I awoke and surveyed her she smiled at me shyly with her dark eyes and I knew that I loved her with all my heart. To win the favor of her family, I gave back all the silver objects that had fallen to my share and kept only the money, which was easy to carry. We left the house well rested and in excellent spirits, and Andy promised our hostess that we would come back that night to protect her honor.

But when we returned in the evening we found that the Spaniards had been there. They had hung the man from a rafter, having burned his feet to make him surrender his money. His wife and son lay dead in a pool of blood, and I found Giovanna's naked body in the bed we had shared. She was no longer beautiful, for they had strangled her.

Better had it been if I had not spared her virginity, but had taken her away by force and defended her, sword in hand.

4

For eight days and nights the senseless pillage continued, and now, should I ever wish to picture to myself the horrors of hell, I have only to call to mind certain of those scenes. The heart of man cannot conceive of any desecration, savagery, or crime that was not committed then. The greatest painters' portrayals of the Last Day are but childish fancies in comparison with the horrors of the sack of Rome.

There was no man, however eminent or holy, but must purchase life with his fortune; no lady, of whatever rank, whose virtue was spared. Mad with blood and wine, the Germans, Spaniards, and Italians vied with one another in ingenious methods of extortion and numbered both papal and Imperial adherents among their victims, without discrimination. Surely after such martyrdom the sufferers need feel no dread of infernal torments. And who were Christians then?

359

The Spaniards raged like savage, soulless beasts and the Germans made of "Lutheran" a hideous byword.

I will not seek to defend myself or play the innocent. For the first three days I thought only of my own gain. Thereafter I sickened of carnage, terror, and the shrieks of the tortured, and awoke one morning from my delirium. That morning is etched in my memory as with acid on copperplate, to be imprinted on the white paper of my soul. I awoke under a colonnade in the Campo di Fiore, my eyes dazzled by the May sunshine. Flames and columns of black smoke rose from two houses near at hand, and the morning air was laden with the stench of blood, soot, and vomit. I could not remember how I had found the way back to our camping place, but my purse was safe, my donkey was tethered to a pillar, and my dog lay with his nose upon the ground as if oppressed with grief, and had not the heart to greet me.

I led my donkey to the banks of the Tiber. I could not drink there myself, for the current brought corpses bobbing along the shores. Among them I saw priests, monks, and nuns, and even the blotched bodies of the sick whom soldiers had torn from their beds in the House of the Holy Ghost, only to slay them and fling them into the river; all because certain rich men had taken refuge among them. I was tormented by an abominable thirst, and stepped into a neighboring church in the hope of meeting with an acquaintance who would give me something to drink.

In the church was a mob of rowdy soldiers who had rolled winecasks in front of the altar and knocked out the heads of them, so that all could help themselves. The sacred vessels served them as drinking cups. Many of them were masquerading in priestly vestments, and they had dressed up two priests in women's clothes. As I came in, a harquebusier seated on the font—which he had befouled—aimed and fired at the crucifix and brought it down in splinters onto the ravaged altar. Others were playing football with the skull of a saint.

As I led my donkey past the citadel of Sant'Angelo I saw a party of priests, monks, and eminent laymen who with unpracticed hands were wielding pick and shovel, digging trenches round about the fortress under the supervision of soldiers who cursed them and struck them with the butts of their lances. A little girl approached the Spanish captain, showed him a bunch of greens, and asked if she might take it to the citadel, as one of its inmates had shouted that the Pope stood in need of fresh vegetables. The Spaniard swore at her, then crossed himself and let the child pass. With eyes shining, she ran to the edge of the moat, and at once a rope was thrown down. She began to fasten her bunch to it, kneeling as she did so and crying in her shrill, childish voice for the Pope's blessing. Some German pikemen shouted and waved their arms. Next moment a shot rang out, the little girl fell with a scream, and lay face downward on the ground, while the bunch of greens rolled into the moat.

I urged on my donkey, and the dog kept close at my heels. We emerged into the great square before St. Peter's, where the decaying corpses of the Swiss Guard polluted the air. But my eyes were for the mightiest temple in Christendom, whose majesty and purity of line filled my spirit with serenity and peace amid the carnage. Some of the Prince of Orange's cavalrymen passed me, leading their horses from watering, and I asked them where I might stable my own beast. Seeing by my dress that I was a physician, they received my question kindly and told me to follow them. To my astonishment they led their mounts up the broad steps of St. Peter's and into the church. I followed, and heard the neighing of many horses beneath the echoing, vaulted roof. There must have been hundreds, but in so vast a building they took up little space. I halted and gazed about me in the utmost wonder, feeling like a little beetle beside those gigantic pillars. Then, following the horsemen's advice, I tethered my donkey to the wrought-iron gates of a side chapel. The men gave me a generous supply of both hay and oats, of which several loads had been brought from the papal stables.

I heard the rumbling of stone and the clang of hammer and crowbar from the interior of the church, and as I wandered among the splendors of this great house of God I observed groups of mercenaries here and there, busily engaged in forcing open the tombs of former Popes, to rob them. Some had begun to break open the tomb of St. Peter himself, but this was too appalling a sight for me. My knees quaked and I fled in horror from the church.

No one hindered me from entering the Vatican through a side gate, where the Prince of Orange had set up his headquarters. The street was white with documents from the archives that the pillaging Germans had flung out of the windows. Two sentries led me to the Sistine Chapel, where the Duke of Bourbon lay in state, pallid and high nosed in the flickering light of wax candles. Thus it was that this prince—traitor to his King and, on the last night of his life, excommunicant—came at last to Rome, as even in his deathbed ravings he had so yearned to do.

Despite the papal ban, two priests were attempting to say a Requiem Mass, but the rending of stuffs and the smashing of panels disturbed the sacred rite. Heedless of this and of their commander's last repose, a number of soldiers were wrenching splendid paintings from the walls. The fellows told me that they had been offered a good price for these works, which were by a painter called Raphael, who was apparently famous. They were only sorry that on the night of their arrival they had burned many pictures and frames just to keep themselves warm. These paintings were indeed very lovely, judging from the few I saw.

When I left the chapel I came upon a party of Spanish harquebusiers smashing a row of stained glass windows with the butts of their guns, and wrenching out the lead. I asked them why they were committing this wanton damage, for the windows were beautiful, and many holy scenes were there depicted. The Spaniards denied that they were doing any damage; rather they were performing a useful task in replenishing their supplies of bullet lead. It was reported that a squadron of the allied cavalry had reached the gates of Rome, and the Spaniards did not mean to let them rescue the Pope without paying his ransom.

I went out into the fresh air of the Vatican hill, and saw clouds of black smoke rising into the clear May sky from the farther shore. A weary hopelessness overpowered me, and I asked myself what profit I had from a full purse, wine, and all the good things of this world, when I did not even know who or what I was, whither I was going, or what I desired from life. The Pope was, as I had sworn to see him, a destitute fugitive. Papal power was broken and would surely never rise again. Yet, if a new world was to be born, what blessings could be expected from this unbridled slaughter, this unprecedented rage to destroy? My oath was fulfilled, but what joy had I of that? It had brought me no nearer Barbara; rather it had lost her to me forever. As I stood watching the heaps of papers in the street being whirled away by the wind, within earshot of the hammerblows that spoke of the desecration of St. Peter's tomb, I perceived that I did not know myself—this naked, forsaken stranger, without home or family, without even a country or a future. I shivered in the May sunshine.

My dog, my only friend, squatted at my feet and bent his mournful gaze upon me. He had lost his mistress, he had been beaten, tortured, and burned; yet he did not lust after revenge. He suffered at the sight of men's savagery. He stared at me in mute prayer, as if willing me to save my soul.

362

Weighed down by these heavy thoughts, I looked out over Rome, where men robbed and tormented one another and in their savage lust for power set not a farthing's value on any man's life or any woman's virtue. And a hideous doubt assailed me of God's very existence. Human understanding could not conceive of a merciful God who, having sent His own son to bear away the sins of the world, could permit the destruction of His Holy City. So to me the fall of Rome presaged the birth of no new era, but rather the end of the world, the loosing of Satan's armies, and the victory of Antichrist in the person of the Emperor.

My heart was naked and empty, but my humble body made known its hunger and led me to hope that my despair was but the result of fasting and immoderate wine drinking. I could find no house that had not been ransacked, though a desolate silence lay upon that quarter of the town. At last I passed through a gateway and found myself among flowering trees in the garden of a little house. I entered one wrecked room after another but found no one, until at last I penetrated into an inner chamber, where a wild-eyed, disheveled woman approached me. Laying a finger on her lips, she pointed to an old man in bed. He was breathing heavily, his lips and cheeks were blue, and I saw that he was suffering from some severe disorder of the heart and must soon die.

The woman pushed me from the room and followed me, and after staring at me for a while she tore open her gown with an expression of weary distaste, lay down upon the floor, and said, "If there be a spark of human pity in you, good sir, have done with me quickly and let me go back to my sick father, to be with him when he dies. I swear by all that's holy that I have hidden nothing in his bed, and I have purchased our lives with our last coin. Make haste, therefore. Afterward you may take with you whatever you wish, so long as you leave me in peace."

I was so full of my own heavy thoughts that at first I did not grasp her meaning. Then I blushed deeply, averted my gaze, and said, "I have no designs on your virtue. I would only ask for food, if you have any, and I will pay you for it. I am a physician and will gladly help your father if I may, though I fear he is already beyond human aid."

My dog went to the woman and licked her hand, and she sat up in astonishment, reddened slightly, and covered her bosom.

"Can it be that I have met with a human being among all the wild beasts?" she exclaimed. "I had lost faith in the very saints. One bar-

barian after another has answered my burning prayers with outrage. They dragged my father from his bed and ripped up the mattress in search of money. But if you are indeed a good man, in God's name fetch me a priest, for my father stands in greater need of him than of a physician. Our servants have fled and joined the marauders, and yesterday when I went in search of a priest myself I was assaulted and robbed in the street and dared go no farther."

I told her that the Pope had forbidden the practice of religion in Rome and that it was doubtful whether any priest would dare to defy the interdict. But she expressed haughty disbelief that the Holy Father would deny the Sacrament of Extreme Unction to one of his most devout and faithful subjects, merely because he himself had been unfortunate. She had risen from her humiliating position and now stood with her head thrown back proudly. She was a lovely woman of about my own age and evidently came of good family.

Her grief moved me to do as she asked, and I said, "I will fetch a priest if there be one left alive in Rome."

Having felt the sick man's pulse and listened to his breathing, I saw that he had not many hours to live, and doubted whether he would be able to receive the viaticum. But I hastened on my errand, and caught a priest just slinking from a church near one of the bridges. I seized and held him despite his struggles and begged him respectfully to come with me and fulfill his sacred duties, but he excused himself on the grounds of the interdict. There was nothing for it but to point my sword at his breast and let him choose whether he would die as a martyr for his faith or live on as a heretic. On reflection, he came to the conclusion that Holy Church had more use for him alive than dead, and that afterward he could win absolution for the offense. So he fetched the sacred vessels and the oil from their hiding place beneath a tombstone and we proceeded silently, ringing no bell, to the bedside of the dying man.

While the priest was engaged with him, and the daughter was praying for her father's soul, I walked about the house. I noted many volumes of the works of ancient Greek and Roman philosophers lying higgledy-piggledy on the floor, together with manuscripts that had been trampled upon by dirty feet. There were also many antique sculptures whose yellow tinge showed them to have been dug up from the ground. But the soldiers had thrown down these pagan divinities from their pedestals, breaking their necks and arms. As my eyes followed the glorious curves of a marble hip, I thought of the artist's hand

—long moldered away before the rise of the Christian Era—and of the chisel that had formed in a pagan world these imperishable images of the perishable human form. That they should meet my gaze now, as the foundations of Christendom collapsed! I shoved the fragments aside with my foot and went into the kitchen, where I found a few heads of garlic and a loaf.

Hardly had I shared the bread with my dog when the woman appeared from the inner rooms and said hesitantly and with downcast eyes that the priest had performed his duties and now demanded six ducats. She asked me to lend her this sum until she could meet with any of her father's wealthy patrons and friends. I gave her the money, but the rapacity of the priest so enraged me that I took the back way through the garden into the street and when he left the house I ran up and struck him a blow on the head so that he fell.

The old man was peaceful and serene now that he had settled his account with God, and he suffered no pain. With a trembling hand he smoothed his daughter's hair as she knelt beside him, and I fancy he knew little of the evil that had come to Rome, for he adjured me in a weak voice to see that he was given honorable burial and that his daughter was conveyed to safety in the palace of the wealthy Massimo. He desired no plumed horses to draw his hearse, but would be content to be carried on a simple bier and laid in consecrated ground. I had not the heart to tell him the truth, and I promised to fulfill his wishes to the best of my power. I then knelt beside his daughter to pray for his soul and to show reverence for death, which robs man of his delight, reduces the mightiest prince to dust, and makes of scholarly labor a vanity.

When the old man had drawn his last breath I rose to close his eyes, prop his jaw with a pillow, and cross his hands upon his breast.

The daughter wept a little, but soon dried her tears and said with a sigh of relief, "My father died a Christian death, which is a great comfort to me. During his lifetime he often neglected Mass and forgot his prayers in studying the writings of the ancient pagans, and he spent more money on relics of antiquity than on the adornment of holy altars. But now his soul is at rest, and it only remains to fulfill his last wish and lay him in consecrated ground."

Her stupid obstinacy annoyed me, and I told her that tens of thousands of bodies lay unburied and pestilent along the banks of the Tiber and before the churches, and that it was vain to expect that anyone would trouble to dig a grave for one poor scholar.

To this she replied haughtily, "I owe you six ducats, but when I have buried my father and you have taken me to Massimo's palace you shall be repaid, with extra for your trouble. Wealthy Massimo will not deny my father's daughter his protection."

I told her gently that Massimo's palace had been plundered and ravaged by both Spaniards and Germans, that Massimo had been bound, and that his two daughters had been raped before his eyes. The girls had then been sent to the sewer to dig up the treasure that the invaders suspected lay hidden there. Therefore I thought that she would find little succor with Massimo or his kin.

The woman bit her lip, and realization of her defenselessness and her dependence upon me brought tears to her eyes.

But after some moments of reflection she said, "For myself I care nothing; my body has been defiled and so my life is of little value. But for my father I desire a decent burial, and if you're a man you will help me."

I know not what it was about this woman that so moved me when she appealed to my manhood, but I promised to do my best and I set forth at once to seek Andy. As luck would have it, I met him on the Ponte Sisto, bearing an old white-haired man on his back and surrounded by a group of shouting, laughing pikemen. He told me that the old fellow was Cardinal Ponzetto, whom they were carrying from palace to palace in quest of ransom money. I explained my errand, and mention of burial gave the pikemen a new idea. Cardinal Ponzetto deserved to be buried alive, they said, for they had not got a penny for him. Lifting him from the ground where Andy had dropped him, they bore him away toward the nearest church. Andy followed them and I perforce followed Andy.

The men laid the cardinal in a coffin that they had somehow found, and this they set upon a bier in the middle of the church. The old fellow lay there more dead than alive as they went through a pantomime of chanting and preaching. Then they pulled up one of the flagstones as if to bury him beneath it. But as even this failed to squeeze a farthing from him, they wearied of the sport, and said they would be guests at his house and hold a banquet instead.

Andy would have gone with them for something to eat, but I begged and entreated him to help me, since Providence had furnished us with a fine coffin and a bier. He induced two pikemen to come with us and by means of a battue in the neighboring houses we rounded up enough men to carry the bier, and two monks to chant. Then in solemn procession and under the protection of Andy's sword we made our way to the scholar's house.

We dressed the old man in a clean shirt, shrouded him, and laid him in the coffin to the accompaniment of psalms. Then the woman led the way to a little burial ground, where as dusk fell the Italians dug a grave. And so the scholar was honorably interred.

When all was over and our helpers had been dismissed with our blessing, the three of us remained alone together by the grave and watched the darkening sky glow red from the fires raging in the city. The woman said a last prayer, then rose, kissed us both, and called us honest men. She begged us to share with her what little food remained in her father's house. On our way thither we ransacked neighboring dwellings for fresh meat, green vegetables, and a little keg of wine, which Andy bore home on his shoulder.

The woman, with unpracticed hand, lit a fire in the kitchen and began to roast the meat, while Andy described his day's adventures and showed me a handful of precious stones, green and red, which he had wrenched from a reliquary in a convent. He said also that he had seen the skull of St. John the Baptist, and would dearly have liked to possess himself of it and send it to Åbo Cathedral. It would have been a praiseworthy action, he said, as there were few valuable relics at home. But someone else had seized it first.

After discoursing for a while on the morbid savagery of the Spaniards, he ended, "They find delight in torturing and in forcing women and even children into serving all manner of vice, whereas an honest man finds his happiness in the kindness and favor of women—and there is no lack of merry-minded girls in Rome who of their own accord are glad to share the soldiers' joys and spoils."

The woman, forgetful of her roast, turned to us and said, "I have lived a quiet and scholarly life in my father's house. A gentleman of eminence would have shown me favor, but as he was to enter the Church he could offer me no more than the insecure position of mistress, and therefore I refused him. Other suitors of lesser rank I disdained. Now God has punished me for my pride and I think I shall never look at a man again without disgust. Perhaps when order is restored and the brigands have been driven from Rome I shall enter some convent whose rule is not too austere."

Andy said, "There will be room enough in the Roman convents, noble lady, and you will have a wide choice. At San Silvestro, for instance, only one nun remains alive, and I last saw her running naked

367

through the streets after the man who stole St. John the Baptist's skull. Let me dissuade you from your hasty and ill-considered plan. No one yet knows which church the Emperor will raise up in place of that which has fallen. But so much I can say: twelve thousand strong men have resolved to elect Doctor Luther as Pope, by force if need be, and Doctor Luther has no love for convents or for celibacy. He married a nun."

At this the woman forgot her roast again and it fell unheeded into the fire. She stared at us open mouthed and said, "Is there then no longer any refuge for a defenseless woman?"

Andy picked the meat from the fire, smelled it, and cut away the charred portions. We sat down at the table and began our meal, though the meat was burned on one side and raw on the other and we were obliged to wash it down with deep draughts of wine.

The woman hid her face in her hands and bewailed her unprotected condition, but Andy comforted her and said, "I understand your grief, but in this world nothing is irrecoverable save human life. When you have had time to reflect calmly, you will see that life can still taste sweet—better at any rate than scorched meat. I understand that some rough fellows have violated you, but be thankful they were not Spaniards, who would have mutilated you to extort money. You are no worse off than a fellow who in a drunken fit has committed every kind of folly and who when he sobers up believes himself the most miserable of all miserable sinners. It would surprise you how quickly that sensation passes after a drink or two to clear the head. And so let me advise you to eat and drink and restore your strength, and remember only that you have given your father a funeral such as not the wealthiest and most eminent corpses in Rome could hope to surpass in these days."

His simple words revived and cheered the scholar's daughter. She did her best to smile at us, and said, "I am indeed ungrateful, and I have neglected my duties as hostess. Your kindness makes me wish that I had spent more time on the art of cooking and less on versification and sacred drama. Perhaps you are right; perhaps God wished to punish my arrogance by degrading the body that I have so jealously guarded from even the tenderest caress. And though there is little consolation in the thought that matters might have been worse, yet like a philosopher I will accept it. My only problem is how to reward you, since I cannot even roast meat to your satisfaction. But if you wish I will repeat some beautiful verses to you, or recite Holy Magdalen's speeches from the Passion play in which I won such great acclaim."

But Andy excused himself, saying that he had neglected his pikemen too long, and urged me to remain for the lady's protection, since I as a scholar would know how to value poetry. And so he went, leaving us alone in the ravaged house which only two days earlier had been home to this lovely girl. We found nothing to say, but sat silent in the light of the two wax candles, until at last she told me softly that her name was Lucrezia, and asked me to converse with her like a brother. She gave me her hands to hold because she was cold and afraid. My dog curled up before the dying fire, and still I was silent.

And the woman said, "My father's heart broke when the soldiers smashed his antique sculptures and maltreated the volumes on which he had spent his whole fortune. I believe he died because he had seen his whole life's work destroyed in an instant. Yet now that he is dead I am free, and afraid of my freedom. I feel like a bird swept by a stormy gust from its cage into a wilder, more terrible, but perhaps more glorious world. Put your arms about me, Michael; warm me, protect me. These two candles are all we have in the house, so let us blow them out. We can talk as well in the dark."

She did so, and I put my arms about her. In the torment of my heavy thoughts I found consolation in the embrace of a being as lonely and forsaken as myself.

In the morning she rose before me. When I saw her again she was pale and silent and dressed in black. When I spoke to her she avoided my eye, and as we broke our fast on what remained of last night's supper she treated me as a stranger or an enemy, and I could not discover what she thought or felt. My conscience would not allow me to leave her alone and unprotected, and so I took her to the pikemen's camp and entrusted her to the care of the sentries. The good-natured Germans had rescued a number of unhappy women from the violence of the Spaniards and had set them to cooking and washing. I could think of no safer refuge for Lucrezia, for my own interests required me to be out and about in the city as long as lawful plundering continued.

But when I came back in the evening bringing food for her, she had left the camp, and the other women said scornfully that the lye in the washing water had proved too harsh for her soft hands and that she had run after some Spaniards in search of a better protector. I was aghast at her folly and sought her at home, but she had not returned.

369

I remained in the little house, which stood near St. Peter's, making it easy for me to keep an eye on my donkey while awaiting her. When the looting was over, Andy joined me, to recover from his excesses. He brought with him a number of his men, so that we were able to defend our quarters against intruders. We laid in stores of flour and dried meat, for it soon appeared that we had by no means captured the fleshpots of Egypt, but were threatened with worse hunger and privation than we had ever known.

5

During those eight days it would have been easy for even a small body of the enemy to penetrate the city and rescue the Pope from Sant'Angelo, for our troops were completely out of hand and given over to looting and debauchery. One day the Prince of Orange, who had ensconced himself in the Vatican to avoid witnessing the hopeless disorders, sounded the alarm in an attempt to frighten the army into unity and obedience. But of thirty thousand men a bare five thousand responded.

At the end of this week of pillage, the spoils were shared out in accordance with the articles of war. Minted gold and silver amounting to ten million ducats had been collected, also gold and silver vessels and precious stones to an equal value. When distribution had been made, there was not a harquebusier or pikeman who had not arrayed himself in silks and velvets and hung gold chains about his neck; the meanest groom had at least a hundred ducats to jingle in his purse. But other property, such as furniture, paintings, books, relics, and costly stuffs, which had either been destroyed or sold in the ghetto for a song, was worth at least as much as that which had been shared out; and the countless houses and palaces that had been set on fire or blown up would have cost many millions of ducats to rebuild.

When enough order was restored to allow hucksters to show themselves again and taverns to open their doors, it soon became clear that wealth had lost all meaning. Barely three weeks had passed before an ordinary loaf cost a ducat and the poorest of the inhabitants were starving to death. No peasant was mad enough to bring food into Rome, and the stocks of provisions in the city had all been either devoured in the first wild gluttony of the insurgents or thrown to the pigs. The air was foul with corruption, rats swarmed everywhere and gnawed the dead bodies, and one day near the Colosseum some Spaniards shot two wolves that had been lured into the city by the stench of carrion.

In the wake of famine came plague, and I who had had no experience of it now had enough to last me for the rest of my days. When the first pikemen began to complain of burning thirst and to finger their tender armpits and groins, I knew what was before us, and in default of remedies I could only bleed them and administer emetics, that they might not run mad with fever and pain and hurl themselves into the river. The pestilence spread even to the citadel of Sant'Angelo, and many feared that the Pope would slip through our fingers.

I seemed to be living in a nightmare. I staggered as I walked, and suffered from giddiness; yet I exerted myself to feed and water my donkey. One morning when I was looking after it in St. Peter's about a hundred pikemen swarmed into the church, untethered the mules, and demanded my beast, which they required for some blasphemous mummery or other. I went with them, not to lose sight of the donkey. When afterward I sought to claim it, they seized me and forced me to go farther with them and find a priest to torment. There were a few priests in Rome who still performed their duties despite the interdict, administering the Sacraments to victims of hunger and plague, tending the sick and comforting the wretched. One of these good men had the ill-fortune to meet us, and the pikemen ordered him to offer the Holy Eucharist to my donkey. But though they struck and thrashed him until blood ran from his nose and mouth, he steadfastly resisted and said he would rather die than desecrate the Sacrament. His firmness drove these devil-ridden men to a frenzy of rage; they murdered him, and trampled the Host into the dirt. My donkey began to bray, and with this noise in my ears I swooned.

I awoke amid an appalling stench, conscious of burning thirst and severe pains. I groped about and grasped a rotting human arm, which tore away from the body. In my delirium I fancied myself among the fires of hell, but gradually my head cleared and I found I had been robbed and thrown naked before a small church, among the corpses of those who had died of plague. Horror lent me strength enough to crawl out into the street and utter a quavering cry for help. Many people were passing, but when they heard my voice they hurried on to avoid me. I felt the boils in my armpits and groin, and they caused me the cruelest agony. My head was misty with fever and I seemed still to hear the shrill bray of the donkey, as I had heard it when the dying priest spread his fingers over the consecrated elements, to protect them from the soldiers' feet.

Sure now that death was near, I fainted again, but awoke after dark to feel a little tongue licking my face—Rael was with me. He had gone astray in the throng but had somehow found his way back to me. Now, seeing that I was awake, he began to utter little cries of joy, and nipped me in the ear to rouse me. Raging fever made me light as a feather, and like many other plague-stricken people I stood up and staggered down the street, leaning against the house walls and often falling on my face.

I had no notion of where I was going, but somehow the dog led me almost to Lucrezia's house. Then I fell again, and this time I could not rise. Rael pulled and tugged at me for a time, and then ran off yelping to wake Andy and bring him to where I lay. Andy picked me up and carried me into the house—an act of selflessness hardly to be surpassed, for even a physician will avoid touching a plague-stricken man and will keep to the other side of the room unless he has to bleed him, and then he washes his hands in salt and vinegar.

I lay sick for several days and my mind wandered, so that I addressed Andy as Mistress Pirjo or Barbara when he brought me fresh water to drink or bathed my swellings with rags dipped in vinegar. While he slept, Rael kept watch over me and chased away the rats. But after five days the boils ripened and burst of themselves and the fever left me, so that I could think clearly once more and understand where I was.

As a physician, I knew I might recover if only I could survive the period of weakness and take enough food. So I made every effort to swallow the gruel that Andy made for me, and sucked dried fruit, whose sweetness revived me. I could not yet get out of bed by myself, and whenever Andy went out to find food for us he left the pikemen on guard, for we still had the greater part of our booty hidden in the house. Yet they often neglected their duty in dread of plague, and relying on the security of our hiding place they would visit the neighboring houses to gossip and amuse themselves with the women. So Andy left a loaded gun by my bed.

Lying one day in that state of utter weakness that accompanies plague, and contemplating my wasted life, I suddenly heard voices. Lucrezia appeared in the doorway and regarded me in astonishment. She wore a flame-colored velvet dress that left her arms and breast bare, and in her hair a rope of pearls was entwined. Precious stones hung from her ears, and heavy rings flashed as she carried her slender fingers to her lips in a gesture of amazement.

372

I fancied at first that my delirium had returned, but then I smiled and cried weakly, "Lucrezia, Lucrezia!"

She crossed herself and said, "Is it you, Michael? Have you the plague? I saw the cross upon the door."

I fingered my bearded, emaciated face and could not wonder that she had failed to recognize me at first. Even this slight effort made me breathless. She approached, but was careful not to touch me, and in so doing observed a crust of bread and a little gruel in an earthen-ware dish beside me.

"There is food here," she called out, and began to gnaw the bread, staring at me meanwhile with her black eyes. A bearded Spaniard strode into the room and gulped down the gruel.

"For God's sake, Lucrezia!" I said. "That is all the food I have and my recovery depends upon it. Have you forgotten all I did for you?"

But Lucrezia turned to the Spaniard and said, "Perhaps he has more food in the bed. And he must have money somewhere."

The Spaniard dragged me out onto the floor by the heels, so as not to infect his hands, and slit open the mattress with his sword. He was a tall, thin fellow with a glossy blue-black beard, and he wore a jeweled pectoral cross on a gold chain about his neck.

Sternly, implacably, he looked at me and said, "Must I burn the soles of your feet with tarred sticks, or will you tell us where you have hidden your food and money?"

"Lucrezia!" I cried. "I could not have believed this of you or of any-one. Is it thus you reward my kindness?"

She said to the Spaniard, "This man exposed me to abominable shame. He violated me when I was helpless in his power and then expected me to wash his shirts. Moreover, he is a Lutheran and it would be an act pleasing to God to slay him."

But the Spaniard was unwilling to touch my plague-infected body. So they left the room, and I heard them overturning furniture and prizing up tiles from the floor in search of our spoils. Meanwhile I succeeded in grasping my weapon, cocked it, and sat on the floor wait-ing with my back braced against the bed. Presently I heard Lucrezia and the Spaniard quarreling together, and the man re-entered the room carrying a blazing brand. But he started and paused when he saw me, which gave me time to aim and pull the trigger. The ball hit him in the chest and he fell backward through the door before he could even swear.

The room was filled with billowing smoke. Lucrezia threw herself upon her knees beside her lover, but when she saw that he was dying she was filled with rage. She drew his sword, rose and took a step toward me, but I pointed the pistol at her and threatened to shoot. God knows how I was inspired to do this. The silly woman forgot that I must reload before I could fire, and dropping the sword on the floor she took to pleading with me to spare her life. I would be wise to remain her friend, she said, or she would send Spaniards to kill me. But I saw that she was afraid, and being unwilling to let her off so lightly I waved my weapon menacingly and ordered her to take off her rings and earrings and lay them on the floor beside the Spaniard. She wept and entreated and tried in every way to soften my heart, but in vain. At last she broke out into imprecations so abominable that I could never have believed any woman, even in Spaniards' company, could have learned such hideous curses in so short a time. I cannot say how the matter would have ended had not the pikemen been alarmed amid their roisterings by the sound of the shot. At this moment they dashed into the house and seized Lucrezia.

At the sight of the Spaniard's body they were aghast, fearing that Andy would flay them alive for leaving the house unguarded. They therefore treated this evil woman more harshly than I expected. They stripped her of her red gown and thrashed her with thorny rods until the blood streamed over her body, and would have no doubt killed her —which would have been the most prudent step—but the sight of her miserable plight induced me to order her release, and they kicked her into the street as naked as she was born. In this respect she was no worse off than many other women in Rome. Her baseness had turned out to our advantage, as there were close on five hundred ducats in the Spaniard's purse, and the pectoral cross alone was worth at least a hundred, from which I judged him to have been a man of rank among his own people.

On Andy's return we left the house without delay. The pikemen carried me to the other side of the river, where we went into hiding in an empty house. Lucrezia would certainly arouse the Spaniards at once and they would search the city for us, to avenge their comrade-in-arms; for these people were as vindictive as they were greedy and never forgot an injury.

But when my swellings were healed and I could stand on my feet once more, I said to Andy, "During my illness I have had leisure to reflect, and I fear we have been accessory to the worst act of brigandage the world has ever seen. The remainder of our lives may not suffice to atone for our share in it. Our punishment has been plague and famine, and I believe that not even the Emperor can escape retribution for the horrible crimes we have committed in his name. Now, therefore, let each man look to his own soul. For us no course lies open but to flee from the city which was once the pride of Christendom and of which we have made a ruin."

Andy replied gravely, "We have indeed reaped as much from Rome as is possible in a city of this sort. True, the Pope has yet to be ransomed, but that will amount to no more than a few ducats for each man, and I fear the high command will pocket the lion's share. So I am ready to leave Rome—and all the readier for the Spaniards whom you have offended. We cannot long elude them. But how we are to get out of this accursed place, and where we are to go, is a knotty problem."

Rael lay at my feet listening as we talked together, and now raising his head he gazed at me beseechingly.

Bodily weakness brought tears to my eyes, and I said to Andy, "We have defiled ourselves with every impurity. We have lost our childhood's faith and can hardly hope for forgiveness. During my illness the conviction has grown upon me that all our misery began on the day when we turned aside from our pilgrimage to the Holy Land. I would not persuade you against your will, brother Andy, but I have resolved to resume that journey now, with or without you, and no power on earth can turn me from my purpose."

"The journey to Jerusalem is arduous and full of danger," said Andy. "We might fall into the hands of the infidels. Could we not as easily find salvation here? One of Schärtlin's pikemen stole St. Longinus's spearhead, which pierced the side of Our Lord. He has bound it to his own pike and swears that with its aid he will fight his way straight to heaven, though a thousand devils stand in his path. Perhaps he would sell it to us if we offered him enough. It could cost no more than the journey to the Holy Land."

I shook my head at his stubbornness and stupidity.

"You don't understand," I said, "and had better hold your tongue. When I was recovering from the plague I dreamed we were walking along a shining road. As we walked, we stumbled over thorn bushes and ruins, but at the end of that road lay the holy Jerusalem, a city of gold. The very day after I had this dream, wicked Lucrezia came to our house with the Spaniard, and I should have suffered a horrible death had not Providence given me grace and strength to shoot the

375

man. It is an omen that cannot be ignored. As for the dangers and difficulties of the journey, you make too much of them, for the Emperor now pays the Sultan twenty thousand ducats a year to protect pilgrims and the holy places, and we have only to apply to the Turks in Venice for a safe-conduct. We can sail comfortably in some Venetian vessel, for we have money enough for that and for laying in good provisions. Providence it was who sent me that Spaniard and his purse, to make up for the loss I suffered when I fell sick in the street and was robbed."

Andy began to see that I was not raving, but had laid my plans with care. He scratched his head and said at last, "The sea should not be too stormy in summer, and I have only pleasant memories of our cruise from Genoa to Spain."

"Excellent, Andy!" I said. "That is the proper way to look at it. You shall undertake to manage our journey as far as Venice, I will be responsible for the voyage thence to the Holy Land, and thus the pious resolve of our youth shall be fulfilled. Let us forget these last errant years and win salvation. The Emperor may answer for his own actions; we will answer for ours."

Two days later we were rowing down the Tiber to Ostia, disguised as porters. With us came Domenico Venier, the Venetian ambassador, and two distinguished ladies from the court of Mantua, also in disguise. I was still so weak that I could scarcely haul on the great oar, but my spirit soared at the sight of Rome gliding away from us and at the freshness of the June air after the stench of burning ruins and rotting corpses. As we left Rome, that plundered carcass, behind us, I seemed to see all Christendom as a wounded, plague-ridden, wailing creature which a man must flee from if he would save his soul.

In Ostia we were safe. Domenico Venier had decided to persuade the Signoria of his mighty republic to lend the Pope money for his ransom; therefore the Imperial forces occupying Ostia did what they could to ease our journey, and when we had come out into the open sea we were protected by the allied fleet under Andrea Doria's command. Thus we came safely to Venice, whence we were to embark for the Holy Land.

I have now described the many strange adventures of my youth, candidly and without seeking to conceal my errors or to present my actions in a flattering light. The story alone is enough to convince a sagacious reader of my good intentions, and my Christian humility after the sack of Rome must also speak for me. Yet I hope that one day

I may find opportunity to tell of our voyage from Venice and our failure ever to reach the Holy Land, and of how instead I was compelled to wear the turban and become a follower of the prophet. I shall thus confute the shameful lies told of me in Christian countries when, after many reverses, I won renown and honor in the service of the Sultan.